Beyond the Truth

Also by Bruce Robert Coffin

Among the Shadows
Beneath the Depths

Beyond the Truth

A Detective Byron Mystery

BRUCE ROBERT COFFIN

WITNESS
IMPULSE
An Imprint of HarperCollinsPublishers

BEYOND THE TRUTH. Copyright © 2018 by Bruce Robert Coffin. All rights reserved. Printed in the United States of America. No part of this book may be used or reproduced in any manner whatsoever without written permission except in the case of brief quotations embodied in critical articles and reviews. For information, address HarperCollins Publishers, 195 Broadway, New York, NY 10007.

Print Edition ISBN: 978-0-06-256953-0
Digital Edition ISBN: 978-0-06-256951-6

Cover design by Guido Caroti
Cover photograph © DenisTangneyJr/iStock /Getty Images (background); © rangizzz/Malivan_Iuliia/nevodka/ Shutterstock (three images)

WITNESS logo and WITNESS IMPULSE are trademarks of HarperCollins Publishers in the United States of America.

HarperCollins is a registered trademark of HarperCollins Publishers in the United States of America and other countries.

FIRST EDITION

18 19 20 21 22   LSC   10 9 8 7 6 5 4 3 2 1

For those who wear the badge.

Man is not what he thinks he is, he is what he hides.

—André Malraux

Beyond the Truth

Chapter 1

VETERAN PORTLAND POLICE officer Sean Haggerty trudged across the deserted parking lot beneath the bright sodium arc lights of the 7-Eleven. His breath condensed into small white clouds before drifting away on the frigid night air. The thin layer of ice and snow covering the pavement crunched under his highly polished jump boots as he approached the idling black-and-white. Only two more hours until the end of his overtime. After four months in his new assignment as school resource officer for Portland High School, it felt good to be back in a patrol car, even if it was only one shift. Balancing a large Styrofoam coffee cup atop his clipboard, he was reaching for the cruiser keys on his belt when static crackled from his radio mic.

"Any unit in the area of Washington Avenue near the Bubble Up Laundromat, please respond," the dispatcher said.

The Bubble Up was in Haggerty's assigned area, less than a half mile up the street, but Dispatch still listed him as busy taking a shoplifting report. Someone had snatched a twelve-pack of beer.

Haggerty unlocked the door to the cruiser, then keyed the mic. "402, I'm clear the 10–92 at 27 Washington. I can cover that."

"Ten-four, 402," the dispatcher said. "Standby. 401."

"401, go."

"And 421."

"Go ahead."

Haggerty knew whatever this was, it was a priority. Dispatch did not send two line units and a supervisor for just any call.

"402, 401, and 421, all three units respond to the Bubble Up Laundromat at 214 Washington Avenue for an armed 10–90 that just occurred."

As Haggerty scrambled into the cruiser, the Styrofoam cup tumbled to the pavement, spilling its contents. The coffee froze almost instantly.

"Dammit," Haggerty said.

He tossed his clipboard onto the passenger seat, then climbed in. Allowing for the possibility of a quick exit, he ignored the seat belt requirement and threw the shift lever into Drive. He powered down his portable radio and reached for the microphone clipped to the dashboard. "402 en route."

"421 and 401 responding from the West End," the sergeant said, acknowledging the call for both backup units.

Haggerty pulled out of the lot onto Washington Avenue, and headed outbound toward Tukey's Bridge. He drove without lights or siren, in hopes of catching the suspects by surprise.

"402," Haggerty said, his eyes scanning the dark sidewalks and alleys. "Any description or direction of travel?"

"Ten-four, 402. We have the victim on the phone. Suspects are described as two masked males. Suspect number one was wearing a black hoodie and blue jeans, carrying a dark-colored backpack. Suspect two was dressed in dark pants and a red hoodie, with some kind of emblem on it. Unknown direction of travel."

"Is the victim injured?" Haggerty asked, trying to decide whether to go directly to the scene, securing the laundromat, or take a quick spin around the area first to try and locate the suspects.

"Negative, 402," the dispatcher said. "Just shaken up."

"What was the weapon used?"

"Standby, 402."

Haggerty caught a flash of red up ahead in the beam of the cruiser's headlights as two figures darted from his right across Washington Avenue down Madison Street. He accelerated, flicked on the emergency lights and siren, and keyed the dash mic again.

"402. I have a visual on the two suspects near Washington and Madison. They just rabbited into Kennedy Park."

"Ten-four. 401 and 421, copy?" the dispatcher said.

"Copy."

Braking hard, Haggerty spun the steering wheel left, making the turn onto Madison. He knew if he didn't stay right on them that he would lose them among the project's many apartments and row houses. The hooded figures sprinting down the hill were already several hundred feet ahead. He punched the gas and the cruiser shot after them. He was beginning to close the gap when they cut left in front of an oncoming car onto Greenleaf Street.

"Greenleaf toward East Oxford," he shouted into the mic, trying to be heard above the wail of his cruiser's siren as he raced through the built-up residential neighborhood.

The Ford skidded wide as he turned onto Greenleaf. Haggerty fought the urge to oversteer, waiting until the cruiser's front tires found purchase on a bare patch of pavement and it straightened out.

The two figures were clearer now, about fifty feet ahead. He was nearly on top of them when they turned again, west, running between rows of apartment buildings.

"They just cut over toward Monroe Court," Haggerty said.

"Ten-four," the dispatcher said. "421 and 401, copy?"

"Copy," 421 acknowledged.

Haggerty accelerated past the alley the suspects had taken, hoping to cut them off by circling the block and coming out ahead of them on East Oxford Street. He turned right onto Oxford just in time to see them run across the road and duck between yet another set of row houses.

He rode the brake, and the pulse of the antilock mechanism pushed back against his foot. The black-and-white felt as if it were speeding up. *Ice. Shit.* The rear end started to swing to the right toward a line of parked cars. He eased off the brake and the Ford straightened out but was now headed directly toward a snowbank in front of the alley—an ice bank, really. Still traveling about five miles per hour, the black-and-white smashed into it with a crunch. Haggerty jumped from the car and gave chase, the door still open, the siren still blaring. He would have to answer for a mangled squad car later, but there was no time to think of that now. The snow piled against the apartment building walls seemed to dance in the flickering blue light of his cruiser's strobes, making the alley look like a disco.

Haggerty could just make out the two hooded figures in the bobbing beam of his mini-Maglite as he ran.

"Police! Stop!" he yelled. They didn't.

He was gaining on them when his boot struck something buried beneath the snow, and he sprawled headfirst to the ground. Scrambling to regain his feet, he stood and quickly scanned the area for his flashlight, but it was gone. He turned and hurried down the dark alley, keying his shoulder mic as he went.

"402, 10–50," he said, referring to his cruiser accident. "I'm now in foot pursuit of the 10–90 suspects. Toward Cumberland from East Oxford."

"Ten-four, 402," the female dispatcher acknowledged. "1 and 21, copy."

Haggerty heard the distorted transmissions as both units responded simultaneously, causing the radio to squeal in protest. He rounded the rear corner of a three-story unit just in time to see the suspect wearing the red hoodie stuck near the top of a six-foot chain-link fence. The other figure had already made it over and stopped to assist.

"Freeze," Haggerty yelled as he drew his weapon.

Neither suspect heeded his warning. Haggerty was at full stride, gun at the low ready position, about fifteen feet from the fence, when the first suspect finally pulled the second one loose. Up and over they went, leaving Haggerty on the wrong side of the barrier.

Damn! Haggerty holstered his Glock, then backed far enough away from the fence to give himself a running start. He hit the fence, left foot out in front, reaching for the top with his gloved hands, and then vaulted up and over it with ease. The suspect in the dark-colored hoodie turned and looked back, giving Haggerty a glimpse of what seemed to be a ski mask made to look like a skull. Thirty feet now. He was closing the distance again.

If they don't split up I'll have a chance, he thought. He heard a dog barking frantically nearby, and the distant wail of approaching sirens. The combination of the cold air into his lungs and the adrenaline surge were beginning to take their toll, sapping his strength. His arms and legs were slowing, despite his efforts.

"What's your 20, 402?" the dispatcher asked. His location.

"Fuck if I know," he said out loud and breathless. He keyed the mic on his shoulder. "Backyards. Headed west. Toward Anderson."

"Ten-four," the dispatcher said. "Units, copy?"

"1 copies."

"21. I copy," the sergeant said. "The call came in as an armed 10–90. What was the weapon?"

"Standby, 21."

Haggerty lost them again as they rounded another building. He slowed to a jog and drew his sidearm again. The alley was pitch-black and he didn't want to risk running into an ambush.

"Units be advised, the original caller was a customer who walked in on the robbery. I have the victim on the phone now. He says the male in the dark-colored hoodie displayed a silver colored 10–32 handgun."

"21, give us a signal," the sergeant said.

"Ten-four," the dispatcher said. The familiar high-pitched tone sounded twice over the radio before the dispatcher spoke again. "All units, a signal 1000 is now in effect. Hold all air traffic or switch to channel two. 401, 402, and 421 have priority."

Haggerty stepped forward carefully, not wanting to trip again. His lungs were burning. He attempted to slow his breathing while waiting for his eyes to adjust to the darkness. He froze in place as he heard a banging sound, as if someone were striking a solid object with a bat. The sound was followed by shouting, but he couldn't make out what was being said.

Peeking quickly around the corner of the building, he saw the figure in the red hoodie kicking at the stuck gate of a wooden stockade fence, while the other had scrambled onto the roof of a junk car and was attempting to climb over the barrier.

"Freeze," Haggerty yelled, aiming his Glock at the dark hooded figure standing atop the car. Red hoodie stopped kicking, but didn't turn back toward Haggerty. The suspect on the car, also facing away from him, didn't move. Haggerty approached the fence cautiously, making sure of his footing as he planted one foot in front of the other. His eyes shifted between the two figures, but he kept his gun trained on the suspect who was reportedly armed. "Let me see your hands. Both of you."

Red hoodie raised his hands high above his head.

The dark figure on top of the car began to turn. His hands were hidden from sight.

"I said freeze." Haggerty sidestepped to his left looking to regain some cover. "Goddammit, freeze!"

The dark figure spun toward him, bringing his right arm up in a pointing gesture.

Haggerty saw a familiar flash of light an instant before he pulled the trigger on his Glock.

Chapter 2

DETECTIVE SERGEANT JOHN Byron stepped out of his unmarked into the chaos. Blue strobes flashing, police radios squawking, and a small crowd had gathered. The brisk night air was like a stinging slap in the face. He'd been asleep for all of twenty minutes when his cellphone had begun to dance across the nightstand. A "police-involved shooting," the dispatch operator had said.

"A cop was shot?" Byron had asked, his brain still fuzzy.

"No," the operator said. "One of ours shot someone."

"Who was the shooter?"

"Officer Sean Haggerty."

Hags, Byron thought. *Damn.*

The 911 operator had provided the address, informing him that it was an outdoor scene. *Of course it is*, he'd thought. Recalling that the weather forecast had predicted single digits for the overnight, Byron had dressed in layers. Now as he stood in the street, feeling the chill creep down his collar and seeing the vapor from his own breath, he was glad for the heavy wool sweater. He reached back inside the car and grabbed his black insulated raid jacket off the seat. He tore apart the Velcro seal and pulled out the reflective back flap that read POLICE, then slid the jacket on.

He paused for a moment outside of the fray to take it all in. Someone in the crowd shouted while someone else wailed in agony. Byron knew the sound of loss. A person so aggrieved by the death of a loved one no words could ever comfort them. Homicide investigations were always intense, but never more so than when the victim is taken down by a cop's bullet. He took a mental inventory of everything he saw. Crime scene tape was up. The evidence van was idling at the curb. Uniforms were holding people back, guarding the scene. *Time to slow it down.*

Byron heard the rapid acceleration of an approaching vehicle. He hoped it was his people and not the clown parade that was likely to follow. An unmarked Malibu with dash-mounted blue lights skidded to a stop directly behind his car, and Detectives Mike Nugent and Melissa Stevens jumped out.

"Sarge," they said in unison.

"Sorry it took us so long to get here," Stevens said, nodding in Nugent's direction. "Car wouldn't start. Somebody left the interior lights on. *Again.*"

"What's the word?" Nugent asked, ignoring his longtime partner's comment and pulling a watch cap down over his clean-shaven dome.

"Don't know," Byron said. "Just got here."

"Hey, John," a somber voice said from the darkness.

Byron turned to see Sergeant Pepin walking toward them. "Andy," he greeted. "Give me a thumbnail. How bad is it?"

Pepin shook his head. "Bad as it gets. Hags shot a kid."

"Shit," Stevens said, echoing Byron's own thoughts on the subject.

"We got an ID on him?" Byron asked.

"Thomas Plummer, seventeen. From Portland."

"Where is the body?" Byron asked.

"Still here. MedCu responded to the scene and called it."

In death investigations having the body still positioned where it was found was usually a positive. "What about next of kin?" Byron asked.

"Already here. Found out through the grapevine, I guess."

"Great," Nugent growled.

"Anyone think to call the victim advocate?" Byron asked as he scrolled through a mental checklist. The victim advocate was a civilian employed by the PD to provide guidance and emotional support to victims and family members during the immediate aftermath of violent crimes and even beyond, throughout the daunting legal proceedings.

"Shit," Pepin said. "Hadn't got that far."

"I'll take care of it," Stevens said as she pulled out her cell and strolled away.

"What do we know?" Byron asked, his attention returning to Pepin.

"Hags was chasing two suspects from an armed robbery at the laundromat around the corner. The Bubble Up. Crashed his black-and-white couple of blocks from here on East Oxford. Chased them on foot after that." Pepin looked back over his shoulder. "Said he cornered them at the end of this alley. One of the suspects took a shot at him. Hags returned fire. Shooting happened before Amy or I could get here."

"Amy?"

"Officer Connolly. We were in the West End just clearing a false burglar alarm when the call came in."

"Where's Connolly now?" Byron asked.

"I sent her up to the laundromat. She's taking statements from the 10–90 victim and another witness."

"And the other suspect?"

"Got away."

"Did we put out an ATL?" he asked.

"Already done."

"And a track?"

"All of our K-9 guys are away at a training."

"That's fucking great," Nugent said, stamping his feet to try and keep warm.

"How about a neighboring department?" Byron asked.

"We tried a half dozen but they're all at the same training. The scene is pretty well contaminated now anyway," Pepin said.

"Where is Hags?" Byron asked.

"We transported him to 109."

"And his gun?"

"Gave it directly to the E.T.," Pepin said, referring to Evidence Technician Gabriel Pelligrosso.

"Good. Where's the shift commander?"

"The lieutenant's off. Sergeant Fitzgerald is acting."

"He's earning his extra pay tonight," Nugent said.

"That's his SUV," Pepin said, pointing toward the empty black-and-white Ford Interceptor with the emergency flashers parked down the street.

"Advocate is en route," Stevens said, returning to the group and pocketing her phone.

"Thanks, Mel," Byron said. "See if you can get the family away from here. Somewhere quiet. Maybe the Munjoy Hill Community Policing Office. Anywhere but 109. I don't want the Plummers running into Haggerty."

"I'm on it."

Byron turned to Nugent. "Grab a couple of uniforms and start a canvass of the crowd and then the surrounding neighborhood. Knock on some doors." He looked back at Pepin. "You have any spare officers available to accompany my detectives?"

Pepin shook his head. "It's Sunday night. We're short. All my people are tied up on this. We've kept three officers available to cover the rest of the city. Priorities only. Dispatch is holding or teleserving everything else."

Byron turned back to Nugent. "Wake up Dustin. Get him in here to help you. And call Sergeant Peterson. Tell him we'll need to use some of his detectives. Canvass the neighborhood. Talk to as many people as you can. Let's get as much intel as possible—what people saw, what they heard, whatever. We can do formal statements later. If you find anyone who witnessed this thing first-hand, take them to 109 and record it."

"You got it, boss," Nugent said. "I'll start with this crowd."

"And let me know if you come up with anything solid. I want to get as many people's stories locked down as we can before the attorney general's investigators get here."

"Will do," Nugent said.

Byron went looking for Sergeant Fitzgerald. Passing the crowd, he saw the woman he'd heard crying. She was wearing a light-colored wool coat and knit hat. Stevens had an arm around the woman trying to calm her. A tall slender man with a mustache stood beside them. The man briefly made eye contact with Byron, then looked away. The pain in the man's eyes was unmistakable. *Plummer's parents*, Byron thought.

Byron knew of nothing on this earth more heartbreaking than watching a parent grieve for a fallen child. Homicide, justifiable or not, multiplied the grief exponentially. Although Byron had no children of his own, he had witnessed the suffering firsthand, time and again. No words ever console, no prayer can give comfort. Even the thoughts of revenge some people cling to eventually ring hollow. The loss of a child crosses all boundaries. The pain is extreme and unending.

Byron knew that finding and bringing to justice those responsible was all he could ever offer in these cases, but it came with no guarantees. Justice, even when served, never soothed the ache, never brought back a son or daughter. And in this case, Byron couldn't even offer the false hope of justice, for the killer had been one of his own. Another cop. Was it a righteous shoot? Who knew? Only time would tell. If Hags wasn't in the right, there would be hell to pay. He scanned the restless crowd as he passed. *In the right or not, there might be hell to pay anyway*, he thought.

Byron located the acting shift commander standing inside the taped-off alleyway, talking on his cell. He recognized the short and stocky sergeant by the rolls of skin at the back of his nonexistent neck. Fitzgerald ended his call just as Byron reached him.

"John," Fitzgerald said. "Glad to see you."

"Tom. How's Hags?"

"Pretty shaken up."

"Does he know the kid's dead yet?"

"I don't think they've told him officially, but I'm pretty sure he knows."

"You assign someone to stay with him? I don't want him sitting alone at 109."

"He's with the union rep. They're calling in a MAP attorney for him," Fitzgerald said.

The Maine Association of Police kept a handful of attorneys on retainer for exactly this type of situation. Byron hoped they were sending a good one.

Byron surveyed the scene up ahead. Evidence Technician Gabriel Pelligrosso was working with another tech, setting up artificial lighting. Byron looked back at Fitzgerald, and pulled out a fresh notebook. "Take me through what happened."

"Sure thing. Dispatcher got a call from the dry cleaner on Washington Avenue."

"I thought the Bubble Up was a laundromat?"

"It's both. Anyway, the manager said he was robbed at gunpoint. Described the suspects as two males wearing hoodies and ski masks."

"What time was that?" Byron asked.

Fitzgerald referred to his own notes. "About forty-five minutes ago. Call came in just after nine-thirty for an armed 10–90. Haggerty, Connolly, and Pepin were assigned. I headed in from Deering as soon as I heard. Before Haggerty got to the scene, he radioed that he had two subjects fitting the description of the suspects running on Washington Avenue. One wearing a red hoodie and the other a black hoodie. When they saw him, they took off down Madison Street into Kennedy Park. Haggerty chased after them in his cruiser until he cleaned out a snowbank. Pursued them on foot after that."

"Pepin said you assigned someone to take a statement from the laundromat manager?" Byron said.

"Yeah. The manager and a customer who walked in during the robbery. I put one of our better officers on it. Amy Connolly. She'll be thorough."

She would need to be. The statements would be vitally important in confirming not only the details of the robbery but the identity of the suspects.

"What happened next?" Byron asked, pausing to look up from his notes as Pelligrosso approached.

"Sarge," Pelligrosso greeted.

"Gabe," Byron said, trying to read his stoic evidence technician's expression, but as usual Pelligrosso gave nothing away. "How's it look so far?"

"Preliminary work is done. I've got Murph helping me."

Murph was Officer Kent Murphy. Brand-new to the lab, Murphy still had much to learn. But he already had a solid reputation for evidence collection, due to his six months of work as a patrol technician. But this was the big leagues.

"Need more help?" Byron asked.

"Wouldn't turn it down," Pelligrosso said. "I've got multiple scenes. They all need working. The cruiser accident, the robbery, and this. Plus, I still have to get up to 109, take some pictures, seize and bag Hags's clothing."

"Okay, I'll get you some," Byron said. "What about this scene?"

"I think we're okay for now. Cramped quarters in there. I don't want anyone else trampling through it. I'm waiting on the M.E. before I do anything more with the body. We've done the best we can to block access, but people are still trying to get a peek."

Byron turned to Fitzgerald. "Can you help with that?"

"John, the captain just lost his shit about the overtime budget last week."

"And?" Byron maintained eye contact while he waited for the seriousness of their situation to sink in. "Tom, Hags just killed a kid."

"Fuck it," Fitzgerald said. "I *am* the shift commander, right? I'll have Dispatch call in more officers." Fitzgerald lifted his cell and stepped away.

Byron readdressed his E.T. "Thanks, Gabe. I'll make sure the other scenes are taken care of. Let me know if you need anything else here."

Pelligrosso stepped in close to Byron and lowered his voice. "There is one more thing you should know."

Byron felt a knot tightening in his stomach. "What?"

"We haven't been able to locate the suspect's gun."

Chapter 3

BYRON TRAILED PELLIGROSSO as far as the scene's perimeter, close enough to get a feel for how it looked, but not so close he might contaminate it further. Plummer's body had been reduced to nothing more than a lump beneath a neon yellow plastic tarp. And despite the ridiculously loud color, covering the body with plastic was simply another attempt at keeping the curious at bay.

"Normally, I wouldn't have used a tarp, Sarge," Pelligrosso said. "But I didn't know what else to do."

"If you hadn't, some asshole would've posted this on social media."

"My very thought."

"Where was Hags shooting from?" Byron asked as he surveyed the scene.

"We walked past it," Pelligrosso said, pointing. "Over there, closer to the street, about thirty feet from the body."

"How many rounds did he fire?"

"Five were missing from the magazine in his Glock. Looks like he struck the suspect at least four times. Once in the head."

Byron's heart sank. He could only imagine how badly a head shot would be perceived.

Officer Kent Murphy approached them, walking on a well-worn trail through the snow. Byron knew the evidence techs had been using the path to keep from trampling any evidence. First rule of crime scene management: pick a route and use it. The young E.T. in training nodded silently. Byron returned the gesture.

Byron spent several moments silently scanning the now brightly lit scene. "Did we get some natural light shots of this yet?"

"First thing," Pelligrosso said. "It was pretty dark, as you already saw, but the ambient light reflecting off the snow showed some detail."

"According to Pepin, Hags said he returned fire. What about shell casings from the suspect?"

Pelligrosso shook his head. "Haven't located anything yet."

"Who else knows about the missing gun?" Byron asked, frowning.

"Besides you and me? Murph, Hags, Connolly, and Sergeant Pepin."

Byron knew how volatile the situation was. A half dozen people in the know was six too many. Soon, someone would begin talking out of school, and word would get out. It always did.

"Let's make sure we keep a lid on the missing weapon for now," Byron said. "Okay? The last thing we need is a riot down here." Byron looked directly at Murphy as he said it, emphasizing his point.

Murphy nodded again. "Got it, Sarge."

"Roger that," Pelligrosso said.

"Have we checked under the body?" Byron asked, recalling several other officer-involved shootings where a weapon wasn't immediately located. In each case, following the ensuing panic by the command staff, the suspect's weapon was eventually found, but not until after the body had been removed.

"Not yet," Pelligrosso said. "We'll be able to once Dr. Ellis arrives."

"Okay, let me know as soon as you do." Byron took another look at the surrounding area. "Do we have any idea how the other suspect got away?" he asked after a moment.

Pelligrosso turned and pointed. "Behind the car, there's a gap under the fence. The snow has been disturbed. Looks like the other robber may have crawled under. I've put a bucket over one really clear sneaker impression in the snow. It doesn't match the tread pattern on Plummer's sneakers. As soon as we move the body, I'll cast it. The kid under the tarp was carrying a backpack, but that's gone too."

Byron looked around, shaking his head in disgust. "All this over a laundromat robbery? How much money could they have possibly grabbed?"

"This might be about more than cash," Pelligrosso said.

"Oh?"

"We found several small Ziplocs in the snow. Might have fallen out of the missing backpack."

"Drugs?"

Pelligrosso nodded. "A couple of them contain white powder. One has about fifty orange pills inside. Looks like Xanax."

"Anything else I need to know?" Byron asked as he made another entry in the notebook.

"Yeah, actually. There is one more thing."

"Why do I get the feeling I'm not gonna like this?"

"There's an iPhone lying beside the body."

"Plummer's?"

"Too soon to say. It's powered off."

"That a problem?" Byron asked, not understanding the issue.

"According to one of the MedCu attendants, it was still on when they arrived."

"So, who shut it down?"

"I think it shut itself down due to the cold. The phone is designed that way to protect the battery. But that's not the problem."

"Okay, what is the problem?"

"According to MedCu, the flashlight was activated when they got here."

BYRON MADE THE calls, waking the remaining evidence technicians, then returned to the street where he had left his car. Despite the bitter cold the crowd had grown. He counted as many as thirty people. As Byron passed by the gathering, a male suffering from a severe lack of originality yelled out, "Pigs!" Someone else laughed. *Only the beginning*, he thought.

He caught sight of his boss, Lieutenant Martin LeRoyer, commander of the Criminal Investigation Division, speaking with Acting Chief Danny Rumsfeld and Lucinda Phillips, a retired state police detective sergeant turned AG investigator. The group stood huddled together near Byron's car. Walking toward them was Sergeant Diane Joyner.

A former New York City homicide investigator, Diane was the PPD's new press liaison. She had previously been one of Byron's detectives; six months ago, she would have been partnered with him on this case. But now, after accepting the chevrons, she was caught in the unenviable position of playing spin doctor for Rumsfeld. Byron wondered how successful Rumsfeld's campaign for a permanent appointment was likely to go following this investigation.

Following Byron's divorce, he and Diane became romantically involved. He missed their daily interactions, both on and occasionally off the job. They made brief but knowing eye contact before she continued on.

Byron heard the muffled ring of his cell beneath his raid jacket. "Byron."

"Sarge, it's Pepin."

"Hey, Andy. What's up?"

"Amy Connolly just texted me a picture of the robbery victim's statement. It's good. The victim said he was closing up for the night when two males entered the laundromat. Both were wearing skull ski masks. One had on a red hoodie and the other wore a dark one. According to the manager, the male in the dark hoodie stuck a gun in his face while the other one stayed by the door, acting as a lookout."

"What about the customer's statement? The one who walked in on the robbery?"

"She's still working on that one."

"Any video?" Byron asked.

"There is a camera, but it isn't hooked up. Only for show."

Byron wondered how many people already knew: full-blown security systems meant expensive monthly premiums. Often, local businesses chose to gamble rather than be bled financially by ADT.

"Did either one of the suspects touch anything inside?" Byron asked.

"Manager wasn't sure," Pepin said. "He's pretty upset."

"Have Connolly stay with him until the E.T. gets there."

"Will do."

Byron pinned the phone between his ear and his shoulder, then pulled out his notebook. He scribbled with the pen on the back of the notepad attempting to get the cold ink flowing, then made some notes. "Could the victim describe the gun?"

"Yup. Said it looked like a stainless revolver with black grips."

A revolver would certainly explain the lack of any visible shell casings, Byron thought. One point in Haggerty's favor.

"Thanks, Andy," Byron said. "Do me a favor. Make sure you have every one of your people write up a supplement before they go home. No matter how small their involvement."

"What about mine?" Pepin asked. "You know, what Haggerty told me."

"Write it up, Andy. Just the way it happened."

"Okay, boss."

Byron pocketed the phone. He took a deep breath, then walked over to LeRoyer.

"Jesus, John," LeRoyer said. "This is a friggin' shit show."

You don't know the half of it, Byron thought.

"John, you know Lucinda Phillips," LeRoyer said, making the introductions. "She's the new investigator for the AG's office."

"Luce," Byron said, shaking her hand. "Sorry I missed your retirement party."

"It's okay," she said. "Wasn't much of a retirement. One weekend to be exact."

Byron and Phillips had enjoyed a good working relationship while she had been with the state police, but now she was working for the Maine Attorney General's Office, the very agency responsible for filing criminal charges against Haggerty should this turn out to be a bad shoot.

"The chief and I were just discussing having the two of you kinda work this together," LeRoyer said. "We thought it might be a good idea."

Byron couldn't imagine a worse idea. Both of their bosses were political animals. It went with the territory. He knew Rumsfeld was desperately seeking a permanent appointment to chief of police. As for Phillips's boss, the attorney general, Byron had no idea what brass ring he might be reaching for.

"No offense, Luce, but isn't that a bit of a conflict of interest, Marty?" Byron said.

Phillips grinned.

"Why?" LeRoyer said. "Aren't we all after the truth here?"

"Police brutality!" someone yelled from within the crowd.

All three investigators turned to look.

Byron turned back to LeRoyer. "Whose version?"

BYRON FILLED IN the lieutenant on *most* of what he knew, mercifully avoiding the acting chief in the process. Byron was not a fan of the man many referred to as Rumpswab. He then drove to police headquarters at 109 Middle Street accompanied by Phillips. Byron wanted to check on Haggerty. While they were en route, Nugent phoned to say he'd located a possible witness to the shooting and would be heading to 109 as well.

Byron pulled off his gloves and cranked the heat, holding one hand at a time directly in front of the dashboard vents as he drove. He opened and closed his fingers, trying to get them working again, and wondered how Haggerty had ever managed to pull the trigger.

"You know I'm still the same person I was when I worked for the state police," Phillips said from the passenger seat.

He glanced at her without saying anything.

"The same detective sergeant you worked well with, remember?" she continued. "We don't have to be on opposing sides here, John."

"No?" Byron asked.

"No, we don't. I have a job to do, just like you. I'm only here to find out what happened."

"What happened is one of our police officers just shot and killed a teenager."

"A teen who had just robbed a business at gunpoint," Phillips countered.

"Yeah? Well, allow me to let you in on a little secret. So far we haven't been able to locate the kid's gun."

Phillips's eyes widened. "Oh Christ."

They spent the remainder of the trip in silence.

PORTLAND POLICE HEADQUARTERS stood at the corner of Franklin Arterial and Middle Street. Constructed in 1972, the oddly shaped four-story pile of bricks had gone through several different renovations—"transformations," they were called—none of which had made the slightest improvement in 109's curb appeal. Compared with the grand architecture of city hall and the federal courthouse, 109 would forever be the ugly stepsister of the Port City.

The Criminal Investigation Division, CID, was housed on the top floor. Comprised of several offices for the supervisory and command staff, a large open bullpen for the detectives, three interview rooms, a conference room, and a glass-walled waiting area, the detective bureau was typical of Maine's larger depart-ments.

Byron's plan had been to drop in and check on Haggerty's state of mind, then head down to the second floor where Nugent was conducting his interview.

"I'm advising you not to go in there, Sergeant," the MAP at-torney barked, briefly interrupting his own conversation with the department's Internal Affairs Sergeant Brad Thibodeau.

Byron turned around and stood toe-to-toe with the portly lawyer, whose name escaped him. He caught the familiar scent of an intoxicant to go along with an almost imperceptible slurring of his words.

"Great. You've advised me, *counselor*," Byron said, enunciat-ing the word as if he'd called him an asshole. "Now, unless you're planning to physically try and stop me, I'm going to check on the well-being of one of *my* officers."

Byron glanced at Phillips and Thibodeau but neither said a word. His gaze lingered on Thibodeau's smug mug. He half ex-pected Thibodeau to say something stupid. The beady-eyed ser-geant had a well-earned reputation as a yes-man, a trait Byron couldn't stand, especially in matters pertaining to internal affairs. IA was the one place in law enforcement with the potential to be more dangerous than the street. In the hands of the wrong IA in-vestigator the pen truly was mightier than the sword.

"This is highly irregular, Sergeant," the mildly inebriated at-torney continued, drawing Byron's attention back to him. "You can be sure I'll be taking this matter up with your chief. In fact, maybe I'll phone him right now."

"Acting chief," Byron corrected. He turned around and con-tinued toward the interview rooms, then stopped. "Oh, and you might wanna consider some mouthwash or a breath mint before speaking with him in person, *counselor.*" Portly had no comeback.

Byron rapped his knuckles against the cobalt-colored door to Interview Room One, then stepped inside.

Sean Haggerty was a cop's cop. In his early thirties and built like a linebacker, he was a gentle giant. A member of the Maine Police Emerald Society, where he and Byron had first met more than a decade ago, he was also a piper with the Maine Public Safety Pipe and Drum Corps. Haggerty was the one uniformed officer Byron wanted to see at every crime scene. Haggerty was smart and he followed the rules. Byron had tried more than once to recruit the veteran cop to CID, but to no avail. Haggerty liked being on the front lines.

On this day, he looked defeated, like someone had let the air out of him. Haggerty bore little resemblance to the formidable and squared away presence that Byron was used to seeing. Seated in a chair on the far side of the round wooden pedestal table, slumped to one side, his head was resting against the wall. He sat up as Byron entered. "Sarge."

Byron saw what appeared to be Plummer's dried blood on Haggerty's uniform pants and shirt. Blood was also present on the black leather jacket lying on the floor.

"How are you holding up, Hags?" Byron asked, already knowing the answer. Alone and scared. Second-guessing himself and wishing more than anything he could somehow turn the clock back and make all of it go away. Byron was glad Haggerty had at least been spared the sounds of the mother's anguish, for now.

"Not too good, Sarge. Feel sick to my stomach."

Byron glanced over at the union representative sitting across from Haggerty. "Give us a minute, would you?"

The officer looked at Haggerty for guidance.

"It's okay," Haggerty said, nodding.

"I'll be right outside," the officer assured him. "Holler if you need me, Hags."

Byron waited until the rep had gone and the door was closed before sliding into the chair across from Haggerty.

"I know the kid didn't make it," Haggerty said. "He didn't, did he, Sarge?"

"No," Byron said. "He didn't."

Haggerty tilted his head back and sighed loudly. "I am so screwed, aren't I?"

"First off, you're not screwed. We're looking into this just like we always do, okay? We'll figure out what happened."

Haggerty looked at Byron. "Have they found his gun yet?"

Byron wished he could say they had, but on that point, he had no comfort to offer. "Not yet."

Haggerty crossed his arms and hung his head. "I'm fucked."

"Listen to me, Sean. I'm gonna do my best to get you out of here as soon as I can. You're gonna get a whole shitload of advice tonight. Some of these self-serving pricks might even try to take advantage of you. Don't let them. You don't have to say a word to anyone, yet. All right?"

Haggerty nodded in silence.

"Only you know what happened out there. I wasn't there, and neither were any of the people gathering in the next room. Only you, Sean. You and your attorney will most likely meet with the investigator from the Attorney General's Office in a couple days.

Her name is Lucinda Phillips. She's good people. It's entirely your decision whether you decide to talk to her about what happened. But for right now, keep your mouth shut, okay? Don't talk to anyone but your lawyer. You got me?"

"Yeah, I gotcha. Guess I shoulda turned down the overtime, huh?"

"Did you get a look at the other suspect?"

"Too dark. I wasn't close enough to him. Did we ID the kid yet?"

"His name is Thomas Plummer."

"Oh Jesus. Tommy."

"You knew him?"

"Everybody knows him."

"Portland High kid?"

"Captain of the basketball team."

Byron hadn't been looking to make Haggerty feel worse. He switched gears. "I called in another E.T. to grab your clothes and snap some photos of you."

Byron watched as Haggerty surveyed his own clothing. Haggerty's face shifted; he knew that his uniform was now evidence.

"Do you have someone who can grab you a change of clothes from your locker?" Byron asked.

"I'll have my rep to do it."

"You want me to call anyone?"

"No. I'll phone my family and my girlfriend after I get out of here."

"You need anything? Coffee? Something to eat?"

Haggerty shook his head. "Don't think I could keep it down."

Byron stood up and moved around the table. He placed his hand atop the younger officer's slumped shoulder and squeezed.

"He shot at me, Sarge. I saw the flash."

Byron resisted the urge to ask a follow-up question. If this was a bad shoot, Haggerty had already said too much. "Just hang in there, okay? You're not alone in this, Sean."

BYRON DEPARTED THE interview room and headed for the stairwell. Phillips remained in CID. He knew she'd at least have to touch base with Haggerty and his lawyers before he was sent home. Byron needed to check in on the detectives taking statements.

He found Nugent and Tran conducting an interview in the police training room on the second floor. Byron motioned through the half glass window wall for Nugent to step out into the hall.

"Hey, Sarge," Nugent said, retreating into the hallway and closing the door behind him.

"Tell me about your witness," Byron said.

"Ha. Well, now that we're getting down to brass tacks, she's not exactly as advertised."

"How so?"

"When I first spoke with her, Mrs. Dietrich claimed to have actually seen the incident happen. Now it comes out that what she actually witnessed was the aftermath. Out walking her dog on Anderson when the foot chase crossed the road up the block in front of her. Says she definitely heard the shots though. She and everyone else."

"She say how many?" Byron asked.

"Maybe a dozen."

Byron raised his eyebrows.

"Her words," Nugent said, raising his hands as if in surrender.

"Gabe told me Hags only fired five rounds."

Nugent rolled his eyes. "So far we've heard everything from two or three to fifteen. Can you say shitty witnesses?"

Byron knew this was not unusual. The bigger the incident, the wilder and less trustworthy the witnesses' stories tended to be. Some people just couldn't help themselves. Some even believed what they were saying.

"How about the canvass?" Byron asked. "Any other people claim to see the shooting?"

"Nope. Mel and a couple of Sergeant Peterson's guys are putting together a list of people, but so far there aren't any eyewitnesses to the shooting itself. I'm sure that will change once the news breaks."

Byron was sure it would too. He watched through the glass as his one-man Computer Crimes Unit interacted with Mrs. Dietrich. Tran seemed to be taking the assignment seriously. Like the rest of the department, CID was down a few bodies, forcing everyone to do more with less. "How's Dustin doing?" Byron asked, nodding toward Tran.

Nugent regarded his temporary partner through the window. "For a geek who spends all his time playing with computers, he's doing okay. Don't worry, Sarge. When I'm through with him, he'll be as suave an interviewer as me."

BYRON MET UP with AG Investigator Phillips and they both headed back to the scene, intentionally bypassing 109's first-floor lobby where Rumsfeld was holding an impromptu press conference, accompanied by Diane and LeRoyer. Byron wasn't worried about the acting chief leaking anything too important, mainly because he didn't know much yet. The problems would begin during the next gathering, most likely late morning, when Rumsfeld would have to field some tough questions.

"How'd it go with Sean?" Byron asked after they were back in the car.

"Okay," Phillips said.

"When is he meeting with you?"

"This afternoon."

This afternoon? Byron turned to face her. "Seriously? I just finished telling him to take some time."

"I suggested the same thing. Sean said he just wanted to get it over with."

Byron hoped Haggerty wasn't making a mistake. Being prodded for details less than eighteen hours after killing a teenager, on the heels of what would likely turn out to be a sleepless night, didn't seem to Byron like the prudent course.

It was after one-thirty by the time Byron and Phillips rolled onto Anderson Street. They parked behind the evidence van and two black-and-whites. The crowd of people gathered earlier had long since departed, along with Tommy Plummer's body. The bitter cold and late hour had been a blessing after all.

Pelligrosso and Murphy were seated inside the rear compartment of the van with the heater cranked, sipping coffee and trying to get warm enough to return to the scene.

"Hey, Sarge," Pelligrosso said as Byron and Phillips climbed in with them and closed the door.

Byron introduced Phillips, then got right to the point. "How's it going?"

"Slow," Pelligrosso said. "The cold is messing with everything. The camera batteries keep dying, even the plaster casting was a bitch. We got it though."

Byron couldn't help but think of the cellphone found next to Plummer.

Pelligrosso addressed Phillips. "Your evidence people just left."

"Yeah, I spoke with them by phone."

"I'll make sure they get copies of everything we generate."

"Thanks," Phillips said. "What were you casting?"

Pelligrosso brought Phillips up to speed, explaining that the sneaker print hadn't matched the soles of the dead suspect's footwear. "Plummer was wearing Adidas running sneakers. The print I found has these two weird angled pairs of squares on the heel and on the ball of the foot."

"What did Ellis have to say?" Byron asked. Ellis was the state's deputy medical examiner.

"Doc said he'll schedule the post for Monday, late afternoon. Figured we'd still have too much to do down here tomorrow morning." Before Byron could correct him, Pelligrosso checked his watch. "Make that today."

"Any problem getting the body out of here?" Byron asked. "We're not gonna see him on Facebook, are we?"

"We managed to keep that from happening, I think. Had a hell of a time getting him bagged though."

"What do you mean?" Phillips asked.

"Body heat," Pelligrosso said. "He'd already frozen to the ground."

Phillips grimaced.

"What else do you need done tonight?" Byron asked his senior evidence tech.

"Still gotta gather up our equipment. I want to come back during daylight hours and take additional photos and measurements."

"I'll get the shift commander to hold a couple of officers down here until you're ready to release the scene."

"Plus, we need to double-check that we've recovered all the evidence there is to find."

"Speaking of which, I'm assuming we didn't find a weapon?" Byron said.

Pelligrosso downed his last swig of coffee, tossing the empty Styrofoam cup into the dingy white five-gallon bucket, doubling as a trash receptacle, tethered to the inside wall of the van. "We did not. Another reason I want to scour the area during daylight. Haggerty told Pepin that the kid shot at him. If there's something to find, I want to find it."

Byron did too. "What about the robbery money?"

"We found a ten and three ones in the left front pocket of his jeans."

"That's it?" Byron asked.

"That's it," Pelligrosso said.

"How much was taken in the robbery?" Phillips asked.

"Victim said they got just over six hundred," Pelligrosso said.

Phillips gave Byron a look that didn't need translating.

"I wanna do a quick group meet-up in CID to go over what we have so far," Byron said. "109 in twenty?"

"We'll be there," Pelligrosso said.

BYRON TOOK A cellphone call as he and Phillips were heading back to their respective cars.

"Sarge, it's Mel. Just finished with Plummer's parents."

"How'd it go?"

"About like you'd imagine. They didn't really hit it off with the advocate, but they were okay with me."

Byron hoped, with Stevens's help, they'd be able to establish a working relationship with the Plummers before things spun totally out of control.

"They say where Tommy got the gun?" Byron asked.

"Said he didn't have one."

"Did they have any idea who he was running with tonight?"

"They didn't."

"How did you leave it with them?" Byron asked.

"I told them you'd want to meet up with them midmorning. I also said we'd let them know of any new developments before we put anything out to the public."

"Good. Where are you now?"

"Heading into 109. I got some paperwork to start and I figured you'd want to meet up as a group."

"Thanks, Mel. I'll be in shortly."

BYRON AND PHILLIPS pulled into the rear parking garage of 109, armed with fresh coffees and two boxes of donut holes from Dunkin' Donuts. LeRoyer was waiting for them as they entered the CID lobby.

"John, we need to talk," LeRoyer said.

"Meeting with my detectives in the conference room right now, Marty. You're free to join us if you'd like."

"Actually, they're *my* detectives," LeRoyer snapped. "As are you, Sergeant." He pointed toward his office like he was ordering a canine to obey. "You and me, right now."

"I'll meet you in the conference room," Phillips said wisely as she took the boxes from Byron. "I gotta check in with my boss anyway."

LeRoyer trailed Byron into the CID locker room where Detective Luke Gardiner, one of Sergeant Peterson's property crime detectives, was changing footwear.

"Give us a second," LeRoyer said.

"Sure thing, Lieu," Gardiner said, quickening his pace.

Byron removed his coat and sweater and hung them in his locker as he waited for the new detective to depart and for his high-strung commander to make his point.

"How long were you gonna leave me in the dark about the Plummer kid not having a gun?"

"We don't know for sure he didn't have one, Marty. Besides, until I knew the gun wasn't hidden beneath something, I wasn't about to say anything." Byron grabbed a small bottle of green-colored mouthwash off the shelf in his locker and headed for the sink. LeRoyer followed, then paced the floor behind him.

"The chief is really pissed off," LeRoyer said.

"Acting chief," Byron corrected before taking a swig. "And I'll be sure and add that to the list of things I don't give a shit about."

"Dammit, John, it isn't funny."

Byron gargled the minty liquid, then spit the rinse into the sink and recapped the bottle. "Don't see me laughing, do you?" Byron said.

Byron and LeRoyer had worked the same city streets together for many years. Byron knew it was only their history that allowed him the leeway of telling his boss exactly what he meant without fear of reprisal. In a paramilitary organization like the Portland Police Department, it wasn't a luxury afforded to many subordinates.

"The chief is meeting with the city manager right now, at his house, about this morning's press conference," LeRoyer said.

"A shame Perkins couldn't be bothered to visit us here," Byron said, returning to his locker with LeRoyer hot on his heels.

"Can it, John."

"Look," Byron said. "I didn't tell you because I knew you'd jump to conclusions, which is exactly what you *are* doing. All of you."

"Yeah. The same conclusions the public is going to come to. Billingslea has already been sniffing around. He's called me twice, in fact, and he was at Rumsfeld's briefing less than an hour ago."

Byron had no love for Davis Billingslea, the nosy police beat reporter from the *Portland Herald*. Too much water had passed beneath the flimsy bridge connecting Byron and the Woodward-and-Bernstein-wannabe.

"You can add Billingslea to my list too," Byron said, grabbing a tie off the hook, which was nothing more than a bent piece of a wire clothes hanger twisted through the vents of his locker door. "Listen, Marty, not finding the suspect's gun isn't the same thing as him not having one, and you know it. Two suspects fled this robbery. Tommy Plummer had an accomplice. An accomplice who may well have removed the gun from the scene."

"If there ever *was* a gun," LeRoyer said, giving his hair a quick pass with his fingers, his telltale nervous tic. "*Shit.*"

Byron considered telling LeRoyer about the cellphone MedCu had noticed, but decided against it for the time being. There were far too many people making premature judgments to suit him.

"Unlike AC Rumpswab, I deal in facts, not spin," Byron said.

"I'm warning you, John. Watch yourself."

"No, you watch it! Listen to yourself, Marty. How long have we known Hags? Ten years? He's a good beat cop. He's smart, uses good judgment, and he's good with people. Hell, if he wasn't all of those things they never would've made him the SRO for Portland High," Byron said.

LeRoyer remained silent while he paced the locker room.

"He deserves our support on this," Byron continued. "The benefit of the doubt while we try and figure out what happened. If Sean says he was shot at, I believe him. And I'll do due fucking diligence to follow up on every possible lead."

LeRoyer said nothing.

"Would you do less if it were me?" Byron asked.

"Of course not."

"Is Haggerty still here?" Byron said, trying to bring the tension down a notch.

"No. Sent him home twenty minutes ago."

"Don't give in to their pressure, Marty. Let me do my job. Let my detectives do their jobs. If there's something to find, we'll find it." Byron moved past him toward the locker room door.

"And if you're wrong?" LeRoyer asked from behind him.

Byron pulled the heavy wooden door open, pausing a moment as he turned to face the lieutenant. "Then we're all fucked."

Chapter 4

Monday, 3:00 A.M.,
January 16, 2017

ACTING CHIEF RUMSFELD blew warm air into his hands as he waited on the darkened stoop for Portland City Manager Clayton Perkins. As instructed, Rumsfeld had sent Perkins a text from the driveway so as not to wake Mrs. Perkins by ringing the bell. He was beginning to wonder whether his text had been received when the overhead light came on in the kitchen and a bathrobe-clad Perkins shuffled into view.

Perkins crossed the kitchen and opened the door for Rumsfeld. "Come inside and close the door," Perkins said gruffly. "Coffee?"

"Coffee would be great," Rumsfeld said. "Thanks."

Rumsfeld pulled out a chair at the kitchen table and sat down to wait. This dance between him and Perkins was still new, and the acting chief did not want to step on his boss's toes. So, he remained silent while waiting to be led.

"Tell me about the kid," Perkins said as he shuffled around the kitchen.

"He attends Portland High, or rather he did. Seventeen years old."

"Jesus," Perkins said.

"Yeah."

"What's his name?"

"Plummer. Thomas Plummer. Family lives on the east end of the peninsula."

Perkins opened the fridge and retrieved a carton of milk. "What's your take on the shooting?" he asked as he placed the carton on the table.

Rumsfeld knew he had to tread carefully as everything he said would be taken as gospel by his boss. Perkins had a reputation for shooting from the hip before getting all the facts. And Rumsfeld couldn't afford to say anything that might later make Perkins look bad. Rumsfeld's career aspirations might well drown under that wave.

"I don't know yet," Rumsfeld said. "The owner of the laundromat said they displayed a gun."

Perkins arched a brow. "They?"

"There were two of them."

"Where is the other one now?" Perkins asked.

"We don't know. He got away."

"So, we may have an armed assailant out roaming the streets, is that what you're telling me?"

"I don't think there is any threat to the general public here, Clayton."

"You mean other than the armed robbery and police shooting?"

Rumsfeld, realizing he'd slipped already, did not respond.

"What did the cop involved in the shooting say?" Perkins asked.

"Sean Haggerty. Said the Plummer kid fired at him first."

"But we don't have a gun."

"No, sir, we don't," Rumsfeld said.

"Who's working this?"

"John Byron and his detectives are working the robbery and the events that led up to the shooting."

"And the shooting itself?"

"Standard protocol, the state Attorney General's Office has jurisdiction, but they will be working alongside of Byron's team."

The Keurig sputtered its last. Perkins delivered two steaming ceramic mugs to the table and sat down.

Rumsfeld picked up the mug and held it between his open palms. The heat felt good on his cold skin. He waited as the city manager regarded him silently.

"You're thinking like a cop right now, aren't you?" Perkins asked.

"Sir?"

"You're thinking about how you're gonna spin this when you have to tell the press about the missing weapon."

"I wouldn't say spin exactly. I'd say it's likely the other suspect—"

The manager held up his hand. "Let me stop you right there. I know you want to be more than just the acting chief."

Rumsfeld nodded but remained silent.

"Dan, this is one of those moments where I'll see what you're made of. Being the chief of police means you are responsible for leading the officers, of course. But it also means you're responsible to me, and to the citizens of this city. You follow?"

Rumsfeld wasn't sure what Perkins was getting at, but he wasn't about to show uncertainty to this man. He nodded again.

"This shooting investigation is likely to go very badly," Perkins said. He inhaled deeply, then let out a long sigh. "Great leaders are forged by adversity. All eyes will be on you to see how you handle this."

As Rumsfeld listened to Perkins wax motivational, he couldn't help but wonder what Vince Lombardi would've looked like in a bathrobe.

Perkins continued. "You'll be expected to walk a fine line on this and, if need be, come out in support of the community and not necessarily of your own department. Think you can do that?"

Rumsfeld paused for only a moment, trying to project just the right amount of thoughtfulness before answering. "Yes, sir. I know I can."

IT WAS THREE-THIRTY by the time all the investigators had assembled in the CID conference room. Standing room only. The space smelled of stale coffee and unwashed hair. Byron walked in and sat down in the only empty seat remaining at the long laminate wooden table, beside Phillips. He wondered if the chair had been left vacant because they'd been seen together or because nobody wanted to sit next to her.

Melissa Stevens was adding names and details to the whiteboard as each of the detectives read them off. Every investigator wore the same sullen expression, as did the evidence technicians. They all knew exactly what was on the line.

"That everything?" Stevens asked as she scanned the room.

"All I've got," Nugent said.

Several other detectives confirmed it was all the information they possessed as well.

"This represents everything to this point, Sarge," Stevens said, addressing Byron.

Byron studied the board trying to take it all in. Under the heading Witnesses were a dozen names, including two marked with the letter *V*, designating the laundromat manager and customer as victims.

"Who processed the robbery scene?" Byron asked.

"I did, Sarge," Albert Junkins said.

Junkins was the most senior member of the crime lab. On the heavy side of stout with wavy black hair and a bad case of dandruff, Junkins was second in ability only to Pelligrosso. His lesser skill set was the primary reason Byron hadn't assigned Junkins to the shooting scene. Byron had learned long ago that on a major case you always wanted your best working the worst aspect, or at least the part with the most at stake.

"Pepin told me the surveillance camera inside the laundromat was a dummy," Byron said to Junkins. "Anything worthwhile from the robbery scene?"

"I lifted a few partial prints from the area near the office safe," Junkins said. "But, based solely on the victim's statement, they most likely belong to the kid Haggerty shot. He's the only one who approached the counter."

"What about the second suspect, the one acting as lookout?" Byron asked. "Did the victim see him touch anything?"

Junkins shook his head, causing his meaty jowls to flap, reminding Byron of a dog. "Victim said he was wearing gloves. Stayed right by the door."

"Any other cameras nearby that might have picked up our suspects either coming or going from the robbery?" Byron asked.

"I did a cursory sweep of the businesses along Washington Avenue," Junkins said. "Figured I'd go back during daylight hours and check with each one individually."

"Dustin, you go with him," Byron said, addressing Detective Tran, the police department's computer virtuoso. "I want to make certain we don't lose something to a system overwrite."

"You got it," Tran said. Dustin usually went for a surfer dude persona; he was fond of calling Byron "Striped-One." But not today.

"In the meantime," Byron said, still addressing Tran, "I want you to download and copy everything Dispatch has surrounding this. All radio traffic, including CID response traffic, MedCu traffic from fire side, the original 911 call from the laundromat customer, and any emergency phone calls regarding shots fired. Everything."

"Consider it done, boss."

Byron turned to Pelligrosso. "Gabe, can you give everyone a thumbnail of your scene?"

"Sure thing, Sarge."

Pelligrosso spent the next ten minutes providing a rundown of the scene in the alley. Using a printed aerial map of Kennedy Park, Pelligrosso drew a red line extending from the scene of Haggerty's 10–50, the code for an accident involving a police vehicle, along the pursuit trail. The line twisted and turned through the housing project, ending at the scene of the shooting.

"Did we recover any shell casings from the area where the suspects were standing when the shooting happened?" Lieutenant LeRoyer asked from the doorway.

Pelligrosso shook his head. "No, but the laundromat manager described the handgun displayed by the robber as a revolver, so there may not have been."

Byron looked to Stevens. "Mel, wait until seven, then reach out to the Plummers again. Let's set up a nine o'clock at their home. I want you to introduce me."

"Okay."

"We need to try and soft-sell a search of Tommy's room and belongings for any evidence he may have had a gun."

"Not sure how cooperative they'll be," Stevens said.

"We need this, Mel," Byron said. "We need to emphasize the importance of what we're trying to do here. If somebody did supply Tommy with a weapon, we want to find out who. Also, let's make sure we revisit his friends with them. They must have some idea who he may have been with last night."

"You got it. I'll let you know the time."

"You know who Tommy Plummer is, right?" Nugent asked Byron.

"Should I?"

"He's the reason Portland High won the state basketball championship last season."

"And the reason they've been picked to repeat this season," Junkins said.

"I'll be sure and congratulate his parents," Byron said.

Junkins's face turned a deep shade of crimson.

Byron slowly scanned the room. "I know this goes without saying, but I don't want any details getting out."

LeRoyer chimed in from the doorway. "All requests for information are to go through me or the chief's office. Everybody clear on that?"

The room gave a collective nod.

"How long before the press dam breaks?" Tran asked.

"Acting Chief Rumsfeld is planning a conference for noon," LeRoyer said.

Several detectives groaned.

"We've got a lot to do today, people," Byron said, checking the wall clock. "It's almost four. I suggest each of you use the next hour or so to take care of any personal business."

Byron knew, as they all did, that any plans they may have had, both professional and personal, were now indefinitely on hold. Uncovering the truth about what had transpired in the alley the previous evening was the only thing any of them would be focused on for the foreseeable future.

"Any questions before we dig in?" Byron asked.

Stevens spoke up. "What about the weather, Sarge?"

"What about it?"

"They're predicting as much as a foot of snow starting sometime this evening," Pelligrosso said.

"Shit, that's right," Nugent said.

Byron had completely forgotten about the forecasted storm. "Can you finish all of the outside processing before then?" he asked Pelligrosso.

"We'll have to."

"Contact the M.E.'s office and delay the autopsy if you need to," Byron said. "We can always do it tomorrow."

Pelligrosso nodded. "Okay. I'll see how it goes."

Byron addressed the rest of the room. "I want a door-to-door sweep through Kennedy Park looking for potential witnesses. Let's make sure we don't overlook anyone."

Detective Gardiner, the latest addition to Sergeant Peterson's property crime unit, spoke up. "What if they say they didn't see or hear anything, you still want a statement?"

"Absolutely," Byron said. "Lock them in. I don't want anyone making up shit later just to get their fifteen minutes. No wiggle room."

"Consider it done, sir."

Byron studied Pelligrosso's map again. "Also, let's sweep the route Haggerty took chasing the suspects. We're looking for anything that may have been dropped or tossed along the way. And we're still missing Haggerty's flashlight."

THE GROUP OF detectives broke up and headed in opposite directions. They went home to shower and change, or to talk with their spouses, who would be manning the fort solo until further notice. Investigator Phillips headed to the Spring Street Holiday Inn with her go bag to check in before meeting Byron for breakfast.

Byron slid his unmarked into a vacant space in front of Becky's on Commercial Street. Portland's landmark waterfront diner operated 362 1/2 days a year, opening at four o'clock in the morning to serve the predawn fishing crowd and the occasional police investigator. Byron had just stepped out of the Malibu's warm interior when his cell rang. He answered mid-ring. "Byron."

"Hey, John," Diane said. "How goes it so far?"

"If I'd had to imagine a scenario, I'd have picked a different one," he said.

"Can you talk?" she asked.

"Have you eaten?"

TWENTY MINUTES LATER, Byron was seated at a booth across from Sergeant Diane Joyner and AG Investigator Lucinda Phillips. Aware of the sensitive nature of their discussion, all three did their best to keep their voices lowered.

"What did your boss have to say?" Byron asked Phillips.

"I think the first word out of his mouth was *shit*."

"Gets right to the point, doesn't he?" Byron said, sliding his mug toward the young waitress who'd stopped by for coffee refills.

"What do you think, John?" Diane asked. "You don't really think Haggerty shot an unarmed kid, do you?"

Byron carefully sipped the steaming mug of black coffee before returning it to the table. "No, I don't," he said. "My guess? The other suspect made off with it. But, at this point, that's all it would be. A guess."

"You're hoping that's what happened," Phillips added.

"Aren't you?" Byron said, making no effort to hide his irritation.

The waitress returned with their orders, balancing several plates on one arm. For the next few minutes they ate in silence, enveloped in the gray cloud of the day that lay ahead.

Byron broke the silence. "What's Rumpswab planning to tell the media?"

Phillips was unsuccessful at hiding a grin.

Diane washed a bite of her breakfast sandwich down with a swig of orange juice before answering. "As little as possible. He won't mention the missing gun. He's planning to give out the description of the second robbery suspect again. And to acknowledge the victim's family and the loss of their son."

Byron bristled. "*Victim?* Don't you mean suspect?"

Diane frowned. "You know what I mean, John."

Chapter 5

Monday, 7:00 A.M.,
January 16, 2017

MICKY CAVALLARO REACHED out blindly, attempting to silence the incessant ringing. His head was still buried in the pillow. In one smooth motion he rolled onto his back and held the receiver to his ear.

"What?"

"Good morning, Michael," an all too familiar voice greeted. "I understand you had some excitement last night."

Cavallaro, now fully awake, sat up and leaned against the headboard, rubbing the sleep from his crusted eyes. "How did you hear about that already?" he asked, knowing better than to use the man's name over the phone.

"I would think the more important question would be, why didn't you contact us?"

He swallowed nervously, knowing that the outcome of this

phone call would likely determine not only the future course of his life, but how long it might continue.

"Am I correct in assuming that you took a rather large hit?"

"Yes."

"How large?"

"All of it."

The long pause in the conversation did nothing to assuage the laundromat owner's fears.

"And you thought it prudent to involve the police?" the voice asked at last.

"I didn't," Cavallaro said. "A customer walked in during the robbery. He called the police." Even as he spoke the words, he knew how little they would matter to the man on the other end of the phone.

"Who did this, Michael?"

"I don't know. The police shot one of them but they haven't released any names yet."

Several moments passed before the caller spoke again.

"I'm sending someone to talk with you."

THE SUN HAD risen over Casco Bay. The fiery ball of vermillion portended the approaching storm. Sea smoke rose from the ocean like rainwater hitting hot pavement. A by-product of the single-digit temperature. Byron sat alone in his unmarked, jammed in workday commuter traffic on his way back to Kennedy Park. A local talk show droned on the radio, but he wasn't listening. His focus was on the investigation. He glanced up at the Chapman Building on Congress Street, and the familiar winter warning caught his eye. *Snow. Ban.* One at a time the words cycled through the lighted billboard messaging system atop the landmark high-rise, also known as the Time and Temperature Building. Only two words, but the message was clear. Any cars left on the street overnight would be towed. Parking in downtown Portland was scarce enough when the weather was favorable. And a storm threatening to dump more than a foot of the white stuff was anything but favorable.

Byron made the left turn onto Anderson, nearly colliding with a tow truck whose driver was operating partially on Byron's side of the road and treating the stop sign as if it were a yield.

"Watch it, asshole!" Byron shouted as he swerved to the right while making eye contact with the young male driver.

The wrecker was a flatbed type hauling what looked like a junk car. The long-haired driver gave Byron a sheepish look and continued his right turn onto Cumberland Avenue.

A moment later Byron pulled over and parked behind an idling black-and-white. Moisture-laden exhaust curled up and around the rear of the cruiser forming a small cloud that hung in the still air, a reminder of just how cold it was, not that he needed one. Farther down the road, two local news vans were parked in front of their own plumes, waiting like vipers about to strike. As Byron exited his unmarked Chevy he saw Nugent approaching on foot. The bald detective's pace suggested there had been a break.

"Gabe is looking for you," Nugent said. "Think maybe we found something."

"Hang on a sec," Byron said as he approached the officer seated inside the cruiser.

"Morning, Sarge," the officer said, quickly stepping out to greet him.

Byron recognized the sandy-haired rookie instantly. "Officer Cody, isn't it?"

"Didn't know if you'd remember me," Cody said.

Nugent piped up. "Not remember *you*? Kid, you're a legend. Passing out during the Ramsey autopsy was priceless."

Cody blushed. "Sir, how is Officer Haggerty?"

Byron was impressed with the rookie's genuine concern for Haggerty's well-being. Haggerty had been Cody's first field training officer after graduation from the Maine Criminal Justice Academy in Vassalboro. *Perhaps there's hope for the "me" generation after all*, Byron thought.

"Having a pretty rough time of it, I imagine," Byron said.

"Think he'd mind if I called him?"

"I think he'd appreciate hearing from you."

Byron made a show of pointing toward the news vans, as he knew they were watching. "See those vultures parked down there, Officer?"

"Yes, sir."

"Don't let those assholes anywhere near my scene."

Cody grinned. "You got it, Sarge."

Byron followed Nugent across the street and down an alley between two buildings. Pelligrosso was standing on an upside-down five-gallon bucket, which looked suspiciously like the one Byron had seen doubling as a trash receptacle inside the evidence van only hours earlier. Byron made a mental note to request additional evidence funding. The flattopped E.T. was photographing something near the top of a cyclone fence while Murphy looked on.

"Nice ladder, huh?" Nugent said.

"What have you got, Gabe?" Byron asked.

"A torn piece of fabric," he said, lowering his hands to allow Byron to see it.

Red in color, the material was no more than a tiny scrap of cloth.

"Might be from the other robbery suspect's clothing," Pelligrosso opined. "Haggerty said one of the males he was chasing got caught up on top of a fence. We also have those." Pelligrosso pointed to a half dozen yellow markers in the snow.

"Shoe prints?" Byron asked.

"Yeah," Pelligrosso said. "We've got three matches: the dead robber's sneakers, Haggerty's boots, and footwear impressions that match the one we cast last night."

"Our missing suspect?" Byron asked.

"Maybe."

Byron and Nugent looked on as Pelligrosso carefully removed the material and placed it inside the small paper bag Murphy was holding.

"I'll go over this for hairs and fibers later," Pelligrosso said.

"We locate anything else?" Byron asked.

"Not yet. Still need to find Haggerty's mini-Mag, and I want to comb through the shooting scene again. If the gun described by the laundromat manager wasn't a revolver, and Haggerty was right, there may be a shell casing still hidden in the snow somewhere."

Byron could only hope they would be so lucky. Something as small as a shell casing, at this point in the investigation, might serve to dampen the public outrage that was likely to follow.

"Whatever you need, Gabe," Byron said. "And take your time. With a foot of snow coming, we'll only get one—"

Byron's cell rang, interrupting him. The caller ID identified it as Sergeant Joyner. He stepped away from them to answer it. "Hey, Di."

"Hey, yourself," she said. "Any progress?"

"Not as much as I'd like. Trying to lock it down before the news media blows this whole thing up."

"Actually, that's why I'm calling. Mayor Gilcrest just announced a press conference of her own."

"Goddammit," Byron snapped.

Nugent and the others turned to look at him.

"I knew you'd want a heads-up," Diane said.

"That's all we need," Byron said, trying to lower his voice. "Any idea what she's planning to say?"

"No, but I'm betting it's not gonna be good. She's upstaging the chief by holding her presser at eleven, an hour before his."

Byron knew exactly what Mayor Patricia Gilcrest was capable of. No fan of Portland's finest, she'd spent four years chairing the public safety committee and had had more than her share of public battles with former Chief Michael Stanton. Gilcrest had been elected mayor in a landslide and was now rumored to have her sights set on the governor's mansion, perhaps as soon as the following year. And if Gilcrest had stood up to Stanton, she'd eat Acting Chief Rumpswab for lunch. As if the impending snow wasn't enough, they would now have to contend with the storm brewing at city hall.

"I just thought you should know, John," Diane said. "I gotta run."

The call had no sooner ended when his phone rang again. It was LeRoyer.

And so it begins, Byron thought as he answered it. "Byron."

PORTLAND HERALD REPORTER Davis Billingslea drove slowly past the scene of the shooting. A young blond police officer sitting inside a parked cruiser gave him the hairy eyeball as he passed. Billingslea wasn't worried about being recognized. He figured the dark glasses and knit hat hid his face well enough. On the opposite side of the road from the cruiser, he spotted Detective Sergeant Byron among a group of other investigators. Byron was talking animatedly on his cell.

Billingslea parked his car one street over from where he'd seen the investigators working. The aging Honda's hinges protested loudly as he opened the door. He grabbed the newspaper's digital camera off the front passenger seat and stepped out into the cold.

He knew the police wouldn't let him anywhere near the scene; Byron would've already taken care of that. But he needed an edge, something the other news outlets didn't have. He could sit around like a trained circus animal waiting for someone at police headquarters to toss him a few scraps or he could take matters into his own hands. Billingslea backtracked around one of the row houses figuring he might get a peek at what the detectives were doing.

It took him several minutes and one heart-stopping face-to-face with a growling, and thankfully chained, Doberman before he found a decent shaded spot from which to surveil the investigators' activity.

From the building's shadow, Billingslea watched Byron turn and depart the area. It took ten more minutes of standing out in the cold before his patience was finally rewarded. Lifting the camera to his face, he zoomed in on the two evidence techs. They were working on something at ground level. *Footprints*, he thought. Or more accurately, shoe prints. The E.T.s were casting footwear impressions. Perhaps they'd found something left behind by the other robber. Billingslea grinned as he snapped a couple of pictures.

BYRON RETURNED TO 109 before his nine o'clock meeting with Tommy Plummer's parents, meeting briefly in the CID conference room with both his and Sergeant Peterson's detectives for the sole purpose of dividing up the witness list compiled the previous evening. It was time to bang on some additional doors. He wanted written statements from everyone who lived inside Kennedy Park.

"I'm not trying to be a dick, but why are we knocking on every door again, Sarge?" Detective Bernie Robbins asked.

Robbins, one of Peterson's detectives, was known for having a piss-poor attitude. When Robbins led with "I'm not trying to be a dick," Byron knew that's exactly what he was trying to be.

"Because, Bernie," Byron said, drawing on every ounce of patience he had, "I don't want to miss someone only to have them turn up later claiming to be a witness and muddying this up any further."

Locking potential witnesses down to one story would be important, especially if it did turn out to be a bad shoot. Byron knew some people would still claim to have been there once the public learned they hadn't found Plummer's gun. He still remembered his father, Reece, telling him that more people claimed to have been in attendance during game six of the 1975 World Series, when Red Sox catcher Carleton Fisk hit the game-winning home run inside the left field foul pole, than there were seats at Fenway Park. Something like two to one. It was simply human nature to want to be where the action was. And second best to being there was being able to say you were.

THE PLUMMERS' YELLOW Victorian stood at the corner of the Eastern Promenade and Melbourne Street. Overlooking Casco Bay, the grand home screamed of money.

The living room was too warm and too crowded. Tommy's parents, Alice and Hugh Plummer, were seated on the couch opposite Byron and Detective Melissa Stevens. Standing behind and flanking the Plummers were a number of relatives and friends, including an older woman who may have been Tommy's grandmother. The large room was filled with that same uncomfortable silence Byron had experienced inside courtrooms whenever a jury was about to render their verdict on a murder case. The feeling of dread was palpable.

"I can't tell you how sorry we are for the loss of your son," Byron began, addressing the Plummers.

Hugh Plummer gave a stiff nod while Alice, who was dressed all in black, stared off into the distance.

Byron continued. "Detective Stevens and I are still trying to piece together what happened last night. We'd be very grateful for any help you can give us."

Mr. Plummer glared at Byron. "What happened is, your officer killed our son."

"I realize this is extremely difficult for you," Byron said. "And I'm not trying to add to your grief, but we need to know everything that led up to Thomas's death. Do you know where your son was last evening?"

"No," Plummer said curtly. "He had dinner with us, then he went out."

Byron spoke as softly as he could, trying hard to get through the questions without further upsetting the Plummers. "Do you know who he was out with?"

Hugh exchanged a fleeting glance with his wife. It was the first time she appeared to be paying attention. Neither of the Plummers spoke a word, but Byron was sure that something had passed between them. Alice shook her head.

"We don't know," Hugh said.

"Can you think of anyone who might have supplied Thomas with a gun?" Byron asked, intentionally trying to offload the fault of possession onto someone else. It was far less accusatory.

"Tommy did not have a gun," Hugh said, pausing to spit out each word as if it were a sentence unto itself. "No one in this house owns a gun."

"Do you have any idea where your son might have obtained one?" Byron asked, scanning the room as he did so. "Maybe a friend or a relative?"

"I do not," Hugh said. "And I have only your word that he even had a gun."

Byron couldn't refute this. Since no gun had been recovered, Byron had only Haggerty's word.

"I have a question for you, Sergeant Byron," Hugh said.

"I'll answer it if I can."

"When can we have our son back? We wish to bury him properly."

Byron knew he was treading on uneven and dangerous ground. The autopsy was often paramount to any death investigation and rushing through it wasn't an option. But he also knew that the longer they maintained custody of Tommy's body, the more uncertainty and angst they would be creating for the family. By delaying the postmortem examination even one day he was risking a huge political backlash from his superiors if the Plummers objected to it. Byron didn't want to provoke tensions further, but he did have a job to do. And much depended upon him doing it well.

"It's my job to ensure the investigation is thorough, Mr. Plummer. I'll make sure that Thomas is returned to you as quickly as I can. You have my word."

Ten minutes later, Byron and Stevens departed the Plummer home without getting what they really wanted, a look inside

Thomas's room. Hugh Plummer had said that the detectives were more than welcome to look through his son's room with him, but he would rather that they came back later in the afternoon, after he'd had a chance to grieve with his family. Byron, wanting to maintain some semblance of cordiality, hesitantly agreed, saying they would return at four.

COMMANDER JENNINGS STOOD in the doorway to Mayor Patricia Gilcrest's office. Gilcrest was seated with her legs crossed, elbows on the arms of the chair, and fingers tented together. She looked calm and composed, nothing like what he'd envisioned when her text requesting his presence popped up on his private cell a half hour earlier. Regardless of the mayor's casual outward appearance, Jennings knew she was holding court, and he'd been summoned.

"Have a seat, Commander," she said, gesturing to the chair directly across from her.

He entered the palatial space and sat down across from her. "Ms. Mayor."

She gave him a well-rehearsed grin, but her eyes weren't smiling. "Cut the Ms. Mayor stuff, Ed. How are things?"

"Things? Well, they are a bit messy at the moment."

"So I've heard. How is Mrs. Jennings?"

"Don't do that, okay?" he said.

"Sorry. I didn't know you were so sensitive about your marriage." Her expression turned serious. "Tell me about the Plummer shooting."

"How do you know the boy's name already?"

"What? Tommy Plummer? I have my sources, Ed. You know you're not the only friend I have at 109."

"Not sure I'm supposed to be sharing details on this one, Patty.

Besides, I probably don't know much more than you do at this point. Have you spoken with Chief Rumsfeld yet?"

Gilcrest laughed. "I think you already know what Rumsfeld thinks of me. And he's only the acting chief at the moment. I have it on good authority that this is a bad shoot, Ed. Word is the Plummer kid was unarmed. Is my information accurate?"

"Well, we haven't located his gun yet, if that's what you mean. He may have taken a shot at Officer Haggerty."

"May have?"

"Haggerty said the kid fired first."

"Any evidence to back that up?"

Jennings shook his head. "We haven't found anything yet."

Gilcrest stood up, smoothed her skirt, and began to stroll around the office. Jennings admired the way the high heels accentuated her well-toned calf muscles. *If only my admiration had stopped there she wouldn't own my ass now*, he thought. And she did own him, unleashing him whenever she wanted to play or, like now, when she needed something.

"If you haven't located the gun, nor any evidence that the boy had one, then it's a bad shoot in my book," Gilcrest said. "Wouldn't you agree?"

"The guy who runs the laundromat said he saw one of the suspects with a gun. His description matched Plummer."

"Then where is the gun now?"

"We think it's possible that the other suspect got away with it."

"Think? So, you don't really know, right? You're all just speculating."

Hoping, he thought. "It's a theory."

Gilcrest walked behind him. He knew she was intentionally trying to make him uncomfortable. And it was working.

She slid her hands over his shoulders and down toward his chest, leaning in close enough that he could smell her shampoo.

"Whose theory?" she asked.

"Acting Chief Rumsfeld."

"Ah, Danny Rumsfeld, City Manager Perkins's errand boy. The man who will do anything so long as it helps him make chief. He's not called Rumpswab for nothing."

Wisely, the commander remained silent.

"Rumor has it you've thrown your hat into the ring too," she said.

"Yeah. Not like I'll have much of a chance over Danny. I just want city hall to know I'm interested in the job. Maybe one day down the road I'll be considered."

Gilcrest stood, removing her hands from Jennings, and returned to her chair. "Down the road? Why not right now? Why wait?"

"I'm not sure I understand."

"Oh, come off it. You've been around long enough to know how this game works. It's never what you've done that matters. It's what you *can* do."

"What *can* I do?"

"You are aware of my plan to announce my candidacy for governor of this backward-ass state, aren't you?"

"I may have caught wind of that," he said.

She frowned. "You say that like it's a bad thing."

"Not at all."

"I figure the seat will be ripe for the picking as Mr. Incumbent terms out. I'll be running with a capital *D* in front of my name. After these last eight years, the Republicans might just as well wave the white flag now and save their money."

"You really think you can win?" he asked.

"Ha! I already have some major donors and political high rollers backing me. The test polls show that if the primaries were held today I would be the nominee. And the Democrat will be a shoe-in."

"Why are you telling me any of this?" Jennings asked.

"Because I believe in planning ahead. I'm talking with the people I know I could work well with. And you are one of those people, Ed."

"What could Governor Gilcrest possibly want with me?" he asked. Waiting for her answer filled him with equal parts excitement and dread.

"How about the commissioner of public safety?"

He was momentarily speechless.

"Think about it," she said. "You'd be working for me, at the state level. No more dealing with this local shit. No more working for someone the likes of Danny Rumpswab."

She had him and they both knew it. Jennings had secretly hated Danny Rumsfeld for as long as he'd known him. What Gilcrest was offering was beyond anything he could have imagined. It was not only a way up but a way out. But at what cost?

"What do you need me to do?" he asked before he could stop himself.

Gilcrest leaned forward in her chair, intentionally affording him a seductive glimpse of the creamy unblemished valley inside her blouse.

"How long were you the commander of internal affairs, Ed?"

He swallowed nervously, not liking the direction this conversation was taking. "About two and a half years. Why?"

Her grin returned. "Do you still have access?"

Chapter 6

Monday, 9:00 A.M.,
January 16, 2017

BYRON SAT ACROSS from Micky Cavallaro, owner and manager of the Bubble Up Laundromat, in CID Interview Room Two, a cramped eight-by-ten space with cream-colored foam acoustic panels attached to the top half of each wall. The room was outfitted with three mismatched chairs and a round pedestal table straight out of the 1970s. The badly worn table consisted of a heavy metal base attached to a wooden top; a plethora of chewing gum pieces hung like stalactites from its underside. Like most of the chopped-up spaces at police headquarters, CID's three interview rooms were, depending upon the time of the year, either freezing cold or hot enough to raise dough. Today it was the latter. It was obvious that Cavallaro, still upset at having been robbed, didn't quite seem to grasp the magnitude of what had occurred in Kennedy Park following the stickup at his laundromat. Byron took his time reading the man's statement, intentionally trying to keep him off balance.

At first glance, Byron had placed the laundromat owner's age at about sixty. The date of birth entered atop Cavallaro's witness statement confirmed Byron's guess within a year. The shop owner was a large man, sporting a full head of wavy black hair and pock-marked skin, both of which were greasy. Given Cavallaro's size, Byron doubted anyone would have been foolhardy enough to rob the man without a gun. He had no criminal history and according to the PPD computer database his only contacts with the police department were complaints he had lodged against others, mostly bad checks written by dry cleaning customers.

Cavallaro's statement, taken by Officer Amy Connolly, was quite good. Byron was impressed with Connolly's thoroughness. After rereading the three-page statement Byron placed it face-down on the table in front of him.

"So, tell me again what happened last night, Mr. Cavallaro."

"*I was robbed*," he said with obvious exasperation.

"I think we've already established that," Byron said. "But I need you to recount exactly what happened again, okay?"

"I told the officer already. I was trying to close for the night when these two punk kids came into my store and robbed me. They stuck a gun right in my face," Cavallaro said, pantomiming the actions of the robber with his own hands.

"They?" Byron asked.

"Yes, they. There were two of them."

"Both subjects had a gun?"

"I guess so."

Byron wasn't looking for assumptions, only facts. "Describe them for me."

"The robbers? Hoods and ski masks, the ones that look like skulls."

"I'm looking more for their physical characteristics. Tall, short, heavy, thin?"

"Tall. Young, like teenagers. The one wearing the black sweatshirt was as tall as me."

"How do you know they were young?"

"I could tell by the voices."

"They both spoke to you?"

"No, just the one, but the other one yelled at the customer. I think he surprised them."

"Did you recognize the voices? Is it possible you knew either of them?"

"I don't know. I see a lot of kids around."

"You said they were wearing ski masks. Did you see any skin or hair around the openings?"

"No, but the one who made me empty the safe was white. He wasn't wearing gloves." Cavallaro thought for a moment. "And I think his eyes were blue."

Byron scribbled another note. Plummer had blue eyes.

"What about the other one? The red hoodie. Did you get a look at skin color or eye color?"

"No."

"What about his hands?"

"He was wearing gloves."

"Did they both approach the counter?" Byron asked.

Cavallaro shook his head. "No, no. Only the one in the black sweatshirt."

"And the one wearing the black sweatshirt pointed a gun at you?"

"That's what I've been saying."

"Was the dry cleaning customer already in the store when the robbery happened?"

"No. He came in in the middle of it."

"And which one of you called the police?"

"He did. Right after they ran out."

"Tell me again who opened the safe?"

"I did. He pointed the gun at me and told me to open it."

"How did he know about the safe?"

Cavallaro paused to consider this. "I don't know."

"Is it possible that one of your employees told him about it?"

"I guess it is. I have two full-time employees and two part-time. They work the counter and do the dry cleaning."

"Was there anything else of value in the safe? Something besides money?"

"No, only cash. Nearly six hundred dollars."

Byron studied Cavallaro's face, looking for any sign of deception. Seeing none, he pressed on. "Did all of the people who worked for you know that the security camera was just for show?"

Cavallaro frowned. "Yeah. They all did."

Byron slid a file folder across the table to Cavallaro. "I'm going to show you a photo array. There are six similar-looking males depicted here. The pictures are numbered one through six. Please take your time and look carefully at each of the photos. When you have finished I want you to tell me if you recognize any of the people depicted. Okay?"

"All right." Cavallaro flipped open the folder and spun it to face him.

Byron waited as the shop owner studied the pictures that Detective Stevens had compiled. The lineup had been more difficult than usual to put together due to Plummer's young age. Typically, they could assemble an array from jail booking photos or from the database at the Maine Bureau of Motor Vehicles. In this case, the detectives were limited to booking photos only as Plummer did not have a license, only a permit. Luckily, he had a juvenile record, affording them one semirecent picture.

"No," Cavallaro said at last. "I don't recognize any of them."

"You're sure?"

"Yes, I'm sure," Cavallaro said. "Did one of them rob me?"

"That is what we're trying to establish." Byron retrieved the folder and flipped it closed. "Thank you, Mr. Cavallaro."

"You're welcome," he said, his tone indignant.

"Tell me again what the other suspect looked like?"

"I already told that lady cop."

"I know you did," Byron said. "But I'd like you to tell me."

"He was tall, like the other one. Thinner, I guess."

"You guess? Why do you guess he was thinner?"

"Because of his sweatshirt. It was baggy," Cavallaro said. "Like it was too big for him."

Byron made a note in his notebook. "Did the suspect in the red hoodie display a gun?"

"He didn't point one at me, if that's what you mean."

"Then how do you know he possessed one?"

Cavallaro paused for a moment as if trying to decipher his own riddle, then shrugged. "I guess I don't. I assume they both did. They came into my store to rob me. Why wouldn't they both have guns?"

"But you didn't actually see the second person with a gun?"

"No. I didn't *see* it."

Byron decided to switch gears for a second. "Tell me about the gun you did see. Describe it for me."

"The one the guy stuck in my face?"

"Yeah," Byron said. "That one."

"It was a revolver, metal-colored. Silver."

"Stainless steel? Or reflective like chrome?"

Cavallaro thought for a moment. "Stainless."

"What else can you tell me about it?"

"Not much. It was just a gun."

Byron handed Cavallaro a clean sheet of paper and a pen. "Would you mind drawing the gun you saw?"

"I'm not too good at drawing."

"That's all right. I just need a rough idea of what you saw. It doesn't have to be perfect."

"Okay."

Cavallaro took the pen and began to draw. Byron made several quick entries in his notebook while he waited.

When Cavallaro had finished, he slid the pen and paper back across the table. "Here you go."

"And you're sure this is what the gun looked like that was pointed at you during the robbery?"

"Yes. The drawing is not very good, but that is like the gun I saw."

WHILE BYRON WAS at 109 conducting the follow-up interview of Cavallaro, Detective Melissa Stevens sat across from Attorney Clifford Stebbins in one of the conference rooms on the second floor of the Cumberland County District Courthouse.

"I apologize for having to meet you here, Detective, but my schedule is a little crazy right now."

"Not a problem. I just wanted to go over your statement concerning the robbery last night."

"I still can't believe it, you know? I mean, you read about these things happening in the papers but to actually walk in on one. It's crazy."

Stebbins had set his leather attaché case on the table in front of him and was leaning on it with his forearms. He repeatedly clicked the pen in his hand, a nervous tic apparently brought on by nerves as the attorney relived the previous evening's encounter.

"In your statement you stated that you didn't realize what was happening until you were fully inside the laundromat. What did you see?"

"I saw the person in the red sweatshirt first. The skull mask kind of threw me. Then he started yelling for me to get down on the floor."

"Did you comply?"

"Not immediately. I don't know if it was shock or if I just didn't believe what was happening. But I looked up and saw the second robber, the one wearing the dark-colored hoodie, standing behind the counter pointing a gun at the owner of the business, Micky. That's when I knew."

"And that's when you got down on the floor."

"Yes."

"Was the voice of the person in the red hoodie male or female?"

"Definitely male. Sounded young."

"Anything else you can remember about the voice?"

"I guess that's it."

"Did Red Hoodie have a gun too?"

"I never saw one. Just the dark-hooded figure behind the counter."

"Can you describe the gun you saw?"

"Sure. It was a semiauto, silver colored."

"And you're positive it was a semiauto and not a revolver?"

"Detective, I don't mean to sound condescending, but I do know the difference. I have a membership to a gun club in Windham. I shoot once a month."

"What kind of gun do you have?"

"A Glock 40."

BYRON AND DETECTIVE Stevens drove back to Kennedy Park to check in on the evidence-gathering progress.

"How can their descriptions of the handgun be so different?" Stevens asked.

"I don't know, Mel," Byron said. "Cavallaro was positive it was a revolver. He even drew it for me."

"Maybe both robbers had guns after all."

Maybe, Byron thought.

Stevens was checking her phone.

"Shit," she said.

"What's up?" Byron asked.

"I missed a call from Hugh Plummer while I was interviewing Stebbins."

"Did he leave a message?" Byron asked, hoping they could get back to check Tommy's room sooner than four o'clock.

Stevens checked her voicemail as Byron waited impatiently.

"Dammit," Stevens said.

"What?"

"He canceled our four o'clock."

"Canceled or rescheduled?"

"Canceled."

Shit, Byron thought. "Did he say why?"

"No."

Byron was beating himself up now. He should never have allowed Hugh Plummer to talk him into coming back. The voluntary search of Tommy's room was most likely off the table now, and he knew obtaining a search warrant wasn't an option. Warrants by their very nature require the police to have probable cause. In this case the information they did have was shaky at best. They hadn't recovered a gun from the scene of the shooting. Not even a shell casing. Hell, the only evidence to suggest that a gun had been fired were the bullets from Haggerty's gun, evidence that was now lying in a cooler at the state medical examiner's office in Augusta. Cavallaro had said that the person who'd pointed a gun at him during the robbery was wearing a black hoodie and had blue eyes, but that didn't mean Tommy Plummer still possessed it when he was shot by Haggerty. Not to mention the fact that the two witnesses to the crime couldn't even agree on the type of handgun displayed. Pelligrosso had located drugs at the scene, but there was no way of knowing whose drugs they were. Had they come from Cavallaro's safe? Was the laundromat just a front for a drug distribution network? Or had the drugs belonged to one of the robbers? Maybe the laundromat wasn't the only robbery they had committed. He could speculate all he wanted but it made no difference. None of the information they had was likely to persuade a judge. Byron would have had an easier time getting a warrant to search Haggerty's bedroom than Tommy Plummer's.

Their only hope was that the aggrieved family was delaying access. Something was beginning to gnaw at him though. What if something else was going on? Had the Plummers located some evidence of their son's guilt? If so, what would be their next move? Destroy the evidence? Contact an attorney? If they had, their cooperation was likely over.

Byron drove up Munjoy Hill, bypassing Kennedy Park.

"I thought we were going back to the scene?" Stevens asked.

"I want to check in personally with the Plummers first. Saying no is always harder in person."

DAVIS BILLINGSLEA SAT in his cubicle checking his social media accounts on the *Herald* desktop. He had just put the finishing touches on his police shooting update and forwarded it to his editor, Will Draper. The surreptitious photograph he'd taken earlier was already posted to Twitter on both his and the newspaper's feeds. It was receiving a fair number of likes, but more important were the retweets. The word was spreading and that was good. He pulled up the webpages for several of the local news agencies, but none had posted any new information on the story. Most were still speculating on the incident and regurgitating what little Acting Chief Rumsfeld had provided at the predawn conference in the PD lobby. Billingslea's page was the only one that depicted the police collecting evidence at the scene. He was wondering how quickly Byron's team might be able to match up the footwear when his editor hollered to him.

"Davis!"

"Yeah, boss," Billingslea said as he quickly closed out his internet page and headed over to Draper's desk.

"Your piece looks good," Draper said. "I'll put it out."

"Thanks."

"Now, I need you to get your ass over to city hall."

"What's at city hall?" Billingslea asked.

"Mayor Gilcrest called a press conference. Ten minutes. Go."

Billingslea went.

BYRON AND STEVENS stood on the front porch waiting for someone to answer the door. He knocked a second time. During their earlier visit a half dozen cars had occupied the driveway; now there was only one.

"What do you think, Sarge?" Stevens said.

"I think we've worn out our welcome."

Byron pulled a business card from the inside pocket of his overcoat, penned his cell number on the back, then stuck it between the storm door and its frame.

"Your move, Hugh," Byron said as they turned and headed back to the car.

MICKY CAVALLARO LOOKED up as the front door to the laundromat opened. With a blast of cold air from outside, a large man entered. He was carrying a suit jacket and pants on a hanger. He recognized Alex instantly. Alexander Bruschi, always dressed to the nines, was a fixer, and Micky's situation was in dire need of fixing.

Bruschi approached the dry cleaning counter, casting a quick glance about the place to make sure they were alone. The only other person present was a young woman wearing sweats and a ski jacket sitting in a chair reading a magazine. The woman was wearing earbuds and humming to a tune that neither man could hear, while she waited for the clothes dryer to finish its cycle.

"Good day, my old friend," Bruschi said. It wasn't and they weren't.

"Alex," Cavallaro said, smiling broadly in an attempt to hide his nervousness. "It's good to see you."

A predatory grin spread across Bruschi's face, just above the deep cleft in his chin. "I understand you had a little trouble recently. Delivery issues?"

A chill ran up Cavallaro's spine as he wondered which thing Bruschi had been sent to fix.

"A little short on product, are we?"

Micky nodded.

"How short?"

"All of it."

Bruschi shook his head in disapproval and made a clicking noise with his tongue. "That's most unfortunate. Have the police caught the other man? The one who isn't dead."

"I don't think so, no."

Bruschi reached out and laid the suit across the top of the counter. "I need to have this cleaned. Can you do that?"

"Of course," Cavallaro said.

"I put the instructions in the inside pocket. You should follow them *exactly*." Bruschi tugged on the cuffs of his black leather gloves, pulling them on tighter. "I understand the officer who killed the boy is the same one assigned to the high school."

"Haggerty, yes."

"Quite a coincidence, wouldn't you say, Micky?"

"Now that you mention it, yes," Cavallaro answered slowly, not at all liking the question or its implications.

Bruschi fixed him with cold calculating eyes as he tapped the suit with his index finger. "Remember. Follow my instructions, to the letter. I'll return when it's done."

"I thought you might fix this thing for me?"

The grin reappeared. "Have you forgotten who it is you work for, Micky?"

Cavallaro shook his head. "No."

"This is your mess. And you need to clean it up. After this thing is behind us, we will talk again."

Cavallaro nodded his understanding.

"Good to see you again," Bruschi said, patting him on the cheek, a little firmer than necessary.

Resisting the urge to call out and ask when his product would be made whole again, Cavallaro watched Bruschi turn and stroll back out through the door to the sidewalk, relieved that he was gone.

Cavallaro hung Bruschi's suit on the rack behind the counter. He reached inside, checking the jacket pockets until he felt a piece of paper. He pulled the paper out and unfolded it. His eyes widened as he read the note. The instructions were very specific. His supplier was going to make him pay for the loss. And pay mightily.

Cavallaro picked up the phone and dialed downstairs to the basement where Roni was working on the dry cleaning. She answered on the first ring. "I need you to cover me on the desk," he said. "I've gotta go out for a while."

BILLINGSLEA STOOD INSIDE city hall's grand first-floor rotunda, crammed between several taller members of the audience, one of which he recognized as Lee Reynolds, the weekend desk anchor for WGME, the local CBS affiliate. Billingslea nodded and said hello but Reynolds pretended not to recognize him. The young reporter wondered what it would be like to be so well-known that you could simply become an asshole. *Or maybe he was an asshole before fame came calling*, Billingslea thought as he fixed the anchorman with an insincere smile.

Attorney Roger Bertram stood with the Plummers, slightly to the right of the mayor at the bottom of the massive winding marble staircase with the gleaming brass railing that led to city hall's second floor. Accompanying the news media, and effectively blocking the building's main entrance and the hallways to both the building's wings, was a sizable crowd of city employees. Digital camera flashes and video spotlights bathed everyone in harsh light, casting monstrous shadows upon the walls. The high ceilings and stone surfaces amplified and distorted every footfall and spoken word, turning the space into an echo chamber.

"I am greatly disturbed and saddened to have to be here today," Gilcrest said, drawing out her words as she scanned the crowd. Her expression was pained, and sincere. "Last night the injustice and brutality, experienced time and again by the rest of the country, reared its ugly head in our beloved city. Thomas Plummer, a seventeen-year-old Portland High School student, was shot and killed by a Portland police officer."

Mrs. Plummer burst into tears, while her husband did his best to console her. Another barrage of flashbulbs illuminated the rotunda. Gilcrest, taking full advantage of the drama, waited a full ten seconds before continuing.

Davis Billingslea scribbled in shorthand as quickly as he could, not wanting to miss a single word.

"Tommy was a bright young man who didn't deserve what happened to him. Many of you will remember that he led the Portland High Bulldogs basketball team to a state championship last year. With Tommy's help, Portland was expected to make another run this season. Tragically, that is no longer possible. The police in this country are out of control. Lethal force by law enforcement is on the rise, in spite of the fact that they now possess more nonlethal options than ever before. Tasers, pepper spray, beanbag rounds—there are so many other options than death."

"Hear, hear," a male voice shouted from within the crowd.

Billingslea craned his neck, searching for him. He made a mental notation to locate and interview the man.

The mayor continued. "I want to assure Hugh and Alice Plummer, and all of the citizens of this great city, that I will avail myself of every resource to get to the bottom of what happened last night. And while I understand that what has happened cannot be undone, I am making a promise to seek justice for Tommy. I will personally be meeting with police department officials this afternoon to discuss this matter fully. I want answers as much as you do."

Gilcrest turned to the Plummers. "I want to offer my heartfelt condolences to you and your family."

Mr. Plummer nodded silently.

Gilcrest faced the cameras again. "I am prepared to take a few questions."

Billingslea's hand shot up before all others.

Chapter 7

WHILE THE TECHNICIANS raced to recover evidence left at the scene, and the detectives were busy recanvassing Kennedy Park for witnesses, Byron regrouped. With no chance of getting another crack at the Plummers, it was time to turn his attention toward identifying the second robbery suspect. Tommy's lookout. He dropped Stevens off at 109.

Byron needed to figure out who Tommy Plummer usually hung with. Who would he have been with on a Sunday evening when one of them got the not-so-bright idea to pull an armed robbery and, assuming Haggerty was right, shoot at a cop? Surely someone at Portland High School knew, but Haggerty, who had already been placed on suspension, would have been his best source for figuring out who. Byron's second-best option was Detective Luke Gardiner. Prior to joining the bureau at the end of the summer, Gardiner had held Haggerty's liaison position at Portland High for the previous three years. Byron figured Gardiner would still have a good handle on who the problem children were at the high school, even though he hadn't been there during the last four months.

Detective Gardiner was currently assigned to the property crimes unit under Sergeant Peterson, but given the nature of the case they were working, and the fact that most of the other investigations had been put on hold, Peterson readily agreed to temporarily assign Gardiner to Byron's team.

ESTABLISHED NEARLY TWO hundred years ago, Portland High is the second oldest public high school in the United States. Constructed from brownstone and granite, the massive Italianate building covers an acre of land on Portland's in-town peninsula. In a school of about a thousand kids, Byron knew that they had their work cut out for them.

They passed through the center of three ornate archways. Byron pulled the heavy wooden door open, gesturing for Gardiner to enter first. "After you, Detective."

They found Assistant Principal Paul Rogers in his office, reading the riot act to a sullen-looking male student who sported a long greasy-looking black ponytail and a silver-colored chin stud. *Some things never change*, Byron thought. He and Gardiner stood in the office reception area, waiting until Rogers had finished.

The chastised student walked by wordlessly a moment before Rogers exited his office and greeted the detectives with a big smile.

"Luke," Rogers said, giving the former SRO an enthusiastic handshake. "Or should I call you Detective now?"

"Luke's fine," Gardiner said as his cheeks turned rosy. "How have you been, Paul?"

"Nothing ever changes around here. You know that."

"Paul, this is Detective Sergeant John Byron," Gardiner said.

"Pleased to meet you," Byron said, extending his hand.

"Likewise, Sergeant. What can I do for the two of you? Am I correct in assuming this has to do with the death of Tommy Plummer?"

"I was hoping we might speak in private," Byron said, casting a glance at the office staff and the young female student with the silver nose stud working the copier. She had been eyeing the detectives since they first arrived.

"Certainly," Rogers said before he led them to his office and closed the door.

Byron got right to the point, explaining the reason for their visit.

"As Luke probably told you, we are very familiar with Tommy," Rogers said. "I'm sure you are aware of his athletic abilities. He was our star basketball player. Many of the students are taking the news of his death pretty hard."

"What kind of a student was he?" Byron asked. "Was he a problem child?"

"He was an average student. Definitely full of himself. He knew how much he meant to our basketball team. But Tommy hadn't been in any real trouble since his sophomore year."

"What kind of trouble did he get into then?" Byron asked, thinking about the shoplifting arrest that Melissa Stevens had uncovered.

"He actually had a couple of different incidents that year. The first was when he got caught dealing marijuana on school property."

"And the second?"

"He got into an altercation with another student who he believed ratted him out."

"Altercation?"

"He beat the other kid pretty badly."

"Why weren't any charges filed?" Byron asked.

"Tommy's parents took care of the medical bills and the boys resolved their differences."

"Pardon my bluntness," Byron said. "But maybe if Tom Terrific been held accountable for any of this behavior he wouldn't have been committing an armed robbery and shooting at a cop last night. What happened to the drug trafficking charge?"

Rogers's face reddened. "Principal Larrabee elected to handle that in-house without involving the police."

Byron shot an accusatory glance at Gardiner before turning his attention back to Rogers. "Can you think of anyone Plummer hung out with regularly who might have been with him last night?"

"You mean besides the entire boys' varsity basketball team?"

Until that moment Byron hadn't realized how big a task finding the second robber might be.

"There are four students who immediately come to mind. Scott Henderson, Nate Freeman, Abdirahman Ali, and Mohammed Sayed," Rogers said, counting on his fingers.

"Are they on the basketball team too?" Byron asked as he jotted the names into his notebook, noting that several of the names were the same ones Gardiner had provided on their way to the school.

"Abdi is, but none of the other three are involved in any school sports."

"Any of them ever get into trouble like Tommy?"

"Oh yeah, Henderson and Sayed are regular visitors to my office. Luke could tell you."

Gardiner nodded. "Yup."

"What kind of stuff?" Byron asked.

"Typical stuff," Rogers said. "Disrupting classes, mouthing off to teachers, and occasionally vandalizing a locker or something. My money would be on one of those two. But it's hard for me to imagine that either one of them would be dumb enough to pull a robbery."

"Armed robbery," Byron corrected. "And would you have imagined that Tommy Plummer was capable of it?"

Rogers shook his head. "Before today? No."

"What about Freeman and Ali?" Byron asked.

"Nate Freeman is actually Tommy's cousin but he's never been in any trouble. Abdi Ali is one of our best students. Abdi's only a sophomore but he's got some serious skills on the basketball court. Made the varsity team this year. Only underclassman to make the cut. He's never been in any trouble that I know of."

Byron wondered if that underclassman might have been trying to score some brownie points with his new teammate, by pulling a robbery.

"Are they all in school today?" Byron asked.

"Let's see." With the click of a mouse, Rogers quickly checked a computerized absentee list. "Henderson, Freeman, and Ali are here. Looks like Mohammed Sayed is out with the flu," Rogers said, rolling his eyes. "Want me to fetch the three that are here for you?"

"We'll want to speak to them separately," Byron said, glancing at Gardiner for guidance.

"Let's start with Scott Henderson," Gardiner said.

MICKY CAVALLARO SAT at a metal visitor's table inside the prison with inmates at nearby tables. He caught bits and pieces of conversations drifting by, but most of the people were speaking in hushed tones, making it difficult to eavesdrop. He glanced at the two guards across the room. In addition to the guards, the room had several security cameras mounted high up on the walls. Cavallaro had been here several times before, and he used the memories of each visit as a reminder not to get caught. He wondered how anyone could spend their days caged like an animal and not go completely batshit crazy.

A door banged open and Derrick Vanos was led into the room by yet another prison guard. Wearing the standard issue dark navy pants and robin's egg blue collared shirt, Vanos shuffled over to where Cavallaro sat waiting.

"No touching," the large guard cautioned as Vanos settled into a chair across from Cavallaro.

"Got it, big guy," Vanos said. "Wasn't planning a conjugal visit anyway."

The guard turned and walked back through the door he had previously entered, giving a nod to the room's two monitors as he left.

Vanos's shirtsleeves were rolled up nearly to his shoulders, revealing bulging biceps and a few tattoos. His nose had several distinct crooks in it, having been broken more than once when he was younger. A four-inch scar bifurcated his left eyebrow and his head was shaved smooth. He looked like a cross between an aging heavyweight boxer and Mr. Clean.

"Mick," Vanos said, grinning warmly. "Good to see you. Though I can't say I'm surprised."

"You saw the news, then?" Cavallaro asked.

Vanos's grin disappeared. "I did. How much did you lose?"

"An entire delivery."

"Holy shit. Do you know who was behind it?"

"The kid the police shot was a senior at Portland High. They haven't released his name."

"The news said there were two."

"The other asshole got away. Apparently the cops don't know who it is. At least, not yet."

"And you're here because you need my help with some muscle."

Cavallaro wished it were that simple. He stole a quick glance at the guards before answering. "More than muscle this time, I'm afraid."

Vanos raised a brow. "You've never made such a request before, Micky. You sure you want to go down this road?"

"I don't have a choice. Either I fix this thing or my supplier will fix me. They want a clear message sent."

"To the other robber?"

He shook his head. "To the cop who shot the kid. Haggerty." Cavallaro saw the muscle in Vanos's jaw twitch.

Vanos slammed his hand down on the table in anger. Both guards ceased their conversation and looked over at him.

Vanos raised his hand and forced a smile to show that everything was fine. After several moments the guards returned to their chat.

"He's the reason I'm in here," Vanos growled.

Cavallaro knew this and was hoping for a discounted rate.

Cavallaro and Vanos had grown up next door to each other in the southern Maine mill town of Sanford. Vanos, always the larger of the two, had looked out for him, kicking the shit out of anyone who dared to mess with Cavallaro. They remained close even through high school, but as they aged Vanos became more violent and unstable, to the point that even Cavallaro had begun to fear him. Still, his side business had required that he avail himself of Vanos's services every now and again. Vanos had friends who would keep people in line for a price. And now that Cavallaro's gambling problem had dragged him into a forced partnership with an out-of-state entity, he needed Vanos more than ever.

Vanos glanced over at the guards, but neither were looking in their direction. He turned his attention back to Cavallaro. "Why the cop?"

"They think he was involved."

"Do you?"

Cavallaro shrugged. "I don't know. It is a hell of a coincidence."

"When do they want it done?"

"As soon as possible. How much is this gonna cost me, Derrick?"

Vanos's lips twisted into a cruel grin. "Let's call this one a gift."

Chapter 8

Monday, 11:30 A.M.,
January 16, 2017

BYRON, LUKE GARDINER, and Scott Henderson were all seated in the guidance counselor's office.

Henderson was tall for his age. Six feet and sinewy with a face covered in freckles, he reminded Byron of Patrick Renna, who played the catcher in *The Sandlot*.

Prior to conducting the interviews, Byron had instructed Gardiner to surreptitiously photograph each of the students' shoes using his cellphone camera. Gardiner would pretend to check his phone as he took the photos. Seizing the shoes or asking to look at them would only serve to tip off the students if they were still in possession of the pair worn during the robbery.

"I'm assuming you know why we're here, Scott," Byron said. "You have heard about what happened to Thomas Plummer last night, correct?"

"Of course I have. Everyone's heard about it," Henderson said. "Can't believe you guys killed Tommy."

"He was fleeing the scene of an armed robbery, Scott," Byron said, incredulous at the teenager's comment. "Any idea who he might have been with?"

"Nope. All I can tell you is it wasn't me. I was home all night. You can check with my mom, if you don't believe me."

"Now why wouldn't we believe you, Scott?" Gardiner asked.

Henderson scoffed at the question.

Byron slid a blank piece of paper and pen toward Henderson. "Write down her phone number and we'll call her."

"What? Right now? She's at work. She'll be pissed if you call her now."

"It's your call, Scott," Gardiner said. "We either call her to confirm your whereabouts last night, or we can show up at her workplace and ask her. What do you think, Sarge?"

"I bet her employer will be delighted that we stopped by," Byron said, playing along.

Henderson sighed. "All right." He scribbled a number onto the paper and shoved it back toward Byron. "Here. But she's gonna be mad as hell."

"We'll chance it," Byron said as he handed the sheet of paper to Gardiner. "I'll hang here with Mr. Henderson while you check. We've still got a few things to talk over. Don't we, Scott?"

Byron spent the next ten minutes grilling Henderson on anything he might know about other robberies that Plummer may have done, or where Tommy might have come by a handgun. The delinquent teen either didn't know or was already proficient at lying. Byron even checked Henderson's phone but all the information had been wiped clean, call history, text messages, everything.

Byron came away with nothing but attitude. And Henderson's mother had backed up his alibi. According to her, Scott had been home all day Sunday, throughout Sunday night. Scott had failed to mention that he had been grounded the previous week. As he watched Henderson walk out of the office, Byron couldn't help wondering how long it would be before the smug teenager would find himself acquainted with the adult version of the criminal justice system.

FOLLOWING HENDERSON'S RETURN to class, Rogers personally escorted Abdirahman Ali to the detectives.

"Have a seat, Abdirahman," Byron said, gesturing across the table. Rogers had been right about Ali. He was tall but thin.

Gardiner stood leaning casually with one shoulder against the wall and his arms folded. "Hey, Abdi," he said. "Remember me?"

"Yes. Officer Luke. How are you?"

Ali was stoic but polite, and didn't appear the least bit nervous.

"Do you know why we're here, Abdi?" Gardiner continued.

Ali nodded. "Is it about Tommy? They made a morning announcement saying that he died last night."

"Yes," Byron said. "He was shot and killed fleeing the scene of an armed robbery."

Ali said nothing.

"Did you know Tommy very well?" Byron asked.

Ali nodded again. "We played basketball together."

"That's right," Byron said. "I understand you're the only underclassman on the varsity team. Congratulations."

Ali's sullen expression brightened a bit. "Thanks."

"Did you only know Tommy from playing basketball or did you hang out with him outside of school too?"

"Mostly basketball. Tommy was a senior. Seniors don't hang out with sophomores."

Byron smiled for Ali's benefit. "I guess they don't."

Ali turned his head toward Gardiner. "Is it true that Officer Haggerty was the officer who killed Tommy? That's what everyone is saying."

Byron answered for him. "I'm afraid it is true, Abdi."

"Did you ever know Tommy to carry a weapon?" Gardiner asked.

"No," Abdi said.

"You're sure?" Byron asked.

"I am sure," Ali said, although his tone suggested otherwise.

"Aren't you at all curious about the kind of weapon?" Gardiner asked.

Ali looked over at the newly minted detective. "Why would it matter? I never saw him with any weapons."

Gardiner grinned at the young man's attempt at projecting an attitude.

"Where were you last night?" Byron asked, shifting gears.

"At home. Studying."

"All night?"

Ali nodded.

"I didn't catch that," Byron said, cupping a hand behind his ear for effect.

"Yes. I was home all night."

"Can anyone verify that?" Byron asked.

Ali shrugged. "My parents didn't get home until late."

"Then you were home alone?" Gardiner said.

"Nadi, my younger sister, was home too."

"N-a-d-i?" Byron asked, pausing to enter the name in his notepad.

"It's short for Nadiifo."

"Do you have a cellphone, Abdi?" Byron asked.

"Yeah."

"May we see it?"

Ali began to reach into his pants pocket, then stopped. "Why do you wanna see my phone?"

"I'm just a curious guy," Byron said. "Curious about why you wouldn't want to show it to me. Is there something on there you don't want us to see?"

Ali's Adam's apple bounced up and down. "No."

"Did you call or text Tommy recently?" Byron asked.

"No."

"Then you shouldn't have anything to worry about, right?" Gardiner said.

Ali pulled the cell out of his pocket and, after punching in the key code, handed it to Byron.

Byron went right to the text history. It was blank. He glanced up at Ali, but said nothing. He punched up the call history and voicemail, and just like Henderson's phone it had been erased. Byron recorded the cell number into his notebook, then handed it back to Ali.

"Know what else I'm curious about, Abdi?"

The boy shrugged his shoulders.

"I'm curious about why you would erase all the history from your phone."

Ali shrugged again. "I do it all the time. Can't be too careful about your phone falling into the wrong hands."

"That you can't," Byron said, grinning. "That you can't."

BYRON AND GARDINER drove away from Portland High School with a list of every student on the varsity boys' basketball team, two alibis, and the address of the Eastern Halal Market, the business owned by Abdirahman Ali's parents. Tommy Plummer's other known associate, Mohammed Sayed, reportedly down with the flu, would have to wait. Byron checked the time and wondered why he hadn't heard anything from Diane about Mayor Gilcrest's press conference.

"What do you think, Sarge?" Gardiner asked. "Nate looked a little nervous."

"Yeah, he did," Byron said. "Had an answer for everything too."

They had interviewed Nate Freeman last. Freeman should have been a senior like Tommy Plummer, but he'd been held back a year due to his grades. Unlike the other two, Freeman didn't own a cellphone. Like the others, he claimed to have no knowledge of the robbery. Freeman claimed to have been at home all night watching a movie. Said his mom was home too.

"*Starship Troopers,*" Gardiner said. "You ever see it?"

"Missed that one," Byron said.

"It's good. And it's available on Netflix."

"Which means what?" Byron asked.

"If you have the streaming service, you can watch it anytime."

"Streaming?"

"Yeah, it's like movies on demand. Like they have in hotels. You find the one you want to watch and it just plays."

Byron considered it for a moment. "Then we really wouldn't know for sure if he was watching it Sunday night, right?"

"I guess. There should be playback history. He's always been such a quiet and polite kid though. Hard to believe that he would have been involved in something like this."

During Byron's twenty-two years on the job, many people had said the exact same thing about one suspect or another. If there was one thing police work had taught him, it was to never underestimate what people are capable of. He'd met many good people who had done some pretty horrible things. The priests of Byron's youth had been fond of saying that God forgives us our sins. Byron wondered which of Tommy Plummer's friends might need absolution.

"What's up with the cellphones being erased?" Gardiner asked. "You ever see anything like that?"

"Not with teenagers," Byron said. He wondered if they'd have better luck with Plummer's phone.

THE EASTERN HALAL Market stood near the top of Munjoy Hill on the north side of Congress Street in the shadow of the Portland Observatory, a seven-story watchtower constructed in 1807 to monitor approaching ships. In Byron's youth, long before the word *halal* appeared anywhere in Portland, he and his friends had played inside the observatory until the landmark structure fell prey to post beetles and dry rot and was shuttered. Closed to visitors, the tower became a popular surveillance spot for Maine's Bureau of Interdiction and Drug Enforcement (BIDE) and later for Maine Drug Enforcement Agency (MDEA) detectives monitoring the East End's bustling illegal heroin and cocaine trade in the 1980s and '90s. As Byron pulled into a loading zone just down the street from the market, he wondered if any of Portland's residents from the 1800s had ever envisioned the city's future diversity of culture.

The strong scent of exotic spices enveloped the two detectives as they entered the overly warm market. Several female customers eyed them suspiciously, as did the balding dark-skinned middle-aged male standing behind the register.

"May I help you?" the man asked as they approached the counter.

Byron produced his credentials with all the smoothness of a veteran detective, then turned and waited as his temporary partner, who until recently had always worn his badge pinned to his chest, fumbled with a stiff leather ID case.

"I'm Detective Sergeant Byron, and this is Detective Gardiner. Are you Mr. Ali?"

"I am Ahmed Ali. What is the problem?"

"I wonder if we might ask you a few questions about your son, Abdirahman?"

Ali's eyes narrowed. "Has something happened to Abdi?"

"Not at all," Byron said, returning his ID to his inside coat pocket. "In fact, we just spoke with him at the high school. He's fine. Did you know a boy by the name of Thomas Plummer?"

"Tommy, yes. He played basketball with Abdi. I heard he was killed by police."

"How well did you know Tommy?" Byron asked.

Ali turned and hollered something in a foreign dialect toward the back of the store. Ali readdressed Byron. "We should talk in private, Sergeant."

A short stout woman wearing a bright tangerine-colored hijab appeared from somewhere in the back, wordlessly swapping places with Ali behind the counter. Byron took her to be Ali's wife.

"Come," Ali said. "We shall speak in my office."

As they followed Ali, Byron still felt the eyes of curious customers upon them.

Cramped and packed floor to ceiling with boxes and paperwork, Ali's office more closely resembled a walk-in closet than a true workspace. There were only two chairs. Ali offered one of them to Byron, then he cleared off a wooden crate and gestured for Gardiner to sit. Byron, unsure if the chair had been presented to him as a recognition of rank or simply one of age, hid a smile from the young detective.

Byron sat down and flipped open his notebook. "What can you tell us about Tommy Plummer?"

"He was trouble. Or as you say, bad news."

"What makes you say that?"

"I can't explain it, just a bad feeling."

"According to the school, your son was often seen hanging out with Tommy."

Ali frowned. "Yes. It is true. I did my best to stop him, but Abdi is very much like his mother, stubborn. Abdi continued to see Tommy outside of school even after I told him not to."

"Was Abdi out with Tommy last night, Mr. Ali?" Byron asked.

"No. He was upstairs studying for school."

"Are you sure he was here all night?"

"Yes. I am sure."

"Were you here all night, Mr. Ali?"

"No. I was attending a meeting at the East End Community Center."

"And your wife, was she here?"

"She was with me."

"So, there is a chance Abdi could have snuck out without your knowledge, right?" Byron asked.

"No," Ali said. "I would know. Besides, he was babysitting our daughter, Nadi."

"Nadiifo," Byron said.

"Yes," Ali said with obvious surprise. "Abdi was watching her. He would not have left her alone."

Byron didn't possess the same level of confidence as Abdi's father. "Is Abdi a good student?"

"Yes. He gets high grades in school."

"Has he ever gotten into trouble at school or elsewhere?" Byron asked.

"No. And I do not want him to."

"Has he ever used illegal drugs?"

"Of course not. Why would you ask that?"

"Just trying to be thorough. Do you know the names of any of the other kids that Abdi hangs around with?"

"He has many friends."

"Anyone in particular that he spends time with? Someone he is close with?"

"There are many. I do not know all of their names."

"How did you know Tommy Plummer?"

"Because he was popular in the school. Abdi talks about him all the time."

"Does anyone in your family have access to a gun, Mr. Ali?"

"No. No one."

"And you're positive Abdirahman was home all night?" Byron asked again.

"I already told you. Yes."

Byron maintained eye contact with the store owner, then nodded his understanding. Realizing that they would get nothing further from Ahmed Ali during this first visit, Byron stood up and closed his notebook. "Thank you for your time, Mr. Ali."

IT WAS FIFTEEN minutes before the scheduled start of Acting Chief Rumsfeld's press conference when Sergeant Diane Joyner learned of the amount of damage Mayor Gilcrest had done. Diane successfully managed to avoid the three different reporters who had attempted to corner her as she walked through 109's hallways, but not before getting a taste of the direction the questioning was likely to go. Rumsfeld, who had been in a closed-door with the police attorney during Gilcrest's press conference, had given orders not to be disturbed. Diane could only hope that he knew about Gilcrest.

Diane stood just outside the double doors to the auditorium, waiting as Rumsfeld approached from the elevators. The chief appeared to have aged ten years in the hour that had passed since she'd last spoken with him.

"You heard about the mayor's grandstanding?" Diane asked.

"Yes," Rumsfeld growled. "Not every detail, but I know she skewered us."

"You ready for this?" Diane asked as she pulled opened one of the auditorium doors.

"Do I have a choice?" he said.

All eyes turned to watch as the two of them entered the packed room.

Diane followed Rumsfeld up to the front of the auditorium where a tangled bank of microphones and wires had been arranged directly in front of the PD's glossy wood podium. Displayed upon the front of the podium were the city seal and motto, Resurgam: *I shall rise again.* Diane wondered if perhaps, given the nature of the press conference, there should have been a question mark following the Latin word.

Rumsfeld removed the prepared notes from his suit jacket and set them atop the podium. Several of the cameramen activated their lights, literally bathing the acting chief in the spotlight. Relegated to second banana on this briefing, Diane gladly stood off to one side.

"Thank you all for coming today," Rumsfeld began. "As you all know by now, last night one of our uniformed patrol officers shot and killed a local teenager. The officer was pursuing two suspects believed to have committed an armed robbery moments before at the Bubble Up Laundromat on Washington Avenue. As a matter of routine, the officer has been placed on paid administrative leave pending the outcome of an investigation into this shooting by the state Attorney General's Office and of this department. I will attempt to answer a few questions, but please keep in mind that this is an ongoing investigation, and as such I am not at liberty to discuss certain details."

Diane looked on as members of the press shouted and raised their arms attempting to get Rumsfeld's attention like some crazed mob of adoring fans. The acting chief quickly scanned the room before pointing to a middle-aged male reporter sporting a bad complexion and an equally bad toupee.

"Chief, will you be releasing the name of the officer involved in the shooting?" the reporter asked.

"We released that earlier this morning," Rumsfeld said. "His name is Officer Sean Haggerty."

"Is this the first time Officer Haggerty has used excessive force?" the same reporter asked.

Rumsfeld glanced over at Diane. His exasperation was obvious.

"Who said anything about excessive force?" Rumsfeld asked the reporter.

"Mayor Gilcrest mentioned that she felt this was another example of overzealous policing."

Rumsfeld ignored the comment and pointed to Davis Billingslea, police beat reporter for the *Portland Herald*.

"What can you tell us about Officer Haggerty's history with the Portland Police Department?"

"Officer Haggerty is a ten-year veteran of this department. He is an excellent police officer. He has been very involved in our Police Athletic League working with area youth. Currently, he is assigned to Portland High as the school resource officer."

"So, it's possible he knew Tommy Plummer, the boy Haggerty shot?" Billingslea asked.

"We haven't released the victim's name," Rumsfeld said. "I don't know where you're—"

"Mayor Gilcrest announced his name at her press conference. Can you tell us if Haggerty knew Plummer?"

"Next question," Rumsfeld said, pointing out a different reporter.

"Chief, is there a number witnesses should call?" a short dark-haired female television reporter asked.

"Yes. We are asking anyone who may have witnessed this incident to call the Criminal Investigation Division." Rumsfeld provided the crowd with the main number to CID, then repeated it.

"So, you want them to contact the police department and not Mayor Gilcrest, is that right?" the female reporter asked.

Rumsfeld shot another glance at Diane before turning back to face the crowd. "They should contact the police department, as always."

A young male reporter Diane did not recognize appeared at the front of the crowd.

"Chief, you stated that Officer Haggerty was pursuing two

armed robbery suspects. Can you tell us about the weapon used during the robbery?"

"Yes," Rumsfeld said. "According to the robbery victim, one of the suspects displayed a handgun during the commission of the crime."

"Has the handgun been recovered?"

"I'm afraid I can't answer that. As I said, this is an ongoing investigation."

The unknown reporter continued, shouting to be heard above the fray. "Chief Rumsfeld, I have received information that the Plummer boy shot by Haggerty was unarmed. Can you confirm that?"

"I don't know where you're getting your information, but I have no comment on that," Rumsfeld said.

The reporter persisted. "So, you won't confirm that he didn't have a gun?"

Rumsfeld glared at the reporter before recomposing himself and addressing the rest of the room. "Thank you, that's all I have to say at this time."

"Chief, Chief," a half dozen reporters shouted as Diane and Rumsfeld pushed through the crowd on their way to the exit.

"Where the fuck did he get the information about the gun?" Rumsfeld said as they reached the hallway. "What the hell is Gilcrest thinking?"

"Honestly? I'd say she just declared her candidacy," Diane said.

Chapter 9

Monday, 12:30 P.M.,
January 16, 2017

BYRON AND DETECTIVE Gardiner arrived back at Kennedy Park looking for an update from E.T.s Pelligrosso and Murphy as well as the detectives still working on the canvass. As Byron and Gardiner stepped from the car, they were approached by Investigator Lucinda Phillips.

"The press knows about the missing gun," Phillips said.

"Shit," Gardiner said, echoing Byron's very thought.

"How the hell did that get out already?" Byron asked.

"I don't know," Phillips said. "But somebody leaked it. One of the reporters put Rumsfeld on the spot with it at the press conference."

"Gilcrest?"

"She never mentioned it during her press conference."

"Did Rumsfeld confirm it?" Byron asked.

"He gave them a no-comment."

Byron knew the leak could have come from a dozen different places. Like every small city, Portland could be a sieve when something juicy happened. Gilcrest had already shown her willingness to grandstand; maybe she had put word out quietly. Or Rumsfeld himself might have leaked the information, trying to get out in front of it. The longer the acting chief waited, the more of a jam he would be in when the story finally broke. But regardless of where the leak originated, it meant the detectives had just run out of time. Byron knew there would be protests, confrontations with police, and likely worse. Every crazy son of a bitch within driving distance would likely crawl from the woodwork, hoping to score their fifteen minutes in the spotlight. CID's ability to investigate unfettered from outside influence had just evaporated before their very eyes.

"Shit," Gardiner said again, staring at the screen on his phone.

Both Byron and Phillips looked at him.

"What?" Byron asked.

"Have you seen the *Herald*'s Twitter page?" Gardiner asked.

"I'm not on social media," Byron said. "What is it?"

"Here," Gardiner said, handing him the phone.

Byron looked at the photograph and the accompanying tweet. "Dammit."

"What?" Phillips asked.

Byron handed her the phone. "The *Portland Herald* just tipped our missing robber to get rid of his sneakers."

Depicted under the photograph taken by Billingslea were the words: *Police collect footwear impressions at scene of shooting.*

"Well, that's helpful," Phillips said as she handed the phone back to Gardiner.

The three investigators trudged in silence across the yard to the outside edge of the crime scene tape where Pelligrosso appeared to be packing up his equipment.

Pelligrosso acknowledged Byron with a nod. "How did the press conference go?"

"Which one?" Byron said.

The evidence technician looked perplexed.

"Where are we at?" Byron asked.

"I'm finished. We've scoured the entire area. Can't find so much as a bullet hole or shell casing anywhere. Well, except for Haggerty's casings."

"And we checked all of the buildings behind Haggerty for holes?" Byron asked.

Pelligrosso nodded. "The buildings, the plastic play set, even a couple of metal sheds. There's nothing here to find, Sarge."

Byron exchanged a wordless glance with Phillips.

Could Hags have been wrong? Byron wondered. *Did he only imagine a flash in the heat of the moment? Was there some other explanation? The flashlight on Plummer's cellphone?*

Haggerty wasn't prone to overreaction. Haggerty's size and easygoing demeanor had served him well. He was very good at getting people to comply with minimal force. It wouldn't have been like Hags to read a situation so badly as to shoot an unarmed man. *Or kid.* So, what did happen?

"How did you leave it with the M.E.?" Byron asked Pelligrosso.

"Dr. Ellis is going to post later this afternoon. Said he was thinking three-thirty-ish."

"All right," Byron said as he surveyed the area one last time. "I'll meet you there."

As Byron headed back to 109 to drop off his temporary partner, his cell rang. It was Stevens.

"Hey, Mel," Byron said. "How are we making out with the canvass?"

"All the detectives are back at 109. Looks like we've contacted at least ninety percent of the units along the route that Haggerty chased the suspects. Still waiting on callbacks from the others."

"Did we put a call into Portland Housing for an active list?"

"Got it in my hot little hands, double-checking as we speak."

"I've got another assignment I need you to take care of."

"Shoot."

"I'm heading to Augusta for the post, but before I go I'm dropping Gardiner off at 109 with a list of the boys' varsity basketball players. They have an afternoon practice today. I want you to head over to the high school and interview all the players. Find out if any of them knew what young Tommy was up to and where they were last night."

"And if any of them tell me to pound sand? They are juveniles after all."

"Then we'll focus harder on the ones who do. Find the coach and charm the pants off the guy so he'll let you talk with them." Byron stole a glance over at his solemn-faced passenger. "Take Gardiner with you. Show him the ropes."

A smile appeared on Gardiner's face.

"Want Nuge to accompany us?" Stevens asked.

"You ever known Nuge to be charming?"

"Good point. Just Gardiner, it is."

TWENTY MINUTES AFTER the telephone call from Uncle Derrick, Terry Alfonsi pulled the candy-apple Mitsubishi Eclipse into the garage bay, killed the engine, and closed the overhead door. It had taken him five minutes to jump-start the car that had once belonged to his best friend, before the heroin overdose that took Arnold's life two years earlier. Tricked out with a loud exhaust, tinted windows, a state of the art stereo, with a trunk-mounted subwoofer that took up most of the car's small trunk, the Eclipse was what Arnie had called "bitchin'." It would be a shame to burn it.

He spent the next hour prepping the car for the little errand Vanos expected him to do. He scraped off the inspection sticker, removed the front registration plate, and changed out the rear, exchanging it with one from a stack of old plates hidden in a wooden box under the workbench. He checked the tire pressure, changed the oil and topped off fluids, replaced the battery, and made sure that the lightbulbs all worked. It wouldn't do to be pulled over on the way back from the job.

The engine appeared to be running all right, but he'd have Vinnie tune it up tomorrow. The car would need a coat of primer. Flat black would blend in better than the car's current shade. Vanos wanted the hit to be public for maximum effect. Said he wanted to send a message. Terry was all for sending messages, but candy-apple red would make disappearing from the scene next to impossible. Besides, this wasn't just anyone his uncle wanted to waste. This was a cop.

THE SOUND OF squeaking sneakers echoed throughout the Portland High gymnasium. Ten players ran up and down the hardwood floor, while several others stood in front of the bleachers watching the scrimmage, awaiting their turn. Detectives Stevens and Gardiner stood beside Coach Rick Miller as he shouted commands to the players. Gardiner had given Stevens the heads-up about Miller being "kind of a dick," but talking to him in person was a study in arrogance.

"Coach, I understand you need the kids to stay focused," Stevens said. "But we're investigating a robbery that resulted in the death of one of your players. We'd like a little cooperation."

"Stay with him, Pat," Miller yelled as one of the players went baseline and sunk a shot from the corner. "Are you gonna do that in a game? Come on! Don't let him get outside like that."

"Coach?" Stevens said.

Miller turned to face them. "Look, I get it. You need to talk with my players. But I need to get this team ready to win another state championship, and that's a tall friggin' order now that our best player is gone." He turned back toward the court to watch the team wearing gray T-shirts set up on offense. "Slow it down, Abdi. Give him time to set the pick."

"Coach Miller!" Stevens shouted, having lost her patience. "Are you going to let us talk to your players or not?"

"Yeah, yeah. Okay." Miller blew the whistle and called the players over to the stands. He addressed Stevens directly. "Take one at a time and use my office if you want."

Miller looked back at the group. "Guys, these detectives have some questions to ask you." Miller pointed to the player he'd been yelling at before, a tall gangly kid with sideburns. "Pat, since your brain isn't in the game anyway, why don't you go first. The rest of you get back out there." He looked back at Stevens. "Happy?"

"Overjoyed."

SEAN HAGGERTY SAT beside his attorney, Eugene Pomeroy, in one of the firm's conference rooms overlooking Congress Street. Haggerty had given depositions before. What was unusual was coming to the table to be questioned by an investigator from the state Attorney General's Office. While doing the job the city paid him to do Haggerty had killed a man. Not even a man—he had killed a teenaged boy. In the line of duty, protecting the citizens from armed robbers like Tommy Plummer and his unknown accomplice, he had killed a kid. And now he would be expected to justify his actions.

Haggerty felt nauseous. The room was suddenly much too warm. He tugged at his collar. The sweat was beading up on his forehead. Maybe Pomeroy was right. Maybe it was too soon. But Haggerty badly wanted to get it over with. To move on with his life and return to the work he loved.

"You okay, Sean?" Pomeroy asked. "Are you sure you're ready?"

"Yeah, I'm good," Haggerty lied. "Let's do this."

Phillips and Pomeroy exchanged nods. Phillips activated the digital recorder sitting between them on the table.

"My name is Lucinda Phillips and I am an investigator for the Attorney General's Office of the State of Maine. Today's date is January 16th, 2017, and the time is 3:05 P.M. The interview is being conducted in the conference room of the law offices of LeClair and Pomeroy. Also present are Officer Sean Haggerty of the Portland Police Department and Attorney Eugene S. Pomeroy. Mr. Pomeroy is representing Officer Haggerty in the matter of the shooting death of Thomas Plummer, which occurred on or about January 15th at 9:35 P.M. within Kennedy Park in Portland, Maine."

Haggerty sat quietly as she spoke. He was having difficulty understanding what Phillips was saying. Her words seemed to run together. This was surreal. Sitting in this room, needing an attorney while being questioned by an investigator from another law enforcement agency, for what? Doing his job? He felt like a criminal.

"Do you understand everything I've said, Officer Haggerty?" Lucinda asked, snapping him out of his funk.

Haggerty looked to Pomeroy. The attorney nodded his approval to proceed.

Haggerty turned to Phillips and gave a nod of his own.

"I'll need a verbal response for the recording, Sean," she said.

"Sorry," he said. "Yes. I understand."

"And do you also understand that this interview is in no way connected with any internal investigation that may be subsequently conducted by the Portland Police Department?"

"Yes."

"And you are making this statement voluntarily and of your own free will, correct?"

"Yes," Haggerty said again.

Lucinda nodded at him. "Let's begin, then. Officer Haggerty, take me back to the start of your shift on Sunday, January 15th, 2017."

Pomeroy placed a hand gently at the center of Haggerty's back. Sean looked over at him again. Pomeroy nodded and gave a half smile.

Haggerty turned back to face Phillips. "My shift—" The words caught in his throat. He felt his eyes watering and closed them. He heard liquid being poured into a cup. He opened his eyes again. Pomeroy handed him a clear plastic cup of water. Haggerty took it and drank. He set the half-empty cup back on top of the table, cleared his throat, and began again.

"My shift started at fifteen hundred hours."

BYRON STOOD SILENTLY off to one side of the examination table while Ellis worked and Pelligrosso moved around the room snapping photos. Byron had attended more autopsies than he cared to remember. He had seen every conceivable manner of death.

Some taken by others, some lives extinguished by the victims themselves. Byron had seen bodies that had been stabbed, shot, hanged, electrocuted, sexually assaulted, asphyxiated, dismembered, drowned, even one memorable case where the body was run over repeatedly and intentionally by someone driving an automobile. He had spent more than two decades bearing witness to this depraved indifference to human life. And to Byron, too, on the autopsy table, lives were reduced to nothing more than evidence-collecting expeditions. Bodies, once life vessels, were methodically cut, examined, weighed, and preserved until all available answers had been obtained.

The one thing Byron had never acclimated to was seeing the body of a child on that table. And at seventeen years of age, despite his size, Tommy Plummer was still only a child. Lying faceup and naked, head cradled in a stand, on full display, was a life wasted before it had even begun. And while it may have been Plummer's own actions that played the largest part in his ultimate demise, his life was cut short by bullets from a cop's gun. Haggerty's gun. And Byron knew that Haggerty's life also depended upon the outcome of this investigation. There was more at stake than just whether the shooting was righteous. Justified or not, Haggerty would be forced to live with the decision he'd made for the rest of his life.

"Sarge, you still with me?" Ellis asked.

Byron climbed back out of his own head to find Ellis and Pelligrosso both staring at him. "Yeah. Sorry, Doc," Byron said, shaking it off. "You were saying?"

"I said two of the five rounds that struck Plummer were fatal. The one in the head, obviously." Ellis pointed to one of the entry wounds in the left side of Plummer's torso. "But this one here actually nicked the pulmonary artery causing massive internal bleeding. Even without the head wound, it's likely he would have bled out before receiving medical help."

"What about direction?" Byron asked. "Can you give me something definitive?"

"Each of these bullets was fired at an upward angle, which matches what you told me about Plummer standing on top of a car. And they were all traveling front to back. There is no question that he was facing the officer at the time he was shot."

"So, the only thing missing is evidence that Plummer possessed and fired a gun," Byron said, thinking out loud.

Ellis carefully peeled off his gloves and turned to face Byron. "My boy, as we both know, the trace evidence left behind on a person's hand after they've fired a gun is extremely transient. Given the conditions you were working in, and the fact that *if* Plummer had a gun he may have only fired one round, it's not surprising we can't confirm anything by paraffin testing. At best this test is inconclusive."

Byron knew what the media, and by extension the public, would do with the word *inconclusive*. *It's the term police use when they haven't the first clue about what happened,* he thought. In a word, Haggerty was still fucked.

DIANE SAT IN Rumsfeld's office, occupying the same chair she had for most of the day, listening as the acting chief consulted with every single member of his command staff about the best way to move forward publicly.

Jesus, make a decision already, she thought.

Her cell vibrated inside the pocket of her suit coat. She removed it to find a single line of text from Davis Billingslea. Still looking 4 quote re missing gun.

Waiting until Rumsfeld was fully engrossed in sharing yet another angle with Commander Jennings, she responded, NO COMMENT!!!

Thirty seconds passed before Billingslea sent his response. Source says Plummer unarmed. Can we meet?

She was preparing to shut him down with something snarky when Rumsfeld surprised her by addressing her directly.

"Diane? What do you think of that idea?"

SEAN HAGGERTY LEFT the law offices of LeClair and Pomeroy exhausted. An empty shell, he was completely drained of every emotion. He wondered if it was possible for a person to use up all their allotted give-a-shit and in so doing be unable to replenish it. Would he just stumble through life not caring about anything or anyone ever again?

Investigator Phillips had hammered him on the missing gun. "How do you know the subjects you were chasing were actually the robbers? If they were the robbery suspects, how can you be sure they didn't toss the gun while you were chasing them?" Again and again she had forced him to recount the events that led up to the shooting. "Was there any other course of action open to you other than discharging your firearm, Officer? Tell me again about the flash of light you saw. You never heard a shot though, correct? Can you describe the weapon Thomas Plummer pointed at you?"

Haggerty didn't know exactly what he had expected the interview to be like, but he now wished he had listened to Byron and waited. He had told himself that getting out in front of this, giving the interview to the attorney general's investigator, would be a good thing, removing a great weight from his shoulders. After all, he had nothing to hide. But it hadn't been a good thing. And he didn't feel better. He actually felt worse but didn't know why. He had gone into the interview nervous but confident in his actions. Now everything was blurry and confusing. Phillips's last question rattled him to the core. "If you had it to do over again, would you have done anything differently?" How was he supposed to answer that?

Listening to the news reports had been another mistake. Many people were already second-guessing him, tagging him an over-zealous cop, calling for his resignation and for charges to be filed against him. *How had he become the bad guy?* he wondered. All he had done was his job, chasing down two robbers from the scene of a crime, one of them armed. And he had killed the armed one, in self-defense, exactly as he'd been trained. It should have been the end of story. Except it wasn't the end and he knew it. He had killed a teenager and regardless of the circumstances, or the outcome, he wasn't sure how to live with that. This felt like the beginning of a long real-life nightmare. A nightmare from which he might never awaken.

IT WAS NEARLY five o'clock when Byron began the hour-long drive back toward Portland. Daylight had long since departed, its passing hastened by the blackened clouds of the advancing storm front. He was in the process of merging onto the southbound lanes of I-95 when his cell rang. It was Diane.

"Didn't know if you'd still be at the post or not," Diane said.

"Headed back now," he said.

"You sound tired."

"I'm okay."

"How did the autopsy go?" she asked. "Any surprises?"

"The holes were all in the right places and in the right direction. Still can't put a gun in Plummer's hand at the time of the shooting though."

"His hands didn't test positive?" Diane asked.

He sighed. "Is it ever that easy?"

"Murphy's law," she said.

"Yeah, well, Murphy's alive and well. Anything new down there?"

"That's why I'm calling," she said. "The protests have begun."

IT WAS HALF past six by the time Byron made the turn off Franklin Arterial onto Middle Street. A light snow had begun to fall. The sidewalk directly in front of police headquarters was jammed with several dozen protestors. He lowered the front passenger window and drove slowly past the front of 109. Some in the group were carrying homemade signs while others shouted at passing cars, including Byron's. The common themes seemed to be *not above the law* and *legalized murder.*

Byron held no ill will toward the protestors, at least not the ones who were concerned that the police might have overstepped their authority. Hell, he'd spent a career questioning his so-called superiors. No, his issue was with the vultures who showed up to every protest rally as if it were a party. Troublemakers looking to start shit regardless of the cause. People who made his job infinitely more difficult. He continued around the block, then entered the PD's rear parking garage from Newbury Street. Not wanting to take part in a confrontation, he quickly crossed the plaza and entered 109 through the rear door.

He trudged up the four flights of stairs toward his office, intentionally bypassing CID's main lobby where he knew Shirley, who had previously agreed to work late, might still be lying in wait to remind him about the scores of people looking for him. Byron wasn't in the mood to listen to bullshit from anyone.

He tossed his coat and gloves into one of the visitor's chairs in his office, then plopped down in his own chair behind the desk. A stack of pink message slips stood sentry before him. The voicemail indicator on his office phone was illuminated. He closed his eyes and rubbed them with his fingertips. Fatigue was finally setting in. Byron hadn't realized how tired he was until this very moment. He had already managed half a week's workload and it was only Monday.

"Hey, Sarge," Melissa Stevens said from the doorway. "Didn't know you were back."

"Just arrived," Byron said as he opened his eyes. "How did it go at the school?"

Stevens entered the office and sat down across from him. "Well, Gardiner and I just spent the last two hours interviewing every sweaty teenager on the Portland High School boys' basketball team. Jesus, teenagers stink. Remind me never to have any. Go Bulldogs."

Byron grinned. "And?"

"Aside from Coach Miller, who by the way is a first class asshole, most of the players didn't care too much for Tommy. Sounds like Tommy thought he was a one-man show. 'Ball hog,' one kid called him. It also sounds like it was pretty common knowledge that Tommy Plummer was the go-to if you wanted to score some drugs."

"How the hell could he get away with that? Wouldn't the teachers or coaches have put a stop to it?"

"Doesn't sound like anyone was looking too closely?" Stevens flipped open her notebook. "One kid we talked to, a Patrick

Mingus, said Tommy's parents spent a lot of time running interference for him. They knew some of what Tommy was into but helped cover it up so it wouldn't screw up his chances to get into a big-name college. Apparently the scouts had been swarming the place and there were already offers on the table. Mingus also thought Tommy had a guardian angel at the school."

"I'm not following. Someone that kept him out of trouble?"

"That. But Mingus said it felt like someone inside the school was supplying the drugs to Tommy."

"How does Mingus know that?"

"He wouldn't say, but I think he was trying not to implicate himself in any drug use."

Byron nodded as he jotted Mingus's name into his own notebook. "Did all of the players talk with you?"

"Yup. Not one holdout."

"Any of them with Plummer on Sunday night?"

"No one would admit it."

"Alibis?"

"Gardiner and I will tackle those tomorrow. We've got contact info for all the parents."

After Stevens departed the office, Byron made a halfhearted attempt to read some of the message slips. Halfway through the second one he stopped and tossed them back on the desk.

The adrenaline flow that began with the previous night's call from Dispatch, and had carried him through the last twenty hours, was tapped out. He knew the fog beginning to envelope his brain was a sure path to making mistakes on the case, and if he was feeling it, then so were the others. There were still several administrative tasks needing his attention, but he knew which one of those was most important. He picked up the handset on his desk phone and punched in a number. It was time to send his people home.

IT WAS NEARLY ten by the time Byron departed 109. He drove past the vacant sidewalk in front of the station. The protesters had also called it a night. The roads were already coated with several inches of the white stuff as he navigated through the snowy darkness and blinking traffic signals toward his North Deering condo. Snowflakes raced past the beam of his headlights, making him feel like a space traveler. Aside from the plow drivers, and Byron himself, traffic was sparse.

The storm couldn't have come at a worse time, he thought, worried that they may have overlooked something. Some vital piece of evidence that would be buried under more than a foot of snow by morning. Evidence that might have cleared Haggerty of any wrongdoing would be lost forever.

Byron couldn't shake the nagging feeling that he was heading in the wrong direction, as if driving away from 109 at this point in the investigation was a mistake. One that couldn't be undone. But there was simply nothing else he could do. The storm was calling all the shots now. He would just have to hunker down and ride it out like everyone else. They all needed a good night's sleep, himself included. He had to have each detective at the top of their game in the days to come.

As he slowed to make the turn into his driveway he noticed the familiar shape of a vehicle half-hidden beneath a thin blanket of snow. It was Diane's unmarked.

Before accepting the promotion to sergeant, Diane had been Byron's partner on every homicide case. Her experience investigating murders in the Big Apple made her a valuable asset. At first their relationship had remained purely professional, in spite of the obvious mutual attraction. It wasn't until after Byron and Kay, his ex-wife, made their year-long separation permanent that Byron and Diane acted on their feelings for each other.

But it had been nearly a month since he and Diane Joyner had spent any meaningful time together outside of work, let alone an actual night. Her abrupt departure from CID had dramatically altered the dynamics of their relationship. They were now free from the restraints that had existed while working together within the same unit, requiring them to keep secret their personal relationship, but the once symbiotic nature of their formerly shared professional lives was gone. Byron's days were still occupied by the complexities of homicide investigation, while Diane's were now spent writing press releases, holding press conferences, and working to maintain the department's professional image in the news and on social media feeds. As far as Byron was concerned, her considerable investigative talent was being wasted on PR.

Diane was waiting for him in the living room as he entered the condo. She had made herself comfortable on the sofa, enjoying the warmth of the gas fireplace, a glass of wine, and his latest Krueger mystery novel. Dressed in one of his white button-down shirts, and not much else, she had his full attention.

"Hey," he said as he pulled off his wet boots and removed his overcoat, hanging it on the rack in the entryway.

"Hey, yourself," she said, taking a sip from her glass. "Thought you might want some help shoveling out in the morning. And perhaps a bit of company tonight."

Normally it would have been the last thing he would have wanted at this point in an investigation. Once his brain was dialed into working a case everything else became a burden. But there was nothing he could do about the weather, and if he was being honest with himself, he had missed being with Diane more than he cared to admit. He couldn't conceive of a more welcome distraction.

"Unless you'd rather I go," she said when he didn't respond right away.

"Not on your life," he said, approaching the couch in his stocking feet. "Is that what you envisioned wearing while helping me shovel?"

"Think it's too much?" she asked.

"I think it's perfect," he said before bending over her and delivering a lingering openmouthed kiss. He tasted the sweetness of the wine on her tongue. She slid a warm hand around to the back of his neck and pulled him closer.

Byron remained in that awkward position until his lower back began to protest. He broke away from her embrace and stood upright, catching his breath. "I should probably slip into something more comfortable," he said.

Diane slid off the couch and pressed herself against him. "Or, if you're looking to get more comfortable, I could help you slip out of these." She maintained eye contact as she slid her hand up his chest and began to loosen his tie.

"Good to have options," he said.

Starting at the top, with agonizing slowness, she unbuttoned his dress shirt, then untucked it from his trousers. When she had finished with his shirt, she began to unfasten the buttons on the one she was wearing, revealing the dark unblemished skin of her breasts. Repositioning both of them, she pushed Byron backward onto the sofa, then climbed over him, straddling his thighs. "Comfortable?" she asked.

"Getting there," Byron said as he felt his desire stirring.

She reached down and unfastened his belt and trousers. "Well, let's see just how comfortable I can make you." Diane leaned forward and delivered another long kiss while her skilled hands went to work on him.

SEAN HAGGERTY AWOKE with a start. His heart was racing, pulse pounding in his temples, and his entire body was soaked in perspiration, as were the bedsheets. Threads of sleep still clung to his consciousness and it took him a moment to realize where he was. He sat up in the darkened room and looked at his alarm clock. The red LED glowed 3:15. It was only a dream.

He had been chasing two hooded figures through an unfamiliar darkened alley during a snowstorm. This alley didn't look anything like Kennedy Park; he wasn't even sure it was Portland. The buildings weren't row houses but high-rises with blackened windows that loomed ominously like abstract art forms. The figures rounded the corner of a building, disappearing from his sight. In the dream, Haggerty followed them through the swirling snow. As he neared the corner he tripped over something and went sprawling, losing his grip on his gun. Exposed and unarmed he searched frantically but the pistol was gone. The hooded figures, no longer fleeing, were now slowly approaching him. He tried to get to his feet to take cover, but his hands and knees were frozen to the ground, rendering him completely helpless. Haggerty looked back at the hooded figures. The luminescence of the snow-covered ground provided enough light for him to recognize the pale chiseled features of skulls. In each of their hands they carried freakishly huge chrome revolvers, the barrels of which would have looked more at home on shotguns. His struggles to free himself from the ground were useless. He looked up at the figures, word-lessly pleading with them. The skeletal faces were grinning. The dream demons raised their arms, pointing the enormous guns directly at Haggerty's head. He screamed as they opened fire.

With the screams still echoing in his head, Haggerty jumped out of bed and ran to the bathroom. He dropped to his knees in front of the toilet and vomited.

Chapter 10

Tuesday, 6:00 A.M.,
January 17, 2017

OVERNIGHT THE SNOW fell with such intensity that Portland's Department of Public Works hadn't been able to keep up. According to the local news, a total of fourteen inches blanketed the Greater Portland area. The accompanying northeasterly winds had created drifts as high as four feet. It would be well after noontime before many of the city's secondary roads were passable. As with any winter storm, parking on the in-town peninsula was a nightmare, the snowbanks rendering parking spaces on many streets unusable.

Byron was up and out of the house by 6:15. He'd cleared off both his car and Diane's before shoveling out some of the pile left by the plow at the end of his short driveway. He grabbed a quick shower, dressed, and was headed for the door when Diane greeted him with a travel mug of coffee and a morning-after kiss. She was wearing his button-down shirt from the night before.

"Here, you'll need this," she said.

"Which?" he asked, giving her a smirk.

"Both. Although I suspect the memory of *this* will outlast the coffee." She rose up on the balls of her bare feet and kissed him again. "Be careful, John," she said, her expression turning to one of concern. "Things are likely to get crazier."

Byron's morning commute normally took ten or fifteen minutes. Today it took forty-five. When he reached 109, he found that nearly a dozen of the protesters from the previous night had already reassembled. The gathering was still low-key and clustered together, many of them holding a Styrofoam cup of Dunkin' Donuts coffee in one hand and a homemade sign in the other. *Every protest begins with Dunkin'*, he thought as he drove past the group and headed to 109's rear parking garage.

While waiting for several black-and-whites to depart the garage, Byron's mind wandered back to the problem at hand. It wasn't as if he hadn't envisioned this very scenario. Hell, every cop in the state had imagined the possibility that a police shooting in Maine might one day have all the necessary ingredients to become a carbon copy of the politically charged incidents seen in other parts of the country. After more than two decades on the job, Byron had witnessed the awesome power wielded by the press too many times to discount it. And that same power to incite was the reason so many people in the public spotlight acted irresponsibly. It was free advertising. Some, like the late Paul Ramsey, Esquire, jumped at any opportunity to try a case in front of the television cameras. *Dr. Phil goes to court*, Byron thought.

Pulling into the garage he wondered what it said about a society that repeatedly condemned members of its police force even before all the facts were in. Didn't public servants deserve the same presumption of innocence that the rest of society demanded? And deserved? The legal standard is innocent until proven guilty in a court of law, not the court of public opinion. This was real life, not *The Gong Show*. These irrational reactions by the public reminded Byron a bit of the Wild West. *Let's break out the torches and pitchforks*, he thought.

As Byron punched in the key code to the rear door to 109 and stepped inside the building, he wondered what would happen if this hysteria continued? Would there eventually come a day when police departments around the U.S. would no longer be able to recruit and retain new officers? As it was, many of the Maine departments were struggling, forced to offer signing bonuses to attract candidates. Even the Portland Police Department, the state's largest municipal agency, was down fifteen officers, a dangerous position to be in. The statewide pool of qualified police candidates had become so depleted that many departments were offering higher starting pay and benefits to entice officers from other agencies into lateral transfers. A self-perpetuating hole in the thin blue fabric of law enforcement. A national shortage of police officers meant there wouldn't be anyone left to keep the wolves away. And as any cop could attest, the wolves are plentiful. It wasn't a comforting thought.

With his briefcase in one hand and the near empty travel mug of coffee that Diane had prepared in the other, Byron stepped out of the stairwell into the fourth-floor hallway. Lieutenant LeRoyer was hovering around the CID lobby, lying in wait.

"John, you got a second?" LeRoyer asked.

"Any chance I could get settled first?" Byron said, snapping back a little more forcefully than he'd intended.

Surprise registered on LeRoyer's face instantly.

Realizing that the Haggerty shooting hadn't exactly been a

picnic for his boss either, Byron backed down a notch. "Sorry, Marty. Guess I'm still overtired. Come on, we can talk in my office."

The pink message slips had grown from a small neat stack to a mountainous pile tossed haphazardly atop his desk. It was Shirley Grant's way of telling him that his voicemail was full again and that she'd had enough of his unresponsiveness to the messages. He shoved the slips to one side and sat down.

"What time did you finally make it home last night?" LeRoyer asked as he settled into one of the visitor chairs.

"Around ten, I guess," Byron said. "You?"

"Maybe an hour before that. Manage any sleep?"

Byron hid a grin behind his coffee cup as he recalled the previous night with Diane. "A little."

"My damn plow guy didn't show. Had to dig myself out. My back is already killing me," LeRoyer said, reaching around with both hands to massage his lower back through his suit coat.

Byron wondered when the lieutenant would end the pleasantries and get to the point.

"You got any good news for me?" LeRoyer asked.

If I did, you'd have it already, Byron thought. "Dr. Ellis confirmed that Tommy Plummer was facing Hags when he was shot. So, when the bullshit about him being shot in the back starts you can use that to douse the flames."

"Not that anything I say will matter," LeRoyer muttered.

Byron, who couldn't argue with LeRoyer's assessment, continued. "Ellis said two of Plummer's wounds were fatal."

LeRoyer did his trademark pass through his hair with his fingers. It was the lieutenant's classic nervous tell and the reason the detectives had nicknamed him Einstein. By day's end LeRoyer's wild hair would no doubt rival that of the world's most famous mathematician. Byron couldn't help but wonder if his boss had ever managed to win a dime at poker.

"The public is gonna lose their shit when they find out Tommy was shot in the head," LeRoyer said. "I can see the headline now: *Police Execute Teen.*"

Byron frowned at the lieutenant's dramatics, but he knew he was probably right. "Ellis said even if the head shot hadn't happened the kid would still be dead. One of the bullets penetrated the chest cavity, nicking the pulmonary artery. He would have bled out internally anyway."

"You think the public is gonna care about that?"

Byron didn't imagine they would, but it wasn't his job to worry about public perception. His mission was simple: find the second robber and fill in the missing pieces of the case. Spin was for someone higher up the food chain than him. It was also one of the reasons Byron had never aspired to a rank higher than that of detective sergeant.

Byron spent several more minutes bringing LeRoyer up to speed on the latest developments before heading down to 109's third floor. He wanted to check in with Pelligrosso. And he had an assignment for Tran.

"Anything I can do to help, Sarge?" Tran asked as Byron entered the computer lab.

Byron still hadn't adjusted to Tran's recent change in demeanor. The computer whiz kid's newfound respect for authority was a bit unsettling. Byron didn't realize how much Tran's surfer dude delivery had become a part of their everyday interactions. Perhaps Tran was maturing, or maybe it was only because of what was at stake with Haggerty's shooting. Regardless of the reason, Byron began to worry he might miss Tran's irreverent streak.

"Actually, I do have something for you, Dustin." Byron handed him a slip of paper with the names and birth dates of the four Portland High students that Detective Gardiner had provided. "I want you to find out everything you can on these kids."

"Who are they?" Tran asked as he read the list.

"Known associates of Tommy Plummer. They hung around with him enough to garner a look."

Tran looked up from the list. "You think one of them might have been with him when the robbery happened?"

"It's possible. Get ahold of Mel. She'll have another list for you. I want you to dig up everything you can find for connections. Relatives, addresses, incident reports, anything that might help us. If Plummer had a gun, I want to know where he got it. Someone could have sold him a gun on the street, but I'd think it was more likely he stole it or borrowed it from an adult. Keep that angle in mind while you're digging, okay?"

"I'll get right on it, boss."

"One more thing. Check for any drug-related history on each."

"In-house or do you want me to make a trip to the DA?"

Byron considered the consequences if someone leaked the fact that Tran was poking around in juvenile records for so many students. "Let's keep it in-house for now."

As Byron departed Tran's office, headed for the crime lab, he cast a quick glance back at his young detective. He was definitely going to miss the surfer dude.

IT HAD TAKEN Terry Alfonsi the better part of two hours to plow the dooryard and driveway to the garage. The actual plowing was easy; it was shoveling out and moving various customers' cars that took so long. By the time he'd finished the chore he was in a foul mood. While he had been outside busting his ass, Vinnie hadn't done a damn thing.

"Comfortable?" Terry asked as he studied Vinnie seated behind the counter playing with his cellphone and munching on a stale donut.

"Very," Vinnie said without looking up. Sugar sprayed from his mouth as he spoke.

"Tell me again why I have to do all the work around here?" Terry asked.

"Simple physics," Vinnie said.

"What the hell does that mean?"

"Means I'm bigger than you."

Terry despised Vinnie's habit of threatening him without actually making a threat. Terry had had his ass handed to him by Vinnie before, and the big lug hardly broke a sweat while doing it. He hated being smaller.

"Have you done anything around here this morning while I've been out killing myself in the yard?" Terry asked.

Vinnie's eyes rolled skyward as if he were trying to recall. "Yup."

"What? 'Cause it looks to me like all you've done is sit there on your lazy ass."

Vinnie looked at him the way he always did, with those disinterested eyes.

"Not true," Vinnie said. "I made the coffee, took a shit, watched a little TV, and tuned that burner over there."

"You tuned up the car already?"

"Yup. Runs like a champ." Vinnie went back to studying his phone.

That was another thing that bugged him about Vinnie. He was a crackerjack mechanic, and body man. Everything came so easy to him. It wasn't fair.

"Yeah, well, don't do shit until I tell you," Terry said. "Uncle Derrick is gonna tell us when to move."

"Already did."

"What?"

"He called while you were outside."

"What did he say?"

"End of the week."

"I'VE MANAGED TO identify the manufacturer and style of sneaker from the tread pattern," Pelligrosso said as he pulled up the image on his computer screen.

Byron leaned in to look at the comparison. The pair of angled parallel squares located on the heel and ball of the tread were the same as the prints left behind at the scene. "So, our missing robber wears Nike basketball sneakers. What size?"

"Nine and a half."

"That's good, right?" Byron asked.

"Not really. Nike LeBron Soldier X is a pretty popular brand of sneaker with the high-school-aged kids right now."

"What about unusual tread wear? Anything we can match?"

Pelligrosso shook his head. "The sneakers that made these prints were fairly new. There's no discernible wear."

"Can you print out a photo of the actual sneaker for me?"

"Sure. This is what they look like," the evidence tech said as he clicked on a link, changing the image.

Byron studied the black-and-gold shoes on the screen. They

were ankle-high, with the familiar Nike swoosh at the back just below what appeared to be a signature.

"Were either of the students you spoke with yesterday wearing anything like these?" Pelligrosso asked.

Byron took out his cellphone and pulled up the photos that Gardiner had sent him by way of text messaging. He compared them to the picture on the screen. The photographs didn't match.

"No," Byron said. "And we were only able to speak with three of them before Davis Billingslea went public with our evidence. Unless our missing robber is completely inept, those sneakers are long gone."

"Most likely," Pelligrosso agreed.

"What about Plummer's cell?" Byron asked.

"I put it on the charger and rebooted it. It works fine. I'll keep it here until you guys get a warrant to go through it."

Given the latest trend among Plummer's mates of erasing all cell history, Byron wondered if that might end up being a fool's errand.

"And the flashlight?" Byron asked. "I read the MedCu attendant's statement about the flashlight being on when they got to the body. Were you able to confirm that when you powered it back on?"

Pelligrosso shook his head. "No. I even tried to re-create the event with my own phone. If you activate the flashlight app, then power the phone down, when you power up again, the flashlight is automatically back in the off position. There's no way to confirm what the attendant saw."

Byron had known it wouldn't be that easy. It never was. "Any idea what the powder is in those baggies you seized?"

"I weighed them and tagged them. Haven't had time for anything more yet."

Byron's cell rang before he could check off the next item on his mental to-do list. The number on the display was blocked. "Thanks, Gabe," Byron said before walking out of the lab to answer the call.

"Byron."

"John. Sam Collier."

Special Agent Sam Collier was a fellow law enforcement dinosaur and longtime friend of Byron's. Collier had worked with him on many sensitive cases over the years and was one of the few people within the FBI that Byron trusted.

"I saw the news, John. How's your officer holding up?"

"He's a tough kid. I think he'll be okay. I'm up to my ass on this though."

"That's why I'm calling. You got time for a quick coffee?"

BY THE TIME Byron walked to Milk Street in the Old Port, Collier was already waiting for him in the back of the Crooked Mile Café with two large coffees, two cranberry scones, and a man Byron had never seen before. Judging by the man's suit and haircut, he was a fed.

Byron stamped the snow off his boots on the mat just inside the door, then walked to the table.

"Breakfast too?" Byron said. "This can't be good."

"Large, black, and your favorite kind of scone," Collier said as he stood and shook Byron's hand. "John, I'd like you to meet Special Agent Mark Lessard."

Lessard stood and shook Byron's hand too. "Pleased to make your acquaintance, Sergeant," Lessard said.

"Mark is up from the Boston field office overseeing a case," Collier said.

Byron took off his wool overcoat, draped in over the empty chair to his right, and sat down. "You're stalling, Sam."

"You know me too well."

"So?"

Collier looked to Lessard. Lessard nodded, a clear indication to Byron of exactly who was in charge. Collier looked around the room. Byron followed his gaze. Only one other table was occupied and it was at the far end of the dining room near a window.

"Cone of secrecy is now engaged," Collier said.

"Of course," Byron said.

"A little bird told me that you recovered some controlled substances at the scene of the shooting Sunday night."

"This bird have a name?"

"You know it doesn't work that way, John."

"Okay. Yeah, we did. Found several baggies. One contained about fifty Xanax. Several others held a white powder we haven't tested yet. Why?"

"You think the drugs belonged to the robbery suspects?" Lessard asked.

Byron, who wasn't about to share more details of PPD's investigation without knowing why, shrugged as he took a bite of his scone. He washed it down with some coffee before proceeding. "Who knows. One of them is dead and the other got away. Why are you asking?"

Collier surveyed the room again, then looked back at Byron and leaned in close. "We think the drugs may have come from the laundromat. Do you know a girl by the name of Christine Souza?"

The name sounded vaguely familiar to Byron but he couldn't place it. "Not sure. Should I?"

"She was a Portland High School cheerleader. Died at a Westbrook party shortly after the school year started last fall. Drug overdose. Cocaine, alcohol, and methylenedioxy-methamphetamine."

"MDMA," Byron said. "Ecstasy."

"Yes. Souza choked to death on her own vomit. This would have been her senior year."

"I remember hearing about it. What does any of this have to do with the laundromat robbery?"

Byron listened for the next several minutes as Collier laid out the intel received by the bureau following Souza's OD. Collier said the drugs may have been coming into the high school from a local laundromat or dry cleaner. The intel also addressed the possibility that someone on the school staff was facilitating the operation from the inside, matching what Patrick Mingus had told Melissa Stevens.

"You're telling me that the bureau has a detail up on the Bubble Up?" Byron asked, wondering why he was only now hearing about it.

"Yes."

Byron could feel his anger building as he looked back and forth between the two men. "And do the Maine Drug Enforcement guys know about it?"

Collier shook his head.

"Not even Crosby?"

"No."

"Sam, don't take this the wrong way, but what the fuck? You guys have known about this since September and you're just letting us know now?"

Roses bloomed on Collier's cheeks and he began fidgeting with his tie. He took another look around the room without answering.

"You're telling me that Haggerty didn't have to go through this shit?" Byron snapped.

Lessard spoke up. "The source of our intel didn't know which laundromat or dry cleaner, only that it was local. Greater Portland somewhere. We had no idea which place to set up on. It wasn't until recently that we discovered which laundromat."

"How recent?" Byron asked.

The agents exchanged glances. "Recent," Lessard said.

"So this wasn't a cash grab?" Byron asked. "It was a drug rip. And Haggerty had no idea what he was getting himself into."

Collier sat back in his chair. "We believe the laundromat is part of an out-of-state OC case."

"Organized crime. Great."

"It took us some time to narrow the possibilities to just a couple of businesses," Lessard said. "Something we could handle without breaking the manpower bank."

Byron was still unsure what it was that Collier and Lessard were holding back. "And?"

"One of the things we've discussed was who the inside contact was at the high school," Collier said.

"You think it might have been the kid Haggerty shot, Tommy Plummer?" Byron asked.

"Maybe. But our intel makes it sound like someone in a position of authority."

"So, what? The principal, assistant principal, head librarian, who?"

"What about the SRO?" Lessard said as he exchanged a quick glance with Collier.

"Get the fuck out of here," Byron said. "Sean Haggerty? You're telling me that you suspect a police officer is the inside guy at the high school?"

"I'm just saying it was discussed," Lessard said. "I know you don't want to believe it, Sergeant. But this influx of drugs didn't hit the school hard until this fall. Haggerty came on board as the new SRO at the same time. Hell, he runs your summer police athletic league. He knows many of these kids."

"Jesus, you've even checked up on him?"

Byron couldn't believe what he was hearing. Ten minutes ago he'd mistakenly believed that his only problems were finding the second robber and trying to clear Haggerty of a bad shoot.

"I'm trying to conduct an investigation into a questionable police shooting and an armed robbery. How the hell do I do that without us tripping over each other?"

Lessard spoke up. "Do what you were doing anyway. So long as you don't confront Cavallaro about the drugs, our investigation will not impede your efforts."

Byron stood up abruptly and grabbed his coat. "You're impeding my efforts right now."

"Look, John, don't shoot the messenger," Collier said. "We're just giving you a heads-up as a courtesy. We wanted you to know what you're up against."

Byron shook his head in disgust as he slid his coat on and grabbed the coffee. "Thanks for the breakfast. Can I assume that any helpful information you guys develop will also be kept from us? Or would it be too much to ask that the bureau actually keep us in the goddamned loop?"

"Not *us*, John," Lessard said. "You. This isn't to be shared with anyone else. We'll let you know if anything develops."

"Yeah, you do that."

AS HE TRUDGED back to 109, Byron wasn't sure which thing he hated most: the fact that he'd been burdened with the additional knowledge of a secret federal investigation, or the possibility that Haggerty might be involved in something so despicable, and the implications which accompanied that possibility. Haggerty's request to leave patrol for the school resource officer position had seemed to come from out of the blue. Byron had tried for years to persuade the veteran beat cop to leave the street and come to CID, but Hags had turned him down time and again, saying that he loved working the street too much to settle for a desk job.

And there were other things weighing on Byron's mind. Had Collier come to Byron as a friend, or had he been elected as messenger by the powers that be inside the Portland Resident Agency or the Boston field office of the FBI? Or Lessard? The one thing Byron was sure of was that the stakes had just risen exponentially.

BYRON STOOD UP to stretch his legs and stiff neck. He had been sitting at his desk doing his best to read through the enormous stack of statements and supplements connected to the shooting, but the conversation with Collier and Lessard kept gnawing at him. He couldn't help but wonder what else they weren't telling him.

The supplements had all been written by officers and detectives while the statements came from the many residents and visitors of Kennedy Park. Most of the latter were people who had heard sirens and loud bangs but not much else. Many of the witnesses thought the noises were kids playing with fireworks, a few described the sounds as a car backfiring. Only a handful had recognized the sounds for what they really were: gunshots. Nothing stood out as particularly helpful.

Byron also spent considerable time reading and rereading the statements from both of the MedCu EMTs who had attended to Tommy Plummer. While one of the attendants made no mention of observing a cellphone lying on the ground with its flashlight activated, the other dedicated nearly an entire paragraph to it.

Why hadn't any of the officers noticed the light? Byron wondered. *Could Haggerty have confused the cellphone's flashlight with the muzzle flash from a gun?* The attendant's statement wasn't doing a thing to quell Byron's unease.

He grimaced as he gulped down the last dregs of cold coffee Collier had purchased, then departed the office to stroll through a mostly vacant CID. Nearing the conference room, he heard the television coming from within and the familiar instrumental intro to the midday news broadcast.

Seated alone at the table, with a stack of paperwork and a sandwich, Nugent was doing the same thing Byron had been doing, except for the lunch part.

"Hey, Sarge," Nugent said.

"Anything worth hearing?" Byron asked as he entered the room, cocking his head in the direction of the television.

"Actually, yeah," Nugent said. "You might want to sit down for it though."

"Really?" Byron said as he pulled out a chair at the end of the table and sat down. He picked up the remote from the table and increased the volume on the television. "Wanna give me a hint?"

"Don't think you'll need to wait that long," Nugent said.

"Good afternoon, I'm Keith Tolan," the news anchor with the bad comb-over said. "Well, that was some storm, wasn't it, Ginny?"

"That is was, Keith," Meteorologist Ginny Wells, wearing too much mascara, affirmed. "And crews are still digging out from what some are calling the biggest storm of 2017. Many areas around Greater Portland received well over a foot of the white stuff. The Portland Jetport reported thirteen and a half inches. And we're already looking at another system moving this way for later in the week. I'll have snowfall totals and more in a few minutes."

"Thank you, Ginny," Tolan said. "But before we get to the rest of our top stories, we have some breaking news to tell you about. Leslie Thomas is live in Portland. Leslie, what have you got for us?"

The screen cut to an attractive twenty-something blonde standing outside on a Congress Street sidewalk. Thomas was wearing a brightly colored knee-length red wool jacket, white knit hat, and matching white mittens. Standing beside her was a short stocky dark-skinned male who appeared to be of Hispanic descent. The man was dressed in sweatpants and a gray hoodie, making him look like a boxer in training. His face looked familiar, but Byron couldn't place him.

"Good afternoon, Keith," Thomas said. "I'm standing here with Lucas Perez of South Portland. Mr. Perez, thank you for agreeing to go on the air with us."

"No problem," Perez said.

Perez. The name didn't ring any bells for Byron.

"Mr. Perez, can you tell our viewing audience what you just told me about the police shooting on Sunday night?"

"Sure thing. I was visiting a friend of mine who lives in Kennedy Park on Sunday night. We were outside having a smoke when we heard sirens coming. The next thing I know these two kids ran by me and a big cop with a gun was chasing them." Perez held his hand up above his head in a gesture designed to indicate that the police officer was somewhat taller than he was.

"What happened next, Mr. Perez?" Ms. Color Coordinated asked.

"These two kids ran up to a fence, but they didn't have anywhere to go. The cop pulled his gun and started yelling at them— 'Freeze,' 'Don't move,' shit like that."

The reporter glanced nervously at the camera before looking back at Perez. "Remember, we're on live television, Mr. Perez."

"Oh yeah. Damn. Sorry."

"Please continue."

"Anyway, I saw both of the kids turn around with their hands raised, you know? Like they were giving up."

"And then what happened?"

"Then the cop just starts shooting at them. About twenty times. I couldn't believe it. This one kid just fell. I knew he was hit."

"Tommy Plummer?" the reporter asked.

"I guess. I didn't know his name."

"What about the other kid?"

"I don't know what happened to him. One minute he was there and the next wasn't. Guess he ran off. I'd have run too," he said, turning to look right into the camera to make his point.

Byron noticed Tolan trying to suppress a grin, as if anyone might find this remotely humorous.

"Did either one of the people being chased have a gun?" Leslie Thomas asked.

"I don't know. Not that I saw."

"What happened next?"

"I ran back inside my friend's apartment. I didn't want to get shot too, you know?"

Byron picked up the remote and muted the television. He could feel his blood pressure rising. "Tell me we already interviewed this asshole," he said.

"I don't recognize the name," Nugent said, shaking his head. "I've been reading all these statements and I haven't seen one from anyone named Perez."

Byron hadn't read anything resembling the account Perez had just provided. He scanned the whiteboard for Perez's name but came up empty.

"Dammit. How did we miss him?"

"Maybe we didn't, Sarge. He could be full of shit."

Byron knew that Nuge might well be right. So many people just couldn't help themselves when it came to a chance at the limelight. But Byron also knew that even if Perez had made up his account of the incident, the damage was already done.

Byron's cell rang. The ID showed that the call was from AG Investigator Lucinda Phillips.

Chapter 11

Tuesday, 12:55 P.M.,
January 17, 2017

IMMEDIATELY FOLLOWING THE midday news, Byron was summoned to the chief's conference room for a one o'clock. From his formidable experience only two things were delivered in that particular room: attaboys and ass-chewings. It was the latter he was envisioning as he entered the room and sat down.

The small rectangular space had the same out of place feel as many of 109's subdivided afterthoughts. The short end bordering the two entry doors was all glass. Windows that only overlooked a hallway were covered by heavy cream-colored floor-to-ceiling drapes. The far wall played host to a large decorative bookcase, which almost succeeded in making the room feel like a study. Displayed on the two long walls were framed sepia-toned Portland police photographs from the 1920s and '30s. A large faux-mahogany wooden table with matching chairs dominated the space. Occupying the chairs were Acting Chief Rumsfeld, Lieutenant LeRoyer, Lucinda

Phillips, Assistant Attorney General Jim Ferguson, Commander Edward Jennings, and a bespectacled Barry Sonnenfeld, the department's legal advisor, who had always reminded Byron of the folk singer John Denver.

Ferguson acknowledged Byron with a slight nod.

"How in hell did you miss this Perez guy?" Rumsfeld barked at LeRoyer.

Byron wondered if the acting chief's pronoun shift from the collective to the singular more accusatory version was by design or a subconscious defense mechanism.

Byron glanced over at LeRoyer. The lieutenant looked as though he might actually melt into the floor like Baum's wicked witch.

Rather than let his floundering boss suffer further abuse, Byron spoke up. "It's my fault, Chief."

Rumsfeld tore his eyes away from the CID commander and fixed them upon his detective sergeant. Byron experienced mild satisfaction at seeing Rumsfeld's clear irritation with him for having the audacity to interrupt this obviously scripted display of his power.

"I thought we'd done a complete canvass of the park," Byron continued. "Evidently, we missed someone."

"*Evidently*," Rumsfeld mocked. "Your incompetence has made this entire department look like shit. First, we hold back on the missing gun, now it looks like we didn't bother to do a thorough canvass for fear that we might actually locate a witness to a bad shooting."

"With all due respect, Chief," Byron said, not really believing the man deserved any, "we don't know any such thing. We're still trying to piece together what did happen."

"And I'm trying to keep this department and city together!"

Rumsfeld shot back. "Maybe you haven't noticed the protestors outside. They're calling for my resignation, for chrissakes."

"That's what this is really all about, isn't it?" Byron said before he could stop himself. "Your *goddamned* promotion to chief."

"*John*, that's enough," LeRoyer snapped.

Rumsfeld's eyes widened, and his mouth hung open. Byron wondered if this was the first time anyone had dared question the acting chief's authority since he'd taken over the temporary position.

None of the room's other occupants made a sound.

Byron noticed Ferguson's raised eyebrows and barely suppressed grin from across the table.

Rumsfeld finally spoke up, only it came out sounding more like a growl than actual speech. "Sergeant Byron, I suggest you get the *hell* out of my conference room and get back to doing your job before I find someone else to do it for you." He pointed at the conference room door, glaring at Byron as if daring him to speak.

Byron glared back while trying to decide his next move.

LeRoyer caught Byron's eye. The lieutenant gave an almost imperceptible shake of his head. Byron knew it was his lieutenant's attempt to keep his senior sergeant from burying himself any further.

Byron had only a second to collect himself. If he verbalized what was on his mind he'd be busted back to the street for insubordination and would no longer be able to help Haggerty clear his name. This wasn't Marty LeRoyer he was screwing with; it was Danny Rumsfeld, the man running the department. Byron and LeRoyer shared a history together and a mutual respect, something he and Rumsfeld would never have. Byron knew that Rumsfeld only cared about himself, and if expediency dictated throwing

Haggerty to the wolves, the acting chief wouldn't hesitate. And if Rumsfeld could cast Haggerty aside that easily, Byron was no more important to him than a squirrel running out in front of his car.

Byron stood, shoving his chair back into the wall, then walked slowly from the room, red-faced, without uttering another word.

BYRON WAS STILL fuming as he retreated to his office. He had planned a return trip to the high school to try and locate Mohammed Sayed, assuming Sayed had recovered from his recent illness, but that would have to wait. Lucas Perez had risen to the top of their to-do list.

A quick search of the PPD in-house computer revealed a possible South Portland address for Perez. Byron grabbed Detective Mike Nugent and the two of them went out in search of the elusive witness and whoever it was he'd been visiting in the project. Prior to departing from 109, Byron had asked Shirley Grant to make a copy of the Portland Housing Authority list of every resident in Kennedy Park. Byron drove while Nugent compared the names and addresses on the list against the statements they had looking for any obvious gaps in their canvass.

"We heard some shouting from the chief's conference room," Nugent said. The provocative tone of his voice was unmistakable. "Care to share, Sarge?"

"No," Byron said. "I don't."

As if conjured by Nugent's comment, Byron's cell rang. He checked the display. LeRoyer. Byron knew precisely why the lieutenant was calling. He thumbed the ignore button and slid the phone back into his jacket pocket.

"I've got some good news," Nugent said. "Wanna hear it?"

Byron looked over at him, trying to get a read on whether he was serious. Nugent had a reputation for delivering inappropriate remarks at the most inopportune times. "If you're thinking about making a bad joke, Nuge, now isn't the time."

"No, I swear. This really *is* good news."

"Go with it."

"I'm gonna be a dad again," Nugent said, his face beaming with pride.

"Seriously?"

"Yup."

"Wow. Congratulations. I didn't know you guys were planning on having any more kids. Thought you said two was more than enough?"

"I know," Nugent said. "We weren't. Guess one must have slipped past the goalie."

Byron saw the look of pure joy on Nugent's face. It was refreshing. More often than not police investigations had a way of sucking all the good out of life. The thought of a third little Nugent running around had left Byron's senior detective beaming. A bright spot amid the darkness.

"How far along is she?" Byron asked.

"Only about three months. We haven't told anyone yet. Well, except for you."

"I'm honored, Nuge," Byron said. "And your secret's safe. Congrats. Give Dee Dee a big hug from me."

"Thanks, Sarge. Will do. Now, let's go find this asshole."

SOUTH PORTLAND'S EARLY American Estates was comprised of a half dozen or so two-story row houses built perpendicular to each other. The exteriors were finished in an impressive mock

Tudor style. Although Byron was confident that any similarities these buildings had to the half-timbered originals ended at their façades.

After scouring the lot, much of which had not been plowed, they located an empty parking space, or at least three quarters of one, near the building marked Administration. Byron shoehorned the Chevy into it.

The detectives entered the office to find an overweight middle-aged man seated with his feet up on a desk. At first glance he appeared to be reading a periodical.

"Help ya?" the man asked, looking up from what now was obviously a soft-core porn magazine with glossy photos.

He wore a sweat-stained long-sleeved thermal undershirt, bright orange insulated snow pants with suspenders, and the familiar tan and brown LL Bean boots from which snow was melting onto the desktop forming dark puddles. A camel-colored insulated field jacket lay over a grungy wooden chair at the end of the desk.

"Portland police detectives," Byron said. "We're looking for the manager."

The man pointed to a sign on the wall behind him. The sign read The Beatings Will Continue until Morale Improves—The Management.

"That's me," he said. "Who is it this time?"

"Don't you want to see our IDs?" Nugent asked, reaching inside his jacket.

"Trust me. No one steps into this place, looking like you do, unless they're cops or selling something." His eyes narrowed with suspicion. "You're not selling anything, are you?"

"No," Byron said. "We're not."

"Good. Who you looking for?"

"Lucas Perez," Byron said. "Does he live here?"

"He in some kind of trouble?"

"He might be a witness to something we're investigating," Byron said.

"We just wanna talk to him," Nugent said.

"Building F, apartment six," the man said. "Perez lives there with his baby mama."

BYRON AND NUGENT stood on the snow-covered steps to unit six. A rusting black metal mailbox dangled on the outside wall by a single screw. The name taped to the front of the box was Perez/Gomez. Byron banged on the storm door with his gloved hand a second time. He'd already tried the doorbell but heard nothing from inside. He was about to slip his card in the door when the inside door opened. A pretty young woman of Hispanic descent stood looking at them through the glass. She held a baby wrapped in a blanket to her chest.

"Yes?" the woman said in a thick accent.

Both detectives displayed their credentials for inspection.

"Good afternoon, ma'am. I'm Detective Sergeant Byron and this is Detective Nugent. We'd like to speak with Lucas Perez."

"He isn't home," she said, concern registering clearly on her face. "Is something wrong?"

"Are you Mrs. Perez?" Byron asked.

"I am Maria Gomez. Lucas and I are not married. Why are you looking for him? Is he in trouble?"

"No, ma'am," Nugent said. "We think he might be a witness to something and we'd like to talk to him."

Nugent had no sooner uttered the words when a beat-up gray Cherokee pulled into a parking spot directly in front of unit six with Lucas Perez behind the wheel.

Perez jumped out of the SUV and began shouting at Gomez. "Get back inside, Maria. Don't talk to them."

Gomez remained in the doorway as if she hadn't heard him, or didn't care what he had to say on the subject.

Perez approached them and yelled at her again. "Didn't you hear me, *mujer*?"

She shouted something back at him Spanish, then turned and retreated inside the apartment.

"You shouldn't talk to her like that," Byron said.

"I'll talk to her any way I like, asshole."

"And you definitely shouldn't talk to him like that," Nugent warned.

"Who the fuck are you?" Perez asked.

"We're police detectives," Byron said, needing every ounce of restraint to not get into the man's face.

"What the hell do you want?" Perez asked as he stepped up onto the sidewalk.

"We came to speak with you about the shooting you witnessed."

"Who says I want to talk to you?"

Byron took a deep breath and counted to three, although he wasn't sure that three was going to cut it. He had hoped it wouldn't go like this. But given the current state of things he probably shouldn't have been surprised.

"We saw your interview on television," Byron said. "We were hoping you might share what you saw with us."

"Yeah? Well, you hoped wrong. I ain't telling you shit."

"You little bastard," Nugent said as he took a step toward Perez. Byron put an arm out, stopping him.

Perez took a half step back but kept his head up and his chest puffed out, trying to maintain his tough-guy routine. It wasn't working.

"We aren't looking to cause you any trouble, Lucas," Byron said, hoping that by using the man's given name he might establish a bit of rapport. "Maybe you could tell us who you were visiting in Kennedy Park the night Tommy Plummer was killed?"

Perez laughed. "Cops have always meant trouble for me. Kinda funny that one of yours is in trouble now, huh? You want my statement? Okay, here it is. Fuck and you. I got nothing to say. Now, I'm going inside my apartment. Try to stop me and I'll have my attorney sue your asses."

Nugent pushed against Byron's outstretched arm again. For just a moment Byron contemplated letting the bald detective go after him. Perez's eyes widened slightly in fear as if he had intuited Byron's dilemma. Finally Nugent relaxed, and Byron lowered his arm. Both detectives stepped aside, allowing Perez just enough room to squeeze past. The instigator eyed them warily before scurrying inside and slamming the door.

As they returned to the car, Byron glanced back toward the apartment and saw Maria Gomez peering at them from an upstairs window. She stepped away, letting the sheer curtain fall back over the glass.

"Well, that was fun," Nugent said as they trudged through the packed snow. "You know, Sarge, there's nothing I like better than fresh air and getting out and meeting folks in the community. It's just so awesome to know that it's our job to protect people like that asshole."

"Protect and serve, Nuge," Byron said. "Protect and serve."

IT WAS NEARLY two-thirty by the time Byron and Nugent pulled into 109's rear garage. They had been monitoring radio chatter about the protesters at headquarters during the return trip from South Portland, but neither was prepared for the swarm of people now marching around the PD's plaza. Byron waited in the car while Nugent moved one of the black-and-whites to allow him a place to park. The shouts of the protesters echoed throughout the garage.

The two detectives trudged up the ramp toward 109 just as Sergeant Pepin was exiting his black-and-white SUV.

"Can you believe this?" Pepin said, shouting to be heard above the chanting.

"Where's-our-jus-tice? Where's-our-jus-tice?"

"That's some catchy shit," Nugent said.

"Have they started a detail yet?" Byron asked, referring to an overtime assignment to keep the protestors in line.

"Ha!" Pepin said. "They're still trying to decide where the money's gonna come from."

Byron looked out at the sea of angry faces and wondered what the cost might be if they didn't get a handle on this uprising.

"Whatever happened to innocent until proven guilty?" Nugent asked.

"Exactly," Pepin said. "They've already convicted Haggerty. That's messed up."

Byron wondered how much Perez, their newfound friend and reluctant witness, had contributed to the chaos.

The three men descended the steps to the plaza, then headed toward 109's rear entry door. Someone in the crowd yelled out, "How about an eye for an eye?"

Byron, who had started to punch in the key code to the door lock, turned around just in time to see a man hurl something large and rust-colored in their direction. "Look out!"

The object caught Pepin squarely in the right side of the head, momentarily stunning him.

"What the fuck?" Nugent said, echoing Byron's own thoughts perfectly.

Pepin reached up to where he'd been struck. When he pulled his hand back it was covered in blood.

Byron maintained focus on the man he'd seen execute the toss. The young white male wearing a mustard-colored field jacket was trying to lose himself by backing into the crowd.

"What the hell was that?" Pepin said.

"A paving stone," Nugent said, bending over and retrieving it from the ground.

"Call for backup, Nuge," Byron said as he headed into the fray. "I'm grabbing this kid before he disappears."

"Hey, don't shove me," a faceless protestor said as Byron passed by.

"Freeze, asshole," Byron said as he saw Yellow Jacket pushing through the crowd toward the steps that led down to Middle Street.

"Careful they don't shoot you," a comedian wannabe shouted.

"Don't tempt me," Nugent yelled back from somewhere right behind Byron.

Byron pushed through the crowd like a lineman as he watched the man slide effortlessly toward his chosen escape route. An unseen foot was thrust out, its owner trying unsuccessfully to trip Byron. He had nearly reached the front of the plaza when the suspect's head disappeared from view.

"He's on the stairs," Byron yelled. "White male. Yellow jacket."

Byron and Nugent reached the top of the stairs nearly simultaneously. Yellow Jacket leapt down onto the sidewalk, skipping the last four steps as he did so, then turned left heading east on Middle Street, dodging several picketers who had stopped to see what was happening. Byron descended the steps two at a time, sliding his hand down the steel tube railing as he went. Yellow Jacket glimpsed back to see if he was still being followed.

"We're gonna get ya, you little shit," Nugent yelled.

"Leave him alone, you big bullies," another protestor yelled. Byron and Nugent reached the sidewalk, then headed toward Franklin Arterial.

Yellow Jacket was halfway past the front of the police station when he cut right to evade his pursuers by crossing Middle Street. He never saw the westbound car that struck him and sent him flying.

Twenty minutes later Byron stood perched on the sidewalk in front of 109, looking on as MedCu attendants and several firemen used a backboard and cervical collar to immobilize Pepin's assailant.

Yellow Jacket turned out to be Jeremy Scott, a nineteen-year-old undergraduate student from the University of Southern Maine. A self-proclaimed revolutionary with three misdemeanor priors for disorderly conduct, Scott had just graduated to a felony.

From somewhere nearby, Byron heard the catcalls and derogatory comments being made about him specifically, and about the

Portland Police Department in general. After more than twenty years on the job he had learned to let it roll off. He'd never understood how a community could be so quick to condemn the police, accusing them of rushing to judgment when in so doing they were themselves rushing to judgment. He didn't have an issue with people getting together to protest whatever they liked, so long as they did it peacefully. Protesting was an American institution going back to the Bostonians throwing tea into the harbor as a not-so-subtle message to the Crown. But bouncing bricks off the head of police officers wasn't a protest; it was an act of aggression. Aggravated assault to be exact. Byron couldn't remember it ever having been this bad. He wondered how much of the antipolice hysteria had been caused by online social media platforms where everyone with a Google app was an instant expert on everything. Sadly, it had become the norm. It was one of the reasons he didn't maintain a presence on social media. The other reason was his disdain for computers.

FIFTEEN MINUTES AFTER the ambulance had departed, Byron stood in LeRoyer's office. The door was closed.

"What the hell happened out there?" LeRoyer barked. "I've got a police sergeant up at Maine Med getting staples in his head and at least a half dozen pissed-off people down in the lobby making out complaints against all the officers involved in this."

"Complaints about what?" Byron said.

"You name it. False arrest. Excessive force. Criminal threatening."

"Criminal threatening? Give me a break, Marty. Who are they alleging made a threat?"

"Specifically? One of the plainclothes officers."

"Well, there were only two plainclothes officers out there, me and Nuge. What did we allegedly say?"

"According to one complainant, one of the cops threatened to shoot him if he didn't get out of their way."

"You're not serious?"

"Yeah, John. I am."

"First off, in case you haven't noticed, Nuge and I look nothing alike. And secondly, if anyone said anything derogatory it was me and what I said was, 'Freeze, asshole.'"

"Is this a joke to you, John? Because I've got multiple people coming forward and they're all saying the same thing."

"And you're surprised by that? Perhaps you didn't notice, but that mob of people outside congregated for the sole purpose of protesting us. Nuge and I chased that Scott kid *after* I witnessed him throw a chunk of brick at Pepin, striking him in the head. I'll bet none of your honest witnesses saw that though, right?"

LeRoyer shook his head. "No. They didn't."

"There's a shock. Next you'll be telling me that someone's accusing us of pushing Jeremy Scott in front of that car."

LeRoyer raised his eyebrows.

"You're not fucking serious?"

Chapter 12

Tuesday, 3:30 P.M.,
January 17, 2017

BYRON WAS SEETHING as he left LeRoyer's office. He wondered how long it would be before Mayor Gilcrest inserted herself in this latest fiasco to bolster her "get the thin blue line back in line" campaign. He shoved the heavy wooden door open and marched into the CID locker room. At the sink he splashed cool water on his face and on the back of his neck. As he reached toward the paper towel dispenser and found it empty, it occurred to him that the old John Byron would have done much more than just splash a bit of water on himself. His thoughts turned to the bottle of spirit-lifter that had previously resided inside the bottom right-hand drawer of the desk in his office. His mouth suddenly felt very dry. He shook the water from his hands and grabbed a wad of toilet paper from the stall to finish the job.

The mini-uprising was nothing but a distraction. Perspective was what he needed, what they *all* needed right now. Staying on point and piecing together what had happened in Kennedy Park. The events that had led up to Tommy Plummer's death were the only thing that mattered. Plummer's death was the match that had ignited the city. And locating the second robber, and ultimately the gun, were the only things that would extinguish the flames.

The locker room door flung open as Detective Nugent marched in.

"What a shit show that turned out to be," Nugent said as he approached his locker and banged open the door. "Did you know they're all downstairs right now filing formal 50s against us?" he asked. 50s were the police code for internal affairs complaints.

"I heard," Byron said as he picked off the last remnants of the toilet paper stuck to his hands.

"That kid's family will probably blame us for the accident."

"How's Andy?" Byron asked.

"Pepin's got a hard head. He'll be all right. Maine Med put a few staples in him. You know that fucking plaza out there, with its loose pavers, makes about as much sense as those quaint little brick sidewalks that this city is so in love with. Jesus. Why not just put up signs that say Free Weapons? Or better yet, Free Burglar Tools?"

The very same thought had occurred to Byron.

Nugent dumped a puddle of aftershave into his palm, then slapped it against his cheeks. "So, what's next, *mon ami*?"

"We get back to work," Byron said. "Someone put a gun in Plummer's hand and I want to know who. I'm gonna see what Dustin has come up with."

"HEY, SARGE," TRAN said as Byron entered his office.

"Any progress?" Byron asked.

"I think I may have found something that will interest you."

"Great. What?"

"Well, I ran a check on each of those names. Then I queried their addresses, looking for relatives, parents, aunts, uncles, grandparents, etc."

"And?"

"I didn't find anything major in-house on the friends list, but when I checked on the relatives a couple of things popped up. First, Tommy Plummer and Nate Freeman are cousins."

"I knew that already. What else?"

"Abdirahman Ali's father, Ahmed, owns a small halal market on Congress Street."

"We were just there yesterday. What about the shop?"

"Ahmed Ali has filed three robbery reports in the last two years. Two of the robberies occurred in the last nine months."

"I'm not following," Byron said.

"I was just thinking, perhaps Mr. Ali got tired of getting ripped off. Maybe he decided to purchase himself a little protection in the form of a handgun. And maybe little Abdi Ali borrowed it to show it off to Tommy Plummer."

Byron considered what Tran was saying. Maybe he had been looking at this all wrong. Byron was thinking that the gun used during the robbery likely belonged to Tommy Plummer or to his father. Mr. Plummer had denied any knowledge of a gun, but then refused to let them search through Tommy's room. Maybe Tran was onto something. Maybe the gun hadn't belonged to Tommy after all. Perhaps one of his schoolmates had come by the gun on the street or taken it from one of their parents. Hugh Plummer had told Byron that he had no idea where his son would have come by a firearm, and maybe that was true.

"Anything in-house on Ahmed?" Byron asked.

"I checked the concealed weapons files as well as the applications. I went back five years. Nothing."

Assuming Tran was right, there were only so many places in town where, for the right price, a shop owner tired of being victimized might get his hands on an equalizer. Pete's Trading Post on St. John or Honest Jimmy's Pawn Shop on India Street were two great possibilities. Neither one of them had a sterling reputation. Byron decided that he would pay a visit to both, beginning with Honest Jimmy.

Byron tore a sheet of paper out of his notebook and wrote down the name Christine Souza. "Add this to the names on your list."

"Any idea where she lives or her date of birth?" Tran asked.

Byron briefly considered giving Tran more background information, but decided against it. "No. But I know she attended Portland High. See if you can find any links between her and the others."

"Okay."

"Oh, and do me a favor. I need you to find the link to her on your own. Understand? I never gave you her name."

Tran grinned, ripped up the paper, and tossed it in the trash. "You got it, boss."

AN ELECTRONIC BELL chimed in the distance as Byron stepped into the narrow front room of Honest Jimmy's stolen goods emporium. He figured the trigger was either connected to the front door or located under the doormat that he'd just crossed. At the far end of the room two teenaged boys stood in front of the counter dealing with the Honest One himself. All three turned to stare as Byron entered.

"Well, if it isn't Portland's finest," Jimmy said in a loud voice, clearly issuing a warning to anyone smart enough to heed it.

"That obvious, huh?" Byron said.

Jimmy grinned and nodded before turning his eyes back to the boys.

Byron watched the teenagers quickly scoop up the electronic gear from the counter and stuff it into the brightly colored knapsacks they were carrying.

He approached the counter. "How's business, Jimmy?"

"Oh, you know me," Jimmy said, lowering his voice to a normal level. "I can't complain. What can I do for the Portland Police Department?"

"We've had reports of teenagers trying to sell stolen goods from car break-ins. Haven't seen anyone like that around here, have you?"

Both boys hurried past Byron, giving him a wide berth as they headed toward the store's entrance as if flames were licking at their heels.

"Nope," Jimmy said. "You know I don't buy hot stuff. Have a nice day, boys."

The fake bell chimed again as the teenagers made a hasty exit, slamming the front door behind them.

"Anyone ever tell you you're bad for business?" Jimmy asked.

Byron pulled out his credentials and held them up.

Jimmy studied the ID. "Detective Sergeant, huh? You're like royalty. Usually I only get the younger detectives stopping by to harass me." He folded his arms and leaned against the table directly behind him. "Must be something really important."

Byron returned the wallet to the inside pocket of his suit coat. "I'm wondering where someone might go to purchase a gun."

"A gun? You looking to buy a gun?"

"Not me," Byron said, playing along. "I have enough guns already. It's for a friend."

"We sell guns. Everything by the book. Waiting period, paperwork, background checks. You know. Everything neat and tidy, Sergeant."

"Yeah, I know. What I'm looking for is a place someone might skip over all those requirements. Buy something off the books. Know anyplace like that, Jimmy?"

HAGGERTY HAD SPENT the morning shoveling the driveway. The physical labor was soothing; it helped him focus. But now he was going stir-crazy. He could feel the walls beginning to close in. He needed something to take his mind off the shooting. Television wasn't an option, as he didn't have the attention span to watch anything for longer than ten or fifteen minutes. And the local networks kept running promos for their latest coverage of the Plummer shooting, each time displaying Tommy's senior class photo. The all-American boy gunned down by police. It was heartbreaking. He couldn't escape it.

He thought about phoning his parents again but didn't want to rehash the incident or upset his mother more than he already had. According to his father she had been glued to the internet looking for news updates and then crying whenever she found one. Besides, his attorney, Eugene Pomeroy, had advised him not to discuss the incident with anyone. What he really wanted was to go visit Sharon, his girlfriend, think about something pleasant for a while. But Sharon had made it clear that as long as this thing went unresolved she couldn't see him.

"It isn't something I want to be a party to," she'd said.

"What the hell does that mean?" he'd asked her. "Are you breaking up with me?"

Sharon said she didn't have to explain herself and that he should just respect her wishes.

Although they'd only been dating for a month, he had expected her to be a little more understanding. *So much for being supportive*, he thought. *Fuck it. I gotta get out of here. Get some more fresh air. Maybe walk around the block a couple of thousand times.*

He walked through the kitchen to the home's side door, slipped into his boots, then grabbed his coat and hat. As he stepped outside he nearly ran over an attractive young blond woman standing halfway up the stairs.

"Excuse me," she said.

There was something vaguely familiar about her, but Haggerty couldn't place the face.

"Can I help you?" he said.

"I was looking for someone who lives around here." She smiled and stuck out her hand. "I'm Leslie."

"Sean," he said, shaking it. "Nice to meet you, Leslie. Who are you looking for?"

"Actually, this is a little embarrassing. I was hoping to find you."

"Me?" he said, taken aback.

"You're Officer Sean Haggerty, right?"

It hit him like an anvil. He knew why he'd recognized her. Leslie Thomas was a field reporter for one of the local news affiliates. He looked past her toward the street where a salt-covered news van sat idling at the end of his driveway. A large bearded man wearing a puffy blue coat stood next to the van aiming a shoulder-mounted video camera in their direction. Haggerty looked back at her. "How the hell did you get my home address, *Leslie*?"

"Please don't be mad," she said. "I just want to get your side of the story."

"*My side?* Since when does anybody give a shit about my side? Get the hell off my property." Before she could respond, Haggerty turned and retreated into the house, slamming the door behind him.

He stood at the front window, peering out around the curtains, watching as the reporter retreated to the street. She spent the next several minutes talking on her cell while looking back at his house. Eventually, Thomas and Grizzly Adams climbed inside the van and drove away.

Haggerty turned from the window and sighed deeply. He really was trapped, a prisoner in his own home.

It took Byron all of ten minutes and fifty bucks to get a name from Jimmy: Daniel Sewell. The irony was that Sewell's Second Hand was Honest Jimmy's only real Portland competition when it came to fencing stolen merchandise on the peninsula. It turned out that Jimmy had only one rule in his less than ethical playbook. He didn't skirt the gun laws and sell off the books. Sewell, at least according to Jimmy, didn't have the same high moral standards.

Sewell's shop, located on Marginal Way near Play It Again Sports, was new to Portland, having only been open since October. Byron knew there was no way a brand-new dealer would ever admit to selling illegal firearms. The way Byron figured it, he had two options. He could bust one of Sewell's friends for something and put them to work, but that would take time, and time wasn't a luxury they possessed. The more expedient option involved getting one of Crosby's out-of-town drug detectives to pose as a buyer. Someone that Sewell would never recognize, and hopefully never suspect.

Byron pulled out his cell and punched in the number for Sergeant Crosby.

Kenny Crosby held the same rank as Byron, detective sergeant, but Crosby was on loan from PPD to MDEA where he supervised all of the drug investigations in Cumberland County. The two men had never gotten along. Byron neither respected nor trusted the smart-mouthed, misogynistic gym rat.

"Crosby."

"Kenny, it's John Byron."

"Well, if it ain't the AG's best friend."

"What's that supposed to mean?" Byron asked.

"Word on the street says you've been working a little too close with one particular ex-trooper on this Haggerty thing. What are you, like IA now?"

Byron wondered how it was that every time he was forced to deal with the egocentric drug sergeant all he could think of was caving Crosby's face in. Even Crosby's voice grated on him. Byron thought about telling Crosby what he could do with his opinion, but he needed his help. Like it or not, Byron had to play nice.

"You're a real riot, Kenny," Byron said. "Listen, I need one of your guys to work a gun buy."

"Trying to jam up Haggerty on something else?"

Byron felt the blood rush to his cheeks. He took a deep breath and gritted his teeth before responding. "Next time we meet up remind me to tell you all about it. Are you gonna help me or just keep busting my balls?"

"Gotta tell ya, that second one sounds like a lot more fun, but I guess I have to. I've got a guy on loan from Lowell PD. When do you need this thing to happen?"

"ASAP. How about this afternoon?"

"No can do. My Lowell guy is tied up on a buy until after midnight. I can send him to you tomorrow though."

Byron wondered if the detective really was busy, or if Crosby was still screwing with him. He also wondered why the feds wouldn't have given Crosby the heads-up on the OC connection with the laundromat. *Or, despite their denials, perhaps they had and Crosby wasn't aware that Collier had tipped Byron.* Either way, Byron wasn't about let on that he knew.

"Tomorrow will have to do," Byron said.

"How do you wanna do the contact?" Crosby asked.

"Give him my cell," Byron said. "Have him call me." Better to remove Crosby from the equation straightaway. Byron needed the help of his undercover, not Crosby.

"You got it. Oh, and give my best to Trooper What's-her-name." Crosby disconnected the call before Byron could respond.

Byron looked at the phone. "Asshole."

TERRY ALFONSI WALKED out of the spray booth and removed his breathing mask and goggles. His hands were spattered with traces of the flat-black primer he had layered onto his late friend's Mitsubishi.

Vinnie was sitting with his feet up on the counter watching the television.

"Finished?" Vinnie asked.

"Yup."

"How's it look?"

"Like a Mitsubishi covered in black primer."

"Wow. Someone's got a shitty attitude."

"Whatever," Terry said, sounding as dismissive as he could. He entered the bathroom and soaked down several paper towels, then wiped the sweat off his head. He kicked off his sneakers, then shimmied out of the paint-smeared coveralls, hanging them on a wall peg. After taking a piss and not bothering to flush the grungy toilet bowl he walked back into the garage. Vinnie was still glued to the TV.

"What's eating you anyway?" Vinnie asked.

"It's the cop thing. We've roughed up some dirtbags before, and you've probably done more than that."

Vinnie grinned but said nothing.

"But this is a cop we're taking out here," Terry said.

"Yeah. So? He bleeds same as everyone else."

"And you think we've planned this out enough?"

"What else is there? I'll follow him around until I have a good opportunity to waste him. You wait in town with the flatbed for my call. We load it, cover it, tow it to the sandpit, and torch it. Easy peasy."

Terry still didn't like it.

"Oh, by the way," Vinnie said. "Derrick called again while you were in the booth."

"What did he say?"

"Had some more information to pass along. Said our boy is a regular at Fitness World on St. John Street in Portland." Vinnie struck a pose, flexing one of his arms like a competitive body builder. "Sun's out, guns out."

Chapter 13

Tuesday, 7:30 P.M.,
January 17, 2017

BYRON RETURNED TO 109 to find uniformed officers posted at both ends of the plaza. One was located at the top of the stairs that led down to Middle Street, the other at the entrance to the rear garage where Byron had just parked.

"What's up?" Byron asked as he approached the officer.

"New directive from up on high. No protests in the plaza."

After this afternoon's incident Byron couldn't find any fault in that order. Removing the threat of violence against officers coming and going from police headquarters would certainly cut down on the number of complaints against officers, and injuries, on both sides. He wondered who had come up with the mandate. Rumsfeld?

"Might have been nice if they'd taken this step before Sergeant Pepin got split, huh?" the officer said.

Byron mounted the stairs to the third floor where he found Tran.

"Anything new?" Byron asked.

"I'm working on it," Tran said. "So far, three names you gave me have accepted my friend requests."

"Which three?"

"Scott Henderson, Nate Freeman, and Abdirahman Ali."

"How does that help us?"

Tran spun around in his chair to face Byron. "Good old-fashioned data mining, Sarge. After they friend me I have access to their friend lists, photos, posts, you name it. You wouldn't believe the stuff these kids put on social media. If there is anything to find, I'll find it."

"Assuming I know nothing about this Facebook stuff, because I don't, how are you getting these kids to friend you?" Byron asked.

"Haven't I ever shown you my profile?"

Byron shook his head.

"Look," Tran said as he pulled up a new screen.

The profile photo was of a cute teenaged-looking Vietnamese girl named Phuong Nguyen.

"Who is that?" Byron asked.

"Jade. She's my cousin."

"Tell me you're not using a photo of an actual teenager."

Tran smiled. "Fear not. My cousin is twenty-three and lives outside of the U.S. She helped me set up this profile to go after pedophiles."

Byron studied the page information and images. He noticed the friend total. "She has over a thousand friends?"

"Not her, me. And this is only one of my fake profiles."

"How many do you have?"

Tran grinned proudly. "Twenty-three."

Byron shook his head in disbelief. "Keep at it."

"Oh, and I found Christine Souza. Did you know she was dead?"

PPD's DAY SHIFT had long departed for home as Commander Jennings walked casually down the back hallway of 109's second floor. In his left hand he held a legal-sized manila envelope containing nothing but blank sheets of paper that he'd taken from the copier outside his office. He wanted to give the appearance that he was delivering something on the off chance he ran into someone working late.

Lining the hallway were doors to the offices of the training sergeant, payroll manager, grant coordinator, community prosecutor, and internal affairs, which comprised three offices and a storage room. Jennings found all the office doors closed. Passing by each he looked down at the floor for any light spilling out. There wasn't any. He stopped at the door to the internal affairs case storage room and pulled a key from his front right pocket. Standard operating procedure mandated that the key was to have been turned over to the IA lieutenant after Jennings was reassigned. But like so many other administrative mandates at 109, it got lost in the shuffle and never happened.

Jennings took one last look up the hallway, then inserted his key into the lock and slipped inside.

BYRON RETURNED TO his office. Amid the growing pile of supplements and statements was a newly formed mountain of pink slips from Shirley Grant. He sat down and began to organize them when his cell rang. It was Diane.

"Hey, lady," he said, answering it.

"Lady, huh?" she said. "I like that. How goes it?"

He sighed and collapsed back in the chair. "Give me a word that's worse than *slow*?"

"*At a standstill?*"

"That's actually three words, but they'll do," he said. "Have you eaten?"

"Just finished. Chief Rumsfeld held an off-site dinner meeting."

"Strange I didn't garner an invite. Intimate dinner?"

"If five is intimate," she said. "A lot of brass there."

"Glad I wasn't invited, then. I've got an allergy to brass."

"I thought it was gluten?"

"I get 'em confused."

"One of the local news reporters showed up on Haggerty's doorstep this afternoon," Diane said.

"How the hell did they get his home address?"

"I don't know."

"Dammit. Can we move him somewhere? Maybe put him up in a hotel outside of town?"

"We tried. Hags doesn't want to leave his house. He's gonna stay inside for the time being. Only Channel 8 has made it out there so far."

Byron knew as well as Diane that sooner or later the other news agencies would have Haggerty's address and come calling. Information like the shooter's home address was chum in the water, especially when the shooter was a cop. The sharks would come circling soon enough.

"Will I see you later?" she asked.

He wanted nothing more than to say yes, but there was still so much to do. "Not tonight. I'm planning to burn the midnight oil on this. I'm way behind on the paperwork."

"Okay. Talk to you tomorrow?"

"Count on it. G'night, Lady Di."

Byron ended the call with Diane and dialed Haggerty's cellphone, but it went straight to voicemail. "Hey, Hags, it's John Byron. Just checking in to see how you're holding up. Heard about your afternoon visit. Give me a call when you get a chance."

He had just slipped the cell back into his pocket when Lucinda Phillips appeared in the office doorway.

"Am I interrupting anything?" Phillips asked.

"Not at all. Come in."

"Making any headway?" she asked as she sat down opposite him.

Byron looked down at his desktop. "Hard to tell. You?"

"Collecting data. Same as you."

Byron nodded.

"Wondered if you might want to catch a bite to eat?" she said.

He considered the work in front of him and the ribbing he had taken from Crosby, both of which were strong reasons to decline her invitation.

"My treat, John."

"Okay, let's go."

THEIR TABLE AT Street & Co., a cozy bistro in the heart of Portland's Old Port, was situated against a rustic brick wall, upon which hung an iron candleholder. A small cinnamon-scented votive cast a warm glow over the table.

Byron checked his cell as the waitress refilled their water glasses and took their orders.

"Am I keeping you from something?" Lucinda asked.

"No, I'm just expecting a call."

"Haggerty?"

"It's related."

She paused after taking a sip of wine. "I'm not the enemy, you know."

"I never said you were."

"You didn't have to. You act like I'm some kind of pariah whenever I'm around."

"I don't mean to, it's just—"

"It's just that you're worried about your friend and want to see him get a fair shake, right?"

"Right. And it doesn't feel like he's getting that."

"From the AG's office?" she asked.

"From anyone. The media, the city, and maybe the AG." He wanted to add the FBI, but held back. "Just feels like everybody is jumping to conclusions."

"What about you? Aren't you jumping to the conclusion that it was a righteous shoot, John?"

Byron said nothing.

"I'm sorry," Lucinda said after a moment. "That was out of line. It's the wine talking. How about we change the subject?"

"Works for me."

"Have you eaten here before?"

"Not really in my budget," he said as he scanned the restaurant for familiar faces. "The state must pay better than I thought."

"Hardly. I couldn't do this either, not without my pension check. Where do you normally dine?"

"Ha. I'm not sure I'd call it dining. It's usually either Thai takeout at my condo or a burger in the car."

"The glamorous life of a homicide detective."

"Something like that."

Lucinda gazed at him over her wineglass. "So, what's the story with you and Diane?"

"More wine?" the waitress asked, appearing in the nick of time.

ALTHOUGH IT WAS nearly 10:00 P.M., Davis Billingslea still occupied his workstation at the *Herald*. He was trying to put the finishing touches on the piece he was writing about Tommy Plummer. It was a human-interest piece entirely designed to highlight the tragic irony of a local basketball star looking toward college, only to watch those dreams shattered by a cop's bullet.

He had been struggling with the wording on the third paragraph for the last half hour and was growing increasingly frustrated when he was saved by the bell, literally. He picked up the desk phone on the second ring.

"Newsroom, Billingslea."

"Davis Billingslea?" a male voice asked.

"The one and only. To whom am I speaking?"

"A concerned citizen."

Concerned citizen, my ass, Davis thought. He tried to place it, but didn't recognize the voice. "So, what can I do for you, Mr. Concerned Citizen?"

"I'm sending a PDF to your email address. In it, you will find information regarding the cop involved in the Kennedy Park shooting."

"What kind of information?" Billingslea said, playing along. "And how do I know that you're—"

Davis heard a click as the call was disconnected. He held the receiver up, looking at it for a moment before hanging up. "Fruitcake."

He returned to his story. Back to that infernal third paragraph. Five minutes later, as he was reading through his edits and thinking that the story was as good as it was likely to get, his email alert chimed. The message header identified the sender as "Concerned Citizen." Billingslea clicked the message bar and it opened. There was nothing in the subject line or body of the email. There was a PDF attachment labeled badcop.pdf. He went up to the sender box and right-clicked, hoping to see an actual address that identified the sender, but all it gave was no_reply@gmail.com. He closed out the pop-up and went back to the original email. The cursor flashed above the file. He paused with his hand resting lightly on the mouse. There was always the possibility that someone was screwing with him. Even in his short tenure at the *Portland Herald*, he had made a few enemies. *Could this be someone hoping to infect the newspaper's computer system with a virus?* he wondered. If that's what it was, would they have called first? He thought about it for a minute. *Maybe they called knowing that you wouldn't be able to resist opening it. The suspense would absolutely kill you.*

"Screw it," he said as he clicked on the file. "No guts, no glory." He waited as the file downloaded to his computer, then opened it.

It took him a moment to realize what he'd been sent. He quickly skimmed through the first few pages, noticing that they were out of order. After locating the page that should have been the first, he began to read the entire document carefully. At first glance it looked to be some kind of internal investigation from the Portland Police Department, only it was hard to tell because the headers had been removed and some of the information redacted. Someone had drawn over portions of the document with a black marker. Blacked out or not, there was still enough information present for him to decipher what this was, and his excitement was building. It was a complaint against Officer Sean Haggerty, probably several years old. The complainant had alleged that Haggerty had used excessive force against him while making an arrest. The complainant also claimed that both the traffic stop and arrest were unlawful, further stating that the reason he was pulled over to begin with was a ruse because of his out-of-state plates. The unnamed complainant was from New York.

Billingslea checked the time on his cell: 10:15. *Way past time for the print edition*, he thought. *But plenty of time for the web. There was always time for the internet.* He snatched up his desk phone and punched in the number for his editor. He was smiling. Scoop Billingslea was back.

IT WAS NEARLY ten o'clock as Byron pulled to the curb and parked in front of the Holiday Inn on Spring Street.

"Thanks for dinner," he said.

"You're most welcome," Lucinda said as she released her seat belt. "Care for a nightcap?"

"I appreciate the offer but—"

Before he could finish the thought, Lucinda leaned over and kissed him squarely on the lips. She had caught him off guard, but he didn't resist.

After several moments Lucinda pulled away slightly but maintained direct eye contact. "John, I may regret this tomorrow—maybe it's the wine, or maybe it's you—but I want to spend the night with you."

Byron paused a moment before answering. There was no question that he had always found her attractive. Very attractive. Any unattached heterosexual male in his position would not have hesitated for even a second before taking her up on her offer. "I am flattered, Luce. But I can't."

The disappointment clearly shown on her face. "Diane?"

He nodded. "I don't know what it is that Diane and I have exactly, but I do know I don't want to screw it up."

Lucinda smiled and lightly touched the side of his face. "She's a lucky woman."

Byron returned her smile. "Good night, Luce."

"Night, John."

Byron waited until she'd made it safely inside the hotel lobby before he pulled away from the curb. The scent of her perfume lingered inside the car. He was wondering why he'd agreed to go to dinner in the first place when his cell rang.

"Byron," he said, answering it on the second ring.

"Sarge, it's Randy Cameron from Lowell PD. Sergeant Crosby said you might need my help with a gun buy."

Chapter 14

Wednesday 6:45 A.M.,
January 18, 2017

SLEEP HAD ELUDED Byron for most of the night. Predictably, the five-thirty alarm ripped him out of the deepest slumber he had been able to achieve. As in any high-profile investigation his brain wouldn't shut down, but the robbery and the Haggerty shooting weren't the only things inside his head. Lucinda Phillips was also taking up considerable space.

Byron slid the unmarked into an empty space on Middle Street and got out. Three protesters—one male and two females—stood on the sidewalk in front of 109. Byron assumed their diminished numbers were due to the early hour. The protesters stood huddled together talking and holding cups of coffee. Their signs were stuck into a snowbank. A middle-aged woman wearing aqua-colored mittens gave him a cursory but disapproving glance before returning to the conversation. Byron mounted the steps to the plaza.

The message indicator light was lit on Byron's desk phone. He tapped the speaker button, then dialed his voicemail password.

"You have twenty-one new messages," the computerized feminine-sounding voice said. Detecting more than a trace of condescension in her tone, he pressed Play.

"Hello, Sergeant Byron. This is Gerry Humboldt again. I'm a reporter with the *Boston Globe* and I am still hoping to get a few minutes of your time regarding the police shooting of Tommy Plummer. You can call me at—"

Byron deleted the message from Humboldt without so much as a second thought, the equivalent of rolling up the car window before it began to rain.

"Sergeant. Austin Graves calling from the *Bangor Daily News*. Wondering if you might call me—"

"Keep wondering, Austin old buddy," Byron said.

He punched the speaker button with his index finger, ending the session and telling himself that he'd listen to the rest of them later but knowing he likely wouldn't. He grabbed the coffee off his desk and headed for the CID conference room.

"War room" described the scene to a T. The long wall-mounted whiteboard was packed with information written in multiple-colored markers. Yellow and blue sticky notes and full sheets of paper covered nearly every inch of the whiteboard's wooden frame. Atop the conference room table stood stacks of file folders, computerized printouts, blue notebooks, and several Portland High School yearbooks. Their entire investigation was here, but it was as if someone had dumped a pile of puzzle pieces onto the table before absconding with the box cover.

Unlike Byron's usual murder cases, they already knew how

this one began and ended. What they still didn't know was the identity of the other suspect and what had become of the gun. *And who was the inside man, or woman, at the high school?* He studied the board, rechecking their progress while he sipped from his large hot coffee.

Shortly after seven, the detectives began to trickle into CID, chattering with each other and checking their own voicemails by way of speakerphone. The workday had started, and Byron's brief moment of solitude was gone.

Nugent walked into the conference room and tossed two large yellow envelopes on the table directly in front of Byron. On the front of each, stamped in red letters, was the word *Confidential*. Rectangular white labels bearing his typed name had been affixed to both.

"These what I think they are?" Byron asked.

"Yup. A formal invitation to the annual IA ball from Sergeant Bradley K. Thibodeau. Got mine too."

"Fabulous," Byron said without opening them. His attention returned to the whiteboard.

"Any idea what we should wear?" Nugent asked.

Byron ignored the question.

"Where do you want to start today, boss?"

"Call the school. Let's find out if Sayed has recovered from his illness yet. It's time we spoke with him."

"You got it." Nugent departed the room a moment before Melissa Stevens appeared in the doorway.

"Hey, Mel," Byron said before taking another sip of coffee.

"Have you seen the *Portland Herald* online this morning?" Stevens asked.

"No. Why?"

"I think you'd better look at it for yourself."

BYRON STARED AT the computer screen. The headline of the *Portland Herald*'s lead story read *Portland Cop Accused of False Arrest, Excessive Force.* The story written by Davis Billingslea covered the details of a five-year-old internal affairs investigation, launched following Haggerty's arrest of an intoxicated motorist. The driver had filed the complaint with the chief's office alleging that Haggerty had only stopped him because he was from out of state. It went on to describe how the cooperative complainant had been manhandled by Haggerty and even punched in the face and falsely accused of resisting arrest. The *Herald* article even included a file photo of Haggerty in uniform with a particularly intimidating expression on his face like that of a cage fighter entering the ring.

"They're not gonna give him a fair shake, are they, Sarge?" Melissa Stevens asked.

Byron didn't know what to say. He knew that he shouldn't have been surprised by what some in news media would stoop to in order to sell copy, but this was so far from decency, even for Billingslea. Byron remembered the case distinctly. The complainant turned out to be a New York City businessman with big-time connections and a history of driving drunk. The charges against the man were eventually filed for one year by the district attorney with the understanding that the defendant would not get into trouble for the next year, nor would he sue the department. According to the news article, the fact that the complainant refused to be interviewed by the internal affairs investigator, or that the allegation against Haggerty had been cleared as unsubstantiated, had no bearing on the DA's decision. Nor did it matter to the editorial staff at the *Herald*. The only thing that mattered was smearing Haggerty's name further. *But Billingslea couldn't have written this story without help*, Byron thought. Through waves of anger it gradually began to dawn on Byron who had most likely requested the information be leaked to the press. *Rumpswab*. But Byron knew the acting chief wouldn't have dirtied his own hands. He would have left that chore to another. *A weasel of lesser rank*. And Byron was confident he knew exactly who that weasel was.

BYRON DIDN'T BOTHER knocking on the closed door before he barged into Internal Affairs.

"What the fuck?" Sergeant Thibodeau barked. "I'm in the middle of a goddamned interview here, John."

Byron glared at the irate sergeant before turning his attention to the wide-eyed young male uniformed officer seated opposite Thibodeau.

"Give us a minute, would you, Officer?" Byron said.

"Now wait just a goddamned minute," Thibodeau said from his chair. "Who the hell do you think you are?"

The officer, who barely looked eighteen, was up and out the door before Thibodeau could finish protesting.

"Why did you do it?" Byron asked, taking a step toward him and holding up a printout of the newspaper article in front of Thibodeau's face.

"Do what?" Thibodeau asked, his face flushed.

"Really? You're just gonna sit there and play stupid? You think I don't know where the *Herald* got this old IA information on Haggerty?"

"I don't know what you're talking about."

"It was a bullshit case too. Wasn't it?"

Thibodeau began shuffling the paperwork on the table in front of him, trying to avoid Byron's gaze. "I don't give a damn what you think, the paper didn't get anything from me."

"You don't think Haggerty's going through enough right now? You're just gonna keep piling it on, right?"

Thibodeau said nothing.

"Know what, Brad?" Byron said. "You're a lying piece of shit. Why don't you stand up and face me like a man?"

Thibodeau glanced toward the door. Byron looked back to see what had caught his attention. Both internal affairs office assistants stood in the hallway, mouths agape.

"What are you gonna do, John, hit me?" Thibodeau asked.

Byron turned his attention back to Thibodeau. "Nothing would make me happier than to lay your ass out. Tell me, whose bidding are you doing now? Rumpswab's? Or maybe Governor-wannabe Gilcrest's?"

Thibodeau said nothing.

"You're pathetic," Byron said.

The internal affairs sergeant glanced toward the door again. Byron figured he was checking to make sure his witnesses were still present. Thibodeau slowly stood and faced Byron.

"You know why they never assigned you to IA?" Thibodeau asked, his voice cracking. "Because you couldn't cut it. You'd have to follow the rules. And everyone knows you just make your own. Don't you?"

Byron clenched his jaw, bearing down so hard he wondered if his teeth might crumble like chalk. He leaned in, invading Thibodeau's personal space until their noses were mere inches apart. Byron took some satisfaction in watching Thibodeau give a slight flinch.

"You're goddamned lucky we've got an audience," Byron growled, intentionally holding his position a few seconds longer, hoping to add to Thibodeau's discomfort.

Thibodeau's Adam's apple bounced up and down as he nervously swallowed, but he wisely remained silent.

Byron crumpled up the printout and hurled it into the plastic trash bin standing next to Thibodeau's desk. He walked toward the door to the hallway where the office assistants stood frozen in place. He stopped before reaching them and turned around to face the flustered internal affairs sergeant.

"And you're wrong," Byron said. "You know why they'll never assign me to this office? It's because I won't put up with people telling me how my cases should turn out before I've even investigated them. Fuck you, Brad."

BYRON NEARLY COLLIDED with Mike Nugent as he exited the stairwell onto the fourth floor.

"Hey, Sarge. I just got—Are you okay?"

"Fine. What's up?"

"I just got off the phone with the high school. Mohammed Sayed is still absent, but Dustin located a work address for his old man, Sameer."

"Where?"

"Sam's Taxi, on Anderson."

BYRON PARKED ACROSS from the taxi depot on the lower end of Anderson Street near its intersection with Gould. Several green-and-white sedans bearing the business name and number were parked on the street directly in front of the brown corrugated steel building, which was nothing more than an oversized garage set on a slab. The rusted metal sign bolted to the front of the business read Sam's Taxi Service. Below the sign a large overhead door stood open revealing several additional taxis inside. Byron entered the building.

Three males of Middle Eastern descent stood beside one of the taxis. The men were engaged in what appeared to be a heated discussion, but they ceased talking as Byron approached.

"What do you want?" the largest of the men asked gruffly.

"I'm looking for Sameer," Byron said as he flashed his credentials.

"I am Sameer," another man said. "You are police?"

"Yes. Detective Sergeant Byron."

"What is the trouble?" Sameer asked.

"I want to ask you a few questions about your son, Mohammed," Byron said.

Sameer waved the other men away, then led Byron to his office at the back of the garage. The office, which had no ceiling, was constructed of plywood on three sides. The back wall was the interior surface of the building's metal exterior wall. One desk, three chairs, and a table rounded it out. The light spilled in from fixtures hung from the garage ceiling. Everything was coated in a thin layer of dust. Sameer sat down in one of the chairs and gestured with his hand for Byron to do the same.

"Why do you come to me about my son?" Sameer asked. "Is he in trouble again?"

"I don't know, Mr. Sayed. Do you know where Mohammed was last Sunday night?"

"At home."

"With you?"

"No, I worked Sunday. All day. I was not home until late."

"Is there anyone who can verify that Mohammed was home on Sunday night?"

"His mother, Astur."

"Where would I find her?" Byron asked.

Before Sameer could answer, a woman entered the office accompanied by a tall thin teenaged boy. Both men turned to look.

"This is Astur," Sameer said. "And my son, Mohammed."

Chapter 15

Wednesday 1:25 P.M.,
January 18, 2017

IN TYPICAL MAINE fashion, the weather was as fickle as a teenaged girl trying to decide on a dress for the prom. Two days prior it had been meteorological Armageddon. Reporters hoping one day to land their own air-conditioned news anchor desks had subjected themselves to doing live feeds outside in blizzard conditions, wearing the latest in outdoor fashion, while jamming yardsticks into snowdrifts as plow trucks passed by. The hyped message was always the same: run to the store and buy bread and milk before the world ends. Now, less than forty-eight hours later, aside from the ridiculously high bankings left behind by city plow drivers, there was no evidence that the world had ended. In fact, it was beautiful. Portland was showcasing her virgin white overcoat under a cloudless Prussian sky. All was right in the world. All except for the crowd of protestors in front of 109, and the dead teenager, and the cop who had shot him.

It was nearly one-thirty. Byron and Nugent sat parked in an unmarked on Diamond Street, just around the corner from Sewell's Second Hand. They were awaiting Detective Cameron's arrival. Byron checked his watch again. Cameron was now twenty minutes late.

"You think the Sayeds were telling the truth about Mohammed?" Nugent asked.

"I don't know," Byron said. "Too much time has passed. They could have gotten their stories straight. At the very least they had to know we'd been looking for Mohammed."

"What about the kid's sneakers?"

Byron shook his head. "They weren't Nikes. And they weren't new."

"Shit."

Byron was about to respond when he noticed a beat-up Chevy half ton rolling toward Sewell's. The rusted silver hulk was a match to the vehicle Crosby's loaned detective had described.

"There he is," Byron said.

"Jeez, what a piece of crap," Nugent said. "That has to be a state-owned seizure. Nobody else would drive it."

The pickup turned into the lot and shuddered to a stop in front of Sewell's.

"Think he'll go for it?" Nugent asked.

"We'll know soon enough," Byron said.

DETECTIVE CAMERON STEPPED inside Sewell's and quickly scanned the store. The only customer in sight was a middle-aged man browsing through bins of old vinyl record albums. Behind the counter sat a beady-eyed unshaven man wearing a plaid chamois shirt. Cameron placed the man's age at about thirty-five. Judging from his hand movements and the way he was holding his phone, Cameron was pretty sure the man was playing a video game.

"Help ya," the man said as Cameron stepped up to the counter.

"I hope so. I'm looking for the owner."

"Owner isn't here," the pawnbroker said with barely a glance away from his phone. "I'm the manager."

"Are you the man I'm supposed to talk to?"

"Depends on what you need."

"I'm looking to buy a handgun."

The manager finally tore his eyes from the phone, sizing up Cameron. "Why do you need a gun, friend?"

Cameron smiled. "Protection. Portland can be one crazy-ass city."

"That it can."

"So, are you the man?"

The manager grinned and slipped the phone into his shirt pocket. "I might be able to help you, but I'm gonna need to see two forms of ID and have you fill out some paperwork for the feds." He reached under the counter and retrieved a firearm application form.

"What's this?" Cameron asked, his smile disappearing.

"That's Form 4473. ATF requires you to fill this out."

"ATF?"

"Yeah, friend. You know, Alcohol, Tobacco, Firearms, and Explosives. Guess they forgot about the *E*."

"And I gotta to fill this out?" Cameron asked, turning the paper around to look at it.

"Yup. Then there's the three-day wait for your background check."

Cameron did his best to look saddened by the news. "That's too bad. I was kinda hoping to avoid all that rigmarole."

"Why's that?"

"Let's just say I've got some history."

"What kind of history?"

"The kind the feds frown on."

"What you're asking is illegal. I could get into a shitload of trouble selling you a gun without going through the proper procedures, Mr.—"

"Smith."

The manager fixed him with a knowing smirk. "Well, Mr. *Smith*, like I said, I could get into serious trouble doing something like that. Trouble I don't need."

The bell hanging from the front door clanged as the lone customer left without making a purchase, leaving Cameron alone with his mark.

Deciding to up the ante, Cameron shoved a hand into the front pocket of his jeans and produced a wad of bills. "I got a thousand bucks. Cash."

Beady's eyes widened as he stared at the money in Cameron's hand. "Give me a minute to close up the store."

"PERHAPS YOU DIDN'T understand the question, Mr. Dresden," Byron said. "I asked you if you recently sold a firearm to a gentleman by the name of Ahmed Ali."

The pawnbroker stared back at him from the other side of the table in CID Interview Room Two. Byron knew Dresden didn't have what it took to win at this game. Whether he was experienced in dealing with the police or not had no bearing. The only thing that mattered now were the years of incarceration hanging over his head for trying to sell an illegal gun to an undercover narcotics officer.

"Cat got your tongue, Mr. Dresden?" Byron asked.

"Oh, I heard you, Sergeant," Dresden said. "I was just wondering how long it would be before my attorney got this whole thing dismissed due to entrapment."

"Entrapment? Hmm. I think you may be a bit confused about how that defense works. Our UC simply asked if you knew where he might be able to purchase a gun without all the red tape. It was you who lost your good sense after seeing the flash money."

Byron watched the arrogance drain from Dresden's face. It was obvious that he hadn't thought the whole thing through.

"What kind of guarantees do I get *if* I decide to cooperate?" Dresden asked.

"No guarantees. And everything depends upon what you can give me." Byron waited as the rusty gears slowly turned inside the young man's head.

"I never got a name," Dresden said at last.

"What did he look like?" Byron asked.

"Middle-aged. Black."

Byron frowned at Dresden's vagueness. "American-born? Foreign?"

"Foreign, I'd guess. He had a really thick accent."

"Could you tell from the accent which country he might have been from?" Byron asked hopefully.

"Africa?"

Byron briefly thought about explaining to Dresden that Africa is not a country but a continent, which is in fact comprised of fifty-four countries. But after careful consideration, Byron decided to save his breath for more useful pursuits. Like breathing.

"Would you recognize him if you saw him again?" Byron asked.

Dresden shrugged. "Maybe. What if I say I want a lawyer?"

"Your choice," Byron said, feigning indifference. He stood up and moved toward the door.

"Where are you going?" Dresden asked, looking concerned.

"Gotta call the feds to come pick your dumb ass up," Byron said as he opened the door to the interview room.

"Wait. Wait."

Byron paused in the doorway. "For what?"

"Okay. I'll cooperate."

BYRON TASKED MELISSA Stevens with assembling a photo array that included Ahmed Ali's BMV photo. After checking the color photos, to see if they were similar enough to warrant using them, and printing out a copy of the lineup, Byron returned to the interview room and sat down across from Dresden.

"Mr. Dresden, I'm going to show you a group of six photos of similar-looking males. I want you to tell me if you recognize any of them, and if so where you recognize them from. Do you understand?"

Dresden nodded. "Is one of these pictures the guy I sold the gun to?"

Byron, resisting the urge to knock some sense into the low-life gun dealer seated across from him, calmly replied, "The man to whom you sold the gun may or may not be among these photographs. If you would just look at all of them before saying anything, then tell me if you recognize any of them."

"Okay."

Byron waited as Dresden studied the photos. Dresden seemed to pause at and then return to photo number two. The minutes slowly passed as Byron watched Dresden agonize over the array.

"Well?" Byron said at last, tired of playing the game. "Do you recognize any of those men?"

Dresden looked up at Byron. "I can't say for certain, but number two and number five look the most like the guy I sold the gun to."

Byron could feel his hopes dashed at Dresden's comment. Ali's photo was displayed in the number five position, but Dresden's comment, combined with his indecisiveness, amounted to nothing more than a maybe in the eyes of the court. And maybe didn't cut it. It didn't rule out Ali as the buyer, but it didn't give Byron the probable cause he'd need for a search warrant either. He picked up the array and placed it back in the folder.

"How did I do?" Dresden asked as Byron stood up.

"Fabulous," Byron said, making no attempt to hide his condescension. "Stay here and I'll go see about your reward."

BYRON DEPARTED 109 with a newfound determination. Dresden may not have given them Ahmed Ali from the prepared lineup, but his confession about selling a Smith & Wesson revolver to a middle-aged foreign-born black male was the first lead they'd had toward putting a gun in the hand of Tommy Plummer. It didn't take a rocket scientist to figure out that if Ali was the buyer, his son might have had access to his father's gun. Extrapolating even further meant that Plummer, through his friendship with Ali's son, might also have had access. The trick would be getting an admission out of either the elder or younger Ali.

Byron parked at the curb in front of Ali's store and walked inside. Ahmed Ali, who was bagging up groceries for a female customer, looked up as Byron entered the store. His expression was somber, and he began to shake his head as Byron approached. Speaking in Somali, Ali said something to the woman as he handed her her purchases. She took her bags and hurried past Byron and out of the store.

"Good afternoon, Mr. Ali," Byron said. "I wonder if you might have a second to speak with me."

"I am very busy, Sergeant Byron. What do you want?"

Both men turned to the sound of the front door opening again. Abdi, Ali's son, stepped inside accompanied by Mohammed Sayed. Both boys froze at the sight of Byron.

Mr. Ali barked something at his son in Somali. Abdi nodded his understanding, then he and Sayed did an about-face and quickly exited the store.

Byron turned his attention back to the store owner. "What did you just say to your son, Mr. Ali?"

"None of your business, Sergeant."

"Did it have anything to do with your gun?"

Ali glared at him. There was no cultural disconnect in the expression on the shopkeeper's face now. His disdain for Byron, and his question, was obvious.

"Who was that other boy with your son?" Byron asked, testing him.

"Please leave my store," Ali said. "You are not welcome here."

Byron departed the halal store and drove the side streets of Munjoy Hill, hoping to spot the boys, but they had disappeared. He was trying to decide his next move when his cell rang. LeRoyer.

"Hey, Marty," Byron said.

"You mind telling me what in the hell happened in Internal Affairs this morning?"

IT WAS NEARLY eight o'clock before Byron could break away for his impromptu dinner date with Diane. They grabbed a table on the second floor of Bull Feeney's pub in Portland's Old Port. Diane ordered a glass of merlot, Caesar salad, and baked haddock; Byron had a cup of coffee and the lamb stew. As they dined, Byron brought Diane up to speed on the case, including the details of his meeting with the FBI.

"The feds showed their hand?" Diane asked. "I don't believe it."

"Yeah, well, not until after Haggerty ended up in the middle of it."

"You trust Special Agent Collier?"

"After the O'Halloran case, I'd have trusted Sam with anything."

"And now?"

Byron, after burning his mouth on the first spoonful of stew, guzzled half of the ice water from his glass before he spoke. "I don't know. I don't think Sam is calling the shots on this thing. The guy Sam was with, Lessard, seemed to be in charge of what information got doled out to me."

"Who else knows about it?"

"Nobody. According to them, even Crosby is in the dark about this one."

"Why wouldn't they involve MDEA? It's a drug thing, right?"

"Yes, but the underlying investigation is OC."

"Ah. And which crime syndicate are they looking at?"

"They wouldn't say. The implication is that Micky Cavallaro is involved."

"So I guess it's safe to assume they aren't looking at the Russians, then," Diane said as she buttered a piece of Irish soda bread.

"They mentioned Haggerty though."

She stopped buttering. "Hags? What about him?"

"Lessard said they think one of the places being supplied with drugs from the Bubble Up is Portland High."

"And?"

"They have reason to believe there may be an inside guy."

"And they suspect *Sean*?"

"They wouldn't go that far. They only said he'd been discussed."

They ate in silence for the next several minutes.

"Have you asked Hags about it?" Diane asked at last.

"Can't. I'm not even supposed to be sharing this with you."

Chapter 16

Thursday, 7:30 a.m.,
January 19, 2017

BYRON GATHERED THE entire team in the conference room. He wanted everyone on the same page before they began the day's work. After sharing the previous afternoon's illegal gun buy and the possible connection to Abdi, Byron had Melissa Stevens give her report.

"Except for a few stragglers, we've talked with everyone in Kennedy Park," Stevens said.

"Anybody admit to knowing that asshole from South Portland?" Nugent asked.

"He means Lucas Perez," Byron said.

"No," Stevens said. "We couldn't locate anyone who claims to know Perez."

"So he's full of shit," Nugent said.

Not as far as the public was concerned, Byron thought.

Stevens continued. "I tracked down Nate Freeman's mother.

She alibied him as being home Sunday night. Said they watched something on Netflix."

"*Starship Troopers*," Byron said, looking at Gardiner.

Stevens looked up from her notes. "Yeah."

Byron turned his attention to Pelligrosso. "What have you got, Gabe?"

"No matches on the footwear yet. The test results for the powder seized at the scene came back positive for cocaine. Oh, by the way, Ellis called and left me a message last night. Tommy Plummer tested positive for alcohol and cocaine."

"Where are we at with Tommy's basketball teammates?" Byron asked.

Gardiner, wanting to contribute, shot Stevens an anxious glance. She nodded.

"All but two of them had alibis for Sunday night," Gardiner said.

"Which two?" Byron asked.

Gardiner checked his notebook. Stevens gave Byron a knowing grin.

"Stephen Fuller and Patrick Mingus."

"Mingus?" Byron said. "Mel, isn't he the student who told you about Plummer being the go-to drug guy?"

"The very same."

"Think he's deflecting?" Tran asked.

Nugent's head snapped around toward Tran. "Look at you, Colombo. *Deflecting*." He turned to Byron. "See, Sarge, told you I'd turn him into a real detective."

Byron turned to Tran. "Anything to add, Dustin?"

"Still working on the social media stuff, pics, connections, etc. I checked BMV and only a handful of the names you gave me have a driver's license."

"Um, note to you, the robbers fled on foot," Nugent said. "We just went from deflecting to regressing in a span of seconds. So much for progress."

BYRON WAITED UNTIL nine o'clock before heading back to Portland High School. He wanted to make sure that Abdi Ali was in school and not under the protective veil of his father. He had barely gotten through the administrative office doors when he was confronted by the school principal.

"Dana Larrabee," the principal said, extending her hand. "And you must be the detective who disrupted my school earlier this week."

Byron quickly realized that things had changed, and not for the better. The warm welcome afforded by Assistant Principal Paul Rogers had evidentially been revoked. There was nothing warm about the smile painted on Larrabee's face. This woman was all business. Not wanting to escalate the tension, Byron shook the hand that was offered, doing his best to remain cordial.

"Detective Sergeant John Byron," he said.

"Well, Detective Sergeant, I understand that you spoke to a number of my students the other day. Pulled them out of their classes, in fact."

"I'm investigating the police shooting that took place Sunday night."

"Is that the shooting in which one of your officers shot an unarmed teenager?"

Byron could feel his patience slipping. "There were two people running from the police, Ms. Larrabee. One of them attended this school. I am trying to locate the second suspect."

"*Suspect?* These are students, Detective Byron. Do you have some type of warrant for one of my students?"

"No. I just need to speak with one of them."

Larrabee proceeded into a long soliloquy, quoting chapter and verse about the rights of students and about the dangers of Portland becoming a police state. Byron wondered how differently the self-righteous administrator might feel about the situation if Haggerty or even the laundromat owner had been friends or relatives of hers. Wisely, he kept those thoughts to himself.

He noticed that Larrabee made no attempt to move their conversation to a more private location, like her office, though it was clear from the posture and cocked heads of both office assistants seated nearby that they were monitoring every word. Reflecting on it further, Byron realized that it was probably Larrabee's intention to be overheard. The opportunity to showcase her authority to her subordinates was too good to pass up.

As Larrabee droned on, Byron couldn't help but be reminded of Albert Stansfield. Stansfield, one of Byron's professors at Saint Joseph's College back in the late '80s, had lectured in the same irritating, monotonous way. Saint Joe's had some truly great professors. Stansfield had not been one of them.

"Are you listening to me, Sergeant?" Larrabee asked, as if she were dressing down one of her students.

"Yeah," Byron said, wondering if all teachers eventually lost the ability to communicate with adults as if they were adults. "You're saying you'd rather I didn't bother your students during the day."

"It's not *just* that. I must guard against you trampling their rights, Sergeant. While they are here, they are my responsibility. And I wouldn't want the parents complaining."

"Heavens, no. We wouldn't want that, would we?"

Larrabee's mouth hung open in disbelief.

Byron, realizing his sarcasm had caught her off guard, forged ahead. "Is it specifically Scott Henderson, Abdirahman Ali, Nate Freeman, and Mohammed Sayed that you don't want me talking to? Or are there other students that you're protecting?" Byron asked, intentionally trying to provoke a reaction from her.

Larrabee's expression hardened as she worked to control her anger with him.

"I'm afraid I don't respond well to sarcasm," she said.

"That's okay," Byron said. "I don't respond well to people obstructing my investigations."

"You know, Sergeant, I'm not sure I even want you in my school. It's clear that you're intent on being disruptive."

Byron wondered how disruptive she'd found the influx of illegal drugs into the school to be. He reached inside his suit coat and removed a single business card, then slid a pen out of the same pocket and began to write something on the back of the card. When he had finished, Byron handed the card to her.

"What is this?" Larrabee asked.

"It's the name and telephone number of my lieutenant. I figure you'll want to call and complain about me."

"Thank you," Larrabee said with as much inflection as she was apparently capable of. "I will."

Byron turned to go, then stopped, turning to face her again. "Have you ever been to the deli, Miss Larrabee?"

"What?" she asked, lowering her brows and looking confused.

"I should warn you, calling Lieutenant LeRoyer to complain about me is like shopping at the deli. You'll want to take a number."

BYRON DROVE AWAY from the school sure of two things. First, LeRoyer would not be pleased that he had goaded Larrabee into complaining about him. And second, he still needed a way to speak with Abdi without his father interfering. Had Principal Larrabee's only concern been the welfare of her students, or was there something else behind her stonewalling the investigation? The assistant principal had said that Larrabee had been the driving force behind Tommy Plummer's disappearing drug charges. What if the "inside man" Special Agents Collier and Lessard were looking for was actually a woman?

He was trying to decide his next move when his cell rang.

Byron answered it without checking the ID. "Byron."

"It's me," Diane said. "Can you talk?"

What now? he wondered. "Yeah. What's up?"

"Billingslea just called. Someone sent him a copy of the MedCu statement. He knows about the flashlight."

"Shit."

POLICE DISPATCHER JUSTINE Jewett had just returned from a bathroom break and side trip to the basement vending machines for a bag of Cheez-Its and a Diet Coke. She'd popped a handful of the salty crackers into her mouth when the computer screen at her station lit up with an incoming emergency call.

"911, Operator Jewett speaking. What is your emergency?"

"Officer Haggerty is dead meat," a male voice said.

"Excuse me?" Jewett said. "I don't think I heard you right. Could you repeat that?" Jewett looked at the number displayed on the screen. It was an obvious mobile number.

"You heard me. Haggerty is dead."

And with that the line was disconnected. She attempted to redial, but the phone was no longer in service. Jewett looked at the caller ID map. The signal had originated from Portland's West End. The caller had been near St. John Street and Congress

Street when the call was made. Jewett swiveled in her chair, looking for the dispatch shift supervisor.

"Hey, Mary," Jewett said, addressing her boss. "We just got another one."

"DAMMIT, JOHN," LEROYER said as he stepped into Byron's office and slammed the door. "I can't decide what I'm more pissed about, your behavior with Principal Larrabee or the fact that you withheld such an important detail from me."

Byron could have predicted the lieutenant's response. He had heard it more times than he cared to count. It was nothing more than a dance necessitated by LeRoyer's position within the department hierarchy. Byron's job required him to withhold certain case details from his boss while simultaneously punching holes in any investigative barriers until the truth began to leak out. LeRoyer's job was to try and keep his senior sergeant in check. Byron didn't envy him.

"You did that on purpose, didn't you?" LeRoyer asked, the stress showing through on his reddening and tightly pinched face.

Byron, who had been running quickly through his voicemails and still held the desk phone to his ear, shrugged. "Which thing are you referring to?"

"Do not fuck with me, John!"

"Look, Marty, I didn't sign up for this job to make friends." He punched the number six, deleting another message before dropping the receiver back in its cradle. "That self-righteous woman is hiding behind her authority. I'm trying to get to the bottom of what happened leading up to Sean's shooting."

"What about this damn MedCu statement?"

"I'm sure you've read it by now."

"Yeah, I have. As has Rumsfeld. And I gotta tell ya, it looks like shit. You know what it's gonna look like printed in the *Herald*. I can't *believe* you kept that from me."

"Come off it. You know as well as I that I intentionally don't tell you everything when I'm working a case. It's called deniability. And I don't give a damn about the *Herald*. We don't share information on an open investigation with the public. If I'd have told you about the flashlight you would have been obligated to share that with Rumsfeld."

"And I would have."

"Yeah, and he would have done what all administrators do. He would have circled the goddamned wagons and figured out a way to distance himself from Haggerty. He would have come up with a contingency plan to fuck Sean over."

"You don't know that," LeRoyer said.

"Don't I?" Byron pointed toward Rumsfeld's office. "What's he doing right now?"

LeRoyer didn't respond.

"Tommy Plummer had a gun. Haggerty knows the difference between a flashlight and a muzzle flash. He isn't some petrified rookie, Marty. Hags is a seasoned veteran. All I'm trying to do is figure out what happened that night. That is still our priority, isn't it?"

"Of course it is," the lieutenant said, backing down, but only slightly.

"You should be far more concerned with the goddamned mole that's leaking all this shit to the paper."

Defeated, LeRoyer let out a long sigh, then plopped down in one of the visitor's chairs across from Byron. "Tell me where you're at?"

"We're still looking at Plummer's basketball teammates and the four students whose names we got from Assistant Principal Rogers at Portland High the other day."

"You think one of them might be the other robber?" LeRoyer asked, his expression softening.

"It's possible. Plummer hung out regularly with all of them. I've got Tran working on them now," Byron said, intentionally holding back the Facebook angle. "If there is a link, beyond the obvious, we'll find it."

"Just do me a favor. Go easy with the feather ruffling, okay?" LeRoyer said.

"You know me."

"WHAT'S THE BIG deal?" Billingslea said from the other end of the phone. "The information is legit."

"The big deal?" Diane said, squeezing the telephone tighter in her hand and wishing it was the young reporter's scrawny neck. "All you did by running that story was pour gasoline on a fire. That's the big deal. You're implying that the kid Haggerty shot was only armed with a flashlight. Also, the internal affairs case, which you shouldn't have had in the first place, was cleared as unsubstantiated. I noticed that doesn't appear anywhere in your damned story."

"Still shows a pattern," Billingslea countered.

"Of what?"

"Excessive force. Overzealousness on Haggerty's part, and on the part of cops nationwide."

"*What?*" She was so angry that she couldn't speak for a moment. Her mouth wouldn't form the words. "Davis, you're lucky that you're not standing here in my office or I'd probably clean your fucking clock."

"Why are you pissed at me?"

"Do you have any idea how dumb what you just said is? Do you really think police officers get up every day looking for someone to beat up, or shoot?"

"Of course you see it differently. You're one of them."

"So, it's us and them now, is it? Keep this up and I might come over to your office and kick your scrawny ass up and down the newsroom anyway. Then you'd have something real to write about."

"No, I just meant—"

"I know exactly what you meant. You think you have any idea what it's like to do this job?"

"Of course not. I don't know—"

"That's right, you don't know. You don't have the first clue about what it means to be a cop. This media crap about labeling police officers as trigger-happy thugs is beyond ridiculous."

"I don't—"

"Shut up and let me finish, Davis. Or I swear to God I will come find you. Sean Haggerty is not only a friend of mine but my brother. A brother cop. I wouldn't expect you to understand that though. Hags is no more trigger-happy than I am. But you're all painting him that way. You're the reason those people are marching outside the station right now, instead of waiting to see what the facts are. Sean is a good cop and he shot a kid, period. Unlike you, we are trying to investigate exactly what did happen. Either Tommy Plummer had a gun and Haggerty shot him in self-defense or Plummer didn't and it was a bad shoot. That's enough to deal with without you sensationalizing it. Whether you are aware of it or not, Haggerty is suffering right along with the Plummer family."

Davis said nothing.

"Tell me you don't honestly believe Sean took any satisfaction in killing that kid," Diane said.

"I would hope not."

Diane took a deep breath, trying to get a handle on her emotions. "Ever had a gun pointed at you?"

"No."

"Well, then consider yourself goddamned lucky. The question you should be asking is why somebody sent that IA report and the MedCu statement to the newspaper. By the way, not that you care, we're now receiving death threats against Haggerty. And if you print one word of that, you'll have to deal with me. Got it?"

"I got it."

"*Death threats.* Is that what you wanted?"

"No, of course it isn't."

"Take a good long look in the mirror, Davis. Because you helped to create this shit storm."

She slammed the handset down, ending the call. *"Fuck."* Her hands were shaking. She didn't know what she was most pissed about, losing her temper with Billingslea or his infuriating stereotyping of everything. Movement in the hallway caught her attention. She looked up and saw Melissa Stevens standing wide-eyed in the doorway. "How long have you been standing there?" Diane asked.

"Long enough to hear how friggin' awesome you are," Stevens said.

"Wasn't trying to be awesome, Mel. I didn't know I had an audience."

"I could kiss you right now."

Diane felt her rage beginning to dissipate. "While I appreciate the gesture, Detective, I'm not sure how appropriate that would be."

Stevens grinned. "And when have you ever known me to be appropriate, *Sarge*?"

BYRON WAS STILL fuming about the leaks when he received a call from Nugent telling him about the calls to Dispatch threatening the life of Sean Haggerty.

"How many calls?" Byron asked, thinking it was probably only one or two looneys.

"Close to a dozen."

"Dispatch should be able to track those down easy enough," Byron said, knowing that the numbers for all incoming 911 calls were captured.

"That's the problem, boss. Some of these assholes are calling in on Dispatch's nonemergency lines, the others are using burners," Nugent said. "The state police in Gray are getting the same type of calls."

Shit, Byron thought. "Okay, let's get someone to sit on Haggerty's house."

"The shift commander already assigned someone out there 'cause the media was showing up."

"Yeah. I heard. How the hell did they get his home address?"

"Who knows. Somebody here at 109 with a grudge, maybe? Assholes wear badges too, Sarge."

After ending the call with Nugent, Byron dialed Haggerty's cell. An automated message stated that the voice mailbox was full. He hung up, making a mental note to stop by and pay a visit to Haggerty later in the evening.

Byron couldn't believe how quickly the hatred had spread. Born from rumor and innuendo, the facts of what had happened that night in Kennedy Park had quickly been replaced by speculation and outright lies. Even the media had done their part to spread disinformation, airing erroneous accounts from supposed witnesses. Witnesses who refused to be interviewed by the police. And the protests had made a tense situation infinitely worse, adding to the stress within the police department. It was as if the City of Portland had lost its collective mind. A rift had formed between residents. People took either the propolice or the antipolice side of the issue, causing them to act like rabid fans of rival sports teams, reminding Byron of the Red Sox and Yankees of old, before A-Rod and Varitek, back when it was Munson and Fisk. But regardless of the way in which the community was acting, Byron knew that the detectives had to stay on point. Had to stay focused. They couldn't allow themselves to be dragged down into the melee. One-dimensional thinking had never held a place in successful investigations and Byron was trying hard to keep an open mind about what had happened. He wanted Haggerty to be cleared of any wrongdoing, of course, but he wasn't about to cut corners to get at the truth. The FBI had kicked around the possibility that Haggerty could be facilitating the influx of drugs to the school, and although Byron didn't believe it, he hadn't found anything to rule Haggerty out either. Byron had allowed a friendship to cloud his judgment once before and it had nearly cost him his life. He couldn't let it happen again.

Chapter 17

Thursday, 8:05 P.M.,
January 19, 2017

BYRON PULLED INTO the plowed dooryard of Haggerty's brown shingled cape on Olde Birch Lane. He exited the car, exchanging nods with the detail officer seated behind the wheel of the idling black-and-white parked directly across the street. Byron walked up the paved drive past Haggerty's pickup to the side door where an outside light was illuminated. He ascended the crumbling brick steps and observed Haggerty seated alone at the kitchen table. Haggerty saw him too, and waved Byron inside.

"Hey, Sarge," Haggerty said as Byron pushed open the inside door.

Byron could tell instantly that Haggerty was drunk, even before the unshaven man spoke. On the table in front of him sat an impressive quantity of sixteen-ounce Pabst Blue Ribbon beer cans, a half dozen empties, and an unholstered stainless semiautomatic handgun.

"Mind if I come inside for a minute?" Byron asked from the doorway.

"Come on in, Sarge," Haggerty said, motioning awkwardly with his arm and slurring his words badly.

Byron stepped inside and pushed the door closed behind him in hopes that the officer sitting outside would remain there. Cautiously, he walked toward the table while keeping his eyes fixed on the burly officer's hands. Byron was trying to avoid doing anything that might aggravate an already volatile situation. Haggerty was built like a linebacker, several inches shorter than Byron, but stocky, easily outweighing him by forty pounds. Even if he was able to reach the weapon first, Byron knew he'd never be able to overpower the younger officer if Hags resisted.

"How are you holding up, Sean?" Byron asked, knowing full well the answer.

Haggerty seemed to consider the question. "Not very good actually. Nope, not too good at all."

"Mind if I sit?"

"Please do," Haggerty said, waving a hand as if casting a spell, his head bobbing slightly.

Moving slowly and deliberately, Byron pulled out a wooden chair directly across from him and sat down. The eerie similarity between the scene playing out before him and the manner in which he'd found his father decades earlier was not at all lost on Byron. It was as if the past was bleeding through into the present and Byron was a teenager again searching his dad's apartment and finding Reece seated at the table facedown in a puddle of blood, gun at his feet. Byron couldn't help wondering what gruesome scene he might have discovered in Haggerty's kitchen had his arrival been delayed.

"I tried calling," Byron said.

"Shut my phone off," Haggerty said. "Someone gave my number to the press, Sarge. They wouldn't stop calling."

Byron made a mental note to find the person responsible and personally rip their throat out. "What's going on, Sean?"

"Oh, all kinds of stuff. Sharon broke up with me. Did you hear about that?"

Byron wasn't sure where Haggerty was headed, but he decided for the time being to let him lead and not to make any waves. "I'm sorry. I'm sure this has been hard on both of you. Maybe she just needs some time to think it through."

Haggerty grabbed the open PBR he was currently working on and took a healthy swig before setting it back on the table. He fixed Byron with a smile that was probably as forced as it appeared. His eyes had transformed into the weary windows of a much older man. "You're a good man, Sarge."

"You staying in contact with your attorney?" Byron asked, attempting to change the subject to something a bit less dangerous.

"Ha! Mr. Bad Fucking News? Yeah, like every day. Told you I was screwed."

"Sean, all the detectives are giving their best on this. We'll figure it out."

"Well, here's to them," Haggerty said, raising the can and finishing off the contents in several gulps. He banged the empty down on the table, then reached over for a fresh one, knocking several empties onto the floor in the process.

Haggerty fixed Byron with a blank stare that Byron couldn't read. *Was this simply about the shooting?* Byron wondered. *Or was Hags feeling guilt about something else?* Byron thought back to what Collier and Lessard had said about Haggerty. Was his friend capable of something as repulsive as pushing drugs on kids? The truth was he didn't know. But given the fragile nature of the moment, this wasn't the time to press it. Byron would say and do whatever he had to to get Haggerty through this.

"I know how you're feeling, Sean."

"Oh, do you, Sarge?" Haggerty asked, his body visibly tensing. A flare of anger flickered in Haggerty's eyes, momentarily clearing them of their alcohol-induced fog. "You know what it's like to kill a kid?"

"No," Byron said as he thought back to the shooting he had been involved in several years before. And while it hadn't been a teenager Byron had killed, it didn't make the act of taking a life any easier to swallow. "But I do know how it feels to kill another human being. And it sucks. I know you feel like you're all alone. Like there's nobody you can talk to. No one on your side."

Haggerty continued to stare at him, but his body had begun to relax.

Byron continued. "You spend all your time watching the news, listening to everyone saying how you frigged up. How they would have handled things differently. Every talking head is a god-damned expert, right?"

"Yeah," Haggerty said, nodding and drawing the word out as if amazed that Byron actually understood.

"You wish you could turn back the clock to that night and change things," Byron said. "You want to fix it. Like you could make it turn out differently. Right?"

Haggerty shook his head, his shoulders slumped forward. "Every minute of every fucking day since it happened."

"I know how *that* feels, Sean."

Haggerty's bloodshot eyes began to water. Byron could see that all the fight had run out of him.

"I can't sleep, Sarge. And I don't want to. Every time I fall asleep, I dream about that night. Over and over, and fucking over. But every time it's different. Sometimes I'm in the laundromat and Tommy shoots me before I can draw my gun. Sometimes both robbers shoot me. Sometimes Tommy doesn't have a gun. He only points a finger at me, but I still shoot him," Haggerty said, choking on the words. Tears rolled freely down his face now.

Byron remained silent.

"I just don't know anymore. I can't think straight. I'm so fucking tired."

Byron caught Haggerty's eyes as they shifted to the gun lying on the table. "What if I did screw up, Sarge? Maybe those talking heads are right. Maybe he didn't have a gun. Maybe I just overreacted. I read the newspaper article online. Maybe it was the light on his phone."

"Sean, look at me," Byron shouted, intentionally trying to pull the despondent officer's attention away from the gun.

Haggerty looked up, wide-eyed, like a child about to be scolded.

"You did the right thing. That night. You did the right thing."

"How do you know?"

"Because I know you, Sean. I know what kind of cop you are. What kind of man. And so do the others. You've got to trust us. We'll find the other suspect. And we'll find the gun. We just need more time."

"He was just a kid, Sarge," Haggerty countered.

"Yeah, he was. A kid who stuck a gun in a man's face and robbed him," Byron said. "You're not the only one who saw Plummer with a gun that night."

Haggerty glanced back toward the Smith & Wesson Model 4506 lying on the table.

"Why don't you let me hold on to that for you, Sean," Byron said. "Just for a little while. For safekeeping. Okay?"

He waited while Haggerty thought it over. Byron was prepared to lunge over the table if necessary, a scenario that would most likely turn out badly. For both of them.

Byron tensed as Haggerty placed his open palm over the firearm and hesitated.

"Okay," Haggerty said at last. He slid the gun across the table toward Byron. "For a little while."

BYRON DROVE THROUGH the darkened streets of Portland unsure of his destination. He glanced over at Haggerty's .45 lying on the front passenger seat. Voluntarily turning over the gun had really been nothing more than a symbolic gesture of trust and they both knew it. In reality, Byron knew that Haggerty probably had many more guns squirreled away throughout the house. Byron could have brought other people into the situation and forced the issue. They could've searched the entire house, removing all of Haggerty's firearms for safekeeping, forcing him to go to the hospital to speak with a shrink. Byron could have set all of that into motion, but at the end of the day it would have been nothing more than window dressing designed to make everyone but Haggerty feel better. If Hags really did intend on harming himself there was nothing Byron or anyone else could do about it. Byron had asked Haggerty to hand over the gun and he had. Both men knew what the other was thinking, and both of them knew that the only person who could prevent harm from coming to Haggerty was Haggerty himself.

Byron stopped behind several other vehicles at the red traffic signal at Woodfords Corner. He snatched the gun off the seat, then bent forward and slid it underneath his own. His intervention had been as a friend. There would be no paperwork generated, no medical trail to follow Haggerty. Things like that had a way of fucking up the careers of some pretty good cops. Byron knew that Haggerty had enough things working against him, without stepping aboard the crazy train.

The light changed to green and the cars in front of his began to move. As he proceeded inbound on Deering Avenue, his thoughts drifted back to the conversation he'd had with Haggerty about the shooting.

"What if I did screw up, Sarge?" Hags had said. "Maybe he didn't have a gun. Maybe I just overreacted. Maybe it was the light on his phone."

Byron didn't believe that, of course, but it troubled him just the same. He knew it was only natural for an officer involved in a shooting to second-guess their own actions. Taking the life of another was no small thing. But with the entire community picking sides on this one it was far from a typical police shooting. And if it turned out that Haggerty *was* wrong, there would be hell to pay.

A good investigator considered all possibilities when trying to solve a case. This credo had been hammered into Byron's head since the day he'd first made detective and he likewise had hammered it into the heads of every detective he'd trained since. He was doing everything in his power to identify the second robbery suspect in hopes of recovering the gun. *But what if they ditched the gun before Haggerty spotted them?* he thought. *Was it a revolver or a semiauto? The two men inside the laundromat hadn't even been able to agree on the type of gun. What if the flash Haggerty saw was the flashlight on Plummer's cell? What if Collier was right? What if Haggerty was involved in the drug trafficking?* Byron wanted to shove these thoughts under the seat next to Haggerty's pistol, far from view, but he knew he couldn't. All he could do was his job. And his job was to uncover the truth. No matter what that truth might be.

As BYRON NEARED home, he passed Khalid Muhammad's unit. A figure was silhouetted in a first-floor window. Byron continued past, pulling into his own driveway. He opened the car door, then grabbed his belongings, pausing for a moment as he considered retrieving Haggerty's firearm under the seat. He decided to leave it where it was. He swung his left leg out to exit the car when he heard the crunch of snow under footsteps. Someone was approaching. Instinctively his right hand moved toward the gun on his hip.

"Sergeant Byron. It is me, Khalid."

Byron relaxed as his neighbor's face came into view. "Hey, Khalid. What's up?"

"I have been waiting for you."

Byron could see by the somber expression on Muhammad's face that something heavy was weighing on the man's mind. He stepped out of the car and headed toward his condo. "Come inside," Byron said.

Muhammad followed Byron into the condo.

Byron had met Muhammad for the first time the previous spring, when he stopped by to deliver a housewarming present to Byron. Muhammed, who lived several doors down with his family, had told Byron that he was an accountant and a respected member of the Somali community. He had offered his assistance to Byron, if ever it was needed. Byron wondered if this might be the time.

"Can I get you anything?" Byron asked as he turned on some lights and the two men entered the kitchen.

"No. I am okay. Thank you."

Byron set his belongings on the counter. "Have a seat," he said, gesturing toward the table.

"Thank you, Sergeant."

After they were both seated, Byron said, "So, what's up?"

"I am here at the request of a friend."

Byron waited while Muhammad wrestled with whatever it was he needed to get off his chest.

Muhammad continued. "Ahmed Ali is a good friend of mine. He told me that you have questioned him twice about his son, Abdi. Do you suspect Abdi had something to do with what happened last weekend?"

"Khalid, you know I can't share the details of an active police investigation."

Muhammad nodded as if he had expected Byron's answer.

"Having said that, we are talking to anyone who might have been with Tommy Plummer, the student who was killed, on Sunday night."

Byron studied his neighbor's face. He could see the conflict behind it.

"Do you think Abdi might know something that would help you?" Muhammad asked.

"If he does, we need him to come forward and tell us what he knows. If he didn't have anything to do with it, maybe he can help me clear his name."

Muhammad's gazed dropped as if there was something interesting on top of Byron's kitchen table. Byron checked. There wasn't.

"Khalid?" Byron asked, nudging him. "Do *you* know something?"

"No. I have to go now," Muhammad said as he rose from the chair. "Thank you for talking with me, Sergeant."

Byron followed his neighbor back to the front door and watched as he started down the walkway. Muhammad might be the key to gaining Ahmed's trust and, by extension, Abdi's trust as well. "You can trust me, you know," Byron called out.

Muhammad stopped walking and turned back to face Byron.

For just a moment it looked as though he might walk back inside and tell Byron everything.

"And Ahmed can trust me too," Byron continued.

"Good night, Sergeant Byron," Muhammad said, giving him a weak smile. He turned and walked briskly back toward his own condo.

He watched his neighbor's shape fade back into darkness.

BYRON WENT UPSTAIRS and changed into his sweats. Returning to the kitchen, he slapped together a sandwich—thickly spread peanut butter on wheat—then poured himself a glass of milk. He retired to the living room where he took a seat on the couch and flicked on the muted television. Watching muted TV always helped him to think. It didn't matter what was being broadcast; he wasn't really watching anyway. It just seemed better than being alone.

He took a healthy bite out of the sandwich and returned it to the plate. He was beginning to mentally dissect Muhammad's visit when his cell rang. He picked it up off the cushion and checked the ID. It was Diane.

"Hey, pretty lady," he said, trying unsuccessfully to clear away the food before he spoke.

"Didn't your mother ever tell you it wasn't polite to talk with your mouth full?" she said.

"Sorry. Hang on." He took a swig of milk and washed down the remainder of the bite. "Better?"

"Better," she said. "Late dinner?"

"You know me."

"Something nutritious, no doubt."

He considered it. "Three of the food groups anyway."

"How did it go today?" she asked. "Any progress?"

"Not nearly enough. Everyone is hunkering down on this one."

"A lot at stake," she said, stating the obvious. "There's a rumor going around that you got into it with Thibodeau."

"I hadn't heard that one," Byron said. "Crazy what people will make up."

"Riiight."

"I just had an unusual visit from one of my neighbors."

"Some hot divorcée looking for help with her *whatever*?"

"No, I fixed her whatever the other day," he said.

"Mmm," she replied. "Yes, you did."

"No, it was my neighbor Khalid."

"What did he want?"

"He came by on behalf of his good friend Ahmed Ali."

"Abdi's father? The halal store owner?"

"That would be the one."

"What did he say?"

"He didn't really say anything. I think he was poking around to see if I thought that Abdi might know something about the robbery. I don't think Ahmed trusts me."

"Do you think Khalid knows anything?"

"I don't know. I think he's struggling with something."

"With what?"

"With whether or not *he* can trust me."

Chapter 18

THE ELECTRICITY IN Byron's neighborhood had gone out overnight. Comparing the time on the nightstand clock to his cellphone he realized that he'd slept in. After starting the Malibu, Byron climbed out with scraper in hand and went to work on the heavy layer of frost coating every window. As he cleared each surface his thoughts turned to Haggerty.

Haggerty had never shown a propensity for overreacting when faced with a stressful situation, and Byron didn't believe he would have overreacted in this case either. Cops tend to revert to their training when in the heat of the moment. Over time their reactions become automatic. The survival instinct was hardwired. As he thought about his interaction with Haggerty the previous night, he hoped Hags's instincts were still intact. He also hoped that the FBI's suspicions about Haggerty were wrong.

BYRON CIRCLED THE block in hopes of avoiding the throng of protesters standing in front of 109. He drove past Middle Street on Franklin Arterial, turned right on Fore Street, then back up Pearl to Federal. As he entered 109's rear parking garage he realized that his efforts had been for naught. A second group of protestors were camped out in the plaza, effectively blocking both the public entrance to the PD and the rear door, the one most commonly used by the employees.

He locked up the unmarked, then headed for the plaza on foot. Several of the picketers focused on Byron, waving their signs and raising their voices as he approached, but that was as far as it went. Absent were the rabble rousers and violent opportunists responsible for Sergeant Pepin's head injury. This gathering obviously believed in delivering the message peaceably. A welcome development. He waded through the crowd, keyed in the entry code, then entered the building.

He stepped out of the stairwell into the fourth floor, nearly colliding with a cameraman. Byron sidestepped around the bearded man and gaped at the crowd of reporters blocking the entrance to CID as well as the elevators. Rumsfeld was holding an impromptu press conference right there in the hallway. To avoid the media circus, Byron banged a left and cut down the back corridor into CID.

He had been at his desk all of five minutes when a frazzled-looking Lieutenant LeRoyer breezed into the office and sat down.

"Did you see that?" LeRoyer asked. "The mob in the hallway?"

"Hard to miss," Byron said.

"You know what it was about?"

"Don't really care. Although if you took away the cameras and microphones and handed them signs, they could stand in for the mob outside. Speaking of which, what happened to the 'no protestors in the plaza' directive?"

"The chief rescinded it after people complained to city hall that this is a public building and they had a right to free speech."

"I hope they didn't forget to mention that they pay our salaries."

"One of the students you questioned, his parents went out and retained an attorney. They're accusing you of harassment."

"That's ridiculous. Which student?"

"Mohammed Sayed."

Byron paused to consider this unexpected development. His interaction with the Sayeds had seemed nonconfrontational. Both parents vouched for their son's illness and had alibied his whereabouts on Sunday night. Why were they hiding behind an attorney? The last time Byron had seen Mohammed Sayed he'd been with Abdi Ahmed at the halal store, and both boys disappeared right after they'd seen him.

"Sayed was a known friend of Tommy's," Byron said. "They frequently hung out together. That's the reason we're looking at him. And we haven't harassed anyone."

"Well, their attorney says he's a good student who has never been in any trouble."

"Good student? He got kicked off the baseball team last year after he was caught selling weed in school. I don't see Harvard in his future, do you?"

"Dammit, John. Must you joke about everything?"

"I'm not going to have some two-bit ambulance chaser torpedo this case, Marty. Tommy Plummer pulled that robbery with somebody. And it had to be someone he trusted. Right now the entire field is in play. If we rule anyone out it will be because the facts support their innocence, not because we were bullied into backing off."

LeRoyer let out a long sigh and swiped his fingers back through his hair. "At least tell me you're making some progress."

"Maybe. I got a late-night visit from my accountant."

"Your accountant?"

"My neighbor Khalid Muhammad. He's friends with Ahmed Ali. Ahmed had asked him to talk to me on his behalf."

"Did he give you anything?"

"No, but it might mean that Ahmed is looking to help us. Even if he has to do it indirectly."

"Well, if you think he knows who the other robber is, let's get him to tell us. Put some pressure on him."

"Oh yeah, I'm sure that will work. Weren't you just whining about us harassing Mohammed Sayed?"

"This is different. Ahmed Ali is an adult. If he knows something he has a responsibility to cooperate."

"You really think it's that simple? Ahmed is trying to take care of his family and run his business. You think he's gonna risk all of that so he can pursue our justice?"

IT HAD BEEN nearly twenty minutes since the big cop entered the grocery store and Vinnie was becoming antsy. He'd had to piss since before leaving the gym. If Haggerty didn't come out of the store soon Vinnie was going to have to chance pissing in public. He was parked at the far end of the lot, affording himself a clear view of the entry and exit doors to Hannaford's Supermarket.

How long does it take to get a few groceries, for fuck's sake? Vinnie thought.

The Mitsubishi was running well. The rear plate was bogus,

stolen from God knew where. And the black primer paint job wasn't as nondescript as he would've preferred, but it was necessary.

Vinnie turned the key in the ignition and the engine fired up. Once idling, it purred without so much as a hitch. He opened the glove compartment and removed the revolver. Only a fiver. Some bullshit chief's special, designed to be hidden easily. He'd have preferred a semiauto, mainly because they held more rounds. But semiautos sprayed shells everywhere, and shells were evidence trails. Vinnie had no intention of getting caught. He set the gun on the seat between his legs, pressed down on the clutch, and slid the car into gear.

This wouldn't be the first time he'd shot someone, but it *would* be his first cop. Slowly he circled the lot, then pulled into the fire zone, facing the supermarket exit doors. He lowered the tinted window on the driver's door several inches, feeling the cold air on his face, and cranked up the stereo. The adrenaline was beginning to flow through him. He inhaled deeply, then slowly released the air from his lungs. Vinnie lived for this.

HAGGERTY WAS STANDING in the checkout line at Hannaford's, waiting for the cashier to scan his groceries, when his cell rang. He recognized Byron's number instantly.

"Hey, Sarge," Haggerty answered.

"Glad to see you're taking calls again," Byron said.

"Yeah. Feeling a little better about things today."

"Glad to hear it. Perspective tends to do that."

"So does a good workout. I figured getting back into the gym would clear my head."

"Did it?"

"Oh yeah."

"What's that beeping sound?" Byron asked.

"I'm at the grocery store. A man's gotta eat, right?"

"That he does. Any more trouble with the press showing up at your house?"

"Nah, I think I've solved that problem for now."

"How so?"

"I moved into my parents' house. It's vacant for the winter and no one is likely to find me there."

"What about the detail?"

"The department is keeping a black-and-white at my house for another day or so to throw media wolves off my scent."

"Smart thinking. So, you're good?"

"I am. Thanks for checking on me last night, Sarge."

"Any time, my friend. Talk soon."

"Roger that."

Haggerty pocketed the phone just as the cashier scanned his last item.

THE COP EXITED the door farthest away from where Vinnie was parked. He was carrying several plastic shopping bags in each hand. *Perfect*, Vinnie thought. Since he already knew where Haggerty had parked, it would be easy to slide up and pop him. Vinnie waited for a vehicle to pass, then he pulled away from the curb. Slowly he cruised along the front of the store. He paused to let an oncoming car pass by, then he took a left, following the cop up a travel lane away from the store toward Preble Street Extension.

Creeping along at less than five miles an hour, he approached Haggerty from behind. The subwoofer was thrumming from the rear of the car. Vinnie reached for the gun, then lowered his window the rest of the way down. He intentionally avoided making eye contact with several pedestrians as they passed, headed toward the store. Vinnie brought the car up alongside his target and stuck the revolver out the window with his left hand. Haggerty turned his head to the right, surprise registering on his face. Vinnie pulled the trigger at precisely the same moment that things went to shit. He fired two rounds at the big cop. Haggerty dropped the bags and dove to his left. Vinnie wasn't sure if the cop was attempting to take cover or if the bullets had found their mark. Before Vinnie could reacquire his target and squeeze off a few more rounds, the Mitsubishi was violently impacted from the right side. A loud bang, then the crunch of sheet metal. The impact jolted him sideways in his seat, knocking the gun from his hand and out onto the pavement. The Mitsubishi's engine stalled.

"*Shit!*" Vinnie yelled. "*Shit, shit!*"

He turned his head to the right to see what had collided with his car. The passenger side windows of the Mitsubishi had spidered. Tinting film was all that held the glass together. The tailgate of a large pickup was pressed solidly against the Mitsubishi, blocking Vinnie's view through the passenger side windows. He scrambled to restart the car. His eyes darted back to the left, searching for the cop, but Haggerty was nowhere to be found. The starter was turning over, but the engine wouldn't catch. Panic set in like something crawling inside him. He twisted the key forward again and pressed the accelerator pedal to the floor. The engine roared to life along with the stereo. The driver of the truck pulled forward, disengaging from the Mitsubishi, causing the much smaller vehicle to shudder. Vinnie jammed the gearshift lever into First and eased off the clutch, trying hard not to stall it.

As the Mitsubishi lurched forward, Vinnie felt intense pain on his left side, like he was being stung by angry wasps. The pain began in his left shoulder, then moved across his chest. He glanced to his left again. The big cop lurched toward the Mitsubishi, firing at Vinnie. Vinnie knew he had to get out of there or he would die where he sat. He mashed the gas pedal to the floor. The squealing of rubber on pavement was deafening as the Mitsubishi's front drive wheel fought for and finally achieved traction. As the car shot forward, Vinnie felt another sharp pain in the back of his left shoulder and neck. Immediately following was the sound of bullets striking the sheet metal of the driver's door.

Vinnie punched the gas as he exited the lot onto Preble Street Extension, nearly striking two other vehicles. The sports car slid sideways toward the curb on the far side of the roadway as he spun the steering wheel hard to the left, then corrected the skid and moved into the passing lane. Still accelerating, he blew through a red traffic light where Preble Street intersected Baxter Boulevard. As he sped toward Forest Avenue, he reached across his body with his right hand and felt something wet and sticky coating his neck. He pulled his hand back and held it up in front of his face. It was covered in blood.

BYRON WAS PULLING into the rear garage of 109 when he heard the familiar signal 1000 tone blast from base radio speaker mounted under the dash of the unmarked. He backed into a space, increased the volume on the radio, then sat with the car idling, waiting until he heard the call. Byron had heard the emergency signal hundreds of times, maybe thousands, during his twenty-plus years on the job, but something about this one in particular, with everything going on in the city, filled him with foreboding.

Amid a crackle of static, the dispatcher began to speak. "Any units in the area of 295 Forest Avenue, Hannaford Plaza, respond along with MedCu Five for a report of shots fired. We have a caller on the line who is reporting that an off-duty police officer is involved. Units responding please acknowledge."

"1 has it."

"102 copies."

"3 copies."

"21 responding from 109."

"Ten-four, 1, 2, 3, and 21."

Byron's hair stood straight up on the back of his neck. There was an unmistakable urgency in each of the responding officer's voices. He put the car in gear and exited the garage. The feeling of dread had intensified a hundredfold.

"21," the patrol sergeant called out, shouting to be heard above his own siren.

"21, go ahead," the dispatcher said.

"21. Find out from the caller if this is still an active scene. I don't want my people driving into an ambush."

"Ten-four, 21," the dispatcher said. "The caller isn't sure what's going on. We're now receiving multiple calls, Sergeant. There's a possibility that there's more than one shooter."

"21 to 101, 2, and 3, did you copy that?"

"Got it, Sarge," one said.

"Copy that," 2 and 3 said, talking over each other.

"21 to Dispatch."

"Go ahead, Sergeant."

"Have some of the Deering units slide over that way until we know for sure what we have. We made need help with the perimeter."

"Ten-four, 21."

As the dispatcher allocated additional resources, Byron used his vehicle's emergency lights and siren to get through the snarl of traffic at Pearl and Congress. It seemed time had slowed to a crawl.

"101, I'm out."

"Ten-four, 101," the dispatcher said.

The driver of the maroon Audi traveling in front of Byron refused to pull to the right. Byron laid on the Chevy's air horn.

"Get out of the way, asshole!" Byron shouted. "Move it! Move it!"

The Audi swerved to the right, nearly striking the curb. Byron roared past him.

"1. Have MedCu step it up! I've got an officer down, multiple gunshot wounds. Advise 21, it's one of ours!"

Byron refused to let off the accelerator even as he approached the elevated intersection at Pearl and Oxford Streets. The Malibu bottomed-out violently on the pavement, jarring his body forward against the seat belt, then hard against the seat back. He momentarily lost contact with the gas pedal as he struggled to regain his footing. Byron punched the accelerator again and the unmarked shot down the hill toward Somerset Street. He already knew who the victim was.

BYRON KNEW IT was bad. Haggerty was drifting in and out of consciousness and he'd lost a great deal of blood.

"Who did this, Hags?" Byron asked, taking his friend's hand. "Who shot you?"

Haggerty's eyes were open, but he was unresponsive. The paramedic looked at Byron for permission to restore the oxygen mask to the officer's face. Byron nodded silently.

"Hang in there, Hags," Byron said. "You hear me, Sean? Keep fighting."

Byron stepped back out of the way as the paramedics quickly loaded Haggerty into the back of the ambulance. Byron wanted nothing more than to climb inside and remain with his friend, but he knew his job was here at the scene where he could do the most good. He had to find out what happened, and locate those responsible. Byron turned his attention to the uniformed officer who'd climbed inside the ambulance and sat down beside the stretcher.

"Stay with him," Byron said. "No matter what."

"You got it, Sarge."

Byron watched the MedCu unit speed away with lights flashing and siren blaring, a black-and-white leading the way and another right on its tail like some high-speed street parade. He'd been listening to the radio traffic and knew that the hospital had a trauma team at the ready. And the staff at the Maine Medical Center ER was as good as they came. For a man who didn't believe in miracles, Byron had seen them bring more than one person back from the brink of death. As he listened to the sirens fade into the distance Byron hoped they had enough magic in the bag to do it one more time.

Unable to get anything out of Haggerty, Byron knew he'd be forced to rely on the remaining witnesses.

His cell buzzed, and he answered it with shaking hands.

"How bad, Sarge?" Stevens asked.

"Bad," Byron said.

"I'm with Nuge. Where do you need us?"

"Hannaford Plaza."

Chapter 19

As SOON AS the detectives arrived they hit the ground running. Byron had Nugent commandeer the security office inside the supermarket. They'd need the surveillance video as soon as possible. Melissa Stevens interviewed a witness. Byron assigned several uniformed officers to tape off and secure the scene, and several more to take statements from bystanders who claimed to have seen the car drive past them prior to the shooting. Byron spoke briefly with the driver of a pickup truck who'd been the victim of a hit-and-run. According to witnesses the pickup had collided with the shooter's vehicle.

"Did you get a good look at the car or the driver?" Byron asked the gangly teenager who reeked of pot.

"I never saw the driver," the kid said. "The windows were tinted."

"What about the car? Make? Model? Color?"

"Flat black. Like primer. Rad stereo."

"What?"

"It had killer bass."

Byron, resisting the urge to grab the kid by the throat while explaining the far more important nonaudiophile points of the investigation, chalked up his lack of focus to the effects of cannabis sativa.

"Did you get the make of the car?" Byron asked again.

The kid smiled proudly. "Yup. A Mitsubishi."

Byron's cell buzzed with a call from Mike Nugent.

"Give me something, Nuge," Byron said.

"Dark-colored two-door. Outbound on Preble Street Extension after leaving the lot. Might be a Mitsubishi."

VINNIE KNEW HE was in trouble, and it wasn't just the white-hot pain radiating throughout his body. His left side was going numb and blood was running down his torso, soaking through his clothing and into the seat. He was growing light-headed and knew if he pulled off the road to hide he might never get moving again. Their plan to flatbed the car out of Portland under the cop's noses was off the table. He had to get back to the garage fast.

The tinted windows, even the two broken ones, turned out to be a blessing as they prevented the other drivers traveling on Route 25 from seeing into the car. One look at him and the Cumberland County emergency switchboards would have lit up like Christmas trees with calls about a dead man driving through Westbrook. Fishing the cellphone out of his pants pocket took nearly every ounce of energy he had, but he finally managed it. He hit the speed dial for Terry's cell with his thumb, smearing blood on the screen in the process. The call went straight to voicemail.

"Shit," he said. Either Terry was on the phone with someone else or he was in a bad cell area with no reception. Vinnie hung up and dialed the number to the garage. One ring. Two. Three.

"Come on! Fucking answer it already."

He knew Jimmy, their part-time desk guy, was there but he also knew what a slacker Jimmy was when no one was around to keep him working. Jimmy was either out back getting high, on his cellphone with his girlfriend, or spending what he called "quality time" in the john.

After losing track of the number of rings, Vinnie hung up. He was thumbing the keypad, attempting to speed dial Terry's cell again, when the phone, already slick with blood, slipped out of his grasp and tumbled onto the floor of the Eclipse.

"*Fuck*," he screamed. He scanned the floor between his legs trying to locate the phone, but he couldn't see it. At the sound of a car horn, his eyes quickly returned to the road in time to see that he had crept over the center line into the path of oncoming vehicles. Vinnie jerked the steering wheel back to the right, just missing a silver-colored Explorer driven by an angry-looking woman who flipped him off as she passed. The sudden movement hurt him badly and he fought to keep from passing out.

There was no way he could reach the phone without stopping the car, and that wasn't an option. The pain intensified each time he inhaled. He was doing his best to keep his breaths shallow. He saw the town line of Westbrook pass into his rearview mirror. He had made it into Gorham. Less than ten miles to the garage now, where he could hide the car and figure out what to do next. Vinnie wasn't prone to prayer, but right now he was making up for lost time, hoping that the Big Guy really did help those who fucking needed it most.

THE HANNAFORD PARKING lot was a bevy of activity, swarming with customers, cops, and witnesses. Despite the chaos, Byron remained all business, directing the investigation from the heart of the action. He had Pelligrosso collecting evidence at the shooting scene, Stevens on statements, and Nugent retrieving the surveillance video. Byron himself had already provided the suspect vehicle description to Dispatch, who in turn had broadcast a regional ATL, both by radio and computer. LeRoyer was standing near the barricades, alternating between talking to reporters and jousting with the business managers who were pissed about how the parking lot being shut down was hurting their businesses. Normally Byron didn't want the press to know anything about his scenes while he was working them, but in this case briefing each of the local television stations was a necessity and the only way to ensure the suspect information got out to the public quickly.

Everything seemed to be well in hand. The one glaring exception was that Byron wasn't at 22 Bramhall Street in the ER watching as the trauma team worked to save his friend's life.

"I can't believe Haggerty was involved in another shooting," LeRoyer said as he approached Byron on foot.

Byron had no trouble believing it, given the current state of the community. The media, along with help from some of the local politicians, specifically Mayor Gilcrest, had whipped Portland into frenzy. Along with generous portions of threats, protests, and public displays of civil disobedience, an attempt on a cop's life was the next logical step in an illogical situation. Byron wondered where things might go from here.

"You think this was payback for the Plummer kid?" LeRoyer asked.

Byron had to admit, on its face the attack had the bitter aftertaste of retribution. But was it for Plummer? Or had the act only been designed to look like payback? Could this attack on Haggerty be related to the OC case the feds were working? It was too early to say. Or perhaps it was retribution, but for something else entirely. What if the shooter had only used an opportunity created by the current crisis? *Never let a crisis go to waste.* Byron couldn't remember where he had heard that particular turn of phrase, but it described the current situation perfectly.

Pelligrosso approached Byron and LeRoyer.

"Anything we can use?" Byron asked.

"We may have recovered the suspect's gun," Pelligrosso said.

"Where did you find it?" Byron asked.

"Lying beneath a parked car. One of the witnesses saw the suspect drop it out the window as the truck backed into the car. The witness pointed it out to Mel."

"Describe it," Byron said as he pulled out his notebook.

"Smith & Wesson .38. Five shot, chief's special. Looks like the suspect managed to fire a couple of rounds at Hags before he dropped it."

"Serial number?"

"Ground off."

Of course it is, Byron thought.

"Well, we can send it to the feds to raise it, right?" LeRoyer asked.

"Sure," Byron said. "Except we don't have six months to wait."

"I'll check it for prints as soon as I can," Pelligrosso said.

"What about Haggerty's gun?" LeRoyer asked, trying again.

"He emptied his Glock," Pelligrosso said. "In addition to the shooter's gun, I've recovered Haggerty's and all of his shell casings."

"Any indication that Haggerty may have hit the suspect?" Byron asked.

"No way to tell. There are a couple of debris fields on the ground. One is Haggerty's groceries and blood; the other seems like it's all from the accident between the suspect's car and the pickup."

"What are the odds that Haggerty would have missed the guy with every shot?" LeRoyer asked.

Pelligrosso shrugged. "Hags is a good shot. But according to the witnesses he'd already been hit, LT. That tends to change the game."

Byron said nothing, but he secretly hoped the piece of shit was bleeding out somewhere. And in a lot of pain.

VINNIE HAD MANAGED to get behind the one driver in all of Buxton who apparently had all day to get where they were going. According to his speedometer they were traveling at least ten under the limit. The pain hadn't departed but mercifully parts of his body had begun to feel numb and detached, as if they belonged to someone else. No one would ever mistake Vinnie for a doctor, but was he fairly confident that his loss of feeling was not a good sign.

He was trying to decide whether he dared pass the silver Buick when the Mitsubishi began to hiccup. All the dashboard warning lights illuminated at the same instant the engine died. He rolled onto the dirt shoulder on the side of the road and stopped. *So much for prayers*, he thought. He wondered how long it would be before a cop pulled up behind him.

"Dammit," he yelled, wasting what little energy he had left and causing his pain to intensify. Vinnie realized he had two choices: find his cell or prepare for life in prison, if he lived that long.

He leaned forward and reached down with his good hand, screaming as he did so. He slid his hand around on the carpet until his fingers touched the side of the phone. Carefully, he grabbed on to it, then sat back in the seat. The steering wheel was now slick with blood. He closed his eyes, trying to catch his breath while he waited for the pain to subside to a bearable level. After a moment or two he carefully keyed in his passcode and hit the redial for Terry's cell.

BYRON STOOD BESIDE Nugent, waiting for the Hannaford store security supervisor to replay the section of video where they had seen Haggerty exit the front of the store. Byron wanted to see where the Mitsubishi had come from. None of the parking lot witnesses had gotten a look at the vehicle's registration, nor had they been able to agree on the number of doors or make of the car. The only thing recalled by every witness was the deep bass of the car's stereo.

Byron looked at the multiple video clips simultaneously playing on the high-definition screen of the multiplexer. He couldn't help but be reminded of the intro to *The Brady Bunch*.

"There," Nugent said, pointing at the lower left image.

As he followed Hags's progress away from the store, Byron's eye was drawn to a different camera angle. The top right view showed what looked to be a dark-colored sports car creeping along the front of the store, then turning to follow Haggerty up the aisle between rows of parked cars. The video wasn't crisp enough to make out the registration. Byron couldn't even tell if it was an Eclipse or not, but it was definitely a two-door.

Byron's body was knotted with tension as he watched the scene unfold. First, the driver of the Mitsubishi could be seen firing in

Haggerty's direction, after which Haggerty either fell or dove, disappearing off camera. Simultaneous to the shooting, a large pickup backed into the Mitsubishi, violently impacting it. Several more seconds passed before anything noteworthy happened. Haggerty reappeared on screen as he approached the shooter's car. His gait was awkward, staggering like one of his legs had fallen asleep. It was clear that he was injured. Haggerty raised his right arm, pointing in the direction of the Mitsubishi. Multiple flashes appeared from the muzzle of Haggerty's gun. The stoner's pickup pulled forward, rocking the Mitsubishi as the two vehicles separated. Haggerty continued to fire his weapon as the Mitsubishi fled the scene out onto Preble Street Extension. The driver never slowed.

A strange combination of grief and nausea swept over Byron as he watched his friend collapse to the pavement. The same friend who at that very moment was fighting for his life at Maine Med. Several bystanders ran to where Haggerty was lying helpless. Not wanting to show weakness to the other people occupying the room, Byron quickly pulled himself together and turned to Nugent.

"Have Dispatch provide you with a list of responding officers," Byron said. "I want the video from each of the cruiser cameras."

Nugent looked confused. "What are we looking for, Sarge? They're only gonna have video of the scene after the shooter fled."

"It's possible that our suspect drove right past one of the responding units. With a little luck we may get a plate number or a look at the suspect's face."

"I'm on it."

TERRY KEPT GLANCING over his shoulder as he operated the winch. After obtaining Vinnie's approximate location, he had driven the wrecker as fast as he dared to Buxton. He'd located the badly damaged Mitsubishi on Route 202 near Hollis Center. One look at Vinnie and he knew there was nothing else to do but leave him in the car and tow it back to the shop.

The Mitsubishi rolled slowly up the flatbed's steeply inclined ramp, leaving a trail of fluid in its wake. Terry didn't care what was leaking out of it, only that they'd get the car out of here. As he was leveling the ramp he saw the familiar profile of a white York County Sheriff SUV come into view, approaching from the opposite direction. His pulse quickened. *Just keep moving*, he thought. *Nothing to see here.*

His legs threatened to buckle as he watched the patrol vehicle slow, then pull up alongside of him. *Shit, shit.*

The SUV stopped, and the driver lowered his window.

"Afternoon," the gray-haired deputy sheriff said. "Whatcha got?"

"Afternoon, Deputy," Terry croaked. He cleared his throat. "Just a broken-down motorist. Triple A call out," he added, thinking it was a nice touch.

"You all set here?" the deputy asked as he looked over at the Mitsubishi.

"Just getting ready to head out. Thanks."

"Anytime, friend," the deputy said as he pulled away with a wave.

Terry returned the wave, then walked on shaky legs back to the front of the truck, waiting to check the progress of the cruiser until he'd reached the cab. As he reached up to open the door he looked back. The patrol vehicle was already a quarter of a mile distant. Terry didn't exhale until after he pulled away from the side of the road and headed back to the garage.

VINNIE SLOWLY CAME to. He felt weaker than he could ever re-member feeling in his entire life. He recognized the crappy faux-wood paneling and old-time pinup posters on the wall. He was lying on the shitty oil-stained couch in the office. A familiar voice floated in from the garage.

"Jesus, you should see him," Terry Alfonsi said. "It's bad. I mean really bad. I think he might be dead."

"I can hear you, asshole," Vinnie croaked. "And I'm not fuck-ing dead."

Terry whipped around the corner. "Oh, thank God."

Vinnie was pretty sure God wasn't involved. "Is that Derrick?" he asked.

"Yeah."

"Let me talk to him," Vinnie said, unsuccessfully trying to raise his left hand. He turned his head to look. The shirtsleeve was dark with blood and there was no feeling in his arm. It was as if the appendage hanging limply off the couch belonged to some-one else. He raised his right hand and took the phone from Terry. "Hey, Der—"

"What the fuck happened?" Derrick asked.

Vinnie struggled to focus. "This a recorded line?"

"No. Actually, they let me out for the day. I'm hanging out by the goddamned pool waiting for a hottie in a bikini to bring me my beer and nachos. Of course it's *fucking* recorded."

Vinnie closed his eyes, waiting for Derrick to stop being a tool. "You done?"

"What happened?"

"He had a piece. Some asshole backed into me before I could finish it."

"Did you get him?"

"I don't know. Maybe."

"Maybe? If I'd wanted maybe, I coulda sent some other dipshit. How bad are you?"

"What did Terry say?"

"He said you're fucked."

Vinnie looked down at his blood-soaked left side. *That's probably accurate*, he thought. "Pretty sure I'm gonna need some medical help."

There was only silence from the other end of the phone. Vinnie began to wonder whether he'd passed out again and was only dreaming the phone call when Vanos spoke up again.

"Sit tight. I got an idea. Put Terry back on the phone."

Vinnie, wondering where Derrick thought he might go, handed the phone to Terry. "He wants to talk to you."

Chapter 20

BYRON HURRIED INTO the emergency room. LeRoyer was pacing back and forth in front of the nursing station.

"Any word?" Byron asked.

LeRoyer shook his head. "Nothing yet. Anything on your end?"

"Gabe is still working the scene. I've got Dustin looking at tape from all the responding cruisers."

"What about the supermarket video?"

"Captured the shooting, but not the driver. And not close enough to see a plate."

"Goddammit," LeRoyer said, swiping at his hair.

Byron silently agreed. "Did all the media outlets put out our ATL?"

"Yeah, all three of the locals cut in on their programming to put out an update. A couple of the radio stations responded as well."

"Good," Byron said. "Dispatch already put out what little we have to the surrounding agencies. NCIC too."

"What do you think?" LeRoyer asked.

"I think they'll be stopping every black Mitsubishi north of Boston."

Byron's cell vibrated with an incoming text from Dustin Tran.

Found it, call me.

Could it be that easy? Byron wondered, knowing full well it never was. He dialed Tran's number, then lifted the phone to his ear. While waiting for his computer wizard to pick up, Byron caught the disapproving eye of an ER nurse standing behind the counter with her arms crossed. The nurse shook her head and pointed at the No Cellphone sign on the wall.

Byron ended the call and turned to LeRoyer. "I'll be outside."

As he reached the parking lot, Byron redialed Tran's cell.

"Hey, Sarge," Tran said.

"Got your text," Byron said. "You sure it's the same car?"

"Positive. One of the cruisers responding by way of Dartmouth Street caught the Mitsubishi on camera just before the driver turned down a side street. Probably trying to avoid being seen."

"Go ahead with the reg," Byron said, pulling out his notebook.

"I can't get it," Tran said. "I tried to enhance some still frames but the car was just too far away."

Byron could hear the disappointment in Tran's voice. But he had provided them with a direction of travel. It would have to do for the time being.

"Good work, Dustin," Byron said. "Do me a favor and call Dispatch. Have them assign any free units to scour that area on the off chance the suspect dumped the car."

"Already done."

BYRON STOOD ACROSS from LeRoyer in the hallway that led to the ER. Byron was working on his third cup of cafeteria coffee when a thirty-something doctor with dark wavy hair came through the automated double doors. The doctor looked exhausted.

"You guys here for the police officer who was shot?" the doctor asked.

Byron tried to get a read from the man's face, but it was a blank page.

"Yeah," LeRoyer said, answering for both of them. "How is he?"

"Too soon to say. I'm Dr. Levesque. My team and I just spent the last two hours working on him. Officer Haggerty is a fighter. Does he have any family waiting? I should really be speaking to them."

"They're on their way," LeRoyer said. "Flying in from out of state."

"Until they get here, we're Sean's family, Doc," Byron said. "What *can* you tell us?"

Levesque looked back and forth at the detectives. Byron knew he was trying to weigh his legal obligation to the patient's privacy against common sense.

At last the surgeon spoke. "He's suffered two gunshot wounds. The first wasn't serious. Caught him in the thigh. Most of the damage was to muscle tissue and I was able to remove the bullet cleanly."

Byron knew Levesque was holding back on the bad news. It

was standard protocol in the medical field. Give the bad news first and people stopped listening.

"And the second?" LeRoyer asked.

"I made the decision to leave the second bullet inside him for now. It is lodged up high in his torso, near the front of his spine. There are too many vital organs around the bullet to justify causing any additional damage to his insides at this point. We've tried to pinpoint and stop his internal bleeding."

"Tried?" LeRoyer asked.

"I've done the best I can," Levesque said.

"When can we talk to him?" Byron asked.

"It won't be for a while, I'm afraid," Levesque said. "We've stabilized him but we're intentionally keeping him sedated right now. Officer Haggerty's body—"

"His name is Sean," Byron said.

Levesque nodded his understanding. "*Sean* has suffered a great deal of trauma. He needs rest. We want to see him get his strength back. Then we'll reassess."

"Level with us, Doc," Byron said. "What are his chances?"

Levesque looked Byron straight in the eye. "Honestly? I don't know. I've done all I can. The rest is up to God."

And Hags, Byron thought.

BYRON WALKED PAST the uniformed officer guarding Haggerty's room in ICU with a silent nod. He entered the room and stood beside the bed. A maze of wires and tubes were connected to Hags. The beeping electronic monitor displayed his pulse and BP and a number of other things Byron didn't fully understand. Looking down at Hags made him feel helpless. He realized that no matter how hard he worked to catch the person responsible for Haggerty being here, Byron had no control over whether his friend would pull through. The doctor had indicated that it was in God's hands now. Byron would have preferred something more tangible to put his faith in, having had it badly shaken so long ago. Despite the doubts, Byron closed his eyes and prayed silently for his friend.

"I find that never hurts," a male voice said, startling Byron out of his thoughts.

He turned to see a nurse who'd come in to check on Haggerty. The young man was olive-complected, with only the slightest remnants of a foreign accent.

"What never hurts?" Byron asked.

"Praying. Only so much we can do. The rest is up to him and whoever he answers to," the nurse said, pointing to Haggerty.

Byron, who said nothing as the nurse went about his work, turned his attention back to Hags. He contemplated what the nurse had said. It made sense. It never really came down to anything more than what each of us chooses to believe.

The irony of Byron's career choice had frequently occurred to him. Like a priest, he was constantly surrounded by death and questions of faith. He also spent much of his time trying to get people to confess their many sins. Unlike a priest, however, Byron could not offer absolution, only incarceration.

Byron wondered if Haggerty's faith was strong enough to get him through this battle. He turned to ask the nurse another question, but the room was empty.

BYRON DEPARTED FROM the hospital and retraced his route back to Hannaford. The uniformed officer guarding Haggerty provided only a small measure of comfort. Byron knew it was unlikely that anyone else would be brazen enough to make an attempt on Haggerty's life but there was someone still on the loose who had. He wanted them located and held accountable.

He had only driven about a half mile from the Maine Medical Center, approaching Park Avenue on Deering, when he heard the dispatcher call his number over the radio.

"720," the dispatcher said.

He keyed the microphone, clipped to the dash, without unhooking it. "720, go ahead."

"Sergeant, we have a York County patrol supervisor on the phone asking to speak with you. If you call in on the nonemergency line, we'll connect the two of you."

"Ten-four."

After making the turn onto Park Avenue, Byron pulled over across from Deering Oaks Park and stopped. He pulled out his cell and dialed Dispatch.

"Police Dispatch, Operator Gostkowski speaking."

"Dale, it's John Byron."

"Hey, Sarge. Hang on a sec and I'll connect you with Sergeant Milliken. Just gotta put you on hold for a minute. Don't hang up, okay?"

"Thanks," Byron said, opening his notebook.

After several moments Gostkowski came back on the line. "Sarge, you still there?"

"Right here," Byron said.

"Okay, you guys should be hitched up. I'll get off the line."

"Sergeant Byron? This is Sergeant Ed Milliken from York SO."

"Sarge, what can I do for you?" Byron asked as he scribbled down the name and time into his case notes.

"Well, I'm not positive but I believe I may have seen the vehicle you guys are looking for."

"The black Mitsubishi?" Byron asked hopefully.

"That'd be the one. I feel bad 'cause I didn't know about it until after."

"After what?"

Milliken explained that the York County computer link to NCIC had crashed. As a result, they never received the ATL sent out by Portland until after he had seen the Mitsubishi. He told Byron the story about the guy who was hauling it away.

"You happen to catch the name of the tow company?" Byron asked.

"I didn't. Sorry. I've already asked our dispatch center to start calling all the local wreckers to see if one of them grabbed it. I remember the driver saying that it was a Triple A tow."

"I don't suppose you've got video in your vehicle?"

"It's being repaired," Milliken said. Byron could hear the embarrassment in the deputy's voice. "I can describe the wrecker and driver for you though."

After taking down the information, Byron said, "Thanks, Ed. I appreciate you reaching out. Can I get you to write that up and email it to me?"

"Will do. How's your officer?"

"He could use some good thoughts."

"I'll send those along too."

Byron hung up and immediately called Dustin Tran to provide him with the wrecker lead.

As BYRON WAS pulling into the Hannaford Plaza from Baxter Boulevard, his phone rang. It was Diane.

"How's it going, John?" she asked.

"Slow. We might have a lead on the last known location of the

Mitsubishi. A York SO sergeant thinks he may have seen it being loaded onto a flatbed in Buxton about forty-five minutes after the shooting."

Byron waited for the officer blocking the way to the scene to wave him through.

"Did he get a plate?" Diane asked. "Or the name of the tow company?"

"He didn't even get the ATL from Dispatch until a half hour later. York County's link to NCIC crashed. What's happening on your end?"

"Hags's parents are scheduled to land at the jetport within the hour. I'm headed out there now to pick them up and bring them to the hospital."

Byron couldn't begin to imagine what kind of emotional roller coaster Haggerty's parents had been riding for the past several days.

"How're you holding up?" Diane asked.

"Talk with you later," he said, ending the call and answering her question simultaneously.

Byron pulled up next to the crime scene tape that had been strung around the area. A dozen or so vehicles were still parked inside it. As he stepped from the unmarked Chevy he glanced toward another of the officers who'd been tasked with keeping the scene secure. The uniform was speaking with several angry-looking people who Byron guessed were the owners of those vehicles. Compassion seemed in short supply.

The double doors to the evidence van stood open and Pelligrosso was loading items into the back.

"Sarge," Pelligrosso said. "How is he?"

"He's out of surgery, in ICU. Find anything more we can use?"

The evidence tech shook his head. "I've recovered all there is. I was just about to release the scene. You good with that?"

Byron surveyed the area. "Yeah, if you are." He caught the attention of one of the uniformed officers and signaled him to take down the tape. The officer shot him a thumbs-up and began to do just that.

Byron looked back at Pelligrosso. "The surgeon said he removed one of the slugs from Hags. Why don't—"

"Already sent Murph up to the hospital to retrieve it."

"Thank you, Gabe."

TWILIGHT HAD FADED to black by the time Byron returned to 22 Bramhall Street. He parked in his favorite no-parking zone near the front entrance to the hospital and walked inside.

Byron found the lieutenant pacing the hall just outside of the ICU.

"Hey, John," LeRoyer said.

"Any change?" Byron asked.

"No. His parents are in with him now."

Byron studied LeRoyer's tired face. He'd never noticed just how old his boss was beginning to look. Crow's-feet had imbedded themselves at the outside corners of his eyes and a permanent vertical frown line was tattooed onto his forehead just above his nose. Byron knew how much of a toll his own job took, and he wondered how much harder it was for the lieutenant.

"Gabe still working the scene?" LeRoyer asked.

"Just finished."

"Any leads?"

Byron filled him in on the York County contact. "And I've got a half dozen detectives taking calls and running down leads."

LeRoyer nodded.

"I'm gonna head down to the cafeteria for a coffee," Byron said. "You want anything?"

"A coffee might be nice."

"Want anything in it?"

"How about ten extra shots of caffeine?" LeRoyer said, forcing a grin.

"I'll see what I can do."

BYRON WAS SEATED in an uncomfortable molded plastic-and-metal chair in the ICU hallway. He was on his cell checking his office voicemail remotely when his phone buzzed with an incoming call from Melissa Stevens.

"Sarge, I think we might have something," the detective said, sounding breathless.

"Go with it."

"I just took a call from a kid who works at a gas station in Standish, right near the Buxton town line. Says he sold gas to a guy a day or two ago and the guy was driving a primer-black Mitsubishi with a loud exhaust. He said he could smell paint, like the primer had just been applied."

"Did he get a plate?"

"No, but the station has video. Nuge and I are headed out there now."

"Good work, Mel. Anything else?"

"Yeah. The attendant thinks he might even know the guy."

"Keep me posted."

Byron was pocketing the phone when he observed a well-dressed man approaching him from the far end of the hall. He'd noticed the silver-haired man speaking with LeRoyer before heading in Byron's direction. Byron stood up and turned to face him.

"Excuse me," the man said, reaching him at last. "Are you Sergeant Byron?"

"I am," Byron said.

"I'm James Haggerty," he said, extending his hand. "I want to thank you for all you've done for my son, Sergeant."

Haggerty, who appeared to be well into his sixties, had the deeply tanned skin of a Floridian and sad eyes. Byron could clearly see the resemblance to Sean. He shook the elder Haggerty's hand firmly but had no idea what to say. He didn't feel like he had managed to *do* anything. He hadn't located the second robber or the gun, and now he was struggling to find Haggerty's attacker.

"I'm very sorry about your son," Byron said. It was all he could think to say.

"Thank you."

"We're all pulling for him," Byron added. He wanted to say *praying* but couldn't quite bring himself to do it.

"My son talks about you frequently. He told me this morning about your visit to his house last night."

Byron, not knowing how much Hags had shared with his father, remained silent.

"Your friendship means a great deal to Sean, Sergeant Byron. He looks up to you."

Byron nodded even as he grappled with his emotions. There was a brief and somewhat awkward pause in the conversation.

"Well, I don't want to keep you," Haggerty said. "I know you're busy. I just wanted to thank you for being a friend to Sean."

Byron wanted to tell him that Hags was going to be okay. He

wanted to assure him that they would find the person responsible for shooting Sean and bring him to justice. He wanted to promise they would find the other robbery suspect, and the gun, and would clear Sean's name. But he couldn't say any of those things. As bad as they all wanted things to work out, it didn't always go that way. Good didn't always triumph over evil. Byron took the hand that was offered and shook it again.

"It was good to meet you, sir," Byron said.

Haggerty gave Byron a weak smile, then turned and walked back down the hallway.

Chapter 21

Friday, 5:35 P.M.,
January 20, 2017

Detectives Melissa Stevens and Mike Nugent stood crammed inside the tiny back office of the Standish Fill 'er Up. They waited impatiently as the pimply faced young clerk ran back and forth alternating between tending the register and helping the detectives review the security video from two days prior.

"Sorry about that," the attendant said as he returned to the office. "This is the busiest it has been all week."

"Typical," Nugent growled.

The clerk gave Nugent a puzzled look, while Stevens gave the detective a threatening one.

"Not a problem," Stevens said. "We really appreciate the help."

"Okay, this is it."

On the video screen a flat-black Mitsubishi two-door coupe pulled up to the pumps, exactly as the clerk had described on the phone. A lone white male was at the wheel. Stevens flipped out her notebook, jotting down the time and date that was stamped on the recording.

"How did he pay?" Nugent asked. "Credit?"

"Nope. It was a cash transaction. Sorry."

"On the phone you said you might know the guy," Stevens said.

"Well, I don't actually know him, but I've seen him a few times."

"Where?" she asked.

"I think he drives a wrecker for one of the local companies."

"Which one?" she asked, praying that he'd actually know.

"I can't remember."

Nugent spoke up. "Is this the only camera angle you have?"

"No. We have one that gets 'em leaving in case of drive-offs."

Nugent gave Stevens an eye roll followed by a "what the hell is this kid's problem" look. She ignored him.

"May we see it?" Stevens asked.

BYRON WAS STANDING outside the hospital's ambulance entrance in the cold, conversing by cell with Pelligrosso, when the connection broke up with an incoming call. He pulled the phone away from his ear to check the ID. It was Stevens again.

"Gabe, I got a call coming in from Mel. Call me back if you get anything."

"Will do."

Byron switched to Stevens's call. "Hey, Mel."

"Sarge, we've got a plate."

"Go."

Stevens read off the plate and Byron copied it into his notebook.

"Who is it registered to?" Byron asked.

"Well . . ."

Byron shook his head. "Tell me."

"The plate hasn't been used for several years. Actually, it expired five years ago in 2012. It was registered to a guy named Clifford Andrews out of North Berwick."

Byron continued to scribble notes that only he would ever be able to decipher. "I'm assuming by your tone that Andrews isn't our shooter."

"I highly doubt it. The guy has no criminal history, and he's in his eighties."

"Go ahead with his current address," Byron said.

"Um, he lives in Bradenton, Florida."

Byron could feel the tension rising from every part of his body, meeting at the big knot forming at the back of his neck. One step forward, two steps back. It was infuriatingly predictable. "Did you find a phone number to go with the address?" he asked.

"No," Stevens said. "Couldn't locate one. You want me to contact the PD in Bradenton?"

"Yeah. Have them pay Mr. Andrews a visit. Find out what happened to that plate. See if he knows who might be using it now."

"I'm on it."

Byron hung up and headed back inside the hospital to update LeRoyer.

TWENTY MINUTES LATER, after realizing he wasn't doing anything useful at the hospital, Byron returned to 109 to meet with his detectives.

Tran had commandeered a desk in CID to be nearer to the detectives who'd been assigned to work the phones for leads, Luke Gardiner among them. Nugent was talking on his phone but gestured that he wouldn't be much longer. Rather than wait, Stevens and Tran followed Byron into the conference room to bring him up to speed.

"What happened in Florida?" Byron asked. "Did we have any luck locating Andrews?"

"We did," Tran said. "Or rather Bradenton PD did. Turns out Clifford Andrews had an accident in York County, Maine, back in 2010. The plate we're looking for was attached to the car he was driving when the accident happened."

"Who has it now?" Byron asked, attempting to hide his impatience.

"Andrews claims he doesn't know," Stevens chimed in. "I talked to him on the phone. He said his car was towed. The insurance company declared it a total loss."

Maine law required that registration plates no longer in use be returned to the state for reissue. But Byron knew that this requirement was rarely enforced; often, plates ended up hanging on someone's garage walls as a memento or as building material for craft projects, like birdhouses. Anywhere but where they were supposed to be.

"Who towed the car?" Byron asked.

"Marcotte Automotive," Nugent said as he entered the room, waving his notepad. "I just got off the phone with York SO. They investigated the crash in 2010. No one at the sheriff's department had a key to records. I told the on-duty CO why we needed the information and he broke into Records to get it. How's that for customer service?"

"Okay, let's contact the owner of Marcotte," Byron said.

"You can't," Nugent said. "According to Lieutenant Wiggins they went out of business six years ago, after the owner died."

Byron couldn't believe they'd hit a dead end so quickly. He took a moment to consider their next move, running the scenario through his head. "The assets," he said finally. "Find out what happened to the building and all of the equipment. They must have records."

"I'm on it, boss," Tran said as he snapped his fingers and began typing furiously on the keyboard to the laptop in front of him.

Detective Luke Gardiner entered the room.

"Any leads sound promising?" Byron asked.

Gardiner shook his head. The disappointment in his expression said it all. "A dozen calls so far. Mostly whack jobs."

Byron knew how badly Gardiner wanted to be out on the street where the action was, but handling the incoming leads was every bit as important. You never knew when the one tip you needed might come in, or how.

The sound of a desk phone ringing drifted in from the other room. Gardiner hurried out to answer it.

"Stay on it, Luke," Byron called after him.

BYRON RETREATED TO the plaza outside 109 in search of fresh air and privacy. The cold was invigorating, helping him to think more clearly. He was running down a mental checklist of things they had already done, searching for gaps, when his cell rang.

"Byron."

"John. It's Sam Collier."

Byron's defenses kicked in immediately. "Tell me this isn't connected to your case, Sam."

"I'm not sure, but I need to talk with you. Where are you?"

Five minutes later Special Agent Collier's unmarked pulled up in front of 109. Byron climbed in.

"How is Officer Haggerty?" Collier asked as he put the car in gear and drove west on Middle Street.

"I don't know. Doc says he took two rounds. They were able to remove one, but the other—What haven't you told me?"

"John, you know I'm not calling the shots on this OC thing. I'm just a grunt, like you."

"I'll be sure and mention that to Sean's parents. I'm sure your burden will mean a lot to them." Byron could see that his words had wounded Collier, but at the moment he was incapable of caring.

They continued west past Temple Street where Middle turned into Spring Street. Collier pulled into a vacant space at the side of the road and parked.

Collier turned in his seat to face Byron. "These are bad guys we're dealing with, John. I can tell you that the family running this is an out-of-state syndicate. They are into everything. We've got cases that overlap in multiple field offices."

"Micky Cavallaro is some made guy?"

Collier shook his head. "No. We don't think so. He's a boob with a functioning business and a gambling problem. We think he got into debt with these people and they made him an offer he couldn't refuse."

"So, they're using his business as a front for moving drugs into the high school."

"Not just the high school. And his isn't the only business."

"And you think Haggerty is involved?"

Collier sighed. "He's not involved the way you think."

"The way I think? Your buddy so much as said it."

"That was Lessard's call, not mine. He wanted to throw you off the scent so you wouldn't know Haggerty was working with us."

"What the hell are you talking about, Sam?"

It took ten minutes for Collier to lay out the background. They'd approached Haggerty as soon as he had been named the new school resource officer for Portland High. He'd been sworn in as a special deputy U.S. Marshall for the sole purpose of gathering intel for the FBI while acting as SRO.

"Did the PPD command staff know about this?" Byron asked.

"No. No one in your department knew."

"Did Sean know you were looking at the Bubble Up Laundromat?"

"His case knowledge was limited. We informed him about the drugs coming into the school and the fact that there might be an inside man behind it, but that's all. He reported directly to me."

Byron's cell buzzed with an incoming text from Dustin Tran. Got the asset info.

"I gotta go back, Sam. We may have a lead on the guy who shot Hags."

Collier pulled out of the parking space and made a U-turn back to 109. "I don't know if it will help you at all, but Cavallaro paid a visit to the Windham Correctional Center on Monday."

"Who did he visit?"

"I don't know. We couldn't risk blowing our surveillance detail to find out."

AFTER COLLIER DROPPED him back at 109, Byron gathered his team in the conference room for a briefing.

"The assets of the Marcotte Automotive business were sold at auction," Tran said. "The name of the buyer was Derrick Vanos, DBA Vanos Automotive."

"Vanos—why do I know that name?" Byron asked as he navigated his way through a foggy memory.

"Derrick Vanos," Stevens said. "A real asshole. He was charged with and subsequently convicted of elevated aggravated assault after nearly beating to death a guy by the name of William Johnson, in the Old Port."

"Why don't I remember this?" Byron asked as he racked his brain for details.

"It was about five years ago. You were out of state at the time, Sarge," Stevens said. "A training or something. Sergeant Peterson handled it. CID didn't have much to do on that particular case anyway. The arresting officer witnessed the attack."

Facts of the case began to materialize inside Byron's head. "A bar on Free Street, right?"

Stevens nodded. "DaVinci's."

"So Vanos is already out?"

"No," Tran said. "He's still inside. Currently serving time at the correctional center in Windham."

Byron felt his insides roiling. Collier might not know who Cavallaro had met at the prison, but Byron was pretty sure he did.

Nugent piped up. "We think the guy that the gas station jockey saw driving the Mitsubishi might be a wrecker operator for Vanos."

"Which might also explain what the sheriff saw," Stevens said.

"I still don't see what any of this has to do with Hags," Byron said.

"Hags was the arresting officer on the Vanos case," Nugent said.

THE VANOS LEAD generated a flurry of activity. The Portland Police Special Reaction Team was called out to be part of a joint detail with the York County Sheriff's Department's own SRT to apprehend Haggerty's assailant, whoever he might be.

Byron wasn't surprised to see the extent of interagency cooperation. The shooting of a brother or sister officer tends to bring out the best of every agency. An attack on one officer is like an attack on the entire law enforcement family. The petty and childlike territoriality that often exists within the LE community simply vanishes. No longer worried about who will get the credit, or foot the bill, everyone wants to help. And it was likely the reason Collier had approached Byron again. Both the Buxton Police Department and the York County Sheriff's Department were eager to assist. Buxton PD's headquarters was chosen as the site of the command post, mainly due to its proximity to the Vanos property.

As the two SWAT teams began to prep for the operation, Byron performed his own break-in to the PPD records on the second floor of 109. It wasn't that detectives weren't allowed access to the reports within Records; it was more that the manager of the division ruled her domain with an iron fist. If a report got misfiled, there would be hell to pay by the offending party.

The Vanos attempted murder case file had already been relegated to the narrow storage area next to Records where the older reports were kept, which of course required a second surreptitious entry on Byron's part. Five years might not seem like a long time, but in a city the size of Portland, five years' worth of police reports took up a lot of space.

Byron kept control of the investigation while LeRoyer and his command counterparts focused on the apprehension, which of course meant micromanaging the SRT. Byron almost felt sorry for the members of the team. Mike Nugent and Luke Gardiner headed to the Windham Correctional Center to follow up on any recent activity on the part of the elder Vanos while Byron remained in Buxton with Stevens and Tran, sifting through the reports and gathering intel on the entire Vanos clan.

Another whiteboard, not unlike the one hanging in the CID conference room at 109, was utilized as the data display board for all relevant intel. Dustin Tran and Melissa Stevens were preparing to brief the members of the joint apprehension team when Byron walked into the conference room.

"You ready?" Byron asked the detectives.

"I think so," Stevens said.

"Born ready, Striped Dude," Tran said.

It was the first glimpse Byron had seen of his young computer virtuoso's former arrogant self since the laundromat robbery. Byron imagined the change was largely due to Tran's renewed potential to add something helpful to the case, or more specifically the attack on Haggerty. Seldom did the detectives stop and think about how much Tran and his abilities meant to their cases. Out of sight, out of mind. But often Dustin Tran was essential.

Byron was anxiously awaiting word from Nugent. He checked his cell for text messages. Nothing. Nugent's prison snitch had come through before, but this wasn't just another case. This was the attempted murder of one of their own.

DETECTIVES NUGENT AND Gardiner sat across from Delbert Franklin, a squirrelly looking inmate with oily skin and a single clump of hair located at the top of his forehead, giving him the unmistakable comedic appearance of Charlie Brown.

"Derrick Vanos," Nugent said matter-of-factly. "Know him?"

Franklin looked around the room before answering, as though someone might be watching them in the closed office. "Yeah, I know him."

"I understand he had a visitor the other day," Nugent continued.

"Some big old guy named Micky."

"You know who he is?"

"Nope."

"Know what they talked about?"

Franklin grinned, knowingly. "I mighta heard something."

Nugent had performed this dance with Franklin too many times to count. It was a part of their ritual. Nugent knew that if Franklin had information he would be fit to burst if he didn't share it with someone. But Franklin loved to play the part of the apprehensive con, wanting to feel like he was in control. Nugent didn't have the luxury of patience this time. The clock was ticking.

"We go back a ways, don't we, Del?"

Franklin kept grinning even as he nodded.

"You know I'd love nothing more than to sit here and bullshit with you about this, but I'm out of time. I need to know what you know about Vanos's visit. And I need to know right now."

"Gonna get tough with me, Detective?"

Nugent placed his elbows on the desk and leaned forward. "You have no idea."

Franklin flinched. His grin vanished.

THE CONFERENCE ROOM inside Buxton PD looked suspiciously like a place from which the Buxton town hall meetings might have been broadcast. Byron stood leaning a shoulder against the far wall of the room as Lieutenant LeRoyer, Lieutenant Price, Damon Roberts, and a dozen or so other men dressed in black fatigues spilled in. Price was the commander of Portland's SRT, Roberts the department hostage negotiator.

After everyone was seated and the introductions had been made, Tran laid out the intel to the audience.

"Some of you have been partially briefed already, but for the sake of those just getting here I will lay out the up to the moment info." Tran pointed to the large color photograph hanging at the center of the whiteboard. "We have reason to believe that the attack on Officer Sean Haggerty was both deliberate and orchestrated by this man. Derrick Vanos. Derrick is currently serving his fifth year of a ten-year sentence for elevated aggravated assault after nearly beating a young man to death using brass knuckles in Portland's Old Port. Vanos is affiliated with an outlaw biker gang that calls itself The Enforcers. I don't have a lot of information on the group, only that they formed in the late '90s and that they are based out of Harrison, Maine. As the name implies, they aren't averse to using violence to get things done."

Byron noted that several members of the audience were familiar with the gang as evidenced by their exchanged glances and bobbing heads. He also noticed Tran's voice cracking occasionally. Tran hated public speaking.

Tran paused a moment for water before continuing. "We know that Derrick received a visitor at the prison in Windham earlier this week. The visit came just after Haggerty shot and killed a Portland High teenager named Tommy Plummer, who was fleeing an armed robbery."

One of the York County men, sporting a blond flattop, raised his hand. Byron didn't recognize him.

"You have a question?" Tran asked.

"Two actually," Flattop said. "Why would Vanos go after Haggerty for killing a Portland kid? Did he know Plummer?"

Byron stepped in, answering the question for Tran. "We don't have any reason to believe that Vanos knew Plummer. We think Vanos might be using the shooting and the community uprising that followed to his advantage. Much like the Dallas sniper who shot a dozen police officers during a Black Lives Matter protest, killing five, we think he wanted to use the discord as cover, enabling him to seek retribution on Haggerty. Haggerty was the officer who arrested Vanos after witnessing the assault."

"Tran said someone paid a visit to Vanos in prison," Flattop said. "Is it possible that someone else put him up to this?"

Before Byron could answer, the door opened and Nugent and Gardiner hurried into the briefing.

"Vanos was probably hired to kill Haggerty," Nugent said, turning every head in the room.

"What?" LeRoyer asked. "How do you know that?"

"We just came from the prison, Lieu. One of the inmates overheard Derrick Vanos talking during a visit the other day. He didn't hear the entire conversation, but he heard enough to know they were planning a hit on a Portland officer. And Derrick specifically mentioned Haggerty."

"Jesus," LeRoyer said.

"And that's not all," Nugent said. "Vanos's visitor was Micky Cavallaro."

"The laundromat owner?" LeRoyer asked.

"None other."

"Let's get some uniforms to pick that asshole up," Byron said.

"Already made the call, boss," Gardiner said.

Byron made a mental note to strangle Special Agent Sam Collier as soon as this was over.

"So, who is the shooter?" Lieutenant Price asked.

Tran pointed to Vanos's photograph again. "We think the shooter might be a relative of Derrick's. Possibly a nephew. We don't have a name yet, only that he may at one time have been employed under the table by Derrick Vanos."

"What about the getaway car?" asked another man. "Have you found it?"

"No," Byron said. "We believe it may have been towed, then hidden inside the Vanos garage. Also, based on witnesses to the shooting at Hannaford, there's a good chance that some of the rounds fired by Haggerty may have struck the shooter."

A dark-haired man with an air of intensity about him, seated directly behind Flattop, raised his hand. "Have you checked out all the hospitals?"

"Yes," Byron said, resisting the urge to be sarcastic. "We've contacted every hospital in Southern Maine. No one has been treated for bullet wounds, so far."

Lieutenant Price chimed in. "We've already got snipers and spotters set up on the perimeter of the Vanos property. No one has come in or gone out in the past hour."

Byron spoke up again. "We're hoping that they'll either leave the garage to seek medical attention or call someone to respond to the garage to treat the shooter."

Price's cell chimed with an incoming text message. He read the message, then looked over at Byron. "Looks like they went with option number two. A pickup driven by a large white male just drove onto the grounds. The guy entered the garage carrying a duffle bag."

"Let's get out there," LeRoyer said.

THE DRUGS HAD lessened Vinnie's pain, but he still felt weak as hell.

"What do you think, Doc?" Vinnie asked Buddy Dixon. Dixon was a former army medic, and a friend of Derrick Vanos.

"You've lost a lot of blood," Dixon said. "I've stopped the external bleeding, but you've probably got some internal stuff that I can't fix."

Terry looked on nervously. "Jeez, you were a medic, right? Just take out the friggin' bullets."

Dixon frowned. "If it was that simple, don't you think I would have done it already? This guy's got enough lead in him to start his own ammo business. I count at least five holes going in. Looks like only one made it out. He needs a surgeon. And he needs blood."

Vinnie looked up at Dixon. "I'm screwed, aren't I?"

"You are unless you go to a hospital," Dixon said. He turned to Terry. "He's also gonna need antibiotics to fight off infection."

"Fuck," Terry said. "I knew this was a bad idea."

MICKY CAVALLARO FLICKED off the basement lights to the Bubble Up, then set the alarm. He stepped outside, then locked the dead bolt on the steel security door. He turned and scanned the darkened dooryard. With exception of his Cadillac, the small dirt employee lot was empty. He pressed a button on his key fob and saw the parking lights flash as the doors unlocked. Warily he walked the thirty feet across the lot to his car.

He was reaching for the handle on the driver's door when he smelled it. Smoke from a cigarette. Cavallaro spun around.

"Hello, Mick," Alexander Bruschi said, pointing a gun at him. "Nice night for a drive."

Before Cavallaro could respond, an expensive-looking SUV pulled up and blocked the entrance to the lot.

Bruschi nodded in the direction of the SUV. "They're with me."

Cavallaro's mouth was dry. He tried to speak but only managed a croaking sound.

Bruschi's eyes narrowed. "Get in."

Chapter 22

BUDDY DIXON HAD traveled less than a mile from the Vanos garage when he noticed the headlights in his rearview. A vehicle was closing on him rapidly. He continued to recheck the mirror until the trailing car was right on his bumper. He was still trying to decide if the car was bad news for him, or if it was simply some yahoo out for a nighttime joyride, when the strobes and flashing headlights lit up, momentarily blinding him and illuminating the cab of his truck. He glanced over at the left side mirror and saw a second vehicle emerge from behind the first. Then a third police car appeared ahead of him, its lights also flashing, perpendicular to the roadway, blocking him in.

Fuck, he thought. *Cops must have had the garage under surveillance.* Dixon slowed, then pulled the truck onto the gravel shoulder and stopped.

Having once served as a military police officer, Dixon knew

the drill. This would be a felony stop, replete with commands and weapons pointed at him. He killed the ignition, turned on the interior dome light, then placed both of his hands atop the steering wheel. Experience had taught him that compliance with lawful orders went a long way toward reducing the nervousness of those issuing them.

"Driver," an electronically amplified voice said from somewhere behind the lights. "Place both of your hands out through the window. Do it now!"

Dixon did as he was instructed. *Fuck*, he thought again.

THIRTY MINUTES LATER Byron sat across from the stoic ex-soldier, trying to decide if Dixon was being truthful or not. The two men were occupying what passed for an interview room inside Buxton PD, although the presence of shelves and metal file cabinets betrayed its actual purpose as a storage room. Dixon looked back at Byron without speaking; his expression was muted.

If he's nervous, he doesn't show it, Byron thought. Perhaps Dixon's involvement was as limited as he had led them to believe.

"So, you're saying that's all you know?" Byron asked.

"That's it. I told you everything. Derrick's nephew, Terry, called me. Said he needed my help for some medical emergency. I told him to call an ambulance. He said he couldn't."

"Did he tell you what the emergency was?"

"No," Dixon said, arching his back until it made an audible popping sound. "I had no idea until I got to the garage."

"And you just dropped what you were doing and went to go help a guy you'd never met."

"I was doing a favor for an army buddy's nephew."

"That's right. And when was the last time you spoke with your good buddy Derrick?"

"It's been years."

"Hard for me to believe, Mr. Dixon."

"That's because you never served, Sergeant."

Byron's cell rang. He reached for it to silence the ringer but noticed that the incoming call was from Pelligrosso.

"Hey, Gabe," Byron said, maintaining eye contact with Dixon, hoping to rattle the man. "You got something?"

"Sarge, I lifted some good prints from the gun, and the rounds inside it."

"Locate a match?"

"They belong to a guy named Vincent Knauer."

"Who's he?" Byron asked.

"Pretty long sheet. Mostly violent crime. Agg. assault, terrorizing, and weapon possession."

"Can you send me a photo?"

"Check your text messages," Pelligrosso said. "I already sent it."

Byron ended the call and pulled up the picture his evidence tech had forwarded. He looked across the table at Dixon. "Tell me again how many people are inside the garage?"

"Just two. Terry Alfonsi and the guy who's all shot up. Terry called him Vinnie, I think."

"The guy you say you've never met before tonight."

The two men sat staring at each other in silence, each sizing up the other.

"If I were you, I probably wouldn't believe me either," Dixon said at last. "But it's true. I've never met the guy before tonight."

Byron leaned forward and reached across the table, holding out his cell screen for Dixon to see. "Recognize this guy?"

"That's him," Dixon said matter-of-factly.

"Who?" Byron asked, looking to make the ID airtight.

"The guy with Terry. The one who's all shot up. How did you guys do that so fast?"

"Either of them armed?" Byron asked.

Dixon shrugged. "No idea. Guess if they had one gun they probably have others."

"Tell me again how you left it with them."

"I said I was going to try and find an open pharmacy. See if I could find more first aid supplies to help him."

"When did you tell them you'd be back?"

"As soon as I could."

"What did you do for him while you were there?" Byron asked.

"I stopped the bleeding and bandaged him up as best I could. He's in a lot of pain. Told him he needed surgery."

"Did you give him anything for the pain?"

Dixon didn't answer.

"Well?" Byron said.

"What would you have done, Sergeant?" Dixon asked.

Byron ignored the question. He reached across the table and picked up Dixon's cellphone. It was unlocked. He went into the call history, then held up the phone for Dixon to see. "Is this the phone number Terry called you from?"

Dixon looked at it, then nodded.

"Will he respond if you send him a text?"

"I guess."

THE WALL-MOUNTED TELEVISION was on, but the volume was turned down. Terry sat behind the office desk fidgeting with a squeaky-hinged staple remover while he watched Vinnie from across the room. The wounded man was pale and sweating profusely. Thinking back to what Dixon had said, Terry wondered if maybe infection had already begun to set in. He didn't know much about medicine, but he knew what a dying man looked like.

Terry's phone vibrated in his shirt pocket. He slid it out and read the text from Dixon. Tell V u r going outside 4 a smoke, then call me.

"Who's that?" Vinnie asked.

Terry felt his stomach turn as he looked up from his phone at Vinnie. He hadn't realized that Vinnie was paying attention to what he was doing. "My girlfriend," he lied. "She's needy."

"Get a new one," Vinnie said matter-of-factly.

Terry laughed nervously. He hoped it didn't sound as forced as it felt. He stood up and exaggerated the act of stretching. "I'm gonna go outside and call her. I need a smoke anyway."

Vinnie eyed him suspiciously. "Don't be talking shit to her about this. Got me?"

"'Course not. What do you think, I'm stupid?"

Vinnie didn't answer but he kept his eyes on Terry.

Terry grabbed his grubby field jacket and wool hat off the wall peg and headed for the door. "You gonna be okay?"

"Don't I look it?"

LEROYER STARED AT the picture on Byron's cellphone. "Is this the guy we think shot Hags?"

"Nothing gets by you, Marty," Byron said, too tired to stop himself. The SRT commander, Lieutenant Price, who stood with them, tried unsuccessfully to suppress a grin.

LeRoyer fixed Byron with a watch-yourself stare. But it was obvious that he also was too tired to engage in any verbal jousting with his detective sergeant.

"Who is he?" LeRoyer asked.

"Vincent Knauer," Byron said. "A longtime friend of Derrick Vanos. Looks like he works as a body man for Derrick's nephew, Terry. Dixon confirmed that this is the guy all shot up."

"Jesus," LeRoyer said. "What the hell is this world coming to?"

Byron, having recently pondered that very question, remained silent.

"Did Dixon shed any more light on why Knauer did it?" LeRoyer asked.

"Dixon said they didn't go into detail with him. He was contacted by Terry Alfonsi because of his army medic experience. Any word on Cavallaro?"

"I just spoke with Dispatch," LeRoyer said. "He's not at home and the business is locked up tight. They put out an ATL on his car."

Byron wondered if Collier's people were still sitting on him.

The detectives turned at the staccato sound of a status update coming in by radio from a member of the advance team.

"Copy that," Price said in response to the transmission. He addressed Byron and LeRoyer. "Here's the latest on the layout of the building. The office, where our intel tells us the targets are holed up, is at the front right corner of the building. The office windows have been covered over with something like painted plywood and we can't see inside. So, we only have Dixon's word that there are only two men in there."

"Have we located the Mitsubishi yet?" Byron asked.

"It's behind the garage, sitting up on a flatbed wrecker. They made a half-assed attempt at covering it with a plastic tarp."

"Bastards," LeRoyer said.

Lieutenant Price continued. "One of our spotters confirmed the presence of a blood trail leading from the driver's door toward the building."

"Good," LeRoyer said. "I hope he's in some serious fucking pain."

"So how do you want to do this?" Byron asked.

They waited while Price thought it over. "Let's make the approach out in the open."

"Are you crazy?" LeRoyer asked. "Those two guys are likely to come out firing."

Given the circumstances, Byron wondered if that would really be such a bad thing.

"Not if we drive up in Dixon's truck," the commander said.

WHEN TERRY ALFONSI reentered the office, Vinnie was sitting up on the couch. He was slouched awkwardly to one side, still in obvious pain, but he was sitting.

"How was she?" Vinnie asked.

"Who?" Terry said, momentarily forgetting his lie.

"Your girlfriend. You said you were going outside to call her, right?"

"Yeah. Yeah, she's good. Just wondering where I was."

Vinnie eyed him suspiciously. "What did you tell her?"

"I—I told her I was working late, is all."

"Why so nervous, Terry?" Vinnie said. "You didn't do anything stupid like tell her what is going on here, did you?"

"Of course I didn't."

"I hope not, for your sake." Vinnie patted the butt of the stainless semiauto sticking up out of the waistband of his jeans, grimacing as he did.

"Where did you get that?" Terry asked. "I thought you said you dropped the gun at Hannaford."

"I always keep another one stashed here. Never know when I might need it. Never know when someone will try and fuck me."

Terry swallowed nervously.

"What the hell is keeping that guy?"

"Dixon? I'm sure he'll be back soon."

Vinnie looked at him appraisingly. "You sure seem to have all the answers tonight, Terry."

Terry could feel Vinnie's eyes trying to bore inside of him to see what he was thinking. It was almost as if Vinnie really could read his thoughts.

"In case you've forgotten, you're up to your ass in this too," Vinnie said. "If I go down for shooting a cop, you will too."

Terry swallowed again.

BYRON STOOD INSIDE the crowded mobile command post as the SRTs for both departments headed toward the target. The tight space was standing room only as the detectives listened to the radio updates. The SRT had already positioned several snipers with night vision scopes in the woods around Vanos Automotive. The entry team was moving into place.

Following a burst of static, the lowered voice of Lieutenant Price came over the radio. "Alpha One to CP."

"CP, go," the York County communications specialist seated in front of Byron said.

"Team two is in position."

"Ten-four, Alpha One. Alpha Mobile copy?"

"Alpha Mobile en route. Two minutes out."

The young communications specialist swiveled in his chair to address Byron. "Here we go, Sarge."

Byron badly wanted to be out at the scene. There, he might make a difference. Packed sardine-like inside the command post, he felt helpless. *What if this goes sideways and another cop gets hurt?* he thought. Or worse still, *What if Haggerty's assailant slips through the noose and goes on a cop-killing rampage?* He knew it was foolish to think that way, especially with snipers in place, but he couldn't quite seem to quiet the voices inside his head.

"YOU'RE BLEEDING AGAIN," Terry said, pointing at Vinnie's bandages.

Vinnie looked down at the blood-soaked rags. "Fuck," he said. "Dixon will have to replace those."

"Ya think?"

Both men's heads swiveled at the sound of an approaching vehicle.

"Check and see who it is," Vinnie said.

Terry got up and went to the window. He slid the plywood to one side, just enough to allow him to peek outside at the parking lot. "It's him."

"About goddamned time," Vinnie said.

Terry replaced the board and returned to his seat behind the desk.

They both heard the front door open followed by the sound of Dixon stomping the snow off his boots.

"Where the hell have you been, Dixon?" Vinnie shouted toward the darkened garage. There was no reply. "Hey, fuck stick, you hear me?"

Before either of them knew what was happening, two shadows appeared on either side of the doorway. "Police. Get your hands in the air," a male voice commanded.

Terry's eyes widened as he saw the two bright red dots appear on Vinnie's chest, crawling around in tight circles like angry fire ants. Terry immediately raised his hands above his head.

Vinnie looked down at the laser dots targeting him, then turned his attention to Terry. His eyes narrowed until they were no more than slits. "You slimy little cocksucker. You set me up!"

"No. I swear I didn't, Vinnie."

"Hands up, Vincent," the voice repeated. "You've got no chance."

Vinnie looked back at the doorway. "I can't raise my hands, pig. Fuck you!"

Terry watched in horror as Vinnie's right hand slid toward the gun sticking out of his waistband. At the exact moment that Vinnie's fingers grazed the butt of the weapon, the room exploded with rifle fire and muzzle flashes. His body jumped around on the couch as if performing some cartoonish improvisational dance. The gunfire ceased. An acrid cloud of bluish smoke spilled into the office from the garage. Terry stared at Vinnie's now motionless body slumped back on the couch. His lifeless eyes were pointed up at the ceiling. Vinnie was dead.

Chapter 23

Friday, 11:15 p.m.,
January 20, 2017

TERRY ALFONSI SAT handcuffed across from Byron in CID Interview Room Two at 109. According to the officer who transported Derrick's nephew to Portland, Terry hadn't spoken more than two words during the entire trip. They made it through Miranda with the mechanic giving an affirmative response at the end of each section. Byron was surprised when Alfonsi didn't immediately request an attorney.

"When did you last speak with your uncle?" Byron asked.

"Monday."

"We checked the prison call log. Derrick didn't receive or make any calls Monday."

"I don't know what to tell you. He called the garage late Monday morning."

Byron made a note to check with the phone company to see which number had called into the garage. "What did he want?"

"I don't know. He talked with Vinnie, not me."

It took every bit of restraint he had not to leap over the table and beat Alfonsi senseless. Outwardly, Byron kept his cool.

"So the call made from your garage phone to the prison this afternoon must have come from Vinnie too, huh?"

"I guess. I know I didn't call the prison."

"Bravo, Terry," Byron said while slowly clapping his hands together in mock applause. "You're gonna lay the blame for all of this at the hands of Vincent Knauer, the one man who can't defend himself."

Alfonsi shrugged.

"I thought you might be smarter than that. Guess I overestimated you."

"What do you mean?"

"The texts. You knew what was going to happen to Vinnie when you responded to our texts. You set him up."

Alfonsi remained silent.

"Do you even know why Derrick wanted the hit on Officer Haggerty?"

"Who?"

Byron sat back in his chair and stared at Alfonsi. He could see that his current tactic wasn't working. Byron didn't believe that Alfonsi was nearly as tough as he was pretending. Alfonsi had gone along with Dixon's text ruse too readily. He'd been looking for a way out, then. Maybe he still was. "You must be wondering how we found you, right?"

"I figure the deputy who saw me towing Vinnie's car called you. But I just thought Vinnie had broken down. I didn't know anything."

"That wasn't how."

Confusion spread across Alfonsi's face.

"You messed up, Terry. The plate you attached to the Mitsubishi hadn't been used in years. Unfortunately for you it was previously registered to a car involved in an accident. And that car was totaled. Care to guess which tow company removed it from the accident scene?"

"No idea. It wasn't Vanos Automotive."

"That's right, it wasn't. It was a company that went bankrupt." Alfonsi shrugged again.

Byron allowed himself a smile. "Guess who purchased the bankrupt company's assets, Terry?"

The realization of what he'd done began to creep into Alfonsi's expression.

"That's right. It was Uncle Derrick. Let me guess, you grabbed a plate from a box in some dusty old corner of the garage and slapped it on the burner."

Alfonsi said nothing.

"That is what you were planning on doing with the car, right? Burn it. Remove all the evidence that might connect you and Vinnie. Like your prints on the plates. Who knows? You might have gotten away with it. But then everything went to shit. Vinnie got himself shot up. He called you for help when the car broke down. That's when the deputy saw you, right? Was Vinnie in the car when you were winching it up onto the flatbed? He must have been. All those holes in him. All that blood. Wouldn't want that in the truck. Then you called the prison, right? *Uncle Derrick, it's all fucked up. What do we do?*"

Alfonsi avoided eye contact with him, but Byron could see the wheels turning.

"Enter Buddy Dixon, an old army pal of Derrick's who you called. You see, Terry? Your prints are all over this thing. Right from the beginning. I don't really give a shit if you admit anything or not."

Byron stood up and grabbed his notepad and pen as if he was preparing to leave. "I guess the only question is, will this remain a state charge or go federal?"

Terry's eyes widened. "What do you mean?"

"Exactly what I said. If the feds get involved in this you might be looking at life or worse."

"Worse? What's worse?"

"Terry, you just took part in a conspiracy to murder a police officer. You're fucked."

Alfonsi's mouth dropped open as if he hadn't considered this. "What if I wanted to cut a deal?"

"I don't make deals, Terry. Not my job. Why would we cut a deal with a piece of shit like you anyway? We've already got you. Besides, you have to have something to bargain with. And you don't."

Byron stood up and opened the interview room door.

"What if I give you my uncle Derrick?"

"So, we'll be able to charge Derrick and his nephew with conspiracy to commit murder, right?" LeRoyer asked, seemingly distracted.

"Based on Terry's confession, I'd say we can," Byron said. "I couldn't shut him up."

"What about Cavallaro? He set this whole thing in motion, right?"

"It looks that way, although we'd need Derrick to convict Cavallaro. Speaking of which, have they had any luck locating him yet?"

"Nothing yet. Trust me, everyone is looking."

Byron nodded, then stood up to leave the lieutenant's office.

"Where are you going?" LeRoyer asked.

"Gonna head up to the hospital to check on Hags."

"Um, hang on a sec."

"What?" Byron asked, stopping at the door. "Haven't we covered everything?"

"I, um, I have something to tell you, John."

Byron studied the serious look on his lieutenant's face and took two steps back into the office. "Am I in some kind of trouble?"

"I don't know how to say this."

"Spit it out, Marty. What?"

"Hags passed away an hour ago."

BYRON FELT THE rage building within him. He wanted to punch something, or someone, until his knuckles were bloody. And keep on punching until he couldn't lift his arms to punch anymore. Vincent Knauer would've been his first choice, but beating on an already dead murderer wouldn't have brought much satisfaction. Of course, Derrick Vanos, the man responsible for initiating the attack on Haggerty, was still alive. Byron knew that the Windham prison allowed conjugal visits, but he was fairly certain that they would frown on a visit of the more pugilistic variety.

All the work he and his team had done to get to the bottom of what happened the night Haggerty shot Plummer had been for naught. While they'd been scrambling to restore Haggerty's life to some semblance of normalcy, Vanos had been working just as hard to extinguish it.

Byron descended the back stairwell to the plaza. He walked alone to his car, then drove away from 109. This wasn't a time for him to be around people.

Chapter 24

Tuesday, January 24, 2017

DURING THE DAYS following Haggerty's death, the Portland Police Department was shrouded in an emotional gray fog. More than two hundred and twenty-five employees, civilian and sworn personnel alike, roamed the halls of 109 like zombies, each of them consumed by and dreading the event awaiting them at week's end. Sean Haggerty's memorial service. Grim-faced uniformed officers and dispatchers all wore a band of black cloth over their badges. Detectives followed suit with the shields clipped to their belts. The daily briefings given in the squad room were solemn affairs, devoid of the usual lighthearted banter and salty irreverence. The PD family was in mourning.

Byron occupied his time as best he could, going through the motions. He arrived at 109 early each morning, grabbing the ever-present stack of overnight crime reports from the printer, then refilling the paper and waiting for the rest to print. As always, he divided the reports into property crimes and person crimes, giving the former to Sergeant Peterson, while he read and assigned the latter to his own detectives. Working alongside the Attorney General's Office, Byron personally oversaw the process of charging both Derrick Vanos and Terrence Alfonsi for their involvement in the Haggerty murder. Micky Cavallaro remained in the wind. Special Agent Collier told Byron that he'd let him know as soon as Cavallaro was located, but Byron wasn't holding out hope. Physically, Byron attended the various administrative meetings, which he'd always considered a waste of precious time, but mentally he was elsewhere.

AG Investigator Lucinda Phillips returned to her own office in Augusta as the investigations into both officer-involved shootings were no longer deemed a priority, now that all concerned parties were dead. The police protests gradually wound down until finally no one was left. The news media moved on to the next big thing, although Mayor Gilcrest managed to get herself in front of the camera on a couple occasions, each time alluding to the need for the Department of Justice to come in and do a review of the Portland Police Department's use of force policies and practices. Byron had heard it all before. The players' names were different but in the end it was always the same old game being played with people's lives. Lives that would never move past the loss they'd suffered.

CID detectives went back to working on the cases they'd set aside following the laundromat robbery and subsequent shooting, and to catching new ones. During what little free time Byron's detectives had they worked on the Plummer case, rereading statements and supplements, reviewing video and news reports. Even the physical evidence was looked at a second time.

Everyone did their best to carry on despite the huge loss the PD family had suffered. They'd lost one of their own but there was still a job to do. Portland's bad guys didn't call a truce so the men and women in blue could grieve. The job wasn't like that. Criminals kept breaking the law and victims demanded justice.

Byron spent every spare moment studying the Plummer shooting. He knew there had to be something they'd overlooked, something that would lead them to the truth.

LeRoyer stopped by Byron's office on several occasions to ask if he was okay.

"You should talk with someone, John," LeRoyer said during one particular visit.

"No offense, Marty, but spare me the EAP bullshit, okay?" Byron said. "I'm not gonna go all goofy on you because I lost a friend. But don't expect me to let this go either."

"I wouldn't dream of it," LeRoyer said, holding his hands up in mock surrender. "I know you too well."

"There's still a suspect somewhere out there who had a hand in all of this," Byron said. "He was with Tommy Plummer when they robbed the laundromat and again when Haggerty shot Plummer. I *will* find that son of a bitch, and they will answer for their crime."

TUESDAY AFTERNOON, UNDER an overcast sky, Byron drove to Kennedy Park alone. After parking on the street, he climbed the rickety back steps to Erlene Jackson's Anderson Street apartment and rapped on the frost-covered glass of a rusted storm door. He had read her statement at least a dozen times. She claimed to have seen and heard nothing. Jackson had told the detectives that she'd retired to bed early on the night Plummer was shot. At first glance her account seemed entirely plausible. It matched up with the fact that officers and detectives hadn't been able to raise anyone at her apartment during their original canvass of the area. But

Byron had never been one to accept anything strictly at face value. Seldom were things the way they first appeared.

Dustin Tran had researched every resident in the area, and Jackson's story did not jibe with her long history of calling the police whenever something wasn't right. Loud music, squealing tires, fights—over the last several years, both day and night, she'd reported it all. She always called anonymously, oblivious to the fact that her phone number was visible to the dispatcher. So it didn't make sense she could have missed this event. Busybodies were creatures of habit, and Erlene Jackson clearly had such a reputation.

Byron was about to knock again when a middle-aged woman came to the door. She wore a tan wool sweater and an expression of distrust.

"Yes?" the woman said through the glass of the storm door.

"Mrs. Jackson?" Byron asked. "Erlene Jackson?"

"Who wants to know?"

Byron removed his credentials from his jacket pocket and held them up for her to see. "I'm from the police department. My name is Detective Sergeant Byron. I wonder if I might ask you a few questions?"

"What about?"

"Do you mind if we talk inside? I'd rather not do this out here."

"Is this about that boy who was shot by the police?" she asked.

"It is," Byron said, returning his ID case to his inside jacket pocket.

"I already told those other detectives I didn't see nothing."

"If I thought that were true, I wouldn't be here," he said, going all in.

Jackson's eyes widened ever so slightly as if she couldn't believe what she'd just heard.

"You calling me a liar?"

"No, ma'am. I think you're doing what you have to do to survive down here. And I can appreciate how hard it must be for you. But I think you know a whole lot more than what you put in your statement to those other detectives. You seem like a person who cares about what happens in her neighborhood. But I wonder, will you be able to live with yourself if and when more people get hurt over this?"

She stared at him without blinking. Byron waited to see which way she would go with it. He knew he had about five seconds, after which she would either slam the door in his face and get on the horn to LeRoyer or she would let him in and unburden herself. He was going all in on the latter.

Jackson's expression softened, but only slightly. "Why should I tell you anything, Sergeant?"

"Because a neighborhood boy is dead, a police officer was gunned down, and because you know I'm right. More people will be hurt or killed unless we can get to the truth about what happened that night."

Jackson looked away for a moment and inhaled deeply though her nostrils. She let out a long slow sigh. "You're not gonna let this go, are you?" she said as she reestablished eye contact with Byron.

"No, ma'am. I'm not. Not until I get to the truth."

She unlocked the outer door, then took a step back. "You might as well come in, then."

"MARTY, COME IN and close the door," Rumsfeld said from behind his desk, gesturing with his hand as if he were in a hurry.

LeRoyer followed the acting chief's instructions, then looked over to the window wall where Commander Jennings was seated.

They had left a vacant seat between them. The lieutenant walked over to the empty chair next to Rumsfeld's desk and sat down.

"What's this about?" LeRoyer asked.

"It's about Sergeant Byron," Rumsfeld said.

"We think he's becoming a liability," Jennings added.

"I disagree," LeRoyer said. "I know John can be a bit difficult sometimes, but—"

"He's losing his perspective, Marty," Rumsfeld said.

"If you're talking about that thing with Thibodeau, in IA, that's just a couple of sergeants blowing off steam," LeRoyer said. "It's old school."

"Well, that behavior wasn't in my old school," Jennings said.

LeRoyer's head swiveled back and forth between the two men as he attempted to read their faces. The meeting felt like an ambush, a rehearsed one.

"What are you saying?" LeRoyer asked.

Rumsfeld sat back in his chair, a move designed to appear less threatening. He tented his fingers and got to the point. "Marty, city hall thinks that this investigation into the laundromat robbery has gone on long enough, and I'm inclined to agree."

"We're still making progress, Chief," LeRoyer protested.

Jennings chimed in. "I don't mean any disrespect, Lieutenant, but it looks like all you're doing is chasing your tail and wasting city resources."

"How it looks is not my problem," LeRoyer shot back.

"But it is mine," Rumsfeld said. "And so is John Byron. Look, Marty, this is a lot more than just getting in the IA sergeant's face or being insubordinate with me the other day. Byron is losing his way."

"Face it, this isn't the first time he's gone off the rails," Jennings added. "He has a reputation for—"

"Getting to the truth," LeRoyer said, finishing his sentence for him. LeRoyer turned his back on Jennings to face Rumsfeld directly. "Look, Chief, I know this has been a rough one. Haggerty's death has been hard on all of us. But I know John. Yeah, he steps on toes, occasionally even mine, but he's a good investigator. He'll come around. He always does."

Rumsfeld appeared to be mulling it over as he stared out the window. LeRoyer knew this was all part of the act. He could tell Rumsfeld had already made his decision.

"Let's look at what you have so far, Marty," Rumsfeld said. "The two guys inside the laundromat can't even agree on what type of gun. And the owner of the Bubble Up is missing, right?"

LeRoyer nodded.

"There wasn't even video of the robbery," Rumsfeld continued.

"How can we even be sure that Haggerty was chasing the robbery suspects?" Jennings asked. "Maybe he just stumbled across two other kids wearing hoodies."

"And ski masks?" LeRoyer said. "They *were* the robbers."

"Marty, all I'm saying is we're just beating a dead horse at this point," Rumsfeld said.

"Where are you going with this?" LeRoyer asked.

"The families of some of the kids Byron has been harassing have attorneys representing them now. It's just more negative press we don't need. City hall thinks it's best if we settle the Plummer affair and move forward. Maybe we can budget for some additional deadly force training for the officers."

"I can't believe I'm hearing this from you, Chief," LeRoyer said.

"Perhaps it's time for some new blood in CID," Rumsfeld said at last.

LeRoyer said nothing, but he could feel the temperature in

the room rising. This *was* an ambush. They were about to float out the name of a sergeant that they'd like to see replace Byron. And then LeRoyer would do what he always did. He'd stake his own position as CID lieutenant against Byron. If John screwed up after that, they'd both be replaced, and Rumsfeld would have two brand-new CID bosses to do his bidding. It was a routine as old as policing. LeRoyer wondered which lieutenant had been sniffing around for a CID command.

"How would you feel about Diane Joyner?" Rumsfeld asked.

"Look, give me another chance to get Byron back in line, okay?" LeRoyer said. "If he steps out of line you can replace me too." *God hates a coward*, he thought.

Rumsfeld's eyes widened slightly, as if LeRoyer's reaction had caught him by surprise. "Are you sure you want to put your neck out there like that, Marty? You're taking a big chance."

"He's the best investigator I have," LeRoyer said.

"And your friend," Jennings added.

"My friendship with John has nothing to do with it," LeRoyer snapped back without looking at him.

"Doesn't it?" Jennings said.

"All right," Rumsfeld said at last. "Sergeant Byron is your responsibility. Get him under control."

"I will," LeRoyer said.

"Don't let me down, Marty."

FORTY-FIVE MINUTES LATER Byron stepped out from Jackson's stuffy apartment into the cold. He knew they wouldn't be exchanging greeting cards any time soon, but she had provided him with something he needed badly. A witness to Plummer possessing and, more importantly, firing a gun at Haggerty. While Jackson had said at the outset that she would never testify in open court to what she was telling him, Byron figured they would cross that particular bridge when, and if, they ever came to it. The problem now was finding the evidence to back up her account. They hadn't managed to find it so far.

Byron paused on the landing to survey the surrounding area. After several moments he descended the wooden steps, then approached the junk car upon which Tommy Plummer had been perched when Haggerty shot him. Nearly obscured by a new blanket of snow, the vehicle looked less like a mode of transport than a sleeping beast. Standing alone in the frozen yard, Byron looked back in the direction of Anderson Street. He didn't know what he was searching for exactly, but he knew the answer had to be close by. It always was. Not close enough to reach out and slap him perhaps, but close.

His gaze shifted toward the back end of the alley. Buried in the drifts were several wooden pallets leaning against a stockade fence. It took him several minutes before he managed to pry a pallet loose and drag it over to the abandoned car. Deep snow worked its way into his boots. Using the pallet as a makeshift ladder he climbed up onto the hood. Sheet metal buckled under his weight. The snow shifted and slid off the car onto the ground as Byron turned and looked toward the road.

Recalling the crime scene captured in Pelligrosso's photos, Byron searched for anything out of the ordinary. There had to be something they had overlooked, but what? He focused on the area to his right where Haggerty had been standing when the shooting occurred. The snow-covered pile of garbage wasn't high enough to have provided Haggerty with much in the way of cover, not from this height. Realizing that at 6'3" he had a higher vantage point than Plummer would have had, Byron crouched down slightly. He pointed his hand as if it were a gun, sighting in on the spot where Haggerty had been standing. Pelligrosso had said that he hadn't located anything in the way of a bullet, or a hole from a bullet, within the pile. Byron moved his hand slightly to the right. Anything fired in that direction would have struck the siding or penetrated a window of the adjacent building, and the evidence techs would have found it. He shifted his aim to the left. Missing left would have yielded a ground strike, and the odds of ever finding a round fired into the ground amid the debris and snow were somewhere next to zero.

What if Plummer missed high? Byron thought. He redirected his aim slightly above where Haggerty had been standing. A bullet fired high from this angle would have traveled into the yard directly across the street. He holstered his finger, then rose up to his full height. He studied the yard. Something wasn't the same. The landscape had changed.

Byron pulled out his cell and hurriedly scrolled through several dozen scene photos, emailed to him by Pelligrosso. He stopped as he came to the one he was looking for, then zoomed in on the area behind Haggerty's location.

Byron alternated looking back and forth between the screen of his cellphone and the scene directly in front of him. He held the phone up and compared the landscape to the picture. It was different. Pelligrosso's photo clearly showed a snow-covered indeterminate lump the shape and size of a motor vehicle, perhaps a small SUV or wagon. The view in front of him yielded no such lump. Quickly, he climbed down from the car, then picked his way through the littered alley toward the yard on the opposite side of Anderson.

Even with the recent heavy snowfall, the indentation in the yard was as evident as an in-ground pool in winter. Whatever had been parked there, or more likely abandoned, was gone. Byron checked the building number, then retrieved his cell again and dialed.

"Dispatch. Mary speaking."

"Mary, it's John Byron. I need you to check something for me, as quick as you can."

AN HOUR LATER, Byron and Pelligrosso stood at the far end of Frederick Street, waiting as the wrecker operator fumbled with the locked gate to Fat Ricky's impound yard. Judging by the driver's average build, Byron guessed the operator was employed by Ricky, and not the man himself.

The driver yanked the chain free and shoved the large rolling cyclone fence gate out of the way. "If you guys want to follow me inside, I'll take you to the abandoned wrecks we pulled out of the projects at the beginning of the week."

Byron and his evidence tech did as instructed, waiting inside the fenced-in yard as the driver secured the gate behind them.

"So, what's the deal with these?" Byron asked. "Why were you towing these cars out of Kennedy Park?"

"Some city thing. They budget money to remove these eyesores from all the low-income housing projects in Portland. So far, we've hit Riverton, Front Street, and Kennedy Park."

"In the dead of winter?" Pelligrosso asked.

"Hey, money is money," the man said.

"The one we're looking for is the one that came from here," Byron said, showing him the address he'd scribbled onto his notepad.

The driver retreated to the cab of his rig. He reemerged with a metal clipboard. "These are all of the junkers we've pulled from Kennedy," he said. "Give me the number on Anderson again."

"Fifty-two," Byron said.

He flipped through the greasy stack of papers attached to the clipboard. "Fifty-two. Fifty-two. Here it is. An '02 Liberty."

They scanned the rows of vehicles.

"Right there," the wrecker driver said, pointing. "Second row in."

The three men walked over to the Jeep. Pelligrosso walked around it, making a visual inspection.

"We'll need the keys," Byron said to the driver.

"Weren't any. It's unlocked."

Byron opened the passenger door, releasing a cascade of snow from the doorframe. He checked the glove box and console for paperwork while Pelligrosso continued his visual inspection of the outside.

"Did you guys find any papers?" Byron asked the wrecker driver as he closed the door and walked around to the driver's side.

"Nope. No papers, no plates, no nothing. Probably belongs to a former tenant at 52 Anderson. They tend to leave all their shit behind."

Byron opened the driver's door and repeated the process, looking under the seat and above the visor. He knew how frequently the people living in the city's assisted housing moved in and out. Many for violating the rules, breaking the law, or simply tiring of living amid all that. Some, although not nearly as many as he would have hoped, were able to move out as their financial situation improved. As he examined the interior of the dilapidated Jeep, he imagined one of the former scenarios was far more likely.

"Sarge, can you pop the hood?" Pelligrosso asked.

Byron pulled the release handle and exited the wreck. He looked on as his evidence tech climbed over and under the SUV, inspecting it from every angle.

Byron pulled out his phone and rechecked the photo. It was impossible to determine whether the snow pile in the picture was the Jeep in question. He'd have to hope that whoever hooked up the junk vehicle had recorded the addresses accurately.

"Sarge," Pelligrosso said as he climbed out from under the hood. "I wanna tow this back to 109."

"You find something?"

"Maybe."

Byron turned to the wrecker driver. "Can you help us with that?"

"I'll have to move some cars around. Give me a half hour and I'll get a flatbed down here. Want me to call you when I get back?"

"We'll wait here," Byron said.

SEVERAL HOURS LATER amid the sickly sweet smell of antifreeze, as a stream of melting snow trickled toward the floor drain, Byron and LeRoyer knelt down to get a closer look at the metallic object lying on the floor of 109's basement. It was only a tiny hunk of lead amid a jumble of disassembled pieces from the Liberty's front end, but Byron knew how big a piece it might turn out to be.

"Tell me again how we found this?" LeRoyer asked, shouting to be heard as the blower to the ceiling-mounted heating unit kicked on.

Byron recounted the series of events that began with him reinterviewing Erlene Jackson and ended with him climbing atop the car at the shooting scene.

"You climbed up on a car?" LeRoyer asked, as if that were the point of the story. "You're lucky you didn't break your neck."

"I wanted to get a look at what Tommy Plummer would have seen that night," Byron said as he pointed to the Jeep. "This piece of crap was abandoned on the lawn on the opposite side of Anderson Street, directly behind where Haggerty was standing when he fired."

"Why didn't we check it earlier?" LeRoyer asked, looking from Byron to Pelligrosso and back.

"Seriously, Marty?" Byron said, coming to the aid of his grease-covered evidence tech. "In addition to being several hundred feet away from our crime scene, and completely covered with snow, it was towed away Monday morning before we had a chance to finish our sweep of the area."

"The Jeep was facing the street," Pelligrosso said. "The bullet fired by Plummer must have sailed over Haggerty's head, through the grille, and into the radiator."

"Even if it hadn't been covered in snow, there was no visible damage to the exterior," Byron added.

LeRoyer shook his head. "Well, this changes things."

"No," Byron said. "Not yet it doesn't. We still need a ballistics match, and that's gonna be tough to do without a gun."

BYRON LOOKED AWAY from his computer monitor. His eyes felt like two burned-out coals. He closed then rubbed them with his knuckles. He wondered if he was really making any progress or just keeping himself occupied. He opened his eyes and observed Internal Affairs Sergeant Brad Thibodeau standing in the darkened doorway like some bad hallucination.

"What do *you* want?" Byron asked.

Instead of responding verbally, Thibodeau entered the office carrying a manila envelope. He placed it on Byron's desk, then stepped back.

Byron studied the envelope. It didn't bear the trademark confidential stamps of a complaint packet, nor did it have his name typed on a label. He looked up at Thibodeau.

"What's this? Another 50?"

"Open it," Thibodeau said.

Byron studied the IA sergeant's solemn expression. Unlike LeRoyer's easy to read mug, Thibodeau's gave nothing away.

Byron unfastened the envelope's metal security tab, then slid the contents out onto his desk. The envelope contained three eight-by-ten glossy photographs of Commander Jennings carrying a file folder. In the first photo, the commander was walking along a corridor that looked suspiciously like the one on the second floor of 109. In the second, the commander was using a key to unlock a door. The third showed him retreating down the same hallway.

Byron looked up at Thibodeau and tossed the pictures atop the envelope. "I don't get it. Why do I care about these?"

The IA sergeant cleared his throat. "The surveillance camera that captured these images was installed after Jennings was promoted out of Internal Affairs. Only former Chief Stanton and I knew about it."

Byron glanced back at the photos.

Thibodeau continued. "The commander, who shouldn't have a key to IA records anyway, spent forty-five minutes in there. Check the time and date stamp."

Byron checked. Thibodeau was right. "And?"

"He was in there the day before Haggerty's old IA case was leaked to the press."

Chapter 25

Thursday, 10:00 A.M.,
January 26, 2017

BYRON WAS FIGHTING to maintain his composure, simultaneously struggling with his emotions and the weight of the flag-draped casket. The visor of his uniform hat was pulled down low over his eyes. The expression on his face was grim.

The previous evening, he had taken his dress uniform back to the condo to prep for Haggerty's service, alone. He hadn't been in the mood to stand in the superior officers' locker room listening to the other supervisors and commanders proselytize over how they were all supposed to feel about the death of their brother. Byron knew all too well how he felt, and the emotion topping his list was guilt. Guilt at not having resolved the shooting incident before someone made an attempt on Haggerty's life. He knew that locating the missing gun would never end the lingering doubts of some, about the events that had led up to the nighttime police shooting of a Portland teen. Nor would finding the gun have guaranteed that Haggerty would still be alive, instead of being carried by six of his comrades. But none of that knowledge did anything to assuage his guilt.

Trailing Byron were Sergeant Pepin and Lieutenant LeRoyer. On the opposite side of the casket, Byron was flanked by Sergeant Crosby. Rounding out the pallbearers were Officer Curtis and Sergeant Fitzgerald. Every leather surface was buffed, every badge, button, and buckle polished. Ice crunching underfoot called cadence to their every step. Uniformed officers, lining both sides of Myrtle Street from Cumberland Avenue to Congress, stood at attention. Their raised right arms were bent sharply in silent salute. Somber notes played by a lone kilted piper drifted down the street. The instrument's forlorn wail echoed off the walls of nearby buildings. As the six men crossed the wide concrete sidewalk, Byron glanced left toward the top of the street where the Stars and Stripes, suspended between two fully-extended fire department ladder trucks, hung lifeless in the cold morning air. He looked away, then slowly climbed up and over the threshold through the side entrance of Merrill Auditorium.

Byron and his fellow pallbearers delivered Haggerty's casket to the center of the stage before exiting on opposite sides, taking empty floor seats at the rear of the auditorium. LeRoyer sat down next to Byron, wordlessly leaving an empty seat between them. The vacant chair was less about the divide that had grown between the two men than it was a symbolic gesture designed to give both officers a private space in which to grieve. One by one, dignitaries took to the stage. Words of comfort were spoken along with the occasional humorous tale about one of Haggerty's exploits, and there had been many. The crowd's laughter momentarily kept their overwhelming grief at bay. Surprisingly, some of the funniest anecdotes came from the department chaplain, Father Barrett.

Following one particularly uplifting moment, Acting Chief Rumsfeld took to the stage for the final time. Byron had done his best to prepare for this very moment, trying to steel himself against the flood of emotions he knew the ceremonial last radio call would bring to everyone in attendance. A brief squeal of feedback filled the packed hall as the chief was connected to the police dispatcher remotely from the podium.

Rumsfeld keyed the microphone. "Car One."

"Go ahead, Car One," the dispatcher replied.

"Would you please raise unit 932?"

"Ten-four, Car One. 932."

The auditorium was filled with tension, but the only sound was the electronic buzz of the open radio link. After a moment the dispatcher spoke again.

"Headquarters calling 932."

Again, there was a pause and again only silence. Byron, along with every officer in attendance, hoped and prayed for Haggerty's voice to answer loud and clear, telling the dispatcher that he was ten-four. A-okay. Right as rain. Ready for duty. Anything but what he actually was.

"932," the dispatcher called one last time.

The sound of sobbing, coming from various places throughout the auditorium, now accompanied the sound of the open radio link.

Byron made the mistake of looking up at the backs of the officers seated in front of him. The battle-hardened warriors in blue had transformed into a sea of Jell-O. Each pair of shoulders bounced up and down, racked by the sobs of their grieving owners. He stole a sideways glance at his lieutenant. A watery-eyed LeRoyer wasn't faring any better.

Rumsfeld keyed the microphone on his remote transmitter. "Car One, to Dispatch."

"Car One, go ahead," the dispatcher replied.

After a brief pause Rumsfeld pressed on, his voice cracking. "Car One, 932, Officer Sean Haggerty, is ten-seven for the final time."

"Ten-four, Car One. I show 932, ten-seven. Godspeed, Officer Haggerty."

Byron hung his head and wept.

THE AMBIENT NOISE inside the packed Italian Heritage Center function room was deafening. Located on Westland Avenue, behind the Westgate Shopping Center in the Libby Town section of the city, the ITHI banquet hall had been the epicenter of activity for Portland's Italian-American community since 1977. Large framed black-and-white photos of the ITHI's past presidents, several of whom had served on the police force, graced the entry hall.

Byron had lost count of how many police banquets, award ceremonies, and retirement parties he'd attended here over the years. The irony of holding a funeral reception for an Irish cop at an Italian banquet hall was not lost on him. But the gesture, which would not have sat well with his father's generation, now meant nothing more than some lighthearted ribbing between friends. Times change.

Byron sat alone at a corner table far from the buzz of activity at the bar. Still attired in the uncomfortable dress uniform, his shirt collar was open and a gray clip-on tie hung limply from its decorative brass clip. His thoughts were muddled, swirling between memories of his murdered friend and what he might still be able to do to clear Haggerty's name.

Sipping from a diet soda, and wishing the glass contained less ice and something far stronger, aged at least four years, Byron's attention was drawn to a nearby table where Sergeant Kenny Crosby was holding court with a handful of younger officers. Crosby's voice boomed out in typical bravado fashion, making himself heard above the crowd. The two men made eye contact. Crosby shifted gears.

"See Sergeant Byron over there, boys?" Crosby said, amplifying his voice even further. "Sitting with all of his friends?" Crosby raised his longneck to the other officers seated around his table. "Let that be a lesson to all of you. Never forget which team you play for."

Byron turned away, not caring to take the bait nor suffer though any more of Crosby's drunken soliloquy. He caught LeRoyer looking in his direction and gave a slight nod. The lieutenant was standing amid a group of his fellow team commanders, separated from the lesser ranks like a clique at a high school dance. *Bars and stripes*, Byron thought.

"You've got some balls, John." It was Crosby again.

Slowly Byron turned to face the instigator.

Crosby loomed over Byron, leering down at him, flanked on either side by several of the younger officers who had come to watch the show.

"Who do you think you are, turning your back on me?" Crosby slurred. Byron rose from his chair to confront him.

"I'm facing you now, Kenny," Byron said. "And I gotta tell ya, I'm not finding you half as impressive as you seem to think you are."

Crosby's eyes narrowed, as if he hadn't expected Byron to poke back.

"You've got some nerve even being here today," Crosby said. "Helping the AG's office bury a good cop like Haggerty. You're a fucking disgrace to the badge."

Byron grinned, intentionally looking to provoke Crosby further. "Coming from you, that's almost a compliment."

Crosby swung first, but in his inebriated state he telegraphed the roundhouse right so badly that Byron ducked it with ease. Not wanting to risk another swing from the muscled-up drug sergeant, Byron lowered his head and dove straight into Crosby. Wrapping his arms around Crosby's torso, Byron used his legs to drive himself forward, knocking both of them into one of the round banquet tables, upending it. Crosby grunted in surprise as the air was expelled from his lungs. The two men landed hard on the ceramic tile floor, amid the shattering of glass bottles and the clatter of overturned chairs. Byron recovered first, climbing on top of Crosby, then delivering several punches to the face of the stunned provocateur.

"Break that shit up!" LeRoyer hollered.

Byron was grabbed roughly from behind by several pairs of hands and dragged off Crosby.

Crosby sat up slowly, then glared at Byron. Several of the officers tried to help Crosby to his feet, but he shook them off and stood on his own.

"Nice punches, John," Crosby said as he rubbed the left side of his face and jaw. "Still doesn't change the fact that you're a rat fuck." Crosby smiled, then took a cheap shot, jabbing out with his right fist and connecting squarely with Byron's mouth as he passed.

"Knock it off, Kenny!" LeRoyer shouted. "Get him out of here."

Byron, whose arms were still being held by several officers, stood his ground, maintaining eye contact with Crosby as he was led away.

Byron turned his attention to the officers holding him. "Thanks for the help, boys. I think you can let me go now." The officers released him, then righted the table and chairs before returning to their own. Byron stood his ground for a moment, trying to act as though the punch hadn't dazed him as badly as it had. He'd never wanted a drink so badly in his life.

"You're bleeding," LeRoyer said.

"Nothing gets by you, does it, Marty?" Byron said as he wiped the blood off his lips with the back of his hand. "I'll bet the Emergency Broadcast System could use someone with your observational skills."

"What the hell is your problem, John? Maybe I should've let Crosby go to work on you."

"I don't remember asking you to intervene."

Byron turned and walked out of the reception.

BYRON KNEW HE was in a dangerous place, but he didn't care. Crosby's punch in the face had stirred something inside of him that once triggered couldn't be undone. Byron had intended to drive back to his condo and change out of his dress blues, but now he had a different destination in mind. Portland High School. It was time to confront Abdirahman Ali directly. Ali might not have been involved, but Byron was pretty sure he knew something. Something he was afraid to tell.

"I'm sorry, Sergeant Byron, but Abdi is in the middle of history class right now," the principals' office assistant said from behind the counter. "Do you know your mouth is bleeding?"

"Yes, thank you. I was recently made aware. Would that be Mr. Galbraith's class?" Byron asked, remembering the name from one of the placards he'd seen while walking through the hallway previously.

"No, Galbraith doesn't teach history," she said with a perplexed look on her face. "Rebecca Tarbox teaches history."

"That's right," Byron said, completing the bluff. "Tarbox."

"Yes, but that doesn't—"

"Thanks very much," Byron said as he turned on his heels and headed to search for Tarbox's room.

BYRON FINALLY LOCATED the history teacher's room on the second floor. He knocked on the closed door to the classroom, then opened it.

Rebecca Tarbox was standing at the front of the room by the blackboard. "May I help you?"

"Sorry to interrupt your class," Byron said. "I need to speak with Abdi Ali for a minute."

"This is highly irregular," the teacher said, looking more than a little uneasy.

"I know," Byron said. "But it's very important. It'll only take a minute."

Tarbox looked over at Ali. The boy was staring at Byron, wide-eyed, as were all the students.

"My parents said I wasn't supposed to talk with you," Ali said.

"It's okay, Abdi," Byron lied. "I cleared it with your father."

The boy didn't budge. It was obvious that he didn't know what to do.

"I promise, it will just take a second," Byron said.

"Why don't you go with the officer, Abdi," Tarbox said at last.

"I TRIED TO stop him, Dana," the office assistant said to Principal Larrabee. "He just took off as soon as he knew which class Abdi was in."

"It's okay, Barbara," Larrabee said. "It's not your fault." Larrabee pulled out her cell and went to her recent call list. "It's time Sergeant Byron realizes he can't do whatever he pleases in *my* school." After finding the number she wanted, Larrabee pressed the redial button and waited. "Chief Rumsfeld? It's Principal Dana Larrabee. We have a problem."

"I KNOW ABOUT the gun, Abdi," Byron said.

Ali, who stood leaning against a bank of lockers with his hands jammed into the front pockets of his jeans, said nothing, but he didn't need to. His falling gaze said it all. He did know something.

Byron pushed on. "How did it happen? Was it a dare? Was it Tommy's idea? Was Mohammed Sayed involved? Did he know what he was getting into? Were you there?"

Abdi said nothing.

"I know how hard this must be for you. These are your friends. But two people are dead because of this. I can't help you unless you tell me what happened."

Ali raised his head and looked at Byron.

"Let me help you, Abdi."

"That's enough, Sergeant Byron!" Rumsfeld's voice barked from behind him.

Byron turned and saw the acting chief standing beside an equally furious-looking Principal Larrabee.

"Abdi and I were just having a quick chat," Byron said.

"In direct violation of my order, Sergeant," Rumsfeld said.

Byron grinned and stepped toward the acting chief. "Actually, it's Detective Sergeant, *Acting* Chief."

"Yeah? Well, we'll see about that."

Byron watched as Larrabee gathered her stray sheep. She accompanied Ali down the hall, leaving Byron and Rumsfeld alone.

"As of this moment you can consider yourself on suspension, pending an internal affairs investigation into your conduct. I can already think of several charges that I intend to file as I stand here."

"Really?" Byron said. "What might those be?"

"For starters? Conduct unbecoming. I just heard about your little display at the reception."

"If you'd bother checking your facts you might find that was self-defense."

"How about violating the rights of a juvenile witness?"

"Witness? He might well be a goddamned suspect."

"Don't push me, Sergeant," Rumsfeld said.

"A push wasn't exactly what I had in mind," Byron said, leaning in closer. "But while you're at it, why not add insubordination to your list of charges?"

"*Done.*"

Byron began to walk away, then stopped. He turned back toward Rumsfeld. "Oh yeah, I almost forgot. Go fuck yourself, *Chief.*"

Chapter 26

BYRON SLOUCHED ON the secondhand sofa amid the growing gloom of dusk in the open area of his condo that passed for a living room. On the coffee table in front of him sat not one but two bottles of Jameson Irish whiskey. Twin emerald-colored vessels of problem-solving elixir. Nectar of the gods. He glanced at the empty glass standing at the ready, sans ice. His new fridge was equipped with an ice maker, which meant a full complement of cubes were waiting in the freezer, but Byron didn't see the need. Experience had taught him that the pain-numbing properties of his favorite prescription worked just as well uncut, at room temperature.

He was about to break the seal on the first bottle when his cell rang. He paused long enough to pull the phone from his pocket and check the caller ID. It was Diane. His thumb hovered over the Accept Call button while he debated. What would he say when she asked how he was doing? Would he lie to her? Diane wasn't stupid. By now, word of his reception donnybrook with Crosby had no doubt made its way around 109. And if she hadn't heard about his run-in with Rumsfeld, and subsequent suspension, she would soon enough. He moved his thumb to the Ignore button and pressed down, returning the phone to its main menu. He tossed the phone onto the far end of the couch and reached for a bottle. Sweet release.

DIANE JOYNER SAT in her office, listening to the ringing of John's phone at the other end of the line until his voicemail picked up. "You have reached Sergeant Byron's voicemail. Leave a message at the beep."

"John, it's Di. I heard about what happened. Please call me as soon as you get this, okay? I'm worried about you."

She ended the call and stared at her phone. "Dammit, John. Don't you pull away from me. Not now."

LeRoyer appeared in the hallway outside her office door, startling her.

"You got a second?" he asked.

"Of course," she said, quickly composing herself.

The lieutenant stepped in and closed the door.

"What's up?" she asked.

He sat down across from her. "I imagine by now you know about John's suspension."

She nodded. "I just heard. What happened?"

"It wasn't one thing actually. Disobeying the chief's order to stay away from Abdi Ali was simply the straw that broke the camel's back. John has been struggling to let the Plummer shooting go."

"You don't think he should have kept pursuing it?" Diane asked.

"Doesn't matter what I think. John broke the rules. He let his passions get the better of him."

Diane wisely kept her feelings on the subject to herself until she knew the purpose for LeRoyer's visit. "John is a passionate man."

"That brings me to the point of my being here. I know you've been talking with John and that you're up to speed on the cases his people are working."

"Lieutenant, if there's some—"

LeRoyer raised a hand. "Just hear me out, Sergeant."

"All right."

"Chief Rumsfeld and I have been talking about a temporary replacement for John. The department can't afford to leave his position vacant even for a few days and Sergeant Peterson has enough on his plate at the moment. Diane, we want you to step up and fill in for John."

"Temporarily?"

He nodded. "Yes."

"Because I'm not about to—"

"And no one is asking you to. Look, John needs some time to get his head on straight. His detectives respect you. Hell, I respect you. I'm asking you to step in *temporarily*, okay?"

Diane didn't know what to say. She'd been worried about this exact scenario from the start. It had been nine months since City Manager Clayton Perkins had called her into his office about the promotional list for sergeant, dangling the CID carrot in front of her face. Perkins had told her about the creation a new public relations sergeant, the very position she now held. At the time she'd had no interest in being someone's PR puppet and the city manager knew it. But Perkins had also flattered her, saying that "down the road" she would make a great CID sergeant, the very job she had always dreamed of having. Now here was the CID lieutenant, sitting in her office, assuring her that filling in for John would only be temporary. But that was always how these things started, wasn't it? Even in New York City the police department had been like this.

Could she trust LeRoyer? The truth was, she didn't know. She knew that John had always trusted him, even when the two men had been on opposite sides of an issue. But John and LeRoyer shared a history together, a history she and LeRoyer did not have. At least, not yet.

She sat up straight, making direct eye contact with LeRoyer. "I have your word, this is only temporary?"

LeRoyer didn't flinch. "You have my word."

"Then I'll do it."

"Thank y—"

"On one condition."

LeRoyer arched an eyebrow. "I'm not much on conditions, Diane. What is it?"

"I want your word that you'll allow me to continue to follow up on the Plummer shooting."

LeRoyer opened his mouth to protest but this time it was Diane's turn to raise her hand and stop him.

"I won't cross the line. But I am going to do my job."

LeRoyer paused a beat before answering. "The administration doesn't think this case is worthy of continuing."

"What?" she asked, stunned. "How can anyone feel that way? What about the witness John found? Or the bullet Gabe pulled out of the Jeep?"

LeRoyer didn't respond.

"Tell me you don't agree with Rumsfeld on this," Diane said. "Tell me you believe clearing Haggerty's name still matters."

"Of course it matters," LeRoyer said.

"If you want me to fill in for John, *temporarily*, then you'll have to let me continue to pursue the robbery case."

He studied her but said nothing.

"I know where the line is, Lieutenant, and I won't cross it."

"And I have *your* word on that?" LeRoyer asked.

"You do."

"All right. Keep working the case, but do it quietly. You make any waves and it will be all over. For both of us."

BEFORE BYRON COULD do more than inhale the intoxicating scent of the whiskey, his cellphone rang again. *Dammit, Diane*, he thought. His guilt got the better of him. He set the bottle down on the coffee table, then leaned over and grabbed the phone off the other end of couch. But it wasn't Diane. It was a 617 number. *Massachusetts*. Against his better judgment he answered it.

"Byron," he said.

"John, it's Colin."

Byron instantly recognized the voice, and it made his skin crawl. Colin Donnelly was the shill his mother had married following the death of John's father, Reece. Reece was barely in the ground before Donnelly showed up. The voice sounded older, more gravelly than Byron remembered, but it was unmistakably Donnelly. It had been years since the two men had spoken.

"I thought I made it clear that I never wanted to speak with you again," Byron said. "And how the hell did you get this number?"

"John, your mother's gone. She passed away."

Byron opened his mouth to speak, but the words wouldn't come. Like someone had stabbed him through the heart, he felt physical pain. He had known this day would come eventually, but like all the other unpleasantnesses in his life, Byron had managed to bury this one down deep.

It had been four years since he'd seen Molly and at least ten since they had partaken in an actual conversation. The last time he had seen her was during a midweek visit to the high-priced care facility she'd been placed in after the Alzheimer's had gotten bad. The news of her institutionalization had also come by way of a telephone call. It was the last time Byron had spoken to Colin Donnelly. Three weeks after receiving Donnelly's call, Byron had driven to Massachusetts, telling no one. Molly hadn't recognized him during his brief visit. He'd meant no more to her than a new orderly would have. Byron never told her who he was and as he made the return trip to Maine he wondered why he'd even driven down to see her in the first place.

Now here he was being informed of his mother's death by a man he despised. Although if he was being truthful with himself, Byron didn't even know the man. He only knew that Donnelly, and all his money, had taken Molly away, stepping into the role that Reece, Byron's real father, used to play.

"When?" Byron croaked out. It was all he could think to ask.

"Last week," Donnelly said. "The service is tomorrow morning. I almost didn't call you, but I thought you'd want to know."

Last week? Byron thought. *And the bastard is just calling now?* It was just one more reason to dislike the man. Not that he needed one.

"Where and when?" Byron asked matter-of-factly.

"The Church of the Advent on Beacon Hill. The service starts at ten o'clock."

Byron couldn't think of anything else to say.

"I'm sorry, John," Donnelly said after the pause in conversation grew even more uncomfortable.

Byron hung up.

BYRON WAS MIRED in self-pity, but he didn't care. The rest of society seemed to embrace the idea of self-medicating. Some chose pills, others marijuana, or coke, or heroin. At least his chosen drug was legal. Besides, if he didn't do something to dull his senses, and numb the guilt, he would go crazy. The two losses coupled with his suspension and the feeling that he'd failed Haggerty were too much. He wondered if he had failed his mother as well.

Following the death of his father, Byron and Molly had suffered a falling-out. Byron had grown tired of listening to her denigrate Reece. And, if he was being totally honest with himself, he may have held her partially responsible for his father's death, back when he'd still believed it was suicide. Molly remarried, taking her new husband's last name, and moved to Boston, back to the neighborhood of her youth. The rift between them had been so wide that she hadn't bothered to attend his graduation from Saint Joseph's College. The final indignity had been her refusal to support his decision to enter the field of law enforcement. Now she was dead and there would be no fixing what had broken between them. Ever.

He sat alone on the couch, still half-clothed in his dress blues, two fingers of Jameson in one hand and an open photo album on his lap. The album was a hodgepodge of moments in his life. There were pictures of his parents. Photos of Byron and Ray Humphrey when they'd worked together as detectives. He and Kay, back when they were still united in holy matrimony, and content to be so. He even found a picture of himself fishing with his niece, Katie. Only now she was grown, and the childlike moniker had been replaced by her given name, Katherine. The photographs, placed in the album in no particular order, conjured memories that now felt distant and jumbled. Byron turned the page and paused a moment before gently removing one of the photos from behind the album's yellowed protective film and placing it atop the page. It was a group photograph taken at a meeting of the Maine Police Emerald Society on the second floor of Bull Feeney's pub in Portland's Old Port, the same pub he and Diane had shared a meal at nearly a week ago. The color photo, now at least six years old, depicted the culmination of a successful fundraising event. The Emerald Society had held a golf tournament at the Riverside Municipal Golf Course, the sole purpose of which had been to raise money to help Ray and Wendy Humphrey with their medical bills. In addition to being Byron's on the job mentor, Ray Humphrey had been like a second father. Wendy had been battling cancer for more than two years and the Humphreys desperately needed financial help. Byron ran his index finger over the photograph's smooth surface, stopping when he got to where he stood sandwiched between Sean Haggerty and Ray Humphrey. The three of them stood together at the end of the bar with glasses raised, toasting to the good health of Mrs. H.

Tears stung Byron's eyes as he knocked back the whiskey in one throat-searing gulp. The alcohol stung his busted lip, courtesy of Kenny Crosby's cheap shot. He reached for the bottle and poured another. What had once been an album filled with joyous moments and people who had both touched and defined his life was now nothing more than a painful reminder of all the things he had lost. His father, Reece. His mother, Molly, twice. A twenty-year marriage to Kay. Ray Humphrey. And now Sean Haggerty. It was too much to bear.

Beyond his personal losses, Byron had seen more death than he cared to remember. And it stayed with him, always. Every case, every scene, every life snuffed out. Every veteran cop knows the feeling. The growing numbness, the sense of isolation. And the high cost associated with both.

He held the photograph of Sean Haggerty in his hand. Haggerty, who had been consumed by self-doubt and guilt the night Byron had intervened. He had talked his friend down from the edge, possibly saving Hags from taking his own life. And now he was gone anyway. Gunned down by a sick and twisted excuse for a human being outside of a grocery store. Byron couldn't help questioning the sanity of a God who would allow those two conflicting events to occur in a span of hours. And to what end? What purpose did any of it serve?

Carefully, he laid the Emerald Society photo on the sofa cushion adjacent to his own, while absently letting the album slide from his lap onto the floor.

"Here's to you, Hags," he said, lifting his glass to an empty room. "Sláinte."

Chapter 27

Friday, 8:35 A.M.,
January 27, 2017

INBOUND TRAFFIC WAS at a standstill on Brighton Avenue. Diane inched her unmarked along as fast as the morning rush would allow. She dialed John's cell, again, and again got only his voicemail. He hadn't had the courtesy to return even one of her calls. She was oscillating between anger and worry. It was time to pay him a visit.

Fifteen minutes later she turned onto the road that led to John's condo. His car was nowhere to be found. She parked her unmarked in the vacant drive and headed inside for a closer look.

She called out his name, but the condo was empty. A quick search through each room yielded the truth. John had fallen hard from the sobriety wagon. And his unhealthy trip down memory lane did nothing to alleviate her fears about his state of mind.

In the bedroom she saw signs that he had hastily packed for a trip. His overnight bag was missing along with his toothbrush and razor. *Where would he go in such a hurry?* John was in a bad place and she knew it. The one thing she didn't know was how to reach him.

She returned to the living room, trying to decide her next move. She stooped to retrieve one of the open photo albums. Her hand moved over an old wedding photo on the right-hand page. There *was* one person who might know how to reach John. The same person who'd stood beside him for almost twenty years. Kay Byron.

IT WAS NEARING half past ten in the morning when Byron slid unseen into a pew at the back of the cathedral. He was late. Molly Donnelly's service was already under way. Most of the attendees were seated toward the front of the church. He'd spent twenty minutes parked down the street, oscillating between attending the service and driving away. The alcohol still flowing through his veins provided him with just enough courage to enter the church.

Booming bass notes from the pipe organ reverberated through the vast ornate space. The air was filled with the same mystical scents of rose and frankincense that Byron remembered from his childhood when attending services at the Cathedral of the Immaculate Conception in Portland. He and his friends had been convinced that the aroma was what God's cigarettes smelled like. Holy smokes, they had called it.

Already feeling like an interloper, Byron caught the eye of the officiating priest as the robed man rose to speak. In that passing glance it felt as if the man knew of Byron's guilt, of his shame. The priest's voice flowed melodic and soothing throughout the church's many alcoves, but the words gradually faded as Byron drifted off into his own past.

The boyhood memories came in a flood, mixed up in much

the same way his photo albums had been. Warm summer days spent with his Munjoy Hill schoolmates at St. Peter's Church Bazaar, eating cannoli. Sneaking out of the house early on Saturday mornings and bicycling to the East End Beach. Buying Italian sandwiches from DiPietro's store on Cumberland Avenue. Stopping by the police station to visit Reece. Fishing off the docks on Commercial Street. The images came and went like a kaleidoscope. But then they took a darker turn. Finding his father dead at the dining room table in his shabby one-bedroom apartment, the gun on the floor. The seemingly endless arguments with his mother. Hateful words that could never be unsaid.

Ripped from his brief nostalgic escape, Byron was startled by a light touch on his shoulder. He turned to see a short balding man with a neatly trimmed white mustache. Colin Donnelly.

Donnelly was dressed in a dark suit, starched white shirt, and maroon tie. Worry lines cut deep across his forehead. The man had aged a great deal since Byron had last seen him.

"I didn't know if you'd come," Donnelly said.

"That makes two of us," Byron replied as he stood. He was a full head taller than Donnelly.

"Why don't you join the rest of the family, down in front?" Donnelly offered.

"I'm fine right here," Byron said.

Donnelly stood there, searching for the words. "Regardless of what you may think of me, John, I did love your mother."

Byron's jaw flexed but he said nothing.

"I had hoped that we might put all of this behind us now," Donnelly said, extending a hand toward Byron.

"*Now?*" Byron said with a raised voice. "Now that my mother has passed, you mean?"

"Yes. Now that Molly has gone to be with God."

"That's what hope will do for you," Byron scoffed as he brushed past Donnelly and walked from the church.

IT WAS NEARLY noontime as Diane stepped out of the elevator and walked toward the front lobby of 109. As she passed by the information desk she saw the familiar face of Khalid Muhammad, Byron's neighbor. Muhammad was speaking with the desk officer through the bulletproof glass partition.

"Khalid," Diane said as she propped open the lobby door and stuck her head out. "What are you doing here?"

"Sergeant Joyner," Muhammad said as he turned, his excitement at seeing her obvious. "I have come here to see you."

"Me?" she asked. "Why do you need to see me?"

He approached her. "Could we please talk with some privacy?"

Finding the first-floor interview room vacant, Diane led him inside and closed the door. After they were seated, she repeated her question. "So why were you looking for me, Khalid?"

"I heard about Sergeant Byron's troubles. I'm worried for him."

Me too, she thought. "I'm sure he would appreciate your concern, Khalid. But these things have a way of working themselves out." But she wondered even as she said the words if she really believed them. "Is that why you've come to see me, because of John?"

Muhammad shook his head and reached into his coat pocket. "No. I came to give you something." He handed her a plastic Ziploc that, at first glance, appeared empty.

"What is this?" she asked, holding the baggie up and examining it until she saw the hairs.

"I took those from Ahmed Ali's son, Abdi."

"You pulled them out of his head?" Diane asked, sincerely hoping he hadn't.

Muhammad smiled and shook his head again. "No, no, not from his head. During my visit to the Ali home last night I pulled these from the Abdi's hairbrush in his bedroom."

"Why?"

"I watch *CSI*. The investigators are always taking hairs to identify people on those shows. I wore latex gloves too," he said proudly.

"But why did you think we might need them?" she asked.

"Detective Sergeant Byron seems to think that Abdi might know something about the robbery of the laundromat. I know the Alis say he does not, but I thought this might help you to know for sure."

Diane didn't know if they had any DNA samples to compare but she planned to check with Gabe Pelligrosso as soon as she was finished with Muhammad. She assisted Muhammad in writing a statement about what he had done, and couldn't help but be touched by the risks this man had taken to try to help them.

Muhammad signed his statement, then handed it to her.

"Why did you do this, Khalid?" she asked. "Certainly, you must know that your friends will be upset with you if this comes out."

Muhammad hung his head. "Some of them will be. I know you are right. But I am hopeful that this will prove Abdi's innocence."

"What if it doesn't?"

Muhammad smiled weakly. "Then we will have the truth." He paused a moment before he spoke again. "Sergeant Byron is a good man, isn't he?"

"I believe he is."

Muhammad stood up from the table. "Please tell Sergeant

Byron I am very sorry." He pointed to the baggie. "I hope this helps you."

AFTER ESCORTING MUHAMMAD out of the building, Diane headed directly for the third floor. She found Pelligrosso in the lab conversing with Evidence Technician Junkins.

"Hey, Sarge," Junkins said.

No matter how often she'd heard the greeting it never rang quite true. She wasn't sure if it was because her unseen chevrons were still so new or if it was because as the department's PR sergeant, who oversaw no one, she did not feel the least bit like a supervisor.

She held up the bag. "I just had some evidence handed to me. Not sure if it will be of any help to you or not."

"What is it?" Pelligrosso asked.

Diane handed him the bag along with a completed evidence sheet, maintaining the chain of custody. "These are hairs from Abdirahman Ali."

Both evidence technicians' eyes widened.

"You're kidding," Pelligrosso said as he took both items from her.

"Nope. Sergeant Byron's neighbor, Khalid Muhammad, a friend of the Alis, pulled them from Abdi's hairbrush."

Pelligrosso held the Ziploc up close to his face, looking at the hairs contained therein. "I recovered a single hair from a torn piece of fabric stuck to a fence in Kennedy Park. Haggerty said that one of the robbery suspects got caught on the fence when he was chasing them. We think the fabric could be from the suspect who got away."

Junkins looked puzzled. "How can we use that if it was seized illegally? Won't those hairs be considered fruit of the poisonous tree?"

Diane spoke up. "They would if we'd seized them without consent or a warrant. But not if Khalid took them and provided them to us. He was acting on his own, not at our behest."

Pelligrosso jumped in. "Sarge is dead-on, junior. These hairs are as good as if we'd had a warrant." He shifted his gaze back to Diane. "Now, we just need to find out if they match."

"How long?" she asked.

Pelligrosso shrugged. "I'll do my best to light a fire under the guys at the state lab. I'll let you know."

"EVEN IF YOU get a match, I'm afraid the DNA by itself won't be enough," Assistant Attorney General Ferguson said. "A judge will want more before signing off on a search warrant."

Diane had wanted to run her case by Ferguson before approaching the District Attorney's Office.

"Because?" she asked.

Ferguson settled back in his chair. "Because all this evidence would show is that Abdi Ali climbed over the fence in question recently. The boy frequents Kennedy Park because he lives nearby and because he attends a nearby high school and has friends in the area. Kids probably cut through the park all the time."

"But Hags said that he was chasing the suspects from the robbery over that fence and thought one of them might have torn his sweatshirt in the process."

Ferguson removed his reading glasses and set them on the table in front of him. "Diane, I'm not looking to undermine what you're trying to accomplish here. Trust me, I want to clear Haggerty's name as much as you do. But you're ignoring some key holes in the evidentiary chain. Haggerty didn't seize the material immediately after the shooting, so you would have a time gap to contend with. How long between the chase and when the hair was recovered?"

"Close to twelve hours, I'd guess."

"Any defense attorney worth his or her salt would get that evidence thrown out along with anything else you might recover as a result of the bad warrant. I'd hate to chance it and have you lose something even more important, like the gun."

Diane said nothing.

"Did Haggerty actually point the fabric out?" Ferguson asked hopefully.

"No," Diane said. "He told us where it happened and Gabe Pelligrosso found it the next morning."

Neither one of them needed to say it, but they both knew that Sean Haggerty wouldn't be making their case any stronger now that he was dead.

Diane felt hopelessness circulate through her like a powerful drug. She wondered if this was how John was feeling. She knew Ferguson was right. The evidence was useless without something further to bolster it in the eyes of the court.

"What about the sneaker prints?" Ferguson asked. "Did you get anywhere with finding a match?"

"Gabe identified the sneaker brand and size but not the owner."

"I'm sorry, Diane. Keep at it. Bring me something more solid and I'll help you get your warrant."

DIANE RETURNED TO 109. She couldn't believe how quickly her stress level had risen. Not that her position as the department's public relations sergeant wasn't stressful. Dealing with Rumsfeld on a daily basis was extremely taxing, mostly because he enjoyed

listening to himself ramble on about everything. And the idiosyn-
cratic behavior of news media types, like Billingslea, was always
a challenge, but the pressure associated with the cases currently
under investigation by the detectives now under her charge was
ridiculous. What had she been thinking? It had sounded like
such an easy transition when LeRoyer suggested it. All she had to
do was find the missing robber and gun, clear Haggerty's name,
without pissing anyone else off, calm the city's unrest, and put a
bow on the murder case against Derrick Vanos and Terrence Alfonsi, and find Micky Cavallaro. No big deal. *Oh, and if it wouldn't
be too much trouble, see if you can put John back together while
you're at it.*

She glanced at the stack of folders piled atop John's filing cabinet,
reports from the Plummer shooting that had been removed from
the CID conference room after the administration had deemed the
case closed. The conference room had to be cleaned out to prep for
the next major case. *What a bunch of bullshit*, she thought. The city
would probably settle out of court, paying off the Plummers and
their attorney on a wrongful death suit.

She knew they were still missing something. They had to be.
Something that was obscured by the more obvious parts of the
case. But what? *Did the incident go down as Hags had described?*
John certainly believed so, or at least he had believed it enough to
get himself suspended. The bullet Pelligrosso had found tended to
support Hags's version too.

Diane placed her elbows on top of the desk, closed her eyes,
and rested her head in her palms. She wondered if it was possible
to want a case to break so badly that it just happened.

*Please God, give me a sign, something to point me in the right
direction.*

She waited. Nothing. No file folder containing the answer floated magically onto the desk, or fell from the stack and landed on the floor. She massaged her temples with her fingers. "Dammit," she said.

The desk phone rang, startling her. It was Dustin Tran.

"Sorry to bother you, Sarge," Tran said.

"You're not bothering me," Diane said. "What is it?"

"I think I may have something."

DIANE HAD CAUGHT the breathless excitement in Tran's voice when he telephoned. Now that she was standing in his office face-to-face with the computer crimes detective, she could see that none of his excitement had waned.

"You said you might have something for me," Diane said.

"I think I just might," he said.

"What is it?"

"Well, you know that I maintain phony Facebook profiles, right?"

She did know. It was one of the many tools law enforcement agencies availed themselves of in order to catch online sexual predators. "And?"

"And I took the liberty of friending the students that Sergeant Byron was looking at as possible accomplices of Tommy Plummer."

"And they accepted?"

"Of course they did. Most of these kids will accept a friend request from anyone who has a good-looking profile picture."

"Anyway," Diane said, anxious for him to get to the point.

"Right. So, after they accepted my request I began following their friends and figured out which ones went to Portland High and which ones they had the most interaction with. Like possible girlfriends or besties. Check out this profile."

Tran pulled up the page of an attractive auburn-haired girl named Bethany Simpson. The profile photograph captured her in mid-jump wearing a blue-and-white Portland Bulldogs cheerleading outfit.

"This girl is a junior at Portland and among her 637 friends are Ali, Plummer, Freeman, and Henderson."

"How does that help us?" Diane asked. "It looks like she's friends with half the high school."

Tran turned in the chair to look at her. "Bethany is one of those teenagers who wears her heart on her sleeve. You know the type. Every single thought that pops into her head she posts on social media. Well, yesterday she posted this."

Diane watched as Tran scrolled down past her recent posts to yesterday's. The post in question read: "What should a person do if someone they really care about asks them to keep a secret, even if it's something bad?"

"Then, of course, there are the usual responses from friends whenever somebody posts this kind of ambiguous and intriguing stuff. *OMG. What happened? Who is it? What is the secret? Can you DM me?* All the usual BS and emoji trains."

"I still don't see how you're making the connection between Bethany's post and the shooting of Tommy Plummer," Diane said.

Tran wordlessly scrolled back to the top of Simpson's page and clicked on the About link. "She's listed herself as in a relationship. Guess who with?"

"Who?"

"Mohammed Sayed."

Chapter 28

Friday, 2:55 P.M.,
January 27, 2017

DIANE AND MELISSA Stevens drove straight to Portland High. The school day had been over for nearly an hour, but Diane was betting that Bethany Simpson would still be there, attending an after-school activity, like cheerleading. They found her at the gym in the middle of practice. After identifying themselves to Simpson's coach and explaining their reason for the interruption, they pulled Bethany into a musty equipment room where they could talk undisturbed.

"Bethany, do you know why we're here?" Diane began.

"No," she responded with an innocent shake of her head.

"We understand that you're dating Mohammed Sayed. How long have you been seeing each other?"

Simpson's eyes widened noticeably. "Mo and I have been going out since September. Why are you asking about him?"

"Why do you think?" Stevens asked.

"I—I have no idea," Simpson stammered. Her eyes darted back and forth between the two detectives.

"I don't think that's entirely true, Bethany," Diane said.

"Tell me about the secret you were asked to keep," Stevens said.

Simpson crossed her arms defensively. "I don't know what you're—"

"On your Facebook page," Diane said. "You asked your friends a question about keeping a secret. What secret?"

Stevens handed the girl a printed copy of the posting.

Simpson studied the printout as if she hadn't written it, then laughed nervously. "Oh, this. This is about a girlfriend of mine. She told me something in confidence."

Diane wasn't convinced by the young girl's performance. "You're sure it has nothing to do with Mo?" she asked.

"Positive."

Diane saw the roses blooming on the young girl's face, betraying her deceit.

"Bethany, has Mohammed, or anyone else, talked to you about the night Tommy Plummer was killed?"

"No," she said, shaking her head. "And I don't know anything about that either."

Diane and Stevens exchanged a quick glance. She knew Stevens wasn't buying the story either, but this wasn't the time to press it. If Simpson was lying and they pushed her into a corner now, it was far less likely that they would be able to reapproach her for a second interview. Better to let her believe that her lie had deceived them.

Diane forced a smile. "Well, I'm so sorry we bothered you, Bethany. Thank you for clearing this up."

"Any time," Simpson said, a little too cheerfully.

Diane offered her hand and Simpson accepted it with a quick sweaty shake.

"Here's my card if you do hear something," Diane said. "I've written my number on the back."

THE BLACK GULL was located squarely in the center of Portland's west end. It was the local watering hole for the middle-aged drinkers who just wanted to be left alone with their thoughts. Anyone dumb enough to violate another's space at the Gull, and occasionally somebody was, might just get a punch in the mouth for their transgression. Byron sat alone at the bar for the first time in nearly two years. He'd returned to pay homage to the nectar of his forefathers. Sitting before him were three shot glasses topped with Lagavulin. The sixteen-year-old single malt was four times as old and twice as expensive as his usual poison. But if he was celebrating the end of his self-imposed exile from drunkenness he might as well do it in style.

Byron picked up one of the glasses and clinked it against the others for luck, then sipped. He had downed the first few shots just to set himself right, but given the price and the quality of his upgrade he decided that savoring it might be the more prudent option. Byron let his eyes wander about the bar as he took it all in. He enjoyed the fact that the Black Gull remained constant. The smell of stale beer, the dark oak plank flooring worn from years of sliding stools, the cork dartboard in the corner; nothing ever changed. The Gull wasn't a cop bar, far from it. The cop bar had always been the Sportsman's on Congress Street, where Byron's dad and many of the other old-time police officers had hung out, until it closed in 1999.

Byron had been coming to the Black Gull since his first days as a detective. The Gull had been Ray Humphrey's bar, precisely because it wasn't a cop bar. It was where he and Ray had solved all of the world's problems. Byron wished Ray was still around to help with the current problem. Although technically it wasn't his problem any longer, since Haggerty was dead and Byron was on suspension. What did he care if the rest of the city thought of Haggerty as a trigger-happy cowboy?

Not my circus, not my monkey, he thought, recalling a phrase that his father, Reece, had often bandied about when talking about department politics, and a phrase that Byron had never truly understood until he began working at 109. The problem was that he did care. *Fuck the job, this was personal.*

It was true—Haggerty was gone and nothing Byron nor anyone else could do would ever change that. But his name had been sullied. Hags's good reputation had been stripped away. And a cop without a good reputation wasn't a cop at all.

Byron cared because it did matter. It mattered to Haggerty's mom and dad, and to every cop who put the uniform on and went to work each day, and to every spouse who worried that their warrior in blue might not make it home again, and to every kid who believed there was good in the world and that it always triumphed over evil. It mattered because Haggerty was a good cop who had been let down by the very people he protected. It mattered to Byron because Hags was his friend.

Maybe I did let this case get too personal, he thought.

Perhaps he had run a bit roughshod over some people trying to get at the truth. Byron was used to people lying to him. They did it every day. But this time it had been different. Byron had always worked hard to see that only the guilty paid the price for their crimes. All Hags was guilty of was doing his job and for that he had been thrown to the wolves.

Byron emptied the shot glass and placed it on the bar beside the other empty. He slid the last one over and held it up in front of his face, studying it.

The bartender swung by as if on autopilot. "You good, Sarge?"

"Since you're here." He watched as Nick recharged the glasses. "Thanks, Nick."

Byron stared at the glass in his hand as if the answers might be contained therein. *There had to be answers somewhere*, he thought. This was just another case, albeit a very personal one. But pushing that aside, it was still just a case. Like the hundreds of cases he'd investigated before. Had they missed something? Had *he*? He had located Erlene Jackson, the reluctant witness to the shooting. And they had found the bullet. The bullet, intended for Haggerty that had sailed wide of its mark. But they hadn't located the gun, or the second robber. No proof. All he had were theories and roadblocks. Each time he had approached the case from a different direction he met with resistance. Detour signs had been erected at every turn, all directing him toward dead ends. What he needed was a way back. Back to the start.

"Remember what I always told you, Sarge," the voice of his mentor, Ray Humphrey, said as clearly as if he'd been bellied up to the bar right beside Byron. "When you get stuck on a case, go back to the beginning."

Byron turned to look, but of course Ray wasn't there. Ray was never there. Only two empty stools and an unshaven guy wearing brown coveralls staring slack-jawed at the television behind the bar. Ray was dead.

Back to the beginning. Back to the night Haggerty had shot Tommy Plummer. Back to the robbery at the laundromat.

"I guess I shouldn't have taken that overtime, huh, Sarge?" Haggerty had said, his voice still bouncing around inside Byron's head.

"No, Hags, I guess you shouldn't have," Byron said aloud.

Coveralls glanced in Byron's direction for a moment before turning his attention back to the television.

"You shoulda spent more time taking the theft report," Byron said. "Had another cup of coffee at the 7-Eleven."

Byron reached for his glass, then froze. *Where was the shoplifting report?* He thought back to every piece of paper he'd seen generated on this case. Every statement, every supplement, every piece of evidence—he had looked at all of it. But he'd never seen anything from the 7-Eleven. He pulled out his cell intending to call Diane, then stopped. Calling her now, in his current condition, after ignoring *her* calls, was at best foolhardy. He replaced the cellphone and polished off the remaining Irish.

DIANE'S WORKDAY WAS over. And it felt as though it had been nothing but a series of starts and stops. Khalid's visit had given her some hope, but the waiting game for a DNA comparison was a familiar one and, as Ferguson had so aptly pointed out, futile. Tran's lead on Bethany Simpson had also looked promising, but the interview had gotten them nowhere. She was confident that the student was holding back information, but getting her to admit it would take time.

Diane sat in her unmarked, parked at the curb, a good ten minutes before finally approaching the house. She climbed the steps and rang the doorbell, then stood waiting on the front porch. After several moments the porch light came on and the inside door swung open.

"Diane?" Kay said, sounding as surprised as she looked.

"Hello, Kay. Bet you didn't expect to see me."

"Is everything all right?" Kay asked.

Diane forced a smile. "I was hoping we could sit down and talk." She held up a bottle of red wine. "About John."

Kay pushed the storm door open. "I'll get the glasses."

DIANE SAT AT the kitchen table making awkward small talk while Kay poured the wine. "Your home is beautiful."

"Thank you. I haven't been here that long. I'm still trying to decide how I want to decorate it." Kay approached the table, handing Diane her glass, before sitting down in the chair at the end of the table to Diane's left. "Every space speaks with a different voice, don't you think?"

"I guess that's probably true," she said as she wondered what her ramshackle Westbrook home was trying to tell her. Diane took a sip of the fragrant liquid.

"So, what else should we discuss while waiting for you to get your courage up?" Kay asked.

"You think I'm stalling?"

"I know you are."

"I forgot, you're a shrink. I'll have to be more careful what I give away."

Kay smiled politely. "I was also John's wife for twenty years. What's going on, Diane?"

Diane let out a long sigh. "I guess you probably know by now that John and I have been seeing each other, on and off, for a while. And I think—" She couldn't figure out how to continue. It felt wrong to even be here. Like she was doing something behind John's back. Like she had opened a door that shouldn't have been opened.

"Do you care about him?" Kay asked, following Diane's silence.

"Very much."

"But?" The word hung there, punctuating the silence.

"He's impossible to understand sometimes," Diane said at last.

"He drives me so goddamned crazy." Then she couldn't help herself. It all came spilling out. All the things she was afraid of: John's drinking, his explosive temper, his dark side. When at last she finished she was emotionally exhausted. And yet it felt like a great weight had been lifted. She had never shared her feelings about John with anyone but Melissa Stevens. And never to this depth. Diane swallowed the remnants in her glass, then set it on the table. "I don't know why I told you any of that. I have no right. I shouldn't have come here."

"Nonsense." Kay picked up Diane's glass and refilled it. "Here."

"Thank you."

"How is John?"

"Not good. He's been suspended."

"For what? Is this about the officer who was killed? Haggerty?"

Diane nodded. "John was working on the shooting Sean Haggerty was involved in. It was going badly even before Sean was killed. He's in a dangerous place, Kay."

Diane could feel her emotions bubbling to the surface again as the first tear streamed down her cheek. She wiped it away with the back of her hand, then looked up, making eye contact with Kay. "And I don't know how to reach him."

It was quarter after one in the morning as Byron staggered down the sidewalk from the Black Gull toward his car. After several failed attempts to retrieve his keys from his pocket he stopped walking. His coordination was impaired to the point that he couldn't perform both tasks at once.

"Maybe they should add that roadside test to the OUI training at the Maine Criminal Justice Academy."

Byron turned toward the voice and saw LeRoyer with his arms crossed leaning against the door of his SUV.

"You haven't got enough shit piled on your plate, John?" LeRoyer asked. "Thinking of adding a drunk driving charge to your CV?"

"What are you, my—?" Byron stopped himself.

"Hop in, sailor," LeRoyer said. "I'll give you a ride."

Several minutes later they were cruising through downtown with LeRoyer behind the wheel. Byron couldn't shake the feeling that he was the kid who got caught sneaking out of the house late at night.

"Do you have to Armor All everything in this damn car?" Byron asked as his ass slid around on the vinyl seat.

LeRoyer looked over at him. "I heard about your mother, John. I'm sorry."

He opened his mouth to say something spiteful until he saw the sincerity in his lieutenant's face. "Thanks."

"I don't remember giving you permission to self-destruct though," LeRoyer said.

Too drunk to conjure up a witty comeback, Byron ignored the comment. "How'd you know where to find me?"

"You're not so hard to find, John. I heard about Molly, and when Diane told me she couldn't reach you, I knew you'd stop by the Gull eventually."

"You paid the bartender, didn't you?" Byron asked, already knowing the answer. "How much?"

"Twenty bucks."

Byron couldn't stop a silly grin from spreading across his face. "You here to read me the riot act, Marty? Gonna tell me how bad I've fucked up my career?"

LeRoyer glanced at Byron again. "You don't need me for that." His eyes returned to the road. "I'm here as a friend, John. A friend who doesn't want to see you fuck up your life."

Byron said nothing.

"I assigned Diane to cover your duties in your absence," Le-Royer said.

"My absence? You make it sound like I'm out with the flu." Byron wondered if that meant she was still pursuing the laundromat robbery.

The two men rode in silence until they reached the end of Byron's driveway. LeRoyer slid the transmission into Park and waited for Byron to get out.

"I went to see him a few days after the shooting," Byron said.

"Hags?"

Byron nodded. "He was pretty messed up in the head. And starting to doubt his own memory of what had happened."

"What did you do?"

"I took the gun he was playing with. Didn't like the things he was saying."

LeRoyer gave a silent nod.

"But after I left him, *I* began to wonder whether it was a good shoot or not."

LeRoyer sighed. "Just makes you a good investigator, John."

"Yeah? But what kind of friend does it make me?"

LeRoyer said nothing.

Byron fumbled with the door handle until he finally managed to get it open and stepped out of the SUV. He leaned in and looked back at LeRoyer, supporting himself by placing his forearm against the roof. "Thanks for the ride, LT. Does your wife know what you were doing out so late?"

"Yup."

"Square this with her for me?"

"Screw you, John," LeRoyer said. "Square it with her yourself. Oh, and you owe me a Jackson."

Chapter 29

BYRON GRADUALLY AWOKE to a gentle shaking and a woman's voice. "John, wake up." It was Diane. She'd come by to check on him. Slowly he opened his eyes. Daylight. The harsh glare of sunlight streaming through the windows felt like someone was driving spikes into his eyeballs. His head was pounding, keeping time with his pulse.

"Jesus, you look like hell," she said. "I was worried. I couldn't reach you on your cell."

"I shut it off," he said as he slowly swung his legs over the edge of the sofa and sat up. Immediately the room began to spin. He closed his eyes and held his head in his hands to steady it. He was still a little drunk.

"I'll make some coffee," she said as she headed toward the kitchen. "Where do you keep the Tylenol?"

"Bathroom cabinet," he croaked, noticing that he was still

dressed in yesterday's clothes and wondering if something stronger than coffee might be more useful. Scanning the room, he saw the empty bottle of Jameson lying on the floor beside the couch, along with an overturned glass and several photo albums, one of which was open. He couldn't remember having taken the albums out or even looking at them, but he knew what they contained. He reached down and flipped the open album closed just as Diane returned to the living room.

"Here, swallow these," she said, handing him a glass of water and three white caplets. "What's that?" she asked, pointing to the album he'd closed.

"Nothing that matters now," he said. He staggered to his feet without taking either offering and rushed toward the bathroom.

Byron dropped to the floor in front of the toilet and wretched up the sour remains of the prior evening. When he had finished he washed up at the sink. The mirror told the tale. Bloodshot eyes accompanied the deep dark circles of exhaustion. The salt and pepper in his once dark hair and unshaven face made him look more like his father than he'd ever realized.

Moving slowly and deliberately, to keep the room from spinning out beneath him, he returned to the living room where Diane stood waiting.

"Feel better?" she asked.

"No," he said, gingerly lowering himself to the couch.

"Let's try this again," she said, handing him the water and Tylenol.

He washed the pills down.

"Coffee will be ready in a minute," she said.

"Thanks." He laid back on the couch and closed his eyes.

"I heard what happened at the reception."

"It seemed like the thing to do," he said.

"And I heard about your mom. I'm sorry. You could have told me, you know."

He didn't know how to respond.

"Wanna talk about it?" she asked.

"No." He waited for her to share whatever else was on her mind.

"You couldn't have saved him, you know. Hags."

He forced his eyes to open and turned his head to look at her, but said nothing.

"Sean's death wasn't your fault any more than Tommy Plummer's was," Diane continued.

"I know that," he said.

She bent down and picked up the empty bottle. "This won't help either."

"Spare me the sermon, okay?"

She snapped. "Oh, what? You're hurting, John? I got a news flash for you. We're all hurting. Hags was like a brother to all of us. Not *just* you."

Byron said nothing. Her shouting wasn't helping the pain in his head, but he thought mentioning it probably wouldn't improve her mood.

"I get it," she said. "It sucks, big-time. But you know what? We all have to keep going. We're cops. It's what we do, John. There are still cases to solve. Rapists, robbers, and murderers to put away. It doesn't stop just because one of us is gone."

She stormed out of the room with the empty whiskey bottle, but he knew she wasn't finished with him. Not by a long shot.

His brain was fuzzy. There was something he'd wanted to share with her about the Plummer case, but he couldn't quite recall what it was. He made an effort to focus his thoughts, but thinking only made his head hurt worse.

Diane returned to the living room a few moments later. "Here," she said.

Carefully, he sat up and took the hot mug from her. His hands were visibly shaking.

"You wanna feel sorry for yourself?" she asked, picking up right where she'd left off. "Go right ahead. You're a big boy. Go on and lose yourself in that damn bottle if it makes you feel better. Be a self-ish prick if you want. No one gives a shit about John Byron anyway, right?"

He still didn't know how to respond. She really was pissed at him. And if he was being honest, she had good reason. He was being selfish.

"Except your friends and family care, John. Kay cares."

He looked at her, surprised that she had mentioned Kay. *Had Diane spoken with her?*

Diane crossed her arms defensively. Her eyes welled up with tears.

"And you know what? So do I. Okay? I fucking care, John. I care about what happens to you. A lot."

Byron hadn't thought he could feel any worse, but as he watched the tears streaming down her cheeks, he realized he was wrong.

"You keep this up and it will kill you," she said. "Is that what you want?"

All he really wanted was for the pounding in his head to depart and for the room to stop spinning. When he didn't respond, she turned on her heels and marched out of the condo, her exit punctuated by the slamming door.

It took Diane ten minutes to cool down and regain her composure. Was she doing the right thing? She didn't know. Kay had suggested tough love might be the only way to reach John, and Diane had just dished out a shovelful. But she was already second-guessing the tactic.

She pulled into the lot across from the ball field at Payson Park to recheck her makeup. Working carefully, she did her best to remove any indication that she had been crying. Well, except for the puffiness around her eyes. There was nothing for that. She had returned the makeup to her pocketbook and was driving toward 109 to meet Nugent and Stevens when her cell rang. It was Assistant Attorney General Jim Ferguson.

"Morning, Jim," she said, attempting to sound like she was back in control.

"Goooood morning, Diane," he said, mimicking Robin Williams's character from the movie about the DJ in Vietnam. "Didn't know if you might be up for a cup o' joe, on neutral ground."

"I'd like that," she said. "I'm in Portland now, headed to the station. Where were you thinking?"

"I'm still southbound on 95. I'm craving something greasy. How about Miss Portland Diner? Fifteen minutes?"

"I'll grab us a table."

Byron sat staring into the empty coffee mug, as if the answers might be contained therein. They weren't. Diane was right, of course. And he knew it. Deep down he'd known it for a long time. He was stuck in a rut and no matter who he tried to blame for his problems it all came back to him. He was his own worst enemy. He'd always had trouble expressing his emotions. It had cost him his marriage to Kay, and now his relationship with Diane was floundering because of it. He cared about her a great deal, even more than he dared admit, but if grades were given out for showing it he would have scored a big fat *F.* The one thing he'd always been good at, even as a drunk, was being a cop. But now . . . He paused in mid-thought. *A drunk. Is that what I am?*

You did say it, John, the voice in his head said.

"Actually, I thought it," he said to an empty room. "I am a drunk." It was the first time he'd ever said it aloud. "I *am* a drunk." He said it again, putting more emphasis on the present tense of being. It rang true. He was. Sadly he realized that the only things separating him from the men he'd seen on the street were his job and his condo. *Pretty damn thin.* He had never wanted to face it. But Diane was right. If he didn't get help now he'd risk losing everything. Including Diane, the one, perhaps the only, good thing in his life.

He glanced at the clock on the wall; it was nearly ten. The painkiller Diane had given him was beginning to work its magic. The banging inside of his head had dulled somewhat. No longer did it feel like baseball bats smashing against a metal trash can; it was more like drumsticks on a plastic bucket. He forced himself up from the couch and staggered into the kitchen. He brewed another cup of coffee, leaning against the counter while he waited for the Keurig to spit its last. He closed his eyes and sipped the hot beverage, relishing the soothing warmth flowing into his belly. He opened his eyes again, waited for them to focus, then slowly climbed the stairs to his bedroom.

DIANE MANAGED TO score a booth at the far end of the dining car, allowing her a view of the entire space. While the stick-built addition protruding from the rear of the restaurant was far more comfortable, there was something magical about sitting in the original steel structure, next to the long counter and its many chrome stools with inviting padded tops. The Miss P was pure Americana.

It was closer to twenty-five minutes before Ferguson's head appeared at the far end of the diner. Diane exchanged a wave with him. She watched him navigate around the waitstaff and up the narrow aisle toward her table.

"Sorry I'm late," he said as he slid onto the bench across from her. "Any word on our missing laundromat magnate?"

"No. It's like he vanished without a trace."

"Or someone vanished him. Permanently."

They ordered breakfast, then Diane filled him in on the latest.

"So you're still pursuing the Plummer shooting?" Ferguson asked as he sopped up the yoke on his plate with a piece of wheat toast.

"Yes," she said. "The lieutenant has assigned me as John's temporary replacement while he's on suspension."

"Good. Glad to hear it. I tried calling him, but I think his phone is off. How's he doing?"

Not wanting the emotion to show through in her voice, she hesitated a moment before answering. "Not well."

Ferguson pushed his empty plate away, then picked up his mug. "Has he fallen?"

Diane studied his face a moment before answering. She was surprised that he knew and was so casual about it. "Headfirst."

"I was afraid of that," Ferguson said with a sigh. "Haggerty's death has really knocked him back, hasn't it?"

"Not just Haggerty's," she said.

Ferguson cocked his head to one side. "There was another?"

"Molly, John's mother."

"Oh shit."

IT WAS PAST noon by the time Diane arrived at 109. She hadn't so much as stepped into CID when Melissa Stevens and Mike Nugent appeared, each sporting a grin on their face.

"What is it?" Diane asked.

Nugent spoke up first. "Remember the douchebag from South Portland who gave the television exclusive about how he witnessed Plummer surrendering before Haggerty shot him?"

"Yeah, Perez, wasn't it?" Diane asked.

"Lucas Perez," Stevens said as she held up the Cumberland County Jail prisoner list. "The drug guys locked him up for possession last night."

"How does that help us?" Diane asked.

"He couldn't make bail," Stevens said, her grin widening. "He'll be in at least until he goes in front of a judge Monday morning."

"Perez wouldn't let the sarge and me anywhere near his baby mama," Nugent said. "This might be the perfect opportunity to punch a hole in that a-hole's story."

"Go," Diane said. "And good luck."

STEVENS KNOCKED ON the storm door to the Perez/Gomez unit for the third time, then waited to see if Ms. Gomez would answer.

"She just peeked out the window," Nugent said from the sidewalk. "She knows we're here." Nugent joined his partner on the steps.

The inside door swung open, and as before Maria Gomez stood there holding her baby. "Yes?" she said.

Both detectives held up their identification for her to see.

Stevens took the lead. "Ms. Gomez, my name is Detective Stevens and I believe you already met my partner, Detective Nugent."

Nugent gave a silent nod.

"If you're looking for Lucas, he's not here," Gomez said.

"Actually, Maria, it's you we'd like to speak with," Stevens said. "Do you mind if we talk inside?"

Gomez hesitated a moment, then stepped back. "Come in," she said.

BY TWO O'CLOCK that afternoon, Byron had managed to shake off most of the effects of his hangover. A long hot shower and shave made him feel almost human. But he still couldn't remember what he'd wanted to tell Diane, and given their last conversation, if it could even be called a conversation, he wasn't sure she'd take his call anyway.

He dressed in a clean pair of jeans and the wool sweater that Diane had given him for Christmas, then went downstairs to fix something to eat. As he entered the kitchen he saw the empty whiskey bottle standing on the counter next to a sink full of dirty dishes. He was starving, but something else was vying for his attention. A quick peek inside the fridge confirmed that he might be better off going out for food. He found his keys and cellphone, then slipped into his shoes and peacoat. It wasn't until he opened the front door and stepped out into the cool afternoon air that he remembered how he'd gotten home. *Shit*, he thought. His car was still parked on the West End.

DIANE WAS CAMPED out in the CID conference room poring over everything in the case again when Stevens and Nugent walked in.

"Perez's story was total bullshit, Sarge," Nugent said.

"Gomez actually spoke with you?" Diane asked.

"And then some," Stevens said. "Perez wasn't in Kennedy Park last Sunday night. He was making a drug run from Lowell, Massachusetts, back to Portland, with his girlfriend."

"Yeah. Apparently, Perez's baby mama doesn't approve of him catting around."

"Don't call her that," Stevens said as she gave Nugent a punch in the shoulder. "It's Maria Gomez."

"Sorry," Nugent said. "Didn't know you were so sensitive."

"Want another one?" Stevens said, drawing her arm back and balling up her fist.

"Did she say why he went on camera?" Diane asked.

"Can't help himself," Nugent said. "Wanted his fifteen minutes."

"Did she provide a written statement?" Diane asked.

"Right here," Stevens said, pulling the paper out of a folder.

"So, the one damning statement to the media that got everyone whipped up into a frenzy is debunked," Diane said as much to herself as the two detectives.

"Yeah," Nugent said. "Want me to call the news channels?"

If only it were that easy, Diane thought.

BYRON'S FOOD RUN had led him straight back to the Gull. As he watched the bartender top off the glass, Byron wondered when his need for the Irish had transformed itself from social to medicinal. In his early days with the police department it had just been a part of being a cop. Toasting to one another's good health or to an important arrest or successful prosecution was part and parcel to the culture. District attorneys, assistant attorney generals, detectives, even the occasional judge would gather to blow off a little steam. But as he sat there alone on the barstool beside the so-called dregs of society it occurred to him that he had no success to toast. Nor anyone to toast it with. Haggerty was gone, and Byron was wallowing in self-pity. *Was Diane right? Did he need help?* He'd never needed anyone's help before. Or had he? Perhaps he'd just been too damned stubborn to notice, or admit it.

"Is this seat taken?" a familiar voice said from behind him.

"Is that the famous homicide trial attorney James Ferguson?" Byron asked without turning to look.

"None other," Ferguson said. He gestured toward the empty stool next to Byron. "May I?"

"By all means, Counselor," Byron said, fully aware of the slur in his voice and not particularly caring. He signaled the bartender over. "What are you doing slumming around Portland on a weekend?"

"Thought I'd give barhopping a shot. I'm told it's the latest thing."

"My barhopping is limited to hopping up on a stool," Byron said as the bartender approached them. "What are you drinking?"

"Soda water with a lime."

"You're kidding?" Byron said, turning away from the barkeep to look at the AAG.

"Nope."

Byron turned back to the bartender. "You heard the man. Soda water and lime."

The bartender frowned and addressed the newcomer. "We don't have any fresh fruit. Lime juice okay?"

"Fine," Ferguson said. He removed his coat, then settled onto the stool to Byron's left. "So, how you doin', John?"

"Who sent you?" Byron asked.

"What makes you think that I didn't come here of my own volition?"

"For soda water? With lime juice?"

"Hey, don't knock it until you've tried it."

"Was it Diane?"

"I'm bound by a sacred vow not to say."

"What are you now, a priest?" Byron said.

Ferguson chuckled. "Hardly. I'm an attorney, remember?"

"One of the good ones."

The bartender set the full glass carefully in front of Ferguson. Ferguson picked up the glass and held it out toward Byron. "What should we drink to?"

Byron thought for a moment before raising his own glass. "Better days."

"I'll drink to that," Ferguson said as they clinked the glasses together.

Byron knocked the remainder of his whiskey back and set the empty glass on the bar. He looked over at his friend. "Why are you really here, Jim?"

"I came to listen."

"To what?"

"Whatever's on your mind."

"I've got some nosy friends," Byron said.

"No, John. You've got some friends who care about you. More importantly, they care about what happens to you."

Byron said nothing as he raised his hand, signaling to the bartender that he was in need of a refill. He turned back to Ferguson. "Is this the part where you lecture me about alcohol being the devil's workshop and how I need to get a handle on this before it kills me?"

Ferguson picked up his glass and nodded. "You said it. Not me."

Byron looked at what his friend was drinking. "That your normal beverage of choice?"

"It's not normal, but it is my choice."

"How long?" Byron asked.

Ferguson checked his watch. "Fourteen years, eleven months, and seventeen days."

"How the hell do you know that?"

"Easy. In less than two weeks I'll get my fifteen-year coin."

Byron looked at the whiskey in his glass and willed himself not to reach for it. "So, what, now you're gonna try to talk me into joining AA?"

"Not up to me."

"Who is it up to?"

"You, my friend. It's all up to you."

For the next several minutes neither man said anything. It was Byron who broke the awkward silence. "It just seems like such a waste."

"What does?" Ferguson asked.

"A great cop's career derailed by a single moment. Hell, his entire reputation."

"Are we still talking about Sean Haggerty?"

"It isn't fair," Byron said.

"Life isn't fair, my friend."

"Who says I have a problem anyway?" Byron said, hating the implication in his own slurred words.

Ferguson said nothing, as if the question had been rhetorical.

"How do you know I can't stop anytime I want to?" Byron said. "I have before, you know."

Ferguson took a sip of his soda, then placed the glass back on the bar. "Mind if I tell you my story, John?"

Byron shrugged. "Have at it."

"I began drinking in college, like most people, I guess. Weekends. Mostly beer. A lot of keg parties. It didn't really get bad until

I started law school. By then I'd switched to hard stuff: vodka, gin, whiskey, the usual suspects. Just a couple every night to take the edge off. Friday and Saturday nights were for partying. I usually spent Sunday hungover, throwing up, and trying to study. I passed the bar and took a job in the Kennebec County District Attorney's Office. That's where I met Betty. A year later we were married, and I toned it down for a while. At least around her."

Byron stared at his whiskey glass as he listened.

Ferguson continued. "I'm not sure when the wheels first began to come off, but I remember having a couple of high-profile trials. Trials I didn't want to lose. Spent many late nights prepping, and drinking. Started keeping a bottle in my desk at work. Next it was a small flask of vodka in my suit coat, just to give me an edge. I even had a tiny funnel for transferring the booze into the flask. The vodka was great. No odor. I won both trials and kept right on drinking. I guess I thought the alcohol was like a talisman. I'd replenish my stock on the way home from work, never buying from the same store two days in a row. I'd toss the empty bottles in the trash at the gas station and keep a fresh one under the driver's seat in my car."

Byron sat in silence, stunned by the similarity to his own history.

Ferguson continued. "I'd wake up every morning and take a few hits from the bottle I'd hidden in the bathroom cabinet or in the pocket of one of the suit coats in my closet. I'd start the day telling myself I wouldn't drink at work, but as the day wore on and I started to feel sick, like I was coming down with something. I knew of only one thing that would make me better. I told myself a lot of things back in those days. Lied to a lot of people I cared about. Including me."

"What made you finally give it up?" Byron asked, the words tumbling out of his mouth before he could stop himself.

Ferguson turned to look directly at him. "Betty. She sat me down one day and said she'd had enough. Told me she loved me too much to watch me kill myself."

Byron remained silent. But his thoughts were clearer than they should have been given the whiskey. He looked back at the glass, regarding the vessel's contents with a strange combination of longing and revulsion. The cost of his habit had already become incredibly expensive. He'd lost his wife to it. His career was hanging by a thread. And then there was Diane.

"So, you quit?" Byron asked.

"Yup."

"Just like that?"

Ferguson chuckled. "Hardly. I fell on my face a few times. But I finally admitted to myself that I couldn't do it alone. That was the first big step, admitting that I needed help." He paused to take another sip of the soda water. "After that I only had to do one more thing."

"What was that?"

"Ask for it."

Chapter 30

THE EMPTY PAPER tray light was flashing red on the printer as Diane unlocked the door and turned on the lights in the CID lobby. If the report pile was any indication, the patrol units had been out straight all weekend. She replaced the paper in both trays, then grabbed the stack that had already been printed. She headed toward her office, listening to the whir of the printer as it continued to spit out reports, wondering if there was enough toner in the building to finish the task. It took her the better part of two hours to go through all of the cases, and assign them. The additional stack deposited on her desk by Sergeant Peterson at eight o'clock didn't help. Nugent volunteered to handle the in-custody felonies, each of which required affidavits and a signed complaint from the District Attorney's Office, otherwise the prisoners might be released. Diane assigned a Saturday pharmacy robbery to Stevens, then met briefly with LeRoyer at eight-thirty, giving him a thumbnail of the weekend's criminal activity. The lieutenant had asked about progress on the Plummer case, but seemed disinterested as she explained the Gomez interview. She couldn't help feeling that John had been right all along. The command staff had moved on.

As busy as she was, there was one thing occupying her thoughts all morning—the call she'd missed from John the previous night. He'd left her a voicemail, and quite possibly a new lead, something she intentionally withheld from LeRoyer. But lead or no lead, she wasn't happy with John. She realized that the conversation she'd had with him on Saturday morning hadn't changed a thing. Had she really believed that it would? He was clearly drunk on the voicemail. She thought about calling him back, but to what end? Based solely on the background noise, he'd made the call from a bar, most likely the Black Gull. She imagined that some habits died harder than others.

The one upside was that he was still thinking about the case. Still trying to set things right. Regardless of how damaged he was, John was still John. He still possessed that never quit attitude. It was one of many things she loved about him. She only hoped that when he was ready he'd be able to draw on that stubbornness to help himself stay sober. For good.

It was after nine by the time Diane had finished her Monday morning duties, duties that should have been John's. She dropped a stack of statements off with Shirley Grant for typing, then headed for the computer lab.

"Hey, Sarge," Tran greeted as she entered his computerized abode. "What's up?"

"I need you to access an incident report from the mobile database," Diane said.

"From this past weekend?" he asked.

"No. From the night Tommy Plummer was shot."

Tran slumped back in his chair and looked at her. "Anything from that night would already be free of the system. The reports would've automatically printed after the supervisor signed off."

"But not if the report was never completed, right?"

She waited while Tran processed what she was saying.

"No. You're right. Only finished reports submitted to a supervisor for approval would get through the system. If it never got that far it would still be locked in the system. Whose report are you looking for?"

"Haggerty's."

Diane noticed a video running on one of the three computer monitors atop Tran's workstation. "Is that the video from Haggerty's cruiser?"

"Yeah. I'm reviewing everything, hoping we've overlooked something. Can't hurt, right?"

"Right. So, you'll check for that report?"

"I'm on it."

DIANE LEFT TRAN to his own devices in search of the unfinished shoplifting report, assuming that Haggerty had ever been able to even start it, while she headed to the basement of 109.

"Anyone home?" Diane called through the caged upper half of the security door to the property office.

A gruff masculine voice called from somewhere out back. "Who's askin'?"

"It's Diane Joyner, Cowboy."

James "Cowboy" Rollins had been the PPD range officer long before Diane had come to Maine. If the stories about him were true, he'd been a cop in Portland for nearly two decades before she'd even begun her basic police training at the old Gramercy Park academy in New York City.

The handsome white-haired man came into view, dodging boxes and brushing the dust off his hands as he headed toward her. "Hey, Sarge," Rollins said, barely hiding his smile under his signature fireman's mustache. "What brings you down to these parts?"

"Can't a girl just stop by to see her favorite old-time cop?"

He flipped the dead bolt on the cage and swung open the Dutch door to the basement hallway. "Flattery will get you everywhere with me, pretty lady. What can I do you for?"

"I need to get into a locker."

"Lose your key?"

"Sean Haggerty's locker."

IT TOOK DIANE all of thirty seconds to locate what she was after. Haggerty's notebook had been shoved haphazardly, clearly by someone other than Haggerty, into the lower shelf, along with everything else that had been removed from his cruiser following the Kennedy Park shooting. She thanked Cowboy for his help before returning to her office and closing the door.

She sat down at her desk and flipped through Haggerty's duty notebook until she came to the point where the notes ended, and the blank pages began. She turned back a page and read what he had written. *Shoplift. 27 Wash. Ave. Twelve-pack of Bud. S. W, M, husky, young, teens? Freckles, black SS, and black watch cap. Fled E on foot.*

Diane's hopefulness quickly evaporated. John hadn't said what he was looking for specifically, but since both suspects in the Bubble Up robbery had been wearing masks and the missing one was dressed in a red sweatshirt, she didn't think the notes from Hags's unfinished shoplifting report would be of much help after all. She closed the notebook and placed it inside the top drawer of her desk. She called Tran.

"Hey, Sarge," Tran said. "I was just about to call you. There's nothing trapped in the computer from Haggerty."

"Thanks for checking," she said.

She hung up the phone and grabbed her gun and coat. There was still one more thing she could check.

As she walked through CID, headed for the elevators, she caught the eye of Detective Luke Gardiner. She knew that Gardiner had assisted Byron with some of the interviews. Diane veered over toward his desk.

"Morning, Sarge," Gardiner said as she approached.

"Luke. I understand that you and Sergeant Byron worked some of the Portland High interviews together."

"We did. Talked to a few of the students I knew who hung out with Tommy Plummer."

"Wanna take a ride?" she asked.

His eyes lit up at the prospect of getting involved in the case again. "Sure."

THIRTY MINUTES LATER Diane and Gardiner were standing in the computer lab hunched over Tran's shoulders as they stared at the 7-Eleven surveillance video from the night that Plummer was shot.

"What exactly am I looking for?" Tran asked.

"I'm not sure," Diane said. "I know from Haggerty's notes that the shoplifter wasn't the missing robber Haggerty was chasing because he was dressed in a black hoodie not a red one. Guess I'm hoping that they might have cased the 7-Eleven before they hit the laundromat."

"Well, let's see," Tran said. "The time is probably off on this thing. But we should be getting close to when the shoplifting occurred."

The three of them studied the video closely, waiting for something to happen. Several minutes into the tape, a single person entered the store just as the clerk stepped into the back room. The customer's head was down and his hood was up, preventing identification, but his size and clothing generally matched the entry Diane had located in Haggerty's notebook.

She shifted her focus to the upper right-hand part of the screen where the four-camera multiplexer had captured the activity near the beer coolers. The male in the video turned from the coolers, providing the detectives with their first good look at him. He matched the suspect described in Haggerty's notes to a T. Right down to his freckle-covered face.

"I know him," Gardiner said, making no attempt to hide his excitement. "That's Scott Henderson. He's one of the kids who regularly hung out with Tommy. He told us that he was home all night. And his mother gave him an alibi."

Diane turned to Tran. "Print me a still of that ugly, lying mug."

SCOTT HENDERSON'S MOM stood frozen in the doorway to her boss's office. She had one foot in the office and one still in the hallway. Her recognition of Diane and Gardiner as police detectives was obvious. Henderson's eyes shifted from Gardiner to Diane.

"Mrs. Henderson," Diane said as she removed her badge case from her pocket. "I'm Sergeant Joyner and I believe you've already spoken with Detective Gardiner."

Gardiner acknowledged her with a nod.

Henderson's hesitation continued.

Diane gave a predatory smile as she gestured toward the chairs. "Come right in, won't you? Have a seat."

Cautiously, Henderson entered the office and sat down, crossing her arms tightly over her chest. Both detectives pulled chairs up close and sat down facing the woman.

"I imagine you must have some idea why we're here," Diane said.

"It's about Scott, isn't it?" Henderson said, her voice barely a whisper.

"When you previously spoke to Detective Gardiner you told him Scott had been home with you the Sunday night that Tommy Plummer was shot," Diane said.

Gardiner joined in. "You told me that he was home because he'd been grounded, remember?"

"That is what you said, isn't it?" Diane asked.

Henderson nodded. She cast her eyes to the floor, ashamed.

"Why did you lie, Mrs. Henderson?" Diane asked.

"I was afraid of what Scott might have been doing that night. I knew he was out with Tommy. But I swear I didn't know what they were up to."

Neither detective said a word as they waited to see where she would take them.

Henderson uncrossed her arms and began wringing her hands in her lap. She continued. "Scott really was grounded, but I can't control him anymore. It's so hard to work full-time and raise a teenager by myself."

"Were you at home when he returned that night?" Diane asked, trying to get her back on topic.

BEYOND THE TRUTH   357

"Yes. I got home from work about twenty minutes before he showed up."

"Do you remember what time that was?" Diane asked.

"I'm not sure. I guess it must have been around nine."

"Did Scott say anything?" Gardiner asked.

"No. Not really. I asked him where he'd been. He said, 'Out.' Then he went upstairs to his room and slammed the door." Henderson looked up from the floor with tears in her eyes. "Do you really think Scott was involved in the robbery?"

"Do you?" Diane asked.

"I don't know." Henderson put her hands to her face and began to sob. "I'm afraid he might have been."

DIANE OPENED THE door and marched directly into Principal Larrabee's office. Gardiner was right on her heels.

"Excuse me," Larrabee said. "I don't know who you think you are, but you can't just barge in here."

"Oh, I am sorry," Diane said. "Allow me to introduce myself. My name is Detective Sergeant Diane Joyner and I think you already know Detective Gardiner."

"Thank you for introducing yourself, *Detective Sergeant*," Larrabee said, her tone dripping with condescension. "Now I know who to complain about."

"Complain away," Diane said. "But first I need to know which classroom Scott Henderson is currently in."

Diane stood her ground as Larrabee wasted the next five minutes whining, cajoling, and threatening. Finally realizing that the detectives would not be dissuaded, she spit out the room number. Henderson was promptly arrested and transported to 109.

DIANE WENT THROUGH the formality of reading Henderson his Miranda rights before tossing the still photo from the 7-Eleven security video onto the interview room table in front of him. He looked down and in the span of five seconds all the color drained from his young freckled face.

"You said you were home the night Tommy was killed," Diane said. "Check the time and date stamp, sport. Tough to be home when you're out stealing beer from the local convenience store."

Henderson looked back at the detectives, the arrogance returning to his face. "Don't you need to have my mother here if you want to question me?"

Gardiner produced a sheet of paper from the folder he was holding. "She already gave us signed consent."

"So, Scott, you want to tell us what really happened that night?" Diane asked.

Henderson glanced over at Gardiner, then back to Diane. "I have no idea."

"This picture says otherwise," Diane said.

He pushed the photograph away. "This picture says I snatched some beer. Nothing to do with Tommy."

Diane scoffed. "You're telling us that you just happened to sneak out of the house so you could steal some beer, and the timing of your moronic impulse just happened to coincide with the armed robbery your buddies were about to pull less than a half mile up the street?"

Henderson shrugged.

"You don't really think we're dumb enough to believe that, do you?" Gardiner asked.

Henderson scoffed. "I don't know what you're dumb enough to believe. But I don't know anything about a robbery. I was by myself when I stole the beer. Shoplifting's only a misdemeanor. If you're gonna charge me, then go ahead."

Diane could feel her anger rising to the surface. This little shit knew how to push her buttons. She turned and opened the door to the interview room.

"Where are you going?" Henderson asked. "Am I free to leave?"

Before Diane could respond, Gardiner answered for her. "You're the guy with all the answers, Scott. What do you think?"

The detectives exited the room and closed the door.

"How long can we hold him?" Gardiner asked after they were out of earshot.

"We've still got some time. Come on, there's someone else I want to talk to."

AFTER LEAVING SCOTT Henderson in the care of one of the property detectives, Diane and Gardiner found Bethany Simpson right where they knew she'd be, at cheering practice. Simpson's eyes widened at the sight of them.

"Hello again, Bethany," Diane said. "There have been some developments and we need to talk. Let's take a ride."

"Where are we going?" Simpson asked.

"Down to the police station."

Gardiner remained in the gym while Simpson and Diane headed to the locker room.

Diane stood by in silence as Simpson changed into her street clothes. She could see that the girl was becoming emotional.

"I'm sorry," Simpson said as she slid into her coat.

"For?" Diane asked.

"For not telling you the truth."

"About your Facebook post?"

Simpson nodded. Her eyes welled up.

"Did Mo ask you to keep a secret?" Diane asked. "A bad secret?"

Simpson nodded again wordlessly and started to cry.

FORTY-FIVE MINUTES LATER Diane and Gardiner walked into the lab carrying two brown paper evidence bags. They handed them to Gabe Pelligrosso.

"What are these?" Pelligrosso asked as he opened each one and looked inside.

"These are the sneakers and red hoodie that Mohammed Sayed asked his girlfriend to hide for him," she said.

"Holy shit," Pelligrosso said.

"We just recovered them from his girlfriend's closet where they've been stashed since Davis Billingslea posted the picture of you casting the shoe impressions."

Pelligrosso slipped a pair of rubber gloves on and lifted a pair of Nike LeBron Soldier X sneakers out of the bag, turning them over as he did so to examine the tread patterns.

"You think they're a match?" Diane asked.

"They're the right style. I guess we'll know soon enough. What about the hoodie?"

"It's ripped," Diane said. "And there's a piece of material missing."

Chapter 31

Monday, 3:50 P.M.,
January 30, 2017

DIANE FELT LIKE they were finally moving in the right direction but there were still too many pieces of the puzzle missing. Even if the tread from Sayed's sneakers matched the prints that Pelligrosso had recovered from the scene of the shooting, it still didn't put a gun in Plummer's hand at the time he was shot by Haggerty. The shoe would only confirm Sayed's presence at the time the shooting happened. The same was true of the ripped hoodie. They needed more.

Diane had nothing to do but wait for Pelligrosso's call. She decided to take a drive to clear her head. She told herself she had no particular destination in mind, but she knew it was a lie. Twenty minutes later she was at John's condo. The sight of his car in the driveway provided some relief. At least he wasn't at the Gull drowning in booze. She realized that he could very well be inside self-medicating anyway, but maybe he wasn't. Maybe, just maybe, Jim Ferguson had put a dent in that thick skull.

She drove past his driveway and was making the turn onto the adjoining street when her cell rang. It was Pelligrosso. She answered.

"Hey, Gabe. Tell me you've got good news."

"Three things."

"I'm all ears."

"The first is that the sneakers you seized are the very same ones that made the prints I recovered from Kennedy Park."

"You're positive?"

"No doubt. The right sneaker has a staple imbedded in it near the toe. It was angled to match the tread pattern, so naturally I assumed it was part of the tread. It isn't."

She could feel her excitement building. "Great news, Gabe. What else?"

"The material I pulled off the cyclone fence definitely came from this sweatshirt."

They were getting close; she could feel it. "And the third thing?"

"You know the hairs you gave me, the ones from the Khalid Muhammad?"

"Yeah. Abdi Ali's hair." *Please make this less complicated*, she thought. "Tell me they don't match the ones you found on the torn cloth."

"They don't," Pelligrosso said. "The hair I pulled off the cloth aren't Abdi's. They are from a different person."

"Like maybe Mohammed Sayed."

"Let's hope."

BETHANY SIMPSON'S STATEMENT along with the matching sneaker tread and torn sweatshirt were more than enough to obtain a warrant to search Mohammed Sayed's room. Diane stood off to one side of the small bedroom watching as Pelligrosso and Murphy scoured through the boy's belongings looking for any sign of a gun or ammo, or anything that might connect him with the robbery. Diane had assigned Nugent to watch the outside of the Sayed home and to give her the heads-up if Mohammed appeared. Stevens and a uniformed officer were keeping the Sayeds company in the next room.

Murphy had just replaced Mohammed's mattress when Pelligrosso turned to Diane. "Think we may have a problem, Sarge."

"What?"

Pelligrosso held up a pair of sneakers. "These are size ten and a half."

"And?"

"And the ones I just matched to the shooting scene in Kennedy Park are only nine and a half."

Diane scrambled to make sense of it. "Maybe the ones you're holding run big?" she said, aware of how desperate it sounded. "Check the others."

"I have. They're all ten and a half. Whoever was fleeing the robbery with Tommy Plummer had feet smaller than Mohammed's."

Dammit.

FORCED TO RELEASE Henderson, the team decided to regroup. Diane, Stevens, Gardiner, and Nugent sat at the CID conference room table working on two large pizzas from Calluzzo's Bistro. Diane had taken thirty dollars out of the petty cash box in Le-Royer's office to pay for dinner. They were all tired and hungry.

"I don't get it," Stevens said. "Why would Mohammed Sayed

ask his girlfriend to hide clothes used in the robbery if they weren't his?"

After a moment of reflective chewing, Nugent spoke up, "Maybe they *were* his."

Stevens rolled her eyes. "Here we go."

"No, I'm serious," Nugent said.

"What do you mean, Nuge?" Diane asked.

"Maybe the sneakers weren't his but perhaps the sweatshirt was."

"I'm listening," Diane said.

"Well, I've been thinking how close in size Henderson, Sayed, Freeman, and Ali are. Hell, it's like looking at a real estate comp sheet. What if Sayed really was sick the night the laundromat was robbed? Maybe he loaned his hoodie to someone with smaller feet."

"Like Abdi Ali," Gardiner said almost absently.

Stevens spoke up. "Playing devil's advocate here, but why couldn't it be Henderson? You said it yourself, Nuge. They've all got a similar build. Maybe Henderson changed into a red hoodie after he shoplifted the beer."

"What size are Henderson's sneakers?" Gardiner asked.

"Jesus, it sounds like we're making the case for the defense," Diane said.

"Something's been nagging at me," Nugent said.

"What's that?" Diane said.

"Your wife?" Stevens asked.

"Ha, ha. No, I'm serious. The night of the shooting, when Mel and I first arrived, the Plummers were already there. At the scene. How did they know already?"

"The neighborhood grapevine?" Gardiner asked.

"Bullshit," Nugent said. "*We* weren't even sure who Hags had shot yet. So how did the Plummers know already?"

"Maybe the other robber told them," Stevens said, thinking out loud.

"Or a relative," Diane said.

"Nathan Freeman and Tommy are cousins, right?" Gardiner asked.

"They are," Stevens said. "But Freeman's mom alibied him as being home that night."

"Riiight," Nugent said. "And I'm sure she'd never lie to protect her little Nate."

The room grew quiet for a few minutes as they worked on the pizzas and thought it through. Nugent spoke up first. "So if we assume for a moment that cousin Nate is the other robber, he knows that Tommy's been shot. He grabs the gun and the backpack and gets out of Dodge."

Stevens chimed in. "He runs home and tells Mom or Dad that he thinks something bad might have happened to Tommy, down in the park. Mom or Dad contact the Plummers, who race down to the project and find Junior dead."

"Makes sense to me," Nugent said.

Gardiner spoke up. "Maybe Nate Freeman supplied the gun?"

"Maybe," Diane said. "But without some direct evidence that puts them together during the robbery, this is all just speculation."

"I might be able to help with that," a voice said from outside the room.

They all turned to see Dustin Tran standing in the doorway.

"What do you mean?" Diane asked.

"Hey, where's *my* pizza?" Tran said as he entered the room. "I'm starving."

"Help yourself, geek boy," Nugent said, pulling out a chair.

Tran grabbed a slice and shoved half of it into his mouth.

"What are you talking about, Dustin?" Diane said.

Tran struggled to swallow the massive quantity of dough and cheese in his mouth before answering.

"I found something on the video you guys need to see."

Nugent closed the lid on the remaining slices, then picked up the pizza box. "Here," he said, pressing the cardboard carton into Tran's stomach. "Take it to go."

SEVERAL MINUTES LATER the pizza crowd had reassembled in the computer lab.

"What exactly did you find?" Diane asked again, knowing Tran would drag it out at novel length if she didn't keep him on point.

"I started thinking that we might want to keep broadening our search parameters. So, I replayed the 7-Eleven video but this time I backed it up and began watching the outside monitors closely during the half hour before the shoplifting occurred."

"Good thinking," Stevens said.

"And?" Diane said.

"I think your shoplifting suspect—"

"Scott Henderson," Nugent said, cutting him off.

"Yeah, Scott Henderson. One of the gas pump cameras caught Henderson getting out of a car about fifteen minutes before the beer theft. Here, look for yourselves." Tran scrolled over the player with the mouse and clicked on one of the camera views, enlarging it.

"That's Henderson in the dark hoodie climbing out of an older model two-door." Tran continued. "I noticed that same car drive by on Washington Avenue several times before."

"Are there any better angles?" Diane asked.

"Yeah," Nugent said. "Maybe get a better look at the car. See who else was inside."

"Or a reg," Stevens said.

Tran grinned. "Ask and you shall receive. Remember I told you that I was checking to see who had a driver's license? And Nuge made fun of me. I was toying with the idea that the robbers may have parked a getaway car nearby. Well, I think I found it." Tran switched videos. "This is the dash cam video from Haggerty's cruiser. I've cued it up to the point where Hags is going down Madison Street. See the two figures up ahead?"

"We see it," Nugent said. "I'm begging you, get to the point."

"As the suspects cut over onto Greenleaf, they passed in front of an oncoming car." Tran let the video play on, freezing the image just before Haggerty passed by the other vehicle.

"Holy crap," Gardiner said. "That's Nate Freeman behind the wheel."

Diane stared at the still, framed image. The alibi that Freeman's parents had provided was now worthless.

"You want a still of this too?" Tran asked.

"You bet your ass we do," Stevens said.

Diane turned to Nugent and Stevens. "Go find Nathan Freeman and drag him in here."

NUGENT, TRAN, AND Gardiner watched the interview from the monitor in the CID conference room, while Diane and Stevens worked Nathan Freeman for answers.

Defeated, Freeman let out a long sigh. "Yeah, I was out with Tommy and Scott. Mo was planning to go out with us, but he got sick."

"What happened?" Diane asked.

"Tommy and I had talked about pulling a drug rip on the owner of the laundromat. That Micky guy. Said we could make a lot of money and no one would report it."

"How did you know the owner of the laundromat had drugs?" Stevens asked.

"I don't know. Tommy wouldn't tell me how he knew, but he did."

"Was Tommy dealing at the high school?" Diane asked.

Freeman nodded. "Yeah."

"What about you?"

"No. I'm not a dealer. I just smoke a little weed. You're welcome to search my stuff."

"We know that Tommy fired a gun at Officer Haggerty," Diane said.

"That wasn't supposed to happen. I don't know what the hell Tommy was thinking. I really liked Officer Haggerty."

"Where did the gun come from?"

Freeman tilted his head back and sighed again. "The gun came from Abdi Ali."

"Abdi was there that night too?" Stevens said.

"Yeah. He and Tommy did the robbery."

"Why involve Abdi at all?" Diane asked. "Why didn't you and Tommy do it?"

"This girl named Christine Souza died from a drug overdose a few months back. I guess she was, like, Abdi's girlfriend or something. He was pretty upset about it. Tommy told Abdi that he might know where the drugs were coming from."

"Did Abdi know that Tommy was dealing?"

Freeman shook his head. "No."

"What *did* you tell Abdi?"

"Tommy told him that he might know a way to stop the drugs from coming into the school."

"Why would Tommy want to keep drugs out of the school if he was dealing them?"

"He didn't, but he needed Abdi to think that."

"I still don't get why either of you involved Abdi in the first place."

Freeman fidgeted in his chair. It was obvious to both detectives that he didn't want to go where he was headed.

"Tommy knew that the guy who ran the laundromat had a gun. We couldn't go in there to rob him without a gun of our own. We all knew Abdi's dad had a gun. He'd talked about seeing it before."

"Where?"

"His dad's store. Abdi said he kept one in the store for protection."

"What kind of gun?"

"A semiautomatic handgun."

"So, it was Abdi who brought the gun that night?"

Freeman nodded silently.

"We can't hear you, Nate," Stevens said.

"Yeah," Freeman said. "Tommy told him that all he had to do was bring it. We would take care of the robbery. Abdi wouldn't have to do anything."

"But that isn't what happened, is it?"

"No. Tommy took the gun and gave one of the skull masks to Abdi and told him that he and Abdi were going to do the robbery. We figured if Abdi helped he'd have to keep his mouth shut about it."

"Tell us what happened?"

"We drove around in my car. We went past the laundromat to

make sure that it was still open. Then we dropped Scott off at the 7-Eleven to steal some beer."

"Why?"

"We figured the cop working the area would be busy taking the report and wouldn't interrupt the robbery. We had no idea that Officer Haggerty was working."

Diane and Stevens exchanged a knowing glance.

"Where were Tommy and Abdi while you were doing that?" Stevens asked.

"In the car with me."

"What happened next?" Diane asked.

"After Scott grabbed the beer he ran behind the old J.J. Nissen Building. We were waiting for him on Romasco Lane."

"Did you drink it?"

"Yeah, we each had a couple."

Liquid courage, Diane thought. "And then?" she asked, prompting Freeman to continue after a long silence.

"We drove down past the Bubble Up so we could see inside. The owner was still there, working alone just like Tommy said. We didn't see any customers around, so I dropped the three of them off."

"And you?" Diane asked.

"I drove down into Kennedy Park and waited."

"Before dropping them off, did you discuss how it was supposed to happen?"

"Yeah. Tommy had the gun and the backpack. He gave a ski mask to Abdi and said he'd changed his mind. Abdi was gonna help him with the robbery. Said they were doing it for Abdi's girlfriend, Christine. Scott was gonna be a lookout from across the street while Tommy and Abdi did it."

"What happened next?"

"I started getting nervous. Seemed like it was taking too long. Finally, I decided to drive up to Washington Avenue and check on them."

"Did you see them?"

"I never made it that far. Tommy and Abdi came running down Madison, right at me. And a police car with lights and siren was right behind them. I just about shit."

"What did you do?" Stevens asked.

"Nothing I could do. They cut up Greenleaf and the police car followed them."

"Where was Scott Henderson?"

"I had no idea. I found out later that he split. Ran home."

"Where did you go?"

"I parked on Washington Avenue on the side of the road with my lights off. I waited for a while. I didn't know what had happened."

"How long did you wait?"

"A few minutes. Then I heard gunshots. A lot of them. It seemed like every cop in the city was coming. Sirens were approaching from everywhere. I drove home."

"What did you tell your parents?" Diane said.

"I told my mom that I'd seen the police chasing Tommy in Kennedy Park."

"Did you tell her why?"

"No way. She didn't know I was out with him. She picked up the phone and called my aunt." Freeman hung his head.

Diane waited a few minutes for Freeman to compose himself before continuing with the questions. He wiped the tears from his face and the snot from his nose on the sleeve of his sweatshirt.

"What happened to the drugs and gun, Nate?" Diane asked.

DIANE GRABBED GARDINER and headed out to locate Abdi Ali, leaving Stevens and Nugent to deal with booking Nate Freeman on the armed robbery charge. They hurried down the back stairwell toward 109's rear garage. Diane held tight to a manila envelope containing the photograph that Tran had printed of Freeman's car.

"Think we should let the lieutenant know what we've got, Sarge?" Gardiner asked.

Diane stopped abruptly as she reached the landing between the first and second floors. She spun around to face him and the young detective nearly collided with her.

"If I thought that, we would've done it already." She could see that her reaction had caught him by surprise. She tried a softer approach. "Look, I know you're new to this, Luke, but this is the job. The big leagues. You've seen how this thing has played out from the very beginning, right?"

Gardiner's head bobbed up and down. "Yeah, kind of a shit show."

"A shit show is right. Between the leaks and the people intentionally trying to manipulate and take advantage of this thing, it's been a disaster. A friend of mine was murdered because it was convenient. I watched someone I care a great deal about get driven right over the edge into a suspension. Not to mention having to watch as the entire police department was dragged through the muck over a lie. Now, do you want to make a call to the lieutenant asking permission, risking another leak, or worse? Or would you rather we go out and do our goddamned jobs?"

"You're the boss," Gardiner said, raising both hands in mock surrender. "I'm with you, Sarge."

"Good," she said. "Let's go."

DIANE AND GARDINER drove to the Eastern Halal Market on Munjoy Hill, fully expecting to have a confrontation with the elder Ali over the whereabouts of his son, Abdirahman. What they found instead were Mr. and Mrs. Ali speaking frantically with a uniformed police officer.

"What are you doing here?" Diane asked the officer.

"Dispatch sent me up here for a missing-persons report," the officer said.

"Who's missing?" Gardiner asked.

"The store owner's son, Abdirahman."

"He has run away," Ahmed Ali said.

Mrs. Ali barked something at her husband, speaking in Somali. Diane couldn't understand what the distressed mother was saying but it was clear she was angry with Ahmed.

Mrs. Ali turned to Diane with pleading eyes. "We are very worried about Abdi, Sergeant Joyner. Please help us find him."

Diane sat Mrs. Ali down, quickly obtaining as much information as she could. Mrs. Ali told her that in addition to running away, Abdi had also stolen his parents' van. Diane stepped away and called Dispatch from her cell. She gave them the particulars, along with the description of Abdi and the van's registration number. Before Diane could disconnect the call, Mrs. Ali approached her again.

"There is something else," Mrs. Ali said. Ahmed yelled something across the room at his wife in their native tongue. Mrs. Ali shouted back. With slumped shoulders, Ahmed turned away in defeat.

"Hang on a sec," Diane said to the dispatcher. "What is it, Mrs. Ali?"

"My son has a gun with him."

"What kind of gun?"

"A small gun that fits in your hand," she said, pantomiming the act of holding a gun.

"A handgun, like this one?" Diane said, pulling back her coat and revealing her own sidearm.

"Just like that, only it is silver colored."

"Where did Abdi get a gun, Mrs. Ali?"

Ahmed yelled again.

"From my husband," she said.

Diane glared over at the store owner. Ahmed hung his head in shame. She looked back at Mrs. Ali. "Does Abdi have ammo for the gun?"

"Bullets?" Mrs. Ali asked.

"Yes, bullets."

"My husband had a box of bullets. It's missing."

"You have got to be shitting me," LeRoyer shouted as he paced the floor of the CID conference room. "Ahmed Ali lied about having a goddamned gun?"

Diane wondered how the lieutenant could ever have put so much stock in what the store owner had told the police in the first place. If it was in fact his gun that Plummer had fired at Haggerty, Ahmed had probably known all along that his son was complicit. She couldn't help wondering what lies she might have been capable of had it been her son.

"So now Ali's son is missing, and he's armed?" LeRoyer asked.

"Yes," Diane said. "He's also stolen his parents' car."

"Jesus," LeRoyer said. "This just gets better and better. Tell me we've got a shitload of people out looking for him."

"Everyone." *Except for John*, she wanted to add, but didn't.

LeRoyer combed the fingers of his right hand back through his hair. "I gotta tell Rumsfeld." He stopped pacing and turned to Diane. "Find this kid, okay? Alive."

"I'm working on it," she said, wondering if it was even possible but praying that it was.

"Shit," LeRoyer said as he opened the conference room door and marched toward his own office.

Diane plopped down in one of the padded chairs surrounding the table and hit the speed dial for John's cell. The call went directly to voicemail. "You have reached Sergeant Byron's voicemail. Leave a—"

Diane hung up and pocketed her phone.

Someone knocked at the door. It was the same officer who had taken the missing-persons report on Abdi Ali.

"Hey, Sarge," he said. "Didn't mean to bother you but I have the copy of the report you asked for."

"You're not bothering me," Diane said as she reached for the report. "All entered into NCIC?"

"Yes. I delivered it to Dispatch myself. Here's a copy of the file-6," he said. The missing-persons report.

"Thanks."

After the officer departed, Diane turned her attention back to the whiteboard. She sighed deeply. There were now two priorities in her life: locate Abdirahman Ali and find a way to reach John. And she needed to do both things before either of them did something that couldn't be undone.

Chapter 32

"911. OPERATOR GOSTKOWSKI speaking. What's your emergency?"

"This is Vice Principal Paul Rogers at Portland High School. We've got an armed student in Freshman Alley firing a gun into the air."

The hair went up on the back of Gostkowski's neck. "Stay right on the line with me, okay?"

"Okay."

Gostkowski turned in his chair and yelled over at the dispatcher. "We've got an active shooter at Portland High. Start some units."

"Jesus. My kid goes there. Where's the shooter?" the dispatcher asked, wide-eyed.

"Freshman Alley."

"I'm on it," the dispatcher said, spinning in his chair to key the microphone. "Headquarters calling 101."

Gostkowski returned his attention to the caller. Following protocol, he started down the checklist. "Okay, Mr. Rogers. Has anyone been shot?"

"I don't know. I—I don't think so."

DIANE HALF RAN, half jogged to 109's rear parking garage. Nugent and Stevens were with her step for step as they headed to their own vehicle. All three detectives were intently monitoring their portable radios. Diane heard multiple sirens blaring in the distance.

"101. Give me the air!" a male voice shouted over the radio.

"Ten-four, 101," the dispatcher said.

Diane clicked the remote on the Ford's ignition key as she neared her car, unlocking the door and jumping inside. As the Taurus's base radio came to life, Diane powered down her portable and threw it on the passenger seat. A long piercing tone emitted from the base speaker, sounding twice as the dispatcher cleared the air.

"All units: a signal 1000 is now in effect," the dispatcher said. "Units on Cumberland Avenue have priority. All other units switch to channel two."

Diane sped out of the rear garage onto Newbury Street, Nugent and Stevens hot on her tail.

"101!"

"101, go ahead," the dispatcher said.

"101. I need two units to shut down traffic on Cumberland Avenue. One at Elm Street and another one at Stone."

"3. I'll take Elm. Just pulling up now."

"Ten-four, 103."

"2. I've got Stone and Cumberland."

"Ten-four, 102."

"121."

"Go ahead, Sergeant," the dispatcher said.

"I want marked units blocking every entry point to Freshman Alley. We'll need one on Congress Street, one on Elm Street, and one on Cumberland at the west end of the high school. Pull all the Deering units if you have to. Contact the local departments and request mutual aid assistance."

"Ten-four, Sergeant."

Diane was trying to navigate through the traffic on Pearl Street, but her way was blocked by a line of traffic on Congress that had stopped for the eastbound light at Franklin.

"Move it!" she yelled at a woman in a tan minivan who was sitting right in the middle of the intersection. The woman shrugged. "Come on, lady!" Diane yelled. "You're the one blocking the intersection. Move!"

This was one of those moments when Diane wished she'd been a firefighter. She imagined a giant red ladder truck would be much more intimidating than her unmarked Taurus. She laid on the air horn until finally a pickup truck that had been stopped directly behind the offending minivan pulled around it to the left and out of the way. She gave a quick wave to the middle-aged male behind the wheel of the truck and gunned the accelerator. Stevens's car was right on her tail as Diane crossed Congress and headed for Cumberland Avenue.

"100."

"Go ahead, Lieutenant," the dispatcher said.

"100. Get ahold of SRT Commander Lieutenant Price."

"Ten-four. Go ahead for Lieutenant Price. He's standing right beside me."

"Tell him to call out the team and have him contact me on my cell ten-eighteen."

"Ten-four. He has it, sir."

When Diane reached Stone Street she could see the throng of students spilling out of the school onto Cumberland Avenue. *So much for shelter in place*, she thought. The officer blocking the roadway stepped aside, waving both unmarked cars through. She swerved around the cruiser, then made the left turn up Chestnut Street, pulling over where two black-and-whites were parked, blocking the east end of the alley.

She jammed the Ford's transmission into Park and jumped out. The black-and-whites belonged to Elmer Anderson, the day class lieutenant, and Officer Lance Beaulieu, the officer covering beat one. Both officers were standing outside of their patrol cars and monitoring the alley. Anderson was talking animatedly on his cell.

"What's going on?" Diane asked as she and the other two detectives approached Anderson and Beaulieu. Lieutenant Anderson nodded without skipping a beat during his conversation with the SRT commander.

Beaulieu said, "Think we found your missing kid."

"You sure it's Abdi?" Diane asked, craning her neck to get a look down the alley.

"Plate number called in by the school matches the vehicle owned by Ahmed Ali."

"What's he done so far?" Nugent asked.

"He drove the van down into Freshman Alley and started waving a gun around telling students to get out of there. We've got the fire department helping us evacuate the school."

"Any shots fired?" Stevens asked.

"Oh yeah," Beaulieu said. "I heard a few myself. Who knows what he's thinking."

Diane wondered the same thing. Her biggest fear was that Abdi might be considering suicide by cop. Now that he knew he'd been found out and was most likely shouldering guilt over his part in the death of Plummer, and perhaps even Haggerty, it was anybody's guess what he might do.

Diane pulled out her phone and dialed LeRoyer.

"Where are you?" the lieutenant asked, answering on the first ring.

"Chestnut Street. I've got Mel and Nuge with me."

"Is it who I think it is?"

"It's Abdi."

"Be right there."

THE NEXT THIRTY minutes were a blur. Diane and the other detectives stood by in case they were needed but there wasn't much any of them could do. Members of the Special Reaction Team began to arrive and beat officers sealed off the alley from every direction. No one was getting in or out without police approval. Officers cleared the school, searching room by room. LeRoyer stayed close to Price and Rumsfeld. The hostage negotiator, Officer Damon Roberts, had made contact with Abdi on his cell. Roberts was attempting to start a dialogue with Abdi, but the young boy hung up before Roberts could say more than a few words.

"He's upset," Roberts said. "Said he'll start shooting at anyone who comes near him."

"Oh, he's upset?" Rumsfeld said. "Well, fuck him. I'm upset. Does he have any idea how much trouble he's created?"

Neither LeRoyer nor the negotiator responded to the acting chief's rhetoric.

"What the hell does he want?" Rumsfeld asked.

"Abdi," Roberts said upon reestablishing contact. "Don't hang up. I only want to talk."

Diane waited as they all did, focusing intently on Robert's half of the conversation, the only one they were privy to.

"My name is Officer Roberts. I understand, Abdi—Is it okay if I call you Abdi? Good. Okay, so listen, Abdi, I—"

LeRoyer began pacing.

"Well, you can talk with me, okay?" Roberts said. "Why do you need to talk to Sergeant Byron?"

Diane saw Rumsfeld turn his head in LeRoyer's direction. The chief's mouth twisted up as he glared at the CID lieutenant.

"He's not gonna be a part of this, Marty," Rumsfeld growled. "He's on suspension, for fuck's sake."

"He hung up again," Roberts said, looking exasperated. "Says he'll only talk to Byron. He's threatening to kill himself if we don't let him."

There was a commotion at the intersection of Chestnut and Cumberland and they all turned to look. Ahmed Ali, Abdi's father, had arrived. He was shouting and trying to push past the officers.

"Great," Rumsfeld said. "That's all we need."

Roberts looked to the chief. "What do you want to do about Byron, sir?"

Rumsfeld looked at the SRT commander. "Get a sniper in position."

"You got it, Chief," Price said

Rumsfeld turned again to LeRoyer. "Drag that son of a bitch down here."

Chapter 33

Tuesday, 1:30 P.M.,
January 31, 2017

BYRON WAS TRYING desperately to will away his impending nausea as LeRoyer navigated the silver SUV through Cumberland Avenue's slalom course of pedestrians and emergency vehicles. The repeated whooping of the Mercury's siren felt like it might split his head in two.

LeRoyer raced past Portland High School, stopping at the intersection of Chestnut and Cumberland where he laid on the horn. The uniformed officer manning the intersection scrambled out of the black-and-white and ran to the wooden barricades impeding their path.

"Let's go already!" LeRoyer yelled out the window as the young officer wrestled with the bulky wooden structure. "While we're fucking young!"

"Easy, Marty," Byron groaned.

"Hold on," the lieutenant said as he stomped on the accelerator, nearly cleaning out the remaining barricades.

LeRoyer sped along the Chestnut Street side of the high school. The SUV jerked to a stop about two hundred feet in. The east end of Freshman Alley was blocked by two City of Portland fire trucks and surrounded by at least a dozen marked and unmarked cars.

Byron wondered if the PPD garage was empty. His stomach was churning as he stepped awkwardly from LeRoyer's vehicle.

The chaos surrounding them wasn't all that different than what he'd experienced in Kennedy Park more than two weeks earlier. So much had happened since then. The shooting, the protests, the media's three-ring circus, the attack on Haggerty and his subsequent death, Molly's funeral, and Byron's suspension. It was all too surreal. Of course, the coup de grâce had been his swan dive off the sobriety wagon.

He stood swaying on sea legs, then turned to look back as the crowd parted for yet another vehicle. This time it was the PPD's flat-black Special Reaction Team transport pulling in behind them. Three members of the team jumped out, including Kenny Crosby, who ran past carrying a rifle.

Diane jogged over to Byron. Concern etched on her face. "You okay?"

Bile rose in his throat. He swallowed it down before answering. "Not really. How bad is it?"

"Bad. Abdi's threatening to kill himself. He has a gun."

"Where'd he get it?"

"The gun belongs to his father. He and Tommy Plummer did the robbery. You were right, John."

Yay for me, Byron thought. It was a nonexistent consolation after everything that had transpired. His vision was fuzzy. He leaned back against the side of LeRoyer's Mercury, closing his eyes for a moment, trying to concentrate.

She touched the side of his face with her bare hand. "Jesus, John, you're burning up. You sure you're up for this?"

He wasn't sure he was up for anything. The truth was, had the barricaded person been almost anyone else Byron would have done an about-face, taken LeRoyer's vehicle, and driven away. After all, Haggerty was dead. Abdi Ali might not have pulled the trigger, but he and Tommy Plummer had set this whole series of events in motion. As far as Byron was concerned, both boys were both responsible for everything that happened following the robbery at the laundromat. *But still*, he thought, *Abdi's only a kid.* A stupid, scared kid who'd most likely been talked into the robbery by Plummer. Byron couldn't let him commit suicide. Especially not suicide by cop. The madness had to end. Byron couldn't change what had already happened, but he could keep it from getting worse. He worried about what would happen to his city if he couldn't save the boy. What would become of the community? What would become of him? If Abdi died today, would Byron ever be able to face himself in the mirror again?

Slowly he opened his eyes. His vision was a bit clearer, but his legs were rubber and his stomach was still threatening a revolt. The noises coming from Byron's insides sounded more like demonic possession than gastric distress. "Anybody talking to him?" he asked.

"Damon Roberts was, but Abdi keeps hanging up," Diane said. "Says he wants a face-to-face and he'll only talk with you."

Byron nodded his understanding, then wished he hadn't. Nodding did nothing for the spinning taking place inside his head.

"You're sure you can do this?" Diane asked again.

"Got to," he said. Byron scanned the faces in the crowd. He saw Acting Chief Rumsfeld and Commander Jennings discussing the situation with Lieutenant Price and Sergeant Crosby. Rumsfeld fixed Byron with a quick look of disgust before returning to the conversation. Byron looked past Diane and saw commotion. His neighbor, Khalid Muhammad, was in a heated exchange with Abdi's father, Ahmed. Both men were shouting and waving their arms in the air. Byron didn't have to understand what they were saying to each other to comprehend the meaning. He knew Muhammad was trying to get it through the storekeeper's head that Byron might well be the only chance his son had. Muhammad acknowledged Byron by giving him a nod. Abdi's father stopped yelling long enough to turn and see what had captured Muhammad's attention. Ahmed Ali stared directly at Byron, but neither his eyes nor his facial expression communicated any hatred. What Byron saw on Ali's face was fear. It was the same look he'd seen on the face of Tommy Plummer's father on a frigid Sunday night in Kennedy Park. Plummer had already lost a son at the hands of the police. Byron knew Ahmed Ali was afraid that his son, Abdi, might be next. And if Byron couldn't pull this off, he would be.

Willing his legs to move, Byron approached the two men.

"Detective Sergeant Byron," Muhammad greeted.

"Khalid."

"Mr. Ali has something he wants to say to you."

Byron turned his attention to Ahmed Ali.

"I am sorry I did not tell you the truth," Ali said. "About the gun."

Byron said nothing.

Ali looked to Muhammad for guidance. Muhammad nodded for him to continue.

"I am ashamed," Ali said. "My son is very much upset. Please help him."

Byron struggled to control his emotions. He was angry with Ahmed, but couldn't help feeling pity for the man and the position he was in. Ahmed Ali was now forced to rely on the help of a stranger, a man he didn't trust, in an occupation he didn't trust, to save the life of his son.

"I'll do my best," Byron said at last.

"JOHN, THAT'S CRAZY," LeRoyer said. "I'm not letting you go in there without a gun."

In his current condition the last thing Byron felt like was getting into an argument with his boss, but on this issue he would hold fast, even if it killed him.

"It's the only way I'm going in, Marty," Byron said. "You're the one who dragged me down here, remember? You don't like it? Get someone else to try and talk him down."

LeRoyer made a nervous swipe through his hair, making it stand up in front. "Believe me, we tried. He'll only talk to you."

"Then I guess you're out of options, huh?"

"God, you're a prick sometimes."

"Yeah. A prick who's still on suspension, lest you forget."

"At least put this on," LeRoyer said, tossing a Kevlar vest toward him.

Byron caught it reluctantly. There was nothing about a bulletproof vest that Abdi Ali could perceive as threatening but there was no sense in advertising that he was wearing one either. Gingerly he removed his coat before handing it to Diane. He hated wearing a vest, but he wasn't all that keen on the prospect of being shot either. Although, as he pulled the vest over his head and secured the Velcro straps, he wondered if getting shot by Abdi could really make him feel any worse.

Lieutenant Price approached as Byron was slipping the jacket back on. "John, we've got a sniper in position on one of the upper floors of the building directly across from the high school."

"Who?" Byron asked.

"Napijalo."

Napijalo was a squared-away officer. Byron was glad it was Nappi at the other end of the sniper rifle and not Crosby. He knew Nappi would have his back, should it come to that. Nappi would also follow orders, which could either be a good thing or bad, depending on how things were about to go.

"He's got a clear line of sight to the kid from the left," Price continued. "So, try and stay away from that side when you're talking to him. Got it?"

"Yeah, I got it."

"If the kid gives any indication—"

"It's Abdi," Byron said, not liking Price's dehumanizing use of the word.

"What?"

"That kid's name is Abdi."

"Yeah, well, if Abdi gives the slightest indication that he intends to shoot you, he'll be taken out."

Byron, who didn't believe in prayer, composed a silent one in the hopes that neither situation developed into a reality.

"Here," Diane said, cracking open a bottled water and passing it to him. "Drink."

Byron took several swallows, then returned the bottle to her. "Thanks," he said.

Damon Roberts, the negotiator, spoke up. "John, when you're

talking to him, try and focus on the positive. Don't let him drag the conversation down. It's important—"

"I get it, Damon," Byron said, cutting him off. "Don't put more shit in my head than I've already got there." Byron's head was pounding, and this wasn't helping. He wondered if it was possible for a head to ache so severely that it actually exploded. *Marty, grab my brains off the ground, would you?* Byron closed his eyes and sucked air in through his nose.

"Jesus, John," LeRoyer said. "You sure you're up for this?"

"Why does everyone keep asking me that?"

"Umm, 'cause you look like shit."

Byron opened his eyes. Black spots danced across his field of vision, then slowly disappeared. "Gee, thanks for the compliment, Lieu. But you needn't worry. I'm as right as rain."

"Ya, right."

Byron turned to Roberts. "He's a scared teenager, Damon. I know what to say. Call him back. Tell him I'm coming in."

"Okay."

"Be careful, John," Diane said.

Byron gave her a weak smile. It was the best he could muster.

"Good luck," LeRoyer said.

Byron took another deep breath, then skirted the barricades, making the long slow walk up Freshman Alley, toward whatever fate awaited him. And a scared teenager named Abdi.

THE VAN ABDI had stolen from his parents was parked at an odd angle in the middle of the alley. Byron knew the boy was on the far side just out of his sight line.

"Abdi, they said you wanted to talk," Byron hollered. "Here I am."

The boy's head partially appeared above the roofline of the car.

"Don't come any closer," Abdi said.

"Listen to me, okay? I am not armed. But there are people watching us who will shoot you if they think you're a threat to me. Nod if you understand me, Abdi."

The boy nodded. His eyes were darting everywhere, trying to see who might be watching them.

"I'm going to walk around to the other side of the van so we can talk, okay?" Byron asked.

"You won't try anything?"

"You have my word. But you have to do me a favor, okay? I need you to put the gun on the ground while we talk." He waited as Abdi thought it over. "If you don't put the gun down, Abdi, my people will see you as a threat. Do you understand?"

Abdi nodded again, then disappeared from view. His head reappeared a moment later. "Okay. I put it on the ground."

"Is it all right if I walk over there with you?"

Abdi nodded again, then ducked out of sight.

Byron circled the car slowly with his hands raised slightly from his sides, palms forward. The boy was sitting on the pavement leaning back against the car. The semiauto was lying beside him three feet to his right. Byron wondered if he might be able to get close enough to grab it or kick it away.

Byron stopped and stood about fifteen feet away, facing Abdi. It was obvious that the young boy had been crying. His cheeks were still wet with tears.

"Abdi, I know you're upset about Officer Haggerty." The words caught in his throat. "We all are."

"It's all my fault. My fault he's dead."

"No, Abdi. It isn't. The man responsible for killing Officer Haggerty is dead. It's over."

"No, it's not. It's all my fault. I lied to you, Sergeant Byron."

Byron looked around at the buildings surrounding them until he caught a glimpse of the open window on the third floor. He knew Nappi was there, back in the shadows, even if he couldn't see him.

"If I hadn't brought the gun to Tommy, none of this would have happened." Abdi wiped his eyes with the back of his hand. "Tommy would still be alive and so would Officer Haggerty."

Byron took a half step to his left, hoping to get between Nappi and the window.

"Don't come any closer," Abdi warned.

"DAMMIT, I HATE this," LeRoyer said as he paced the sidewalk. He stopped and addressed Lieutenant Price. "What the hell is happening in there?"

The SRT commander keyed the mic. "Cover One, give me a SITREP."

Price's portable radio squawked.

"Byron is talking to him," Nappi said. "The target is sitting on the ground up against the vehicle. The gun is lying beside him."

"Do you have a clear shot?" Price asked.

They waited for several seconds for a response.

"It's tight. I do, if Byron stays where he is. But he's sidestepping into my line of sight."

The commander looked at LeRoyer. "I told you not to tell Byron where we were set up."

Nappi's voice came over Price's radio again. "Byron just moved again."

LeRoyer ran his fingers through his hair. "Goddammit, John."

Price turned to Sergeant Crosby, who was standing with his

rifle slung over his shoulder. "Get up onto the Elm Street Parking Garage. Give me another option."

"You got it," Crosby said. He shot a quick glance at LeRoyer before running off.

BYRON'S LEGS FELT wobblier than when he'd first walked down the alley. Standing in one spot was even harder than he'd imagined. He'd have given anything to be able to lie down and close his eyes, just for a few minutes.

"Officer Haggerty was always nice to me," Abdi said. "He didn't deserve to die."

"Neither do you, Abdi. Hurting yourself isn't going to bring him back. Besides, he wouldn't want you to do this."

"I thought I could help keep the drugs out of the school. If we took them they wouldn't be able to hurt anyone else."

Byron wondered if Abdi knew how shortsighted that logic was, or how badly Plummer and the others had used him. "Christine Souza, the senior who overdosed, she was a friend of yours, wasn't she?"

Abdi's nostrils flared. "I did it for her." He looked down at the ground and his chest began to heave as he broke into fresh sobs.

Byron took another half step to his left.

IT TOOK CROSBY four minutes at a fast jog to circle the block onto Elm Street and ascend the parking garage steps. As he ran, he continued to monitor the radio traffic between Price and Nappi. He knew what Byron was doing.

Crosby had settled into the shadows on the third level of the garage, overlooking Freshman Alley. The crosshairs of his rifle were trained on Abdi.

Byron might have intentionally blocked Nappi's sight line, Crosby thought. *But he won't block this one.*

Crosby adjusted his earbuds and keyed the mic on his radio. "Cover Two is in the nest."

"Ten-four, Cover Two," Lieutenant Price said.

Crosby could clearly see the gun and the boy's right hand. If Abdi made even the slightest move toward raising the weapon at Byron, it would be his last.

BYRON WAS WORKING hard to focus. Normally, this would have been easier. After all, he'd spent much of his professional life talking people down, some of whom had very little to lose. Abdi was only a boy. He had his whole life ahead of him. Yes, he had made a huge mistake, but it didn't have to define his future. After all, Abdi hadn't been the one who pulled the gun on Haggerty or taken a shot at him, Tommy Plummer had done that. All Abdi had done was facilitate a robbery. And although armed robbery was a felony, Abdi was still a juvenile. He would likely get another chance when he turned twenty-one.

"Tommy made his own decision, Abdi," Byron continued. "He tried to shoot Officer Haggerty. But you're not responsible for his actions."

Abdi wiped the tears from his eyes and looked up. He seemed to be trying to decide if Byron was being straight with him. "Yeah, but—"

"No buts, Abdi," Byron said, attempting to take a firmer, more paternal approach with the boy. "Tommy could have surrendered to Officer Haggerty. And you both would have been arrested and charged with robbery. That's it. He'd still be alive. It was Tommy's choice to fight back, not yours."

Abdi looked to his right, down where the gun was lying. "I never should have taken my father's gun. I shouldn't have told Tommy about it. I shouldn't have lied to you."

"What Tommy did isn't your fault, Abdi. And you know I'm right."

Abdi looked back at Byron. "I'm sorry," he said. He hesitated a moment, then he reached for the gun.

"No!" Byron yelled.

As ABDI ALI's hand moved toward the pistol, Crosby reacted. Time slowed to a crawl. The riflescope crosshairs were centered on the right side of the boy's head. Crosby exhaled through his mouth. His index finger tightened on the rifle's trigger. Then he caught a sudden flash of movement from the right. Byron was diving toward the boy. Abdi raised the handgun. Crosby squeezed back on the trigger. The crack of the shot rang out at precisely the same instant that Crosby jerked the rifle.

A GUN SHOT echoed down the alley like thunder, sending pigeons and gulls scattering.

"What the hell was that?" LeRoyer yelled. "What the fuck just happened?"

Ahmed Ali let out an agonizing wail and had to be restrained from running down the alley by Muhammad and a uniformed officer.

Diane was doing her best to remain outwardly calm, but her heart was racing, and the hair was standing up on the back of her neck. It was all she could do not to run down the alley herself. She looked over at Lieutenant Price, who was frantically trying to get an update.

"Cover One, Cover Two, report!" Price yelled into the radio mic.

For what seemed like an eternity only static came back through the radio. After several moments the audio silence was broken by the sound of a radio carrier followed by Nappi's voice. "Cover One, that shot did not come from me."

"Dammit," Price said. "Cover Two, status report!"

CROSBY TOOK A deep breath and slowly removed his finger from inside the trigger guard. He flicked on the safety, then lowered the rifle as if it were made of glass. His hands were visibly shaking.

"Cover Two, standby," Crosby said, his voice cracking as he said it.

He stared down at the alley below him, unsure whether he had successfully repositioned the rifle at the second it discharged, or not. It had all happened too fast. From the illusion of slow motion to out of control speed, as if someone had been playing a 45 record at 33 speed, then suddenly flicked the control to 78. He hoisted the rifle up to his shoulder and peered through the scope, making sure his finger was nowhere near the trigger. Scanning the area, he could only see one of the boy's legs. The rest of him was covered by Byron's motionless body. He spotted Abdi's gun lying on the pavement about five feet away from Byron's right arm, not far from the van's front tire.

Move, Crosby thought, as if willing it might make it happen. *Please God, let them be okay.*

THE PAIN HAD been immediate and intense, worse than anything in Byron's head. Window glass from the car door had exploded and rained down over both of them. A white-hot surge ran up Byron's arm from his now useless right hand. His body was totally shielding Abdi's. The gun, no longer in the boy's grip, had skittered across the pavement and out of reach.

"Are you all right?" Byron asked.

"I think so," Abdi said. "What happened?"

Byron wasn't sure himself. Pushing himself up with his left arm, he crawled off the boy and rose slowly to his feet. He retrieved Ahmed's semi-auto with his good hand and slid it into his jacket pocket. He returned to Abdi and helped him to his feet. The boy hugged him tightly.

"I'm sorry," Abdi said, his voice muffled by Byron's coat. "I'm so, so sorry."

Byron hugged him back. "I know."

Abdi began to sob uncontrollably, his body wracked by grief, and he squeezed Byron even tighter.

"COVER ONE," NAPIJALO said as he keyed mic on his headset and lowered his rifle. "Suspect disarmed. I repeat, suspect disarmed. 720 and the target are both up and moving. Situation secure."

Napijalo gave a long sigh of relief before making the sign of the cross with his right hand.

A COLLECTIVE CHEER of relief spread through the makeshift command post on Chestnut Street.

LeRoyer looked up at the sky. "Thank you," he said.

"That goes double for me," Diane said. "Thank you, God."

Lieutenant Price switched the speaker off and responded to both snipers by radio in private. He turned and gave Diane and LeRoyer the thumbs-up.

"How close was it?" LeRoyer asked.

"You don't want to know," Price said. "Trust me, you do not want to know."

BYRON PUT HIS good arm around Abdi and led him slowly down Freshman Alley toward the command post. He could only imagine the heartache and guilt the boy was probably feeling. The same emotions Haggerty had experienced after killing Tommy Plummer. Regret for actions that couldn't be undone. Sadness for the lives lost. And as Byron knew too well, being justified, as Haggerty had been, never trumps the inevitable deep-seated feelings of remorse. Being a juvenile meant Abdi might not pay the full legal price for his role in all that had happened, but actions always come with consequences. Byron knew that Abdi would have to live with the consequences of his actions for the rest of his life.

As they neared the cluster of people clogging the Chestnut Street entrance to the alley, two uniformed officers broke from the crowd and took custody of Abdi. As the boy was being handcuffed he turned to look at Byron. "I'm sorry," he said.

Byron nodded wordlessly. He stood and watched as the officers led Abdi toward a marked unit.

Diane ran up to Byron. "That was way more excitement than I needed today. We thought you'd been shot."

"I couldn't be that lucky."

"Are you okay?"

Byron winced as he held up his right arm. His hand had swollen to nearly twice its normal size. "Pretty sure my arm is broken."

"Let me see," she said, wearing a genuine look of concern on her face. "Jesus, you did a number on yourself. MedCu is still here. I'll get the paramedics."

Diane turned to leave but he stopped her.

"What?" she asked.

He handed her the gun. "Here. Tell Mayor Gilcrest she owes the Haggertys a fucking apology."

"I'll make sure she knows."

"The backpack is in Abdi's locker. The drugs, money, and the revolver they took from Micky Cavallaro are all inside it."

"I'll take care of it."

"One more thing."

"What's that?"

"I'm ready," he said.

"This isn't really the place, John," she said, grinning. "Have a little class. There are kids here."

"You know what I mean."

She studied his face. "You're serious?"

"Yeah. You're right. I need help. I can't do this by myself."

She reached over and took his left hand in hers. "You're one stubborn SOB, John Byron. How the hell did I ever get mixed up with a salty old dog like you?"

"Bad luck?"

"Not in my book." She leaned in close and kissed him on the cheek.

"Remember, Sergeant, there *are* kids here," he said.

"Too bad. Guess that will have to wait."

"Thank you for not giving up on me," he said.

She squeezed his hand in hers. "Never."

Epilogue

THE ENGINE WAS idling, and warm air flowed from the vents. Byron rode shotgun beside Diane in her unmarked Ford. The dashboard lights illuminated their faces in the darkness. Outside it was raining lightly, the arctic-like temperatures having finally departed. The two detectives watched in silence as vehicles gradually populated the parking lot, and people entered the church.

Byron's broken wrist was throbbing badly. He knew the surgeon would be pissed if he found out Byron wasn't wearing the sling. *C'est la vie*, he thought. He'd never been very good at taking orders from anyone, not even doctors.

"Wished I'd been there to see the assistant principal's face when they pulled him over," Byron said.

"Yeah, the K-9 practically tore the emblem off the trunk lid," Diane said. "They've estimated the street value of the drugs at about fifty thousand. And there was a stainless revolver in the bag. Abdi identified it as the gun Plummer took from Cavallaro's safe. The same gun Tommy fired at Haggerty."

"How did they know Rogers was the one who took the pack from Abdi's locker?"

"Aside from the SRT, Paul Rogers was the only other person inside the school while it was being cleared. He had keys to everything. After the incident was over, one of the teachers reported seeing Rogers remove a Patriots pack back from a student's locker and place it inside a black gym bag. The teacher followed him and watched him place the bag in the trunk of his car."

"What about Micky Cavallaro?" Byron asked.

"I spoke to Collier. He danced around any specifics, but it sounds like they suspect that the out-of-state players in their OC investigation made an example of Cavallaro. They found his Cadillac abandoned in Boston's north end. I asked him to let me know if they find his body. Sam suggested that I shouldn't hold my breath."

Byron stared at the church, knowing what it represented.

Diane held his left hand gently in hers. Her contact was both warm and comforting and the only thing keeping him from fleeing to the nearest bar.

He looked over at her. "Thanks," he said.

"You're not doing this for me, John. This is something you need to do for yourself."

He knew she was right. But he also knew he likely wouldn't have reached this point without her.

"Thank you anyway."

She smiled. "What are partners for, right?"

Their eyes met. "You're more than that," he said. "And we both know it."

Her smile widened, and she gripped his hand a little tighter.

He turned and looked out through the windshield just as another person headed toward the church entrance. The rain had blurred the glass, preventing him from being able to distinguish whether the figure was a man or woman. The wipers cleared his vision, but the figure was gone.

"What time is it?" he asked, licking his dry lips.

"You can do this," Diane said.

Byron looked back at her, unsure. His stomach was in knots, his palms sweating.

"I'll be right here for you," she said. "I promise."

He lifted her hand and gently kissed it before letting go. He reached across his body, opened the door, and stepped out of the car.

Once inside the church, Byron followed several people down a flight of stairs, into what appeared to be a basement cafeteria. About two dozen people were scattered about the room in small clusters chatting and laughing. He'd been worried that he might see someone he knew. He didn't. A circle of metal folding chairs had been arranged in the center of the room. The siren call of strong coffee filled the air. Resisting the urge to run back up the stairs, he approached a side table and poured himself a cup. On either side of the coffee urn was a large tin of sugar cookies and half of a pound cake. Hanging from the wall above the table was a faded purple banner with gold lettering that read You Are Not Alone. Byron considered that for a moment before turning back toward the room. He made eye contact with a young bearded man of about thirty. The man smiled and nodded. People began walking toward the chairs. Byron followed suit, selecting a chair that afforded him a view of the exit.

The meeting started at precisely seven o'clock, led by the same young bearded man.

"I see we have a couple of new faces in the group tonight. Why don't we begin with introductions?" He looked directly at Byron. "Would you like to go first?"

Byron hesitated as he looked around the room at the faces of strangers. Strangers who appeared not to have any commonalities outside of their reason for being there.

"You're among friends here," the young man said, giving Byron another nod.

Byron cleared his throat. "My name is John and—and I'm an alcoholic."

"Welcome, John," they all said in unison.

"Welcome, John," the group leader repeated with a smile.

Acknowledgments

BEYOND THE TRUTH, novel number three in the Detective Byron Mystery Series, is a milestone I wouldn't have dared imagine only a few short years ago. In 2012, I left my old life behind, retiring after nearly three decades in law enforcement, to pursue my life-long dream of becoming a successful published novelist. In 2016, my first novel, *Among the Shadows*, was published, and its publication meant I had achieved my first goal. It was then that I realized I still had no idea how to define success. That, dear readers, is where you came in. I've learned that success is an intangible that writers have no control over. Writers depend upon readers to enjoy our stories, and to keep coming back in large enough numbers to sustain us in our creative endeavors. Because of you, John Byron lives on, and for that both John and I are eternally grateful.

As always, I must give thanks to many special folks without whom I might never have gotten this far: Paula Munier and Gina Panettieri at Talcott Notch Literary for continuing to believe in me and my stories; Nick Amphlett, Christine Langone, Kaitlyn Kennedy, Jessica Lyons, Gena Lanzi, Guido Caroti, and the rest of the Witness Impulse Team at HarperCollins; fellow bloggers at Maine Crime Writers and Murder Books; and the great folks at the many New England libraries and bookstores, too numerous to list.

My beta readers and fact checkers: Kate Flora, Heather Sage, Michael Bennis, Brian MacMaster, Steve Gotlieb, Sara Perrigo, Mike Mercer, Judy LaBonte, and Pat Larrabee. Any mistakes were my own.

My immediate family and friends for their constant encouragement and support along the way.

The many men and women in the field of criminal justice, true professionals, I was fortunate to have served with, as well as those who continue to serve (these are their stories).

John Byron, Diane Joyner, and the rest of the fictional 109 team, who have become as much a part of my life as those with whom I once worked.

Lastly, and most importantly, my wife, Karen, for her love, inspiration, and infinite patience. Without you in my life, there would be no story.

About the Author

BRUCE ROBERT COFFIN retired from the Portland, Maine, police department in 2012, after more than twenty-seven years in law enforcement. As a detective sergeant, he supervised all homicide and violent crime investigations for Maine's largest city. Following the terrorist attacks of September 11, he worked for four years with the FBI, earning the Director's Award (the highest honor a nonagent can receive) for his work in counterterrorism.

Bruce's fiction has been shortlisted twice for the Al Blanchard Award. His story *Foolproof* appears in the Level Best Books anthology *Red Dawn, Best New England Crime Stories*, 2016, and in Houghton Mifflin Harcourt's *Best American Mystery Stories*, 2016. He lives and writes in Maine.

Discover great authors, exclusive offers, and more at hc.com.